# SEARCHING

# FOR

# SPARROW

K.A. Emmons

# PROLOGUE

*2201*

*Sunrise*

DEAD TREES REACHED THEIR GHOSTLY FINGERS TOWARDS THE glowing white moon that was just visible through the tainted atmosphere, lighting our way as we ran.

I glanced over my shoulder. Small fragments of light bobbed after us; the distant drone of a siren cut the thick air. My every pounding footstep rattled through my body. A sudden burst of pain surged through my swollen abdomen, and my knees buckled beneath me. Icarus's arms caught me before the ground could.

"Hawk!" His lips were suddenly pressed to my ear, his words just loud enough to hear over the lonely wails and distant voices shouting across the meadow. "Hawk, it's okay—it's okay. We're almost there—"

I shook my head, catching blurry snatches of his silhouetted face as I clutched his shoulders. "Icarus, it's starting."

I heard him suck in a breath. "Now?"

I leaned forward, my fingers tightening around his T-shirt. "Now."

The wail of the siren escalated. The shouts grew louder. My body was seized in the grip of pain as it ripped down my spine and tightened around my belly. My teeth sank into my tongue, and Icarus lifted me into his arms.

"We have to make it to the foothills," he whispered urgently. "We're almost there."

I drank in the air, sweat sheathing my skin as my head sank against his chest.

"We won't be able to outrun them." I gritted my teeth. "They're too close!"

"Hawk, we have no choice!"

I shook my head. "They're too close…"

Icarus halted among the towering pines, glancing back over his shoulder once more. The flashlight beams drew closer.

"Damnit," he cursed under his breath. "Okay, we'll hide and wait for them to pass. But what about—"

"Never mind," I hissed, my jaw tight. "Just… just—"

I couldn't finish. I swallowed back a moan as agonizing pain slivered through my back. The woods around us became a blur as Icarus ran faster, the thud of his boots muted against the soft ground. Ahead, something wreathed in shimmering ripples of white parted the forest around us. The moonlight, dappled by the shadows of the trees, scattered across what I realized was the surface of a pond as the thuds of my husband's footsteps became splashes.

The air was sucked out of my lungs as cool water suddenly rose over my legs and arms, swallowing us as Icarus waded in. He pressed his lips to my forehead.

Strange voices echoed through the forest now. The barking of orders resonated through the still summer night, accentuated by the crickets and frogs chorusing around us as we waded among the thick marsh grasses and cattails. I shivered, winding my arms more tightly around Icarus.

Icarus pulled me closer, breathing hard. "They're almost on us."

I closed my eyes and focused on my breathing, my beating heart—anything to keep my mind from the escalating ache tightening around my belly. I couldn't see the search party, but I could hear them break out of the forest around us, the thuds of boots against the damp ground. Beams of light swept through the trees.

"They must have turned!" one of them shouted.

The footsteps drew closer and then stopped. "Impossible! We just had them…" White light sliced over the tops of the cattails, just above our heads. Icarus held his breath.

"There's no way to be sure it was them," another responded. I heard boots scuffing to a stop in the dirt. "There's no way to know where—"

"You say that as if there's only a few of them," a throaty voice cut in; the light was still sweeping across the brush. "We're not just dealing with recusants anymore, Corporal. This is a different matter entirely…"

"Sir?"

There was a long pause; then the light clicked off.

"We're dealing with a force of nature." He lowered his voice. "Something that could destroy everything we stand for—everything we've fought and died for."

My throat tightened. I knew Icarus was feeling everything I was as he held me tight. Finally, with the clattering of weapons and a gruff signal from the commander, the search party retreated into the woods, the night swallowing them whole.

"They're gone," Icarus whispered. He straightened now and gasped for air, snapping into action as we waded forward. "They're gone now. Love, are you—"

He didn't need to ask. I was panting for air and writhing in pain as he sloshed out of the water, dropping to his knees in the grass to gently lower me to the ground. I pressed into my palms, struggling up into a seated position. Icarus's eyes were wide and terrified, glinting in the moonlight, his wet hair hanging into his face.

"Hawk, I don't know what to do," he whispered, his voice splintering.

"Neither do I…" I gasped. "I've never done this before…"

Icarus's eyes searched mine. His fingers wound around my hand, and he gripped it tight.

"It's okay," he said, his voice stronger now. "You're going to be fine—you're strong, Hawk…"

The sun was just peeking over the trees, brightening the forest around us to a soft lavender gray as Icarus walked back towards me from the edge of the pond, carrying a bundle wrapped in his own T-shirt. The sunlight washed over his skin, illuminating the black markings wrapping his arms, the ones I'd given him, along with the black band around his finger—the band that matched mine. His blue eyes were wide as he stared down at the tiny anomaly in his arms.

My trembling lips curved into a smile. Icarus came to a stop beside me, kneeling down to gently lower our daughter into my arms. I felt the warmth radiating from the tiny body. I swallowed back the lump in my throat as I gently traced her cheek with my fingertip.

Icarus leaned in and pressed a kiss against my cheek. I returned one to his lips.

"She's just like her mother…" he whispered into my ear. "Perfect."

I swallowed, leaning my head against his shoulder.

"Born at sunrise," I said softly. "That must be a good sign."

"Mmm."

Just then a twig snapped. My muscles tensed, and Icarus jumped to his feet. Two strong arms brushed aside the branches of the faded pines. Fin's emerald eyes locked with mine, and my heart calmed. His golden hair fell over his shoulders, and a scruffy beard swathed his jaw.

"Fin," Icarus sighed, relieved.

"I came as soon as I heard the hunters had—"

"We got them off our trail." Icarus glanced back at me. "Thanks to Hawk."

Fin didn't respond. His eyes had lowered to the tiny sleeping baby girl in my arms. For a moment he just stood there staring; then slowly he stepped closer, sinking to his knees in front of me.

Leaning forward, I gently shifted the baby into Fin's arms. His hands trembled as he took her. He seemed to make a study of the tiny features of her face—her rosebud lips and tightly closed eyes. He gently touched her arm with his finger and, stirring slightly, she seized it in her small, pink hand.

"I wish I could believe she's been born into a better world," Icarus said softly. "But it seems like Earth is darker now than it was before we arrived. Or maybe it just feels that way because now there's no longer any excuse for things to be as they are."

"It is because of us that the RGM no longer has full control of the people. They know we're more than recusants or rebels—they call us what we are: anomalies. *Sliders*," Fin replied.

I swallowed back the lump in my throat as Fin handed my daughter back to me. Her eyes were still shut tight.

"You are both fugitives here." Fin looked from me to Icarus, then to the baby. "We all are—we all must keep our true identities hidden, moving from place to place to avoid detection."

Icarus looked at him. "What about the initiates?"

"They're sworn to secrecy—every portal, every school I've established doubles as something else to throw off suspicion," he explained. "Every one of the new initiates is a force for good—something beautiful that we never even expected to find this far in Earth's future. And there are a few who have something beyond that…"

My gaze shifted to Fin's. "What do you mean?"

"Some students just seem to be naturally in tune with the things they cannot see—they trust. They use their own unique ability to give the Earth back what she has lost. They're the ones who will bring Earth back from death before we lose her altogether." He squinted up at the dead tree towering over us. "They're natural healers."

"How will you go about training them?"

Fin smiled. "I don't think I'll need to… These things seem to simply come when they are given room to grow. Lara, Areos, and I are building something new—a home, not a school—in western America, where the chances of being discovered are very slim…" He paused, glancing down at my and Icarus's new daughter. "You two are not the only ones with a child now."

My eyes widened, but he shook his head and lifted a hand before I could voice my suspicions.

"Galway fell—there was a massacre. I rescued a little boy whose parents were killed. I've adopted him. I know what it is to lose everything—everyone you hold dear…" Fin drew a breath, his green eyes shifting back to the bundle in my arms. His lips curved into a smile. "What have you named her?"

Before I could respond, there was the sound of a distant shot. Icarus tensed beside me, and Fin rose calmly to his feet.

"That can't be…" Icarus stammered.

Fin looked at him. "After New Dublin? They're not going to stop searching for the pair of you—for all of us."

Icarus's face was sheet white. He swallowed. "It's been five years."

"There are bounties on your heads," he said gravely. "They won't stop looking for you until they believe you both are dead."

Another shot sounded in the distance.

Icarus dropped down beside me. "We have to go, Hawk—now."

My heart pounding in my chest, my gaze slid from Fin to Icarus. "We're not supposed to be living in hiding—running every time we meet opposition!"

"I agree—I know," Icarus began. "But, Hawk, if we don't run now, they will find us and kill us, and then what will become of Earth?"

"We can't—not with…" My voice cracked as I looked down at our daughter. "If they capture us…"

Fin stepped forward before Icarus could respond. "Leave her with me and run, Hawk. You have to protect yourselves." He lowered his voice, stepping closer. "We can't risk anything happening to you. We need you…"

The words rang in my ears, along with the pounding of my heart in my head. In the distance I could hear shouts, gunfire, and the distant whir of aircraft approaching. I swallowed hard. Fin placed his warm hand over mine.

"Come to me as soon as it is safe, when things have died down," he quickly whispered. "No one suspects me. She will be safe."

I swallowed hard as I gazed up into his face. I kissed our little girl's head before placing her into his arms, choking back tears.

"Take care of her," I whispered, swallowing a sob. "For me."

There were tears in Icarus's eyes, too, but he made no protest.

"Call her Sparrow," I told him, my voice cracking. "And don't let her forget who she is…"

Fin stared at me for a moment, his green eyes glistening. "You will be back for her, Hawk—you both will see her soon. Believe that."

I nodded, blinded now by tears. "Yes. Yes, we will…"

I could hardly finish the sentence. Fin took my hand in his own, his voice frayed with urgency.

"I will protect her with all that I am," he whispered, holding my daughter against his chest. "Now run."

# PART ONE

# 1

*2218*

"WHOA, WHOA, WHOA—THAT IS A STOP SIGNAL, YOU IDIOT!"

There was a dull thud as the brakes locked up, and the tight steel pod the five of us were crowded into slammed to a halt. Flying over the rails that lined the congested city streets, we rolled through the red light blinking up from the ground in the middle of the intersection. I saw Cal bite his lip as he swung the steering wheel and missed a collision with another pod by inches.

The guy riding shotgun, whose name I was still trying to remember, reached over to smack Cal, cursing.

"Are you *trying* to get us killed?" one of the girls in the backseat with me growled, putting down her window.

"This is how everyone drives in New York," Cal insisted.

I smirked but said nothing as his eyes connected with mine in the rearview mirror.

We rocketed forward over the glossy metallic streets, weaving in among the skyscrapers, then swung a left at the next intersection, sinking below the buzzing city and into a tunnel running parallel with the multiple sets of Bullet tracks. One of the girls lit a cigarette; someone turned some music on. I leaned my head back and cracked my window, taking a deep breath as the wind rushed in, drenching me in the scent of smog.

I rolled my sweaty palms over the knees of my black jeans, my fingertips catching on the wide rips. Neon blurred through the glass to burn my eyes; deep bass and shrill sirens filtered through the night air as we resurfaced above ground. The clusters of soldiers from the Reformed Global Militia, known as the RGM, convening on a street corner were mere flashes of black uniforms among the bright lights.

"Where is this place, anyway?" The girl in the seat opposite mine leaned forward, peering out the windshield.

"Not far."

She grumbled, then reached across the girl between us, offering me her cigarette. I took a long drag before handing it back to her.

We swung into a dirty parking lot illuminated in shades of rust by streetlights. Cal cut the engine, and my worn combat boots thudded against the dinged metal surface beneath my feet. The pod mechanically lowered to the ground with an easy hiss. Cal slammed the driver's door, and a moment later I felt his hand at the small of my back.

"Glad you could get out tonight." He ran a hand back through his jet-black hair, his glossy hazel eyes holding me in a particular stare. "You usually can't."

I gave him a weak grin, shrugging a shoulder. "You know how the rules are at my school."

"Well, they need to lighten the hell up."

I gave a mirthless laugh. "That's not likely."

We were making our way around to the back of a somewhat dilapidated-looking building. Music pumped through a few of the shattered windows, along with the vague scent of smoke. I saw Cal's friend knock on a rusty old door that read "Employees Only" in chipped red paint. It swung open a moment later, and he stepped in, holding it open for the rest of us.

Cal pushed me inside in front of him, and for a moment I was deafened.

The club was tiny, deluged in neon light, and filled with people. Various languages hummed in the air, a band played on a stage at the back of the room, and glasses clattered at the bar.

"Don't they give you any free time at this school?" Cal yelled over the noise, his hand still around my waist. "They treat you like you're still a kid."

"I think they consider seventeen still a kid."

We wove our way through the tangle of bodies and stopped at the far end of the bar. Cal leaned against the long stretch of shiny metal and lowered his head to shoot me a look.

"And, uh… what about you, Sarah?" he asked. "Do you think seventeen is still a kid?"

I rolled my eyes, smirking. "Of course not."

Cal's thin lips curved into a smile that was like a crimson streak against his pale skin.

"Prove it." He jerked his head toward the bartender as she approached. "You order."

"Hey, you're the expert," I came back smoothly. "I'll have whatever you're having." I swallowed, scanning the room for the rest of our group, who seemed to have vanished among the crowd.

Cal ordered and then turned back to me just as the band was finishing up. "So, tell me: how *did* you get out?"

I shrugged and leaned an elbow on the bar. "Window."

"Are you kidding me?"

"I plan on getting back in the same way. I left it open a crack," I explained, leaning closer. "You have no idea how much I envy you—being able to do whatever you want. I could never do that."

Cal's eyebrows furrowed. "Why not? What are they trying to do at that place—hide you from the rest of the world?"

I couldn't help but laugh a little. *If he only knew…*

The bartender slid our drinks in front of us, saving me from having to answer. Among the crowd were several young RGM soldiers.

"You know what?" I said, taking a long sip. "Let's not talk about school, okay? I'm here; you're here… Let's talk about us."

Cal's drink was already gone. He wiped his mouth with the back of his hand and smiled. "What about us?"

I started to reply, but a sudden burst of music severed my sentence as the band came to life once again. Shooting the soldiers a side glance, I laced my fingers through Cal's and tugged him through the crowd, closer to the stage.

The room dimmed; hands, arms, and bodies followed the rhythm of the music. Standing behind me, Cal brushed my hair aside and kissed the back of my neck before leaning closer to talk into my ear. "You should do this running-away thing more often."

Not replying, I took another long sip from the cold glass in my hands. The lights started blinking overhead just as Cal slid his hands down over my hips and spun me around to face him. He held me in a long stare for a moment, his eyes glistening in the low light; then his lips brushed mine.

The lights seemed to bend and dip as we swayed, as his lips pressed harder against mine. It was just a kiss, just a drink, just a club… but it all made me feel, just for a moment, like I was normal. Like I was just a human.

*If only that were true.*

"You can just stop here." I reached over and placed a hand on his arm as I unbuckled my safety belt. The pod slammed to a halt beneath the glow of the floating blue streetlight overhead.

"Are you sure you don't want to just spend the night?" Cal asked, his gaze drifting down my body. I leaned over and laughed into his lips.

"Nah, not tonight, babe." I ran my hands back through his hair. "I've got school in the morning."

"Screw it."

"Easy for you to say." I opened the passenger door. "It's not your problem."

"We've been going out for a while now, you know," he argued playfully.

"Three dates," I corrected him.

"I would love to show you my place."

"Oh, I'm sure you would." I got out on the sidewalk, steadying myself against the pod as blurs of buildings and street signs swirled around me. I turned and leaned through the open window of the pod.

Cal sighed, tapping his palms on the steering wheel. "When do I get to see you again?"

I waved the question off. "Oh, eventually."

Cal bit his lip, tipping his head back against the driver's seat. "Hard to get."

"Of course."

I backed away from the hovering pod, and Cal took off down the street. Once he was gone, I turned and continued down the dimly lit sidewalk, bathed in the sickly glow of the flickering streetlights.

I swung a right and headed down another sidewalk lined with buildings, stopping at a particular set of cement steps to slide off my high-tops. The window to the left of the sleek metal front door was still open a few inches; the curtains pulled shut over the glass swayed in the soft night air. I glanced around, making sure there was no one lingering on the sidewalk. With my free hand, I noiselessly slid the window farther open, hoisting myself up onto the sill and lowering myself inside. The silky white curtains encompassed me. I quickly, quietly lowered the window again, silencing the street noise.

I brushed aside the curtains, stepping out into the open—only to stop dead.

"Fin!" I blurted. "I just—I—I…"

Streetlight spilled across the polished floorboards, illuminating a figure seated on the floor with his back to the wall. A figure with a mess of blond hair and a craggy jawline. His glinting green eyes locked with mine, and his deep voice filled the room with a solitary question.

"Where were you?"

I racked my brain for some kind of explanation, but none came fast enough. My fingers trembled as I stumbled forward a few steps. He rose to his feet to switch on the light, blinding me.

"What do you expect?" My voice cracked. "You never let me do anything! You never let me be normal. You always have to treat me like I'm such a freak!"

He was standing at the opposite end of the big open room now, his back to me.

"Fin, I'm not a child anymore," I began again through clenched teeth. "I have my own life. Why can't you just respect that?"

"Keep your voice down, Sparrow. You'll wake the other students."

"See? See, that's all I am to you—that's all I ever was—"

"Sparrow—"

"A student!" I shouted over him. "All you want is to turn me into something I'm not—a monster, just like the rest of them!"

"Sparrow!"

Fin whirled around so fast I barely saw him move. Suddenly he was in front of me. Wordlessly, he grabbed me by the wrist and pulled open my clenched fingers, instantly channeling my anger, against my will, into a hot red orb levitating just above my palm. Fin's gaze leveled with mine, steel and velvet all at once. Everything I'd been about to yell into his face disintegrated in my throat as I stared at the energy flowing out of my own hand.

"I say that you are different, Sparrow, because you are," he said quietly. "And you cannot keep running from it."

I felt numb. I swallowed, my tongue clinging to my jaw. "You don't understand…"

He held on to my wrist a moment longer before finally letting go. "I understand that something has to change."

I shuffled backward, my eyes widening, still not having disconnected from his. I knew that look—the tone of his voice. We stood at the edge, and I'd pushed too hard—too far.

"No, no, no, no—Fin, please," I slurred frantically. "I don't—I can't—"

His shoulders were back, and his facial expression remained firm. "You have forgotten who you are, Sparrow."

I almost choked as I staggered back a few more steps—hit the wall. "No… no—"

"Sparrow."

"Don't call me that! Don't ever call me that again! I'm not Sparrow—I never wanted to be!" My fingers rolled into fists once more. "I-I never wanted to be like you. I'm not!"

I pressed my hands to my face, avoiding his eyes. Silence swelled in the void my angry words had left, interrupted only by the creak of doors opening upstairs.

"Sensei, is everything okay?" a boy's voice called, echoing down the stairwell.

My hands fell away from my face; they were stained with angry black tears. Through my bleary vision, I still saw Fin's face: that look.

"Everything is fine," he called to the boy, his voice gentle. "Go back to sleep."

The door creaked and clicked shut once again.

Fin closed his eyes for a moment. My throat tightened as he stepped forward.

"Pack your things," he told me, his voice quiet and even. "We leave in the morning."

My lips slowly parted, my eyes widening once again. "F-f-for where?"

Fin studied my face, his jaw set. "To find what you have lost."

# 2

I LEANED BACK AGAINST THE ROUGH BARK COVERING THE dead pine tree, not moving, barely breathing.

The blackened forest around me rolled on for another quarter of a mile and then yawned open into a glade dripping in colors of rust and brown. Beyond that were more trees and then the river. I could hear the muted gurgle from where I stood. A fox crouched in the clearing in front of me. Its coat was dull, and chunks of it were missing.

"I think it's mange," Kateri whispered into my ear, sidling up next to me without making any noise. "And its leg…"

I gave a quick nod. I'd noticed the blood-caked fur. "Think you can get over to that other pine?" I made the slightest gesture with my head. "We'll close him off."

I could see the wheels turning behind Kateri's amber eyes, her golden skin lit by the shafts of dawn. She slung her long jet-black braid over her shoulder.

"All right," she replied. "Be ready."

I nodded, then turned my focus back to the limping fox, which took only a few pitiful steps before stopping again.

*Don't move… don't move… not yet.*

Kateri skirted the glade, her brown leather cutoff leggings and tan tunic making it easy for her to blend into the desolate landscape surrounding us. She slipped deftly into place behind the tree just as the wounded fox limped forward, tripping over its leg.

I let out a soft, lilting whistle.

Carefully I reached into my shoulder holster and pulled out one of my knives. I focused it into levitation over my palm, scoping out my target. I threw the knife in one swift motion.

I watched it rotate forward in a blur, cutting clear across the glade and leaving a long stream of red energy to arch after it. The blade embedded itself into a lifeless birch, and the energy disintegrated into a glittering mist that snowed to the ground, creating a cloudy red curtain.

The fox stopped and then took a limping step backward. A shrill, eagle-like call penetrated the quiet. Scared, it bounded forward again, toward the clouds of red. I watched it carefully, ready to jump forward if needed, but sure enough, it jerked to a startled halt once more before it reached the colorful bursts of energy, letting out a frightened shriek.

In a flash, I dove out from my cover just as Kateri did the same, closing off the wounded fox's escape. Crouching, it bared its teeth, snarling as we got closer.

"Wait." Kateri motioned for me to stop. "He's scared."

"I can see that," I panted, half-crouched in the clearing with my arms outstretched. "Get in there and do your thing before he bites me."

"Pshh—he's not going to bite…" Kateri calmed her voice, shuffling incrementally closer and lowering herself to her knees. "No… no, you're not going to attack, are you, love?"

The fox crouched.

Kateri made quiet clicking sounds with her tongue. The fox's bright greenish-yellow eyes flicked warily from me to her.

"Shhh…" she whispered. "Nobody's going to hurt you…"

Slowly, she extended one hand until it was inches from the fox's snout. Its ears flicked back a little farther, and then, cautiously, it inched forward to sniff Kateri's open palm.

"I know. I know you're not sure…" she told it softly.

I crept a little closer. Its eyes flashed up to mine, and it backed off.

"You're scaring him."

I gritted my teeth. "How am I supposed to heal it if it won't let me near it?"

"He's a he, not an it." Kateri gently traced its snout with one finger. "Let's take him back. You can work on him there. He's too scared right now—he needs to rest."

"All right, all right." I raked my fingers back through my long hair. "Think you can get him to follow us?"

Kateri lifted herself from the ground, her arm still outstretched in front of her. She coaxed the little animal forward, and slowly, limping, it began to follow her. She glanced at me over her shoulder.

"Lead the way," she said softly.

I brushed aside blackened branches and held them for Kateri. We climbed over fallen trees and rotting piles of what used to be logs, brush, and flowers. This was our first time being out this far—nothing was alive. Up ahead, the roasted remains of a rotting sign stuck halfway out of the ground, only half the words still legible:

*… elcome to Yellowstone Natio…*

The sun had just peeked over the ridge, and early white light rolled down the mountainside as we trekked back into the charred remains of the fire-eaten forest. The ashy ground was rough under my bare feet, and the scent of smoke still hung faintly in the air like an invisible memento mori.

Kateri stared up into the treetops as she walked, her lips pressed into a troubled frown. The fox limped at her heels. Slowing to a stop at the forest's edge, I scanned the open meadow. A long curving river split the land into two distinct sections: half was a burnt auburn, and the other a lush green that tapered off into the part of the forest we frequented, thick and dark and rolling like waves. When I was confident the meadow was safe to cross, I motioned for Kateri to follow, and she clucked her tongue for the fox to do likewise.

Faint wisps of what Sensei called "poison" churned in the air, tainting the sky's turquoise shine. The smog was less thick here, in what was now called Section West—the part of the country everyone had evacuated long ago.

"It kills me to walk past," I murmured to Kateri as the charred grass crunched beneath our feet, "without being able to heal every tree I touch. This meadow… it must have been so beautiful once…"

"If too much of the forest suddenly came back, they would spot it from the air."

"Pssh. Let them. What are they gonna do, come find me and lock me up?" I gave a flippant shrug. "Bring it on."

A little smile found Kateri's lips. She reached over and tugged on the small braid that hung a little lower than the rest of my shaggy ginger mane, two feathers tied at the end.

"You have such a temper; I blame the hair."

"I blame the wolf pack Sensei extracted me from."

She almost choked on a laugh.

"My darkest secret: I was raised by wild animals. Not that I mind." I gestured to the fox, which was trailing Kateri peacefully at this point despite its limp. "They're more understanding than most humans I've encountered."

Kateri brushed her long braid over her shoulder. "Things will not always be this way, Keegan."

We stopped when we reached the river. Kateri stooped down and coaxed the fox toward her. She scooped it gently into her arms, and we splashed through the cold, black, waist-deep water.

I could already hear the distant shriek of an eagle and the hiss of cicadas in the tall grass. The scent of pine began to drift into my lungs.

We'd reached *our* part of the forest.

"We've already made quite a bit of progress." Kateri picked the conversation back up, glancing around. "It's good to actually see the fruits of our labors, the very reason why Sensei brought us here—why he transferred us from other schools."

"If only healers were easier to come by." My fingers brushed against the bark on a pine. "How does he know he's choosing the right ones?" I squinted up at the treetops. "I didn't even know I was a healer. I thought I was just a—"

"Mind reader."

"Only when I have to be. You know I don't ever abuse the ability—"

"Relax. I'm only teasing." She knocked me gently with her elbow. "We all have our abilities to use for good or bad… We chose to use them for good."

"Do you miss your old place of training?" I asked. "Section C… your family… I'm sure they miss *you*."

Kateri sighed, a distant look on her face. "You're more like family to me, all of you. Healing has always been what I was made for—what we were all made for."

I followed Kateri as we entered a large clearing encircled by pines that seemed to stand guard around the cabin erected in the center; the cabin Dad, Lara, Areos, and I had built years before: the school for healers. Felled trees with thick notches chopped out had been interlocked to create a two-story dwelling. Moss bloomed over the roof, and creeping myrtle ran wild up the front of the cabin to frame the gabled second-story windows.

Kateri circled around the back of the cabin to the small barn. It was more like a shack, built of pine branches and covered with foliage. She opened the door and led the fox inside. It limped over the threshold. I closed the door behind us. The fox clambered slowly but willingly into Kateri's lap. I knelt down on the soft ground beside them.

Milling around us were other animals from the previous few days: rabbits, squirrels, and even a fawn, who was sleeping quietly.

"All right, let's see…" My tone was soft as I spoke to the fox, letting it sniff my hand for a moment before attempting to lift its injured paw.

I could feel Kateri's eyes on me as I gently closed the fox's paw between my palms. It whimpered and tried to writhe away. She hummed softly as I took a steady breath and closed my eyes. I focused on the matted fur and mangled claws, the wetness of its blood. A glowing warmth began to travel from my chest to my arms and finally into my hands, where it seemed to ignite.

"Shhh, there we go… all done…" Kateri soothed it when I finally pulled away. I found her cradling it in her arms like a baby when I opened my eyes again. She beamed as she held up the fox's tiny paw. It was completely healed now.

"Good." I gave her a little smile, straightening up. "Now we should probably feed these guys…"

Before Kateri could respond, the door burst open. A halo of light illuminated Janna's head of frizzy blonde hair. The fox writhed violently and leapt out of Kateri's arms, and the other animals started.

"You're scaring them," I grumbled, shooting her an annoyed look. "How many times have I—"

"It's okay. I've got it," Kateri cut in, getting to her feet. "Just go outside, both of you—I'll calm them down."

Janna looked sheepish as I stepped outside. She hugged her arms around herself and pulled her hands into the sleeves of a baggy wool sweater.

"Sensei wants you, Keeg," she announced.

"Couldn't you just have told me that through the door?"

She rolled her blue eyes. "Well, sor-ry. I didn't know you guys were healing a baby wolf."

"Fox."

"Whatever."

Following the tall, skinny nineteen-year-old girl around to the front of the cabin, I pounded up the stairs. The scent of pancakes hit me as Janna pushed the creaky screen door open. Lara occupied the rustic old stove at the far end of the room. Rafael was helping set the table.

Striding into the kitchen, I grabbed a warm plate off the butcher-block island and inhaled deeply.

"Man, you're a wizard with a spatula, Lara," I told her.

Lara grinned. I held up the plate a few yards away, and she slingshotted one round, buttery pancake through the air. It almost hit me in the face. Preston, my roommate and best friend, burst out laughing from the table, where he sat eating his breakfast. He was wearing dirt-streaked canvas pants like I was, and a green T-shirt that contrasted with his dark brown skin. He grinned, pointing a fork in my direction.

"Watch your face," he suggested teasingly. "Lara's aim is—"

"Oh, stop it," Lara said, laughing. Her voice had a lilting Irish accent. She forked up one more pancake and took aim. "I was a sniper, for goodness' sake."

I had to lunge for it, which made Preston laugh all the more, but I caught it. I walked over to the counter for butter, sidling up beside Rafael.

"Keegan, do you think we'll have time to throw today?" he asked, his voice edged with a Spanish accent.

"Today?" I paused, resting my hand on his shoulder. "We're heading out into the northeast section of the woods today, bro."

Rafael's lips twisted a little in disappointment.

"Tell you what," I said. "Let me destroy some pancakes, and then I'll talk to Sensei. Maybe we can get an early start, and we'll have time to fit in a lesson before dinner."

His face brightened. "Yeah?"

I clapped him on the back. "Of course." Then I glanced back at Lara. "Has Sensei already eaten?"

"No, he hasn't," Lara replied. "But I'll make him up a plate. He didn't transport back until dawn," she explained, wiping her hands with a dishrag. "I'm hoping he went back to sleep."

"Sensei? Sleep?" I grunted. "Not likely."

"See if he'll eat something," Lara said. "He's always insisting he doesn't need food, but…"

"But he enjoys it like the rest of us," Preston finished.

Lara piled some food on a plate and handed it to me. Putting a hand on my shoulder, she walked a few paces toward the hallway alongside me.

"I just heard from Areos this morning," she told me, keeping her voice low. "There was a capture."

I tensed a little, a cold feeling wringing my stomach.

"Is Areos all right?"

Lara quickly nodded. "Yes, but they got one of his students in Section C."

I frowned. "Still such a dangerous area."

"All the cities are—who knows when it will spread to the country-side…" Lara's blonde eyebrows knitted together. "We're not just recusants to them anymore—they've seen us. They know."

"It feels like such a long time ago that Areos left to teach in Section C." I blew out a sigh. "I know how much you miss him—how much the dreams… bother you." I dropped my voice, looking her in the eyes. "Believe me, I know how it feels."

"I know you do."

"But we're not near any of the occupied cities," I assured her softly. "The RGM has *no idea* we're out here. I'm sure we're safe."

She yielded a stiff nod. "Of course." She turned back to the kitchen. "Of course we are."

There were thousands of words in between the few she actually spoke. Out here in the middle of nowhere, in the forgotten remains of Yellowstone National Park, it was easy to forget that we were in the middle of a war. It was easy to forget that Lara had been an RGM sniper. It was easy to forget what had happened in New Dublin, and that they were still searching for us.

I continued down the hall until I reached the door to Dad's office. We called it his office, but it was more like a greenhouse. I was about to knock when I noticed the tiny vines fingering out from underneath the knotted oak door. I shifted the plates onto one arm and rapped swiftly.

A pause. Then a familiar Irish accent.

"Come on in, Keegan."

I twisted the knob and slipped into what looked like a small forest confined to four walls. Vines of ivy covered the side of the room, baskets of herbs spilled from the windowsills, moss coated the fireplace, and lanky potted saplings grew in the corners, reaching towards the illuminated panes of glass. Wisteria gathered and hung in the center of the ceiling like a chandelier. Dad stood behind a hefty mahogany desk, holding a magnifying glass up to examine the blossoms of a pale-yellow wildflower. Other species of plant clippings were scattered across the desk's surface, and off to one side was a stack of notes. Beside them sat a jar full of pens mixed with faded hawk feathers.

He set down the magnifying glass and sighed, leaning forward on the desk. His green eyes connected with mine, and he smiled, noticing the plate I was carrying.

Though he'd raised me since I was five, it still felt strange when I called him "Dad"—I only called him that when it was just us. Around the other students, it was always and respectfully "Sensei." He looked no older than thirty, even though he was, like, three hundred years old or something like that.

"Thought you might need some pancakes." I stepped forward, setting the plate down.

He laughed a little, rubbing his forehead. "You thought right."

"What are you working on?"

He handed me the sprig of the tiny plant he'd been studying when I walked in. A dried-up stem with faded nectary blossoms.

"Sulphur flower," he explained bluntly, picking up his fork. "They were rare to begin with. They're extinct now."

I twirled the stem between my fingertips, studying it silently.

"We've been here so long," I pointed out. "Yet we haven't been able to save something even as small as this…"

"Things only change because we choose to change them, Keegan," he responded. "Before you were born, before the attack on New Dublin, I spent a year living among the dead mountains in County Wicklow, trying to bring them back to life."

"And eventually you did."

"*Eventually*," he emphasized. "But that's just one forest. One place."

I handed the sulphur flower back to him.

"And though the things directly in front of us can often seem bleak, it's important to recognize the progress we have made," he went on. "We've restored many forests and streams and mountains. Not just in Wicklow."

"I wish I remembered Ireland," I said. "I feel like I'm not even from there."

Dad shook his head, taking a bite of the pancake. "You're not from there."

"I was born there—that's where you found me."

"Yes, but it's still not where you're from, Keegan." He pushed back his chair and got to his feet. "And neither am I." He turned to a wooden cabinet behind him, sliding open one of the narrow drawers and taking out a small canvas pouch. "Give me your hand."

I extended my arm over the desk, and he spread my palm, tapping what looked like a few dried, speckled beans into my hand.

"Seeds?"

Dad nodded. "Where did they come from?"

"The plant they grew from," I answered, bringing them closer to my face to examine.

"Mm-hmm. But what about *that* plant?" Dad asked. "Where did *it* come from?"

"Another seed from another plant…"

"Which grew somewhere else." He picked one out of my hand. "And so did the plant before it, and the one before it—ad infinitum. All seeds, all carried various distances from other plants, from other locations."

I frowned, glancing up at him. "So… they come from nowhere?"

"No." He dropped the seed back into the palm of my hand. "They come from everywhere."

I picked one up and looked at it a little closer as Dad began his morning routine of watering the plants.

"So…" I began slowly. "This is what you wanted to talk to me about?"

He shook his head but didn't answer. I watched him water the plants while I ate my pancakes. Finally, he took the kind of breath that meant an answer was coming. I straightened up a little, already listening.

"I'm transferring a student," Dad started, strangely hesitant. "From New York."

"Cool," I said. "To where?"

He looked at me seriously. It clicked before he'd even answered. My eyes widened.

"Here?" I blurted. "Are you serious?"

"Perfectly."

"When?"

"She arrives today." He ran his fingertips across his forehead. "I came back just before dawn, and I'm planning on transporting back to the school in New York shortly. You could transport there with me if you like," he said after a moment of silence. "You've never seen the training center in New York."

"I'll stay here and help get things ready." I brushed away the thought, picking at the edge of the desk. "I can hardly believe it." I glanced up at him. "Kateri and I were just talking about how we could use an increase in our numbers if we really want to start making an impact—this is exactly what we need! What's her special ability?"

Dad looked at me for a long moment in silence before rising from the desk. He walked to the window overlooking the garden and paused there, rubbing his jaw thoughtfully.

"What is it?" I asked after a moment.

Still, he made no reply.

"Dad?" I pressed the question. "Is there something wrong? I feel like you know something I don't."

Finally, he turned around, seeming to blink back into focus. "She'll be here this afternoon," he answered finally. "You can ask her yourself."

# 3

"SPARROW…"

My eyelids were heavy and unwilling as I lifted them. Raindrops hit my face and blurred the tall, dark trees towering over me. Their naked branches cracked the decaying sky. I stumbled forward, feeling drunk, and a moment later the cold, stiff earth caught me as I fell.

I blinked and squinted, trying desperately to keep my eyes open. I listened for the strange, soft voice that had spoken my name. I craned my neck and peeled my eyes open to find that the trees had turned to angry swirls overhead; their dark, skeletal shapes seemed to stretch on and on.

"*Sparrow…*" came the whispering voice again.

I struggled to climb to my feet. I wanted to ask who was there, but my dry, quivering lips remained sealed. The woods stood like a yawning black void. Just as everything began to flicker, I saw the dark shapes of wings emerge from the treetops, smudging against the sky and vanishing into the angry gray clouds.

"*Sparrow…*"

A sound like the pounding of a drum rattled through my mind, wrenching me into what felt like a whirlwind. Sucking in a startled breath, I bolted upright, my hands tangled in bedsheets.

"Sparrow!"

I sat there for a moment, gasping, taking in snatches of the room around me: wood floors, white curtains, open window. I felt sick to my stomach as I pressed my hand to my forehead, squeezing my eyes closed just as the pounding came again.

"Spaaaarrow," droned the student's familiar voice. "Sensei's waiting for you."

"Just leave me alone!" I snapped, throwing the sheets aside. Sun spilled over the rows of empty beds. "I'll be down in a minute."

I pulled on a pair of shorts and pried open the top drawer of the clunky oak dresser.

The sound of rush hour traffic drifted up from the busy streets below. My gaze fell on the simple, unframed mirror mounted to the wall across the room. My reflection stared back at me: an almond-shaped face, olive skin, thick arching brown eyebrows. Eyes and hair the color of the night: dark, dark brown that wanted to be black. Fingernails painted chipped midnight blue stood out against faded pink as I tugged my bottom lip. Dark circles and smudges of mascara hung below my eyes.

I stood there, studying myself for a moment before walking back to my bed. I pulled my bag out from underneath, unzipped it, and reached inside.

A familiar square of paper brushed my fingertips.

I walked back to the mirror, my tired eyes scrutinizing my reflection once more. Then I looked down at the photograph in my hand.

A young woman with a thin oval face, her skin and long hair the same tones as mine, with arching brown eyebrows to match. Her eyes were like night skies.

Fin had always told me that I "looked so much like her." Finally, he'd given me a picture—the only picture he'd had of her.

I slid the photograph back into my bag and stepped away from the mirror, shoving these thoughts out of my mind.

I pulled a white T-shirt over my bra and raked my hair into a tired ponytail. All I wanted was a hot shower and then three more hours of sleep, but that was never going to happen. I was already running late. I muttered a halfhearted apology as I reached the bottom of the stairs, where Runner, one of our instructors, was waiting.

"That doesn't cut it," he announced, tipping back his head of highlighter-yellow hair. "You're supposed to be at every training session–"

"Every morning, on time, always. Yes…" I dropped off the last step, rubbing my temple. "I know."

"And a bad attitude will get you nowhere, just in case you were wondering."

"I wasn't," I said flatly. "But thanks."

Runner tossed me a disappointed look. "Fin's an awesome guy—and teacher. I was his student too, you know. You should at least *try* for his sake."

I rolled my eyes. "I'm not even attending training anymore, Runner. Didn't you hear? Fin's kicking me out."

Surprise flashed in his dark brown eyes. I nodded.

"He's transferring me—I don't know where to," I continued, leaning back against the wall. "I don't really care at this point, honestly. It could be hell and I'd be okay with it."

Runner snorted. "You don't mean that."

A quiet laugh hummed past my sealed lips.

*You have no idea…*

"Not quite hell…" a voice cut in; I heard the sound of approaching footsteps. Fin appeared behind Runner. I frowned as soon as I saw his irritating expression of resolve—hard green eyes and a tense, craggy jaw. There was no room for negotiation when he looked that way.

"Where?" Runner questioned.

Fin was staring at me. I shifted my gaze to the floorboards and tried to focus on the sound of traffic outside, but his response snapped me back.

"The Homestead."

I almost choked. "*What?*"

"The *Homestead?*" Runner sounded about as flabbergasted as I felt. "Fin, you can't be—"

"I'm perfectly serious."

"Then… you must be losing it," he concluded.

I nodded my agreement. A muscle in Fin's jaw twitched.

"Sparrow is barely passing these *basic* classes, Fin. She hates them," Runner huffed.

"He's right, Fin," I chimed in. "Listen to him."

Fin shot me a severe look. I lifted my chin defiantly.

"You can't just transport her to our most elite place of training." Runner gestured toward me like I was some kind of Frankenstein. "She's the furthest thing from a healer!"

"That's not for us to decide," Fin replied firmly.

"She runs away, stays out all night, and comes home drunk," Runner sputtered.

"Yes, I know," Fin agreed flatly. "And she's going to transfer to the Homestead."

Runner dragged a hand over his face.

"I assume you and Mala can handle taking the classes today?" Fin asked.

"Yeah… yeah, sure. Whatever you say, Fin," Runner muttered. "Whatever you say."

Fin turned to me, still wearing that face. "Follow me."

I trailed after him reluctantly, forcing one foot in front of the other. My toes clenched in my shoes as we stopped at a metal door. Fin unlocked it and focused it open. It swung smoothly on its hinges, revealing a tiny space within—an empty closet. Fin tilted his head, motioning for me to step inside.

I swallowed tightly and pushed myself forward into the darkness. He followed, and the door slammed shut.

"Sparrow, before we transport," Fin began, a disembodied voice in the dark, "there's something you have to know—something you have to promise me."

I rolled my eyes because he couldn't see. "And what's that?"

There was a pause.

"No one at the Homestead except Lara knows anything about you, Sparrow—not even my son, Keegan. You must tell no one at the Homestead who you really are, or that I've raised you," he began, his tone serious. "You must be nothing more than an ordinary student—"

"I know, okay?" I interrupted. "We go through this *every time*, Fin. When have I ever told anyone who I really am?" I lowered my voice to mutter, "Who *you* think I really am, anyway."

"*Promise me*," he said firmly. "For your own protection: not a word."

"Yes, I know. I *promise*."

Fin was silent for a moment.

"Now relax and think of nothing," he said, beginning to focus on the transport. "Think of nothing."

I wanted to think of everything. To think of the city, the skyline, the roaring streets and lights and smoke and beautiful lies that kept me going. I wasn't ready to let go—and I never would be. I wanted to remember last night, Cal, and the stupid, empty conversations.

My back touched the wall, and I closed my eyes.

There was only one consolation in going to the Homestead: I would finally meet Fin's son. I'd never met Keegan before—I'd never been able to. It was weird how I knew about him, but, for my protection, of course, he didn't know a thing about me.

Maybe he would be like Fin. Maybe I would finally become friends with another anomaly.

I could hear Fin's soft breathing close by and feel the touches of energy that seemed to radiate from him as he focused on our destination. I felt the space around us slowly change and expand. The sound of the traffic faded. For a split second, I felt dizzy. I couldn't tell if it was from the transportation or the hangover.

The scent of cedar filled my lungs. Fin began to stir, and a moment later, dusty golden light cut through the darkness, illuminating Fin's strong hand as he pushed the door open. He stepped out into the hallway and gestured for me to follow. Folding my arms over my chest, I slowly stepped out into the sun-drenched hallway.

"This way." Fin strode forward.

Everything was made of logs or wood planks: the walls, the floor, everything. Every window we passed was open, but there were no screens in any of them, just swung-open panes of glass. There was hardly any furniture until we reached the kitchen. A table stood in the middle of the room with a few chairs pulled up; one was occupied by an Asian girl who cradled a guitar in her arms while she scribbled on sheet music. She didn't look up.

"Myung, is Lara around?"

The girl's short brown hair bobbed as she nodded. "She just stepped outside for a second," she said, and then paused, squinting at me suspiciously. "Fresh meat?"

Fin rendered a nod. "Sparrow."

Myung gave me a once-over before lowering her head once again over the notepad in front of her, not saying a word. Fin placed a hand on my shoulder and guided me gently toward the back door.

When the screen door creaked open and we stepped outside, the first thing I noticed were the trees. Tall, tall stretches of gnarled hickory bark and arms of rich green. I'd never seen trees like these—so alive. Everything smelled like... well, something I'd never smelled before. But beyond the trees there was nothing. No houses, no people, no streets. There were shadows and more trees. That was all.

*Hell would have been better.*

"Lara." Fin addressed the young woman who stood at a tree stump with an ax in her hand, chopping wood. She looked up, and her face relaxed.

She looked only a few years older than me. She had green eyes like Fin, with sun-bleached blonde hair pulled back into an untidy bun. A few wisps fell around her face. She smiled when she saw me, leaning the ax against the chopping block.

"This must be Sparrow," she said, looking at me like this happened every day. She stuck out one earth-stained hand for me to shake. "I'm Lara, Sensei's sister."

After a slight hesitation, I shook her hand loosely before folding my arms back over my chest. "I just call him Fin."

There was an awkward pause. Lara's pleasant expression didn't fade. "You'll call him Sensei here, just like the other students," she corrected me.

"That's just it—I'm not a student—didn't Fin tell you?" I said, dragging the toe of my sneaker through the dirt. "I'm a delinquent."

"*Sparrow,*" Fin warned.

"All right then," Lara came back, seeming unfazed. "So is that how you want me to introduce you to the other students at dinner?"

I didn't respond.

"Okay, then, Sparrow," she continued. "You're sharing a room with Myung, Kateri, and Janna—it's upstairs at the far end of the hallway, across from the boys' room. Why don't you go and get settled in?"

I nodded slowly and shuffled backward a few steps before turning around to walk back toward the cabin. My lips twitched miserably as I took it all in. *A cabin—in the middle of literally nowhere.*

The screen door slammed behind me as I stepped back into the kitchen. Myung peered up from the table to shoot me a scowl as I stomped across the room.

"I'm trying to study here," she announced irritably.

I grumbled an insincere apology, barely pausing. I walked back down the hallway toward the closet through which we had entered. I twisted the knob frantically but found it locked.

Gritting my teeth, I quietly walked back through the living room and out the front door. I crept out onto the covered, wraparound porch and halted, scanning my surroundings. Over to one side of the house, a few students worked in between rows of vegetable beds framed by a rough post-and-rail fence.

Descending the steps, I kept my head low and crossed the yard to the tree line where the forest began. A woodpecker drilled nearby, and crickets chirruped in the brush covering the ground. I felt spiderwebs brush against my shins as I trod across the soft blanket of pine needles.

I walked briskly at first, then picked up my pace to a run. A tight, strange feeling seemed to suffocate me from the inside out. A feeling that was as vast and empty as the forest stretching out around me on all sides.

*I can't stay here… I can't stay here… I can't…*

The words ricocheted through my brain on repeat with the pounding of my footsteps; the trees blurred to a meaningless smudge around me, just as they had in my dream. Finally, I thudded to a stop, gripping the bark of a thick, towering pine before slumping back against it to catch my breath.

Aside from my own breathing, there was silence. The air hung thick and humid around me.

Fumbling in my pocket, I pulled out a cigarette and pinched it between my lips. I dug out my lighter, and a tiny click interrupted the silence as I lit the end. Leaning back against the tree, I took a long drag.

"Oh, god, I cannot stay here…" I whispered, exhaling smoke. "I can't…"

The smoke feathered up into the branches, dispersing with the gentle breeze. For a moment I just stood there, gaping up at the empty sky, a tightness burning in my throat with the taste of ash. I lifted the cigarette to my lips again.

Suddenly, a black blur whipped through the air, inches from my face, slicing the cigarette in half. I lurched away from the tree as two powerful arms latched around my torso and tackled me to the ground.

# 4

DAD WAS ALWAYS TRYING TO CONVINCE ME TO TRANSPORT with him to other portals—the other places of training he had helped to establish. Mostly he wanted to show me the ones in cities—Chicago, Lyon, Vienna, Belfast—but I never went. I always made some excuse not to go. There was always something else going on, something I had to be helping Kateri or Preston with. I never had time, but that was not the truth. Dad saw straight past my facade, but never questioned it.

This time my excuse was that I needed to go retrieve the knife I'd left out in the woods earlier. Which meant trekking back to where Kateri and I had tracked the injured fox. It had been the first of its kind we'd tracked in over a year in a place that had once been teeming with foxes, wolves, and elk.

Dad was very particular in deciding whom he would transfer here— who would actually benefit from living out here. I'd watched him bring in each and every student who trained here. Everyone was here for a very specific, necessary reason.

Kateri had been the first anomaly Dad had brought here. It had been just him, Lara, and me for a couple of years; then suddenly we became four. Though I'd been only a young teenager, I could still remember the first time I saw her: this strong, confident Cheyenne girl, beautiful inside and out.

She could talk to animals. I thought it was the coolest thing ever—I still did. She was quiet, listened more than she ever spoke, but she had more to say than I did.

She had taught me how to track, how to read animal behaviors, how to communicate with them through body language. But her gift was a bit like mine: I could read the minds of people; she could read the minds of animals—decipher what it was they were trying to "say" to us. She was so at home in her own skin, and I admired her for it. It seemed so long ago that she'd first arrived.

It had been two years since the last healer had come to the school: Rafael. I wondered what this new student my father was bringing in would be like, what gift she would have, what she would contribute.

I was excited about it. There was extra energy in my steps as I considered how our small group of healers would be growing more powerful.

I wrenched the black metal blade from the pine tree. Dried bits of wood showered to the ground as I levered the knife out of the trunk and slid it into my holster.

Out here, the wind seemed to breathe down the back of my neck and remind me who I really was. Sure, I could heal… but between the forest and me, we knew that wasn't why I was here.

The chirrup of a cardinal filled the air, accented by a few crickets, and then, farther up and into the blue, I caught the shrill, lonely call of a red-tailed hawk. The sounds spun and wove with the scent of pine and dirt and then suddenly slammed to a stop.

I ducked behind the trunk of a tree, holding my breath. I hadn't seen or heard anything yet, but my forehead felt numb. I sensed someone—their thoughts seemed to radiate in the air with the sunlight.

I slowed myself down, calming my breathing. I wasn't sure who was out there with me. I heard the snapping of a twig a moment later. Something crashed through the brush, and then—nothing. A long silence.

A few murmured words came after a moment, though I couldn't make out any of them. A soft rustle followed and then a click. I leaned around the tree just far enough to catch a glimpse of what I was hearing.

Standing in the middle of the clearing was a girl with scraggly limbs, long dark hair and stupid-looking clothes that no normal anomaly would wear out into the woods. A thin feather of smoke rose from between her fingertips.

My blood boiling, I wrenched a knife out of my holster and threw it with fierce accuracy. The blade slashed the end off her cigarette, sparing the tip of her nose by only a hair. She gasped, her whole body clenching as she bolted forward.

Springing out from my hiding place, I tackled her to the ground in a tangle of fighting limbs. Ashy vapor mixed with perfume filled my lungs as I wrenched her onto her back and pinned her hands over her head.

Wide, dark eyes pierced mine, furious and terrified.

"What the hell do you think you're doing?" I yelled into her face. "One spark, and this whole place could go up!"

She responded by folding her knee underneath me and delivering a firm jab to my groin.

Pain shot through my body as I buckled, crumpling to the dirt with a howl of pain. She jumped to her feet and streaked away into the brush. I yanked my knife out of the ground and took off after her, gritting my teeth.

The girl crashed through the brush like an animal being chased. I took a parallel path that was faster, but it didn't compensate for how quick she was. We both emerged into the glade where the cabin stood at exactly the same time, and to my surprise she dashed up the porch steps and bolted through the front door. I halted, staring in bewilderment.

"Keegan!" A waving hand caught my eye. "Who was that?"

I glanced over at Preston, who was working alongside Janna in the garden. Without taking the time to answer, I tore up the porch steps and yanked open the front door. I ran into the house and pounded up the stairs just as the door to the girls' room at the far end of the hallway slammed shut.

I stormed the length of the hallway and twisted the knob. It was locked.

"Open this door, *now!*" I yelled, jerking the doorknob furiously. "Or I swear to god—"

"*Keegan.*" I turned just as Lara stepped onto the landing, basket of laundry on her hip. "What on earth are you—"

I jabbed a finger at the door, striding toward Lara.

"I found a strange girl in the woods, and now she's locked herself in—"

"The woods?" Lara interrupted, quirking an eyebrow. "What was she doing out there? I told her to go upstairs and get—"

"You *told* her?" I croaked, cutting in. "You mean—you *knew* she was here?"

"Yes, I knew she was here, Keegan."

"Who *the hell* is she?"

Lara sighed, looking pained as she rubbed her forehead. "She's the new student."

# 5

I GRABBED A CHAIR OUT FROM UNDER A DESK AND WEDGED it under the doorknob. It began rattling as I backed away, followed by a fierce voice. "Open this door, now, or I swear to god—"

I was still trying to catch my breath when the knob abruptly stopped jiggling. Sweat trickled down my forehead. Something bristled against my leg. Startled, I whirled around.

A small, fuzzy fawn stood in front of me, trembling on its skinny legs in the middle of the bedroom floor. A young woman of Native American descent sat cross-legged on the lower bunk at the far end of the bedroom by the window. Her skin was golden brown, and a long black braid hung over her shoulder. She wore loose, earthy clothing and studied me calmly, not seeming to mind my explosive entrance. She held a pen poised in her fingertips, and a sketchbook lay open in her lap.

"He won't hurt you." She spoke up. "He just wants to say hi."

I stared at her. "Say hi? Really?" I swung a thumb towards the door. "That guy attacked me in the woods! And now he's in the house—Lara and Fin don't even know! We have to stay in here."

The girl seemed puzzled for a moment before breaking into a smile. "I meant the fawn."

My eyes lowered to the small animal in front of me. It gaped up at me with large brown eyes, slathering its snout with its long pink tongue.

"Oh," I said, nonplussed. "Well, I'm talking about the guy out there in the hallway! I was out in the woods for a… a walk, and he jumped me and chased me all the way here!"

The young woman still seemed confused, leveling her gaze past my shoulder to the door.

"It just sounded like Keegan to me."

I stared at her, a weight dropping into my stomach. "Say his name again?"

She seemed puzzled. "Keegan…" she repeated slowly.

*"No one at the Homestead except Lara knows anything about you, Sparrow—not even my son, Keegan."* Fin's words echoed in my thoughts.

I squeezed my eyes shut, wincing. "Keegan is… Fin's son."

She rendered a slow, deliberate nod. "*Sensei's* son, yes," she answered, correcting me. "He's the resident mind reader." She grinned a little, closing the sketchbook. "We work together most days, Keegan and I—you must be Sparrow, I assume."

I rendered a slow, horrified nod.

She swung her legs over the side of the mattress and extended a hand for me to shake. "I'm Kateri."

I inched my way around the baby deer to clasp her hand in a weak shake.

Kateri smiled. "Welcome to the Homestead."

A few loud, consecutive knocks made me turn to the door again.

"Hey, what's up with the locked door!" a muffled voice demanded.

Kateri sprang up and started to pull the chair out of the way.

"No, no, no—don't do that!" I shimmied backward. "He's still out there."

Kateri threw me a glance over her shoulder, pausing for only a moment before continuing to take away my obstruction. "It's only Myung." She turned the knob and pulled the door open. The girl I'd seen at the table downstairs stepped inside, her guitar slung over her shoulder. She was dressed in all black, with a scowl on her face to complete the vibe. She shot me a disdainful glance, but stopped in her tracks when she noticed the fawn.

"Ugh, Kateri," she groaned. "I thought we agreed about—"

"I know, I know, Myung, but he didn't like being out there with the fox—"

"No animals in the bedroom!"

"Myung, *just for tonight,* I promise."

I sidled over to the door, shutting and locking it again before leaning back against it. Out of the corner of my eye, in the mirror, I noticed a twig stuck in my hair. My knees were scuffed with dirt.

Kateri glanced over at me, coaxing the fawn over to her bunk. "You'll have to deal with Keegan sooner or later, Sparrow."

"Why?"

"Because we all work together here," Myung shot back, dropping onto one of the vacant bunks. "We have abilities for a reason, you know— we're supposed to use them to work together..." She paused. "What's yours?"

I froze, a sick feeling twisting in the pit of my stomach. My gaze switched from Myung to Kateri as they both waited for an answer... an answer I didn't have. Another sharp knock saved me.

"Hey, why's this locked?" The voice was Lara's.

Kateri motioned for me to open the door. Fin's sister stood in the hallway, her arms crossed over her chest, sizing me up through glinting green eyes.

"I told you to settle in, not disappear," she said sternly; then her gaze shifted to the fawn. "Kateri... you know the rule about—"

"Okay, okay... I'll sleep in the shed with him, then."

Lara's lips pinched together, pausing. "Fine. *One night*—then he's out."

"Yes, ma'am."

Lara looked back at me. "Come downstairs with me, please."

"No." I shook my head firmly. "I'm staying in my room until I leave."

Lara didn't seem surprised by my reaction. "If you don't come down, you don't get dinner," she informed me levelly.

There was silence behind me. Kateri and Myung had stopped talking, and I could sense their eyes on me.

"Cool," I answered, shrugging my shoulders. "I don't care."

The corners of Lara's lips turned down slightly before she finally drew a breath. "All right. If that's how you feel, Sparrow."

I stayed in the bedroom. Kateri tried to talk me into going downstairs for dinner with her, but I refused. I knew Fin would eventually come up and talk to me, like he always did. He would be wearing his usual disappointed look, and I would explain all the reasons why I wouldn't—*couldn't*—stay; all the reasons why he'd made the wrong decision. No one except Fin, and maybe Lara, knew why I was here. Everyone else thought I'd transferred from the school in New York to this godforsaken Homestead for some kind of divinely ordained reason.

I could still remember how I'd answered Fin the first time he had told me where I came from, back when we lived in France. Who I was.

"No," I had replied.

The memory was made up of messy visions: a fire flickering in the hearth, walls glowing soft pink, and me as a small child, curling up in the folds of Fin's strong arms. He'd tell me stories about a world beyond this one, a place where the sun never set. A place where he'd grown up with my mother.

I'd grin, and he'd look me in the eyes and ask, "What? Don't you believe me?"

And I'd shake my head, giggling like little girls do. Fin would tickle me and smile and say it was past my bedtime. It didn't matter, back then, that I thought it all was a fairy tale. It didn't matter that I didn't believe in this world he told me about, because Fin *was* my whole world. I couldn't imagine anything more: not another dimension, and certainly not my parents. Why did I need parents when I had Fin?

But parents mean something different when you're in that strange place between a kid and a young woman; a child in too-tight skin, fumbling for something that will fit but discovering that the drawers are empty. It was different when we began moving from training place to training place, avoiding the questions the initiates asked: *"What happened to your parents, Sparrow?"*

I didn't know, but I couldn't say that. The words hurt too much. So instead, I just made myself into someone no one wanted to question, someone no one wanted to talk to at all.

Our nights at the fireside turned into nights by the window overlooking the city, with me looking at Fin through a lens of suspicion.

"Fin, tell me the truth," I'd whispered one night. "Am I really yours, and you're just too ashamed to admit it?"

He'd looked at me through the low light from where he sat, his head tipped back against the chair.

"I love you as my own, Sparrow," he'd answered in a voice like tattered velvet: soft, but broken underneath. "I sometimes wish you were."

"If you're not my father, then why didn't mine ever come back?" That bitter question had been my only reply. "Why didn't my mother come back for me—"

"One day—"

"No, no—I'm sick of believing lies, Fin." Tears had stung my eyes. "They abandoned me. Maybe you should just accept that, like I have: they didn't want me."

But Fin would never accept that. Over and over again, Fin tried to tell me what had happened: that my parents had been fleeing the RGM, that they'd left me with him for my own safety, promising to return.

Fin told me my mother was brave. She was graceful. She was a wildfire, he always said, and she had given me the name Sparrow. From that day on, I hated my own name.

"No," I would say when he would try to tell me, again, about the world beyond this one—the one that I could touch if I only reached.

"You don't understand!" I shouted at him. "I don't believe anymore!" The words caught in my throat. "I… I never have."

I'll never forget that day, standing there, watching his face fall—Fin, the man who had once been my whole world. I'd cried into my pillow that night, clutching the back of my head as if it would burst.

*I never have, I never have, I never have…*

"Sparrow?" A soft voice pulled me from the black water of my thoughts.

I was lying in the bunk above Kateri's, staring at the ceiling, studying the cracks in the moonlight as it drizzled in. So lost in memories, I hadn't even heard her come in.

"Sparrow." She repeated my name again, a whisper. "Are you still awake?"

I pressed my eyelids closed, silencing a sigh in my throat.

"No," I replied.

Kateri was silent. A moment later, I heard the thud of porcelain on wood.

"I brought you something to eat," she whispered. "I thought you might be hungry."

I said nothing. Kateri lingered a moment longer before I heard the swish of sheets beneath me as she climbed into the lower bunk.

The room quieted once again, swelling with the echoing chorus of the crickets carried in on the soft wind. After a long silence, Kateri spoke up softly.

"I know it's not an easy transition…" Her words were quiet. "It's hard to leave everything you're familiar with."

I felt a lump tighten in my throat. I studied the crack in the ceiling, listening to the swish of the curtains and the leaves shivering in the wind.

The day rewound and replayed in my head; I could still see Keegan's face in my mind as he'd knocked me to the ground—that angry agglomeration of freckles and wild red mane; those raging green eyes. He'd looked more like a lion than a boy.

*You'll have to deal with Keegan sooner or later…*

I couldn't believe he was Fin's son. Just thinking about it left a sinking feeling in the pit of my stomach.

It was still so strange to me that Fin even had a son—that he'd raised Keegan since he was a boy even as he was raising me, in what seemed like another universe running parallel to this one. I'd heard about him plenty—Fin had always spoken of him so highly. Keegan was this and that, he was capable and smart and kind—and one day I would meet him, so long as I never told him who I was. But this was all Fin had ever told me about him.

Today, I finally had met him—the boy I'd heard so much about all these years.

He was *nothing* like Fin.

"But I think you'll grow to like it here, Sparrow," Kateri continued finally, almost as if on cue with my thoughts. "Just give it a few weeks… It'll start to feel like home."

Something hot stung my closed eyelids, but I swallowed it back.

*I won't be here that long.*

# 6

"PLEASE TELL ME YOU'RE NOT SERIOUS." I LEANED FORWARD on the desk, looking Dad in the eyes. "Please tell me this is some kind of… some kind of—"

"Mistake?" he suggested, cutting in. "Keegan…"

"No, no, no. Don't say my name like that and trail off." I groaned. "That always means you're about to tell me that it's—"

"True, yes," Dad interjected firmly. "Sparrow *is* the new student. The one I told you about earlier, the transfer from the school in New York."

Even after all these years—after living with him and calling him Dad since before I was tall enough to see over his desk—I still couldn't read him. I couldn't read that look in his green eyes: a hollow stare into something only he could see. All my mind-reading skills fell flat when it came to Dad.

"I caught her out in the woods smoking a cigarette." I tried again. "She could have started a *forest fire*." I put extra emphasis on the two words. "This isn't just a game—all of our hard work could have gone up in flames because of her! Do you realize that?"

"I realize that."

"And so?"

"So I will speak to her on the matter," he replied simply. "And it will not happen again."

"Dad, come on—there's no way you can make sure she doesn't sneak off and do it again. You're not even here half the time…" I scanned his face. "I don't think you understand what a liability she could be—I don't understand why you chose her. How long has she even been a student? When did she initiate?"

He pushed back his chair and rose to his feet, walking to the window.

"She has a name, Keegan," Dad corrected me finally, without answering any of my questions. "I expect you to treat her with the same respect you would treat any other student. With the same respect you would treat me."

Sometimes conversations with my father felt like beating my head against a wall.

"Fine," I said at last. "But why did you bring her here? She clearly isn't a healer."

Dad's back was to me as he stood gazing out the window. "Why did I bring you here, Keegan?"

I started to speak, but the words died in my throat.

"Keegan, not everything can be understood, however much you might wish it." His voice softened. "But don't judge… don't forget where you have come from."

"I don't think I could forget even if I tried," I answered hoarsely. "I… I'm reminded of it every night…"

Dad nodded slowly, lines still spanning his forehead. "I know."

"I don't mean to judge her…" I fought back the anger that was still boiling inside me. "I just… she's not what I expected."

"I know, Keegan."

"She's not what *any of us* expected. Who is she, even? Like… where did she come from?"

"Is that important?"

I exhaled hard in frustration. "Is she even a healer? I mean, that's kind of a requirement…"

"That's not for you to ask."

"Dad, seriously… are you sure this is wise?"

"No, Keegan, I'm not sure that it is wise," he answered, resolved. "But I am sure that it is right."

"Don't hold it too tightly—just lightly pinch the handle and let the back of the blade rest against your hand."

Rafael's fingers wound around the handle of the black knife as he readjusted his grip. I tugged on his arm and led him backwards a few paces, putting a little more distance between him and the tall piece of slashed plywood leaning up against the pine tree in front of us.

"The blade's going to make a full rotation about every six feet, all right?" I explained, dragging my shoe through the dirt to make a marker for him. "So right now, we're about twelve feet back, so it's going to rotate twice before it hits the wood."

Rafael's mop of messy dark hair bobbed in a nod. "Got it."

"So bring your arm back like this…" I stationed myself beside him, pulling a knife of my own out of my holster. "Keep your grip nice and easy, and…"

A tight *whoosh* sounded as I threw. The knife swept through the air, nailing into the dead center of the board with a satisfying *thwap*.

Rafael whipped around to stare up at me, blue eyes wide. "Dude…"

I grinned and stepped back. "'Dude,' nothin'—you'll be throwing better than me in no time. Let's see you try."

Rafael licked his lips and shuffled his feet into a wider stance. He wound one skinny arm back and launched the knife forward. It spun through the air and clattered handle-first against the board. He puffed his cheeks out, disappointed.

"Hey, it's all right." I pulled another knife out of my holster, this time with my focus alone. I let it hover in midair next to Rafael, who started laughing as soon as he noticed it floating there.

"Try again, bro," I said, squatting down. "You got this."

Sweat was starting to patch through his dirt-streaked T-shirt, and I was pretty sure I looked the same. There hadn't been a cloud in the sky all day. After a long but satisfying day's work out in the woods, everyone had quit for the day. Preston was lying in the hammock with a book. I could hear the singing of Myung's violin drifting through the open second-floor window, and voices that sounded like Kateri and Janna on the porch. I hadn't seen Dad since our talk, or Sparrow since she'd stormed into the house the day before and locked herself in the girls' bedroom. When I glanced up at their window, I noticed the curtains were pulled shut.

I pulled my gaze back to Rafael as he took position and hurled the knife forward. It hit the board spine-first and thudded to the ground.

Rafael groaned. "I don't think I'm ever going to be any—"

"Hey—what have I told you about that?"

"About what?"

I gave him a knowing look.

"Down-talking?" He sighed.

"Yep," I affirmed. "What have I told you about down-talking yourself?"

"Not to do it?"

I nodded, and he yielded a halfhearted smile.

"Now go pick up the two on the ground and get back here," I said. "You're gonna get this."

Rafael broke into a full grin now. "All right, Keeg."

He sprinted ahead to pick up the knives. I straightened up and stretched my arms over my head. I heard the screen door creak open as Kateri stepped out of the cabin and onto the porch. Her long braid was damp and slung over her shoulder. She wore a loose tan shirt and patterned silk pants. Her feet were bare, and she was holding two tin mugs in her hands.

I smiled, waving. She descended the steps and made her way over to the range. I caught scent of frankincense and lavender as she came up beside me and extended one of the cups.

"Lara made lemonade," she announced. "Thought you both could use some."

I threw back my head and drained the cup in one gulp. I wiped my mouth with the collar of my shirt, and she stared at me for a moment, shaking her head as she chuckled.

"You're the best," I said, setting the cup down on the ground. "Want to try throwing some knives?"

She chuckled. "No, thanks. I'm all set."

Rafael jogged back over and skidded to a stop on the mark I'd drawn in the dirt. "All right, all right. I'm gonna try again."

I folded my arms over my chest and exchanged a glance with Kateri.

"All right, little brother. Let's see it."

Taking a steady breath, Rafael wound up and flung the knife forward. It rotated once, twice, then sliced into the board, sticking. His face lit up.

"All right!" I hooted. "That's how it's *done*."

Rafael punched the air. He repositioned himself to throw again. Kateri stepped a little closer, lowering her voice.

"Sparrow has vowed not to come out of our room," she informed me quietly. "I think Lara's a bit… frustrated over the whole thing."

"That makes two of us," I grunted.

"You really freaked her out—yesterday in the woods." Kateri sighed.

"She was endangering the forest."

"But did you really have to tackle her to the ground?"

"I didn't even know who she was! What was I supposed to do—"

A tug on my sleeve interrupted me. Rafael pulled me forward.

"Come on, Keeg, you try."

Kateri grinned, watching as I relented and let him lead me within range of the target. He watched me with eager eyes as I set up.

For a moment I twirled the blade between my fingers. Then I slowly opened my palm and held the knife in a steady levitation. I closed my eyes and sucked in a deep breath, focusing on the heat slowly traveling the length of my arm and emanating up through my palm.

In my mind's eye I could see the tree and the target leaning against it. I focused on the dead center. With a surge of energy, I launched it forward. A loud crack sounded, and I heard Rafael gasp behind me. I opened my eyes.

The tip of the knife had dug into the target and buried itself deep. I gestured for Rafael to follow as I started towards it. He raced ahead of me and dropped down beside the piece of plywood. Pulling it forward, he checked the back side, and his eyes went wide.

"Dang, Keeg!" He looked up at me with wide eyes. "Look how far it went through!"

The blade had sliced through the wood with the effortlessness of a knife through butter. Only the handle was visible on the front side.

"You gonna teach me how to throw it without touching it?"

I nodded. "In time. For now, keep practicing what I've shown you."

With a swift pull, I yanked the blade out of the wood and held the handle out for him to grasp.

"When did you learn, Keeg?" he asked, studying the blade.

"When I was a little younger than you. I wanted to be able to defend myself. Or somebody I loved…" I trailed off, then cleared my throat. "Come on. Give it another shot."

Rafael didn't say anything. He turned the knife over in his palms, as if there were some secret etched into the blade that I wasn't telling him about. I got up and walked back to where Kateri stood.

"I don't understand why Sensei's doing this." I lowered my voice, dusting off my shirt. "Why did he bring her here?"

Kateri tossed me a glance. "Who am I to question Sensei's ways? I have a feeling Sparrow doesn't understand why she's here, either."

"Clearly."

"Oh, don't be all high and mighty," she scolded me. "It doesn't suit you."

I heaved a frustrated sigh. "It just doesn't seem right. What's the point of it?"

"Don't be so hard on her—making judgments before you even get to know her." Kateri gave me a look. "Give it a few days. Trust that maybe Sensei sees something in her that we don't… something deep down."

I felt the warmth of her hand on my shoulder as she walked past, heading back to the house. I glanced up at the white curtains covering the cabin window, suppressing a narrow sigh.

*Very deep down.*

# 7

THERE'S A PLACE BETWEEN SLEEP AND CONSCIOUSNESS where reality begins to lose its form. Where memories and actuality blend, where you choose which is real and which is the illusion. For a moment I lay in between soft sheets and thought I detected the sound of traffic, the hum and bustle of New York City as she came alive, as the rusty sun peeked over the skyline. For a moment that felt like reality.

Then someone banged on the door.

"Sparrow! Wake up!"

I started fully awake, tangling myself in the sheets. I scrambled to get up as the brash pounding continued.

"What?" I snapped.

"Oh, good. You're still alive in there…"

It was a male's voice, but I didn't recognize it; it wasn't the lion boy.

I rushed to button a soft plaid shirt over my lacy maroon bra. "My god. It's a little early."

"It's five thirty."

I grunted. "Oh, wow… *so late*."

"It is here," he replied. His voice was smooth and deep and already beginning to get on my nerves. I was still working on buttoning my shirt when I swung the door open and put a face to the cocky tone.

A tall, young black guy with muscled arms leaned against the door frame. He wore earth-toned clothes and a loose knit hat. His warm brown eyes scrutinized me. I narrowed mine.

"Look, I'm not used to getting up at the crack of dawn," I explained, folding my arms over my chest. "And I would appreciate you not banging on my door. Ever."

The corners of his lips twitched into a smug grin. "Then you'd better start getting your butt moving before I get up these stairs."

"What are you? A drill sergeant?"

"Nah, that's Lara's job." He jerked his head toward the stairs. "Better get a move on before she comes up to check on you herself."

I shook my head. "No, I'm staying up here until Fin lets me leave."

"Sensei."

"What?"

"*Sensei*," he repeated, his voice firmer. "That's what we call him around here—it's respectful." He straightened up a little. "And you can call me Preston. But I wouldn't wait around for Sensei if I were you."

I stood in the threshold, staring after him as he headed for the stairs.

"Why not?" I questioned.

"Because he's gone," Preston replied. "He won't be back until later."

My stomach sank. "How much later?"

Preston shrugged his broad shoulders. "Who's to say? This is Sensei we're talking about."

I slammed the bedroom door shut behind me and pounded down the stairs after Preston. Lara and a girl with big blonde hair were in the kitchen, which swelled with the scent of cinnamon and butter. Lara looked up as soon as I walked in. Preston jerked a finger in my direction and said, "See? Told you I'd get her down here."

Lara's expression remained neutral. She pushed something around in a frying pan with a spatula.

"Good morning," she said flatly. "I trust you slept well… seeing as you slept *in*."

I resisted the urge to roll my eyes.

"You can get started on setting the table—Janna will show you where everything is."

I scrunched my nose. "We don't even need to eat—what's the point of all this? It seems like a waste of time."

Preston snorted, flipping around to shoot me a look. "Not everything is about time efficiency here."

"Clearly," I muttered.

"It's about learning to create," Janna chimed in, swinging open one of the cabinets. "To make something simply for the enjoyment of it—the beauty of it."

"It's just food," I said.

"It's *art*," Preston objected, stepping over to the counter alongside Lara. "And it also tastes good, so bonus there…"

Janna held out a stack of plates, and after a moment of hesitation, I took them. Trudging over to the table, I began setting one down at each empty place.

"If you all get up so early around here, where the hell is everyone?"

"Everyone's working," Janna explained. "Preston and I have kitchen duty this morning, Kateri and Keegan have been out since dawn, and Myung and Rafael have chores."

"In other words, unlike you, we're not used to sleeping the day away and doing nothing," Preston continued. "Is that what they do at the school in New York?"

My fingers tightened around the two remaining plates in my hand.

"You don't know anything about it," I replied coldly. "It's a different world."

"Apparently so…" Preston turned around to the island, setting down a tray of cinnamon rolls. "But you're not there anymore, in case you haven't noticed."

"Preston." Lara spoke his name like a warning, but it went ignored by both of us.

"Oh, I've noticed." I took a few steady steps forward, forgetting about setting the table. "And you know what? I didn't even like it there. It sucked. Fin's the same there as he is here. Everything is stupid and regulated—"

"Sensei," he corrected me again icily.

"No," I shot back. "Fin—that's all he is to me. *Fin.* Not Sensei, not teacher…"

"Sparrow." Lara stared at me from the stove.

"You can all choose to be indoctrinated if you want." My eyes narrowed to slits. "You can choose to believe that fantasy is reality, to be freaks of nature, living separated from everyone and everything—but not me."

No one said anything for a moment. Silence swelled in the room, and all I could hear was the sizzling of the food as it cooked. Finally, Preston spoke.

"How dare you!" He stepped around the island to my side. "You think you can just come in here and talk about Sensei like that? Think again—"

"How dare I?" I reiterated the question. "How dare I *what*, Preston? *Question?* Question the things that you're so eager to blindly accept?"

"You think we're freaks, Sparrow?" Preston stepped right up in front of me. "You think *we're* the ones with a problem?"

The plates trembled in my hands as I stared up into his eyes; my jaw clenched as he began to slowly shake his head.

"If you want to see the problem…" He lowered his voice, leaning closer to my face. "You should look in the mirror."

Lara's voice cut in, but I didn't hear what she said. The sounds around me became muffled. Preston tipped his head back slightly, looking me straight in the eyes. For a second I merely stood there, my blood boiling in my veins.

Then, in a burst of unbridled energy, the plates shot out of my hands and smashed to the floor. Preston's expression morphed into one of surprise as I got right in his face.

"Go to hell," I growled through gritted teeth.

"Sparrow!" Lara boomed.

Preston didn't back off, but he didn't say anything either. I spun around and strode out of the kitchen, my bare feet pounding against the floorboards. I swung open the front door—and slammed into a blur of red mane and freckles.

Anger flared in his emerald eyes as our eyes locked. I shoved past him, stepping outside and slamming the door behind me.

Running for the woods, I darted and dodged between blurs of trees until the cabin tucked into the pines seemed far off. I trotted to a walk and then collapsed at the base of one of the larger trees. Dark green boughs swayed overhead. My ears were filled with the soft *shhhh* of the wind as it sighed through the branches, almost as if the trees were chiding me for my sudden intrusion. I hated the silence—I *couldn't stand* the silence.

I leaned against the tree trunk, tipping my head back and drinking in the oxygen. Gathering my knees up to my chest, I pressed my face into the palms of my hands. A sob tightened in my throat, but I swallowed it back.

"*Sparrow…*"

A distant voice suddenly interrupted the silence. For a moment I remembered the dream: the voice and the wind and the rain. But then I realized whose voice it was.

I hugged my knees tighter and made no response. I sat still, holding my breath.

"Sparrow?" Fin's voice echoed through the woods. "Where are you?"

Slowly his voice came closer and closer until finally I could hear the pad of his footsteps just behind me. He stopped beside the tree I was seated against.

"I thought you were away," I said flatly.

"I was." He lowered down to sit beside me. "Until now."

I didn't turn to look at him, but I could feel his eyes on me.

I sniffed hard, wiping the back of my hand across my nose. "What do you want?"

"I don't want anything," he replied quietly. "I just came to check on you."

"Are you sure you didn't want to give me a lecture?"

"Do you feel you are deserving of one?"

I made no response.

"It was wrong of you to treat Preston that way," Fin said.

"You didn't hear what he said to me."

"You cannot control what someone else says, Sparrow, but you can control your response. You cannot let someone else's opinion shake who you are."

I turned to look at him. "And who might that be, Fin?"

Fin's deep green eyes studied my face for a moment. "You have been with me all this time, and still you don't know? Sparrow, you are like a daughter—"

"No!" I jumped up, clenching my fists. "I'm not! Don't lie to yourself anymore—I can't be someone I'm not! I'm not your daughter!"

Something sad and heavy flashed in Fin's eyes. His expression went soft, and I heard him take a small gulp of air, as if he'd been punched.

"No," he responded quietly. "No, you're not my daughter, Sparrow."

I stood there rigidly, fists still clenched. Fin's eyes didn't leave mine.

"You are the daughter of the Sunrise and the Sunset," he began steadily. "You are *their* daughter. They entrusted you to—"

"No—no, Fin." I lifted a hand to cut him off, violently shaking my head. "I don't want to hear this story again. I'm done."

"Done? Done with what, Sparrow? With truth?"

"With these made-up fairy tales!" I exploded. "With this false reality you've given me to hold onto my entire life, just to make me feel like I wasn't some useless no-name kid you picked off the street!"

Fin slowly shook his head and rose to his feet. "Do you honestly believe that I've lied to you all these years?"

"You mean do I believe I'm the daughter of a split-soul, holding the universe together? That I—that I'm *special* and *powerful* and here to help restore Earth to its former glory?" My voice dripped with sarcasm as I shook my head. "If I had parents and they loved me and wanted me, why would they have *left me?*"

Fin's face was pale. "Leaving you was the last thing they wanted—"

"Oh, and here we go again!" I spun away from him. "They left me here because they *loved* me, right?"

"Because they knew there was a chance they could be caught, and they wanted to protect you."

"So is that what happened, then?" My voice cracked a little. "They were caught and killed? Is that the truth—are you just shielding me from it?"

"If I knew what happened to them, I would tell you. But the truth is, I have no idea—no one does. The day they left… the day your mother put you into my arms…" He trailed off, pinching his eyes shut as though it were painful to discuss. "I never saw them again."

"Right, right—they just vanished into thin air." My voice came out cutting.

Fin was quiet. The sound of birdsong swelled in the woods around us.

"They knew your purpose, Sparrow. I could see it in your mother's eyes when she put you in my arms. She loved you, Sparrow—"

I whirled back around, trembling as I faced him. "Enough! I've heard enough about—about my 'mother,' about who you think I am, about all of it!" My eyes narrowed as I stepped closer. "You have no idea who I am, Fin…"

Tears crested in Fin's eyes. He looked away for a moment. When he finally spoke again, his voice was tattered. "I don't know how to make you see, Sparrow. I don't know how to make you see anymore."

"I see perfectly," I whispered. "I see that I don't belong here—and never will."

"You're wrong, Sparrow."

"Oh? So I'm supposed to be thrilled to live in isolation and be a screwup?" I shouted, my voice shredding. "With powers that have done nothing but ruin my life?"

"Your power is yours to do with as you choose. Whether you use it for good or evil—whether you use it to 'ruin' your life or change the world…" A tear rolled down his cheek as his eyes leveled with mine again. "That is your decision to make."

"You really don't get it, do you? I don't want to be an anomaly! I just want to…" My voice broke off as hot tears welled in my eyes. "I just want to be normal."

Fin didn't reply. I felt the warmth of his hand on my shoulder. For a moment I stood there, frozen and trembling, my face in my hands. Something inside me wanted to hold on to him and sob. But there was a vise tightening inside me—holding me back. Holding me together.

I jerked back from his touch and walked away, leaving him standing there among the trees.

# 8

PRESTON FOLLOWED ME OUTSIDE, POUNDING DOWN THE porch steps after me. "How on earth can she be the new student? Only healers get transferred here, and I'm fairly certain she is not—"

"I know," I cut in. "But Sensei brought her here, so we have to try to understand—"

"Why he transferred a student who's probably going to start the next wildfire?"

I dragged a hand over my face. "He said she needs to be here—so there must be a reason."

Preston went quiet as we trekked across the yard and into the forest, heading out toward our designated section, a hundred-square-foot area enshrouded in ash and surrounded by the ghosts of trees.

I searched for a sign of Sparrow—after crashing into me on the porch, she'd taken off into the woods, slamming the door behind her.

"You should have heard the way she was talking about Sensei—about all of us. Like she's not even an anomaly herself," he grunted, falling into step beside me.

I wanted to chime in and agree with him, but then I remembered the look on Dad's face and what he'd said about her. About *me*.

"I mean, this isn't a game!" Preston made a wide gesture around us. "We have a mission—I don't know what Sensei's thinking, but I don't see how this girl's going to help us accomplish anything. In fact, it's probable she'll—"

"Slow us down?" I offered, looking over at him. "Don't remind me."

"So what are we going to do?" Preston slowed to a stop, lifting his hands to channel a beam of light between them. "Just… deal with it?"

I placed my hand gently on the trunk of a scraggly dead birch, gazing up into its blackened branches. I closed my eyes and began to visualize.

"She acts like she doesn't even understand what it means to be a healer…" He bent the channel of light between his palms as he thought. I could hear the subtle *bbvvvvvvvvvvvvvvnnnnnn* sound it made. "Maybe she's not…"

I began to feel the pulse of sap flowing beneath the bark under my fingertips.

"But that makes no sense—why would she be here if she's not a healer? She would be virtually useless," he continued.

*Useless.* The word splintered through my mind.

My face grew suddenly hot as new life exploded through the tree with a loud crack—throwing enough energy to send me staggering backward as tiny green leaves burst from the branches above and showered down like confetti. I reached up and snatched a tree branch, catching myself before I fell to the ashy ground.

"What was that?" Preston asked.

"N-nothing," I answered breathlessly.

"That… was definitely something. What were you thinking about?"

"Nothing," I repeated, more firmly now. "I just… I don't think we should make any judgments about her until we've really gotten to know her."

It didn't sound like something I would say, because it wasn't: I'd repeated Kateri's words. I couldn't tell him what I was really thinking…

how I sometimes felt inferior compared to the rest—like I was just here because of the simple fact that I was Sensei's son.

How could I call Sparrow an impostor when I was no better? Sure, I could heal *now*… but it hadn't always been that way. That wasn't why I'd been brought here.

Preston stared at me for a moment, then grinned, flashing the light back into focus and channeling it up into the leaves.

"You know, you sound more and more like Kateri every day." He gave a soft little laugh. "Did you guys have some nice alone time out there this morning?"

I sighed as we moved on to the next tree.

"She's brilliant," I confessed. "Gifted…"

"And hot."

"Do you think I haven't noticed?" I laid my hands on the trunk of the next tree. "But we practically grew up together, Kateri and I. In truth, I've never really thought about it."

Preston snorted. "Bull. You've totally thought about it."

I felt my ears turn red. "I like Kateri. I've always liked Kateri. She gets me like no one else ever has, and I like to think that I get her too, but… I don't think she thinks of me that way, and…" I rubbed the back of my neck. "We're not supposed to get involved. I am not going to get involved."

Preston turned to look at me again. "But you would if you could, right?"

"No, Kateri and I are just friends, Pres. She would never—I would never…" My voice faded in my throat.

Preston quirked one eyebrow. He didn't push it any further, but I could tell he was grinning.

"Where's Sparrow?" I asked as I was setting the table.

"I haven't seen her since this morning." Lara stood in the kitchen, gazing past the window. "Your father transported back from Ireland to talk to her…"

*Ireland.* My stomach twisted into a knot.

"I heard the door slam a couple of hours ago, so she might be upstairs in her room."

"What about her chores?" I asked.

"They're still waiting for her." Lara turned to look at me. "But what's that to you?"

I didn't answer. I kept setting plates down, listening to the sounds drifting in from outside, the soft hum of the crickets and the dull *thwap* of knives hitting the target I'd left up for Rafael. Lara's footsteps joined those sounds as she crossed the room, pausing at the opposite side of the table.

"You all right?" she asked quietly after a steady few moments of watching me go around the table. "You've been acting… different since she got here."

"Yeah, my balls still hurt."

"She kneed you that hard, huh?"

I shot her a look—it was answer enough.

"But that's not it, is it?" Lara continued, prying further.

Lara knew me too well.

I set the last piece of silverware down and gripped the back of the chair in front of me, staring straight ahead.

"No," I answered her finally. "That's not it."

She said nothing, waiting for me to continue.

"You know, Dad wanted me to transport to New York City with him to get Sparrow," I began dryly. "I said no right away—I didn't even think about it. I just said no—made an excuse…"

"Because… you didn't want to?"

"Because I was afraid. Because I *am* afraid—of cities, people, human beings, and the evil, hatred, corruption, and violence that come with them. I know what they're like—I lived in one of their cesspits. I was there…"

My voice felt cramped in my throat. I stopped, staring down at the back of the chair.

"Humans can match all of those descriptions, yes…" Lara agreed quietly. "There is evil and darkness in humankind, Keegan, but within that darkness and evil there is also the overcoming of it."

"Us?"

"Us..." She nodded slowly. "And them... and this great, spinning ball we call home."

"It's hard to imagine anything good coming from humanity." I sighed. "When you've seen them at their worst..."

Lara's face darkened, and I immediately cursed my choice of words.

"What you look for, you will find, Keegan," she answered. "War is an ugly thing—war is *hell*. It brings out the very worst in people... the most atrocious acts the human mind can conjure. But at the same time, war can bring out the best in people..." She looked me in the eyes. "Underneath it all, we were just kids... beams of light, clothed in darkness. I'll never forget a single one of them—RGM soldiers and recusant rebels... We didn't know what we were doing, and neither did they. We were just trying to survive."

I was quiet for a moment, reading her face before saying anything. "I still hear you up most nights... down here, by yourself, while everyone else is sleeping."

Lara didn't seem surprised that I'd noticed this. But then she turned the tables.

"You're obviously awake most nights yourself."

"The memories come back stronger in the dark... the hours before dawn. The faces..." I backed away from the chair, running a hand over my forehead. "I hate remembering—I hate that I can't forget."

Lara walked back around the table, heading for the kitchen. She set a hand on my shoulder as she walked past and quietly said, "Me too."

I could hear the voices from outside growing closer, footsteps approaching. In a moment the screen door would swing open, and everyone would river inside, and Lara and I would have to pretend this conversation had never happened. We only ever talked like this when no one was around to overhear. Lara and Dad were the only ones who knew about the nightmares, and Lara, I often felt, was the only one who understood what it was like to relive something a thousand times in the dark stillness of midnight.

The screen door flung open, and the quiet kitchen burst into conversation, plates clattered, and the aroma of red sauce hung in the air. After talking to Lara about the nightmares, I'd lost my appetite, but I still forced myself to eat. The last thing I wanted was someone asking me what was wrong.

I sat across from Kateri, who passed me a smile when our eyes met. Everyone was at the table except Dad and Sparrow. Somehow, this didn't surprise me. What did catch me off guard was the creaking on the stairs, followed by Sparrow's sudden appearance.

It was the first time I had really had a chance to look at her. I mean, I'd technically seen her out in the woods, but I hadn't really *seen* her. I'd been too angry for that.

She was on the short side, with long dark hair to match her eyes, and thick eyebrows. Her face was like a storm, but pretty in a way. Her lips were pressed together, and her arms were braced over her torso, as if arrows would come flying toward her at any moment.

Kateri and I exchanged a glance, and I noticed Preston checking her out from the other side of the table.

"Sparrow," Lara said between bites, treating her just like she would any of us. "Grab a plate and join us."

Sparrow stood there rigidly for a moment before walking silently into the kitchen and pulling a plate from the stack. The conversation picked up again.

"Keeg and I got quite a bit of work done on that new section today," Preston explained, then nudged Rafael with his elbow. "You'll have a lot of work to do tomorrow," he said, then he nodded to Janna and winked. "Both of you."

Janna snapped her fingers to create a tiny, sparkling prism of water, tossing it into the air and catching it in her palm, where it disintegrated. Wide-eyed, Rafael attempted to follow suit, but succeeded only in splashing Janna in the face.

"Okay, guys, we get it: you channel water. Please stop," Myung grumbled, shielding her food.

Kateri bit back a grin, looking at me from across the table.

"Hey, we don't complain when you're playing the same three chords over and over and over," Preston chimed in, laughing.

"That is *so* different," Myung grunted. "I'm a musician—music is my gift. Not everyone can naturally play every single instrument."

"And they're water… channelers…?" Preston fumbled.

"Yeah, we need to work on a cool name," Rafael agreed. "Although it will hardly measure up to 'mind reader' or 'animal communicator.'"

Kateri waved it off. "Nah, you're much cooler. The trees couldn't grow without you—and then where would we be?"

"Yeah, but the forest also needs animals," Preston came back.

"And light," Kateri said.

"Music is the only thing that isn't necessary to existence." I smirked, shooting Myung a look.

"The wind is music." Kateri pointed her fork at me. "The streams, the bird songs…"

I thought about it, watching out of the corner of my eye as Sparrow came back to the table, carrying a plate with just enough food for a small rodent on it. She sat down cautiously in the vacant chair beside Kateri.

I tried my best to ignore her.

"I think all of your gifts are equally important." Lara spoke up. "Each one of your abilities is necessary. The Earth is a planet, sure, but it's not much different than us. It's really the same. People, planets… they all have lungs to breathe, and hearts that beat to a certain, specific rhythm. Blood flows through our veins. Trees, oceans, rivers, mountains—they all work like organs. They're all part of this orchestra. Everything plays a part." She gestured towards us. "Just like you guys. You all have gifts: abilities that come to you as naturally as breathing."

I had to hand it to Lara: she was pretty great at stepping into Dad's shoes when he wasn't there. If she didn't look twenty, she would feel like the resident mom.

"You're using your gifts to heal," she went on. "Helping the Earth grow again, rescuing what's left—restoring the music to the wind and the streams."

"What about you, Sparrow?" Rafael straightened in his chair. "What's your power?"

Sparrow stiffened in her seat, looking taken aback. She didn't respond for a moment. Her lips slowly parted and then clamped shut again. She set her jaw.

"I don't have one," she answered. Her smoky voice broke a little as she lowered it. "I never have, and I never will."

"Not if you keep talking like that, you won't," I said, picking up my glass of water to take a long swig. "It's ninety percent mindset, you know."

Sparrow's dark eyes locked on mine. "You don't know anything about me."

The table quieted. I swirled the water in my glass and set it back down on the table.

"I know that you're not trying," I replied. "I know that you don't care—about this place, or learning, or being an asset to the mission."

"Oh, and you're such an asset because, what?" Sparrow tipped her head back. "You run around in the woods throwing knives at things?"

"You would have burned down the forest!" I burst out, my voice quickly rising. "Just because you don't want to be here—just because you have to make everything all about you!"

Sparrow leaned forward over the table. "You don't know anything about my life, Keegan. None of you do."

"Sparrow—" Lara began, but I cut in before she could finish.

"Oh, I don't, huh?" I asked, leaning forward too. "Because your life is so complex and difficult? Open your eyes: you run away and hide every time something gets remotely tough!"

"At least I'm not some little choirboy who just bows and scrapes and does what he's told." Sparrow's face was flushed and angry; her brown eyes were huge.

My gut twisted, as if something inside me knew that what I was about to say was wrong. But I said it anyway.

"You know what, Sparrow?" I lowered my voice. "I can agree with you on one thing: you don't belong here."

"Keegan, that's *enough*," Lara snapped, but I barely heard. My eyes were still locked with Sparrow's.

For a brief moment, hurt replaced the anger in Sparrow's eyes. I caught only a glimpse of it, but it was enough to make me regret what I'd just said.

Slamming her hands on the table, she leapt to her feet and threw back her chair. It clattered to the floor behind her, and she stormed out of the room.

# 9

I STARED AT THE CEILING FOR WHAT FELT LIKE HOURS, studying the lines and cracks in the moonlight as I lay there in silence. I missed the sounds of pods racing past my window. I missed the whir of the Bullet train, the pumping music drifting up from the clubs and restaurants. There was so much noise in the city, I couldn't hear myself think, and that was the best part: not having to listen to the whispering chants of all those little voices that lived inside my head, reminding me exactly who Sparrow was:

*A no-name.*

*A freak of nature.*

*An outcast.*

Here, in the quiet of the woods, these whispers became screams. They blared like sirens, howling through the night.

*Screw-up, screw-up, screw-up… No wonder they abandoned you…*

It was laughable, really, the stories Fin had made up about me to make me feel better about myself. How my mother had loved me so much, but had had to leave me with Fin just for a little while, just until she and my "real" father could come back for me. How my mother could shift, my father could rise from a bottomless pit to save the "Dimension," some extra realm hidden within space and time. How they were my real family—part of who I was.

"Such bullshit," I muttered under my breath, brushing back the sheets with my free hand. "I'm sorry, Fin. I love you, but I don't need your fairy tales anymore to help me cope…"

I crept softly over the old floorboards and slid into a pair of cutoff shorts and a black tank top, pulling my hair back into a braid. I slung my bag over my shoulder and reached inside for a tiny slip of paper covered in messy handwriting. An address for an apartment downtown, scented with smoke and cheap cologne, just like he was.

For a moment, doubts rang through my mind:

*Should I… should I… should I?*

Taking a shallow breath, I set the paper down on the nightstand, tiptoed across the room and slipped out into the hallway. Keeping as silent as possible, I took the stairs and padded down the hallway to the broom closet. This time it wasn't locked.

Wrapping my fingers around the cool brass knob, I twisted it and pulled the door open, hesitating when it creaked.

I listened, holding my breath. Then I quickly eased it open the rest of the way and slipped inside, sealing myself into the cool darkness. With my back against the wall, I took a deep breath and closed my eyes.

I had a sinking feeling in my gut, something deeper than the night and churning like a storm on the sea—something that urgently whispered, *Stay, stay, stay.*

I gagged the voice, focusing: imagining the lights of the city, the messy neon chaos of the streets. The apartment building reaching up, up, up into a sky too polluted to yield stars. I imagined the hallway and the long rows of stainless-steel doors until, in my mind's eye, I found the one at the end, just as he had described it so many times when he was trying to coax me to spend the night with him. When I finally opened my eyes, the closet, the cabin, the woods, the world I hated so much had fallen away.

I stood in front of the door to Cal's apartment. A sliver of light drifted out through the crack underneath.

I pushed myself forward, shaking the thoughts away as I flipped my braid over my shoulder. I leaned against the door frame and lifted the back of my hand to knock. I glanced over my chipped nails, a moment passing in an eternity. Then, softly, footsteps; a fracture in the light from under the door. The knob turned, and the door opened.

His hair was a mess spilling over his forehead, over his deep eyes and jagged face. Between his fingers he held a cigarette. He wore gym shorts and no shirt. A slow smile came to his lips. I managed a weak one in return.

"Hey."

He opened the door all the way and tugged me inside by the arm. There was a blur of a messy bedroom and the flickering lights outside— then everything jolted as my back slammed against the door, and Cal pressed his lips against mine.

He pulled back slowly, nuzzling my face with his own.

"You did it again," he whispered. "You're becoming quite the escape artist."

I nodded, reaching up to touch his face.

"Everything all right?" he asked.

"No… no, not really."

He kissed me again and looked into my face.

"What can I do?" he asked. His hand was down on my waist, one finger sliding under my shirt. "Tell me what to do, Sarah."

"There's nothing you can do. I just hate…" My voice crumbled.

He pulled me into his arms, and for a moment I sank onto his shoulder, tears welling in my eyes.

"I hate my life…" I whispered. "I hate who I'm becoming… No, who I've *already become.*"

"Shhh. Don't say that."

I pulled back, steadying my quivering lip as I looked up into his eyes.

"Cal, do you love me?" My voice crept out, broken. "Like… really?"

His eyes scanned my face for a moment. "You know I care about you, Sarah."

My bleary eyes searched his. "But… do you love me?"

Cal took one more drag off the cigarette, lighting up the embers bright orange before he reached over and pressed it into the ashtray. He tipped back his head and let the smoke roll up like a wolf howl before he leaned in and kissed my neck, pressing me back against the door and whispering into my ear, "Let me show you, Sarah…"

I closed my eyes and tried to ignore the pounding of my heart in my head, the sound of that same voice: *Should I, should I, should I?*

Cal pulled me in by the waist. I could feel my toes digging into the soles of my sneakers. He slid my bag off my arm and tossed it aside, pushing the thin straps of my tank top off my shoulders.

I sucked in a breath and gently pushed him away. "Cal…"

"Mmm…"

"I didn't—Cal, I didn't come over for this—"

My voice submerged again as I was pulled under, deep. His mouth covered mine, and his hands wrapped around my thighs, lifting me up and carrying me away from the door.

*Should I, should I, should I…?*

I felt the softness of the mattress at my back as he lowered me down. I jammed my hands against his chest and pushed myself up to sit.

"No," I said softly. "Cal, I… I can't."

Cal's eyes searched mine. "Why? Sarah, what's wrong?"

"Nothing," I sighed. "I just… I came to talk to you."

"We can still talk, but—"

"I don't want to." I cut him off firmly. I swung my legs over the side of the bed and stood, my heart still pounding and my head dizzy.

Cal sat there, looking up at me like I was a different species. My eyes darted around the room as I subconsciously began routing a map around the clutter to the door. But something among the chaos caught my eye.

A familiar black tactical uniform draped over the back of a chair, a matching cap tossed into the seat. My mouth immediately ran dry.

"Sarah, I don't get it."

I could still feel tears burning in my eyes. "Cal, you're..." I almost choked, sucking in a breath. "You're an RGM soldier?"

Cal nodded slowly. "I thought I'd mentioned that before," he replied. "What about it?"

"Oh, nothing. I just..." I swallowed, my heart beating a little faster. "I just didn't realize that."

Cal nodded, rising to his feet to wrap his arms around me again. His hands gently traced my spine.

"Sarah, I need you," he said.

"I need you too," I whispered, swallowing back the lump in my throat. "I just can't..."

"You can," he interrupted, pushing a kiss against my lips. "You can."

He pushed me backwards. I stumbled and thudded against the wall. The lamp on the nightstand flickered as he bumped into it. It crashed to the ground, and everything went dark. I pushed against him, but he didn't let go.

Over his shoulder I could still see the uniform in the glow from the window, hanging there like a warning sign. Sirens were going off in my head. I could already feel tinges of energy trickling through the veins in my arms, coursing through my hands—that strange power I barely knew how to harness.

*Hold it back, hold it back...*

"Cal, stop." I writhed in his grasp. "Please just..."

"Shhh."

"No!" I pushed his hands away as he began to slide the strap of my tank top off my shoulder. "Stop it!"

The air rushed out of my lungs as he pressed me back against the wall again.

"Cal, stop it!" My voice rose from my throat, frantic and ragged. "Stop!"

He didn't; he kissed me hard and grabbed me harder. Then suddenly a deafening crack split the quiet room in half.

The tiny apartment lit up like an explosion as the door burst off its hinges.

# 10

'I SAT ON THE ROOF AND STARED UP AT THE DIM PINPRICKS scattered in the darkness stretched above me. My eyelids sagged, begging for sleep that I refused to yield to. My arms were satisfyingly heavy from the day's work, and nothing would have felt better than a pillow under my head, but I wasn't ready to surrender—not yet.

My mind kept wandering back to the argument at dinner and the look in Lara's eyes when Sparrow had left the table. She hadn't corrected me, lectured me, or asked to speak to me afterward. All she'd said before I'd gone up was a quiet goodnight.

But I didn't need Lara to tell me what I had done was wrong. The heavy feeling in my gut was already taking its toll.

*"You know what, Sparrow? I can agree with you on one thing: you don't belong here."*

My bitter words rewound and replayed in my head until a noise caught my attention. I glanced over my shoulder just as the window at the opposite end of the roof slid quietly open, and someone leaned out.

"Hey…"

The voice was familiar and warm. My shoulders relaxed.

"Kateri."

The outline grew into arms and legs as she carefully slid over the windowsill and climbed out onto the roof.

The rooftop was our place—our refuge. It had always been my haven when the sleepless nights came, and Kateri usually joined me when she heard my window slide open—unless she was already out here herself. I'd lost count of how many sunrises we'd watched from here. From the rooftop everything stretched on in peaceful silence. We had these hours to ourselves, a slice of reality all our own. A place where the waves inside me could crash to a calm, and I could hear the quiet voice of what Dad called Truth.

Noiselessly, Kateri walked the length of the roof and settled down beside me.

"Couldn't sleep?" she asked.

I gave her a little smile. "Sleep is for the weak."

Kateri gave a quiet laugh. "Are you afraid of it?"

"Sleeping? No." I leaned back on my elbows, craning my neck to stare up at the sky. "Just... the memories it brings..."

Kateri was quiet, but I could feel her looking at me.

"I just can't seem to fall asleep without being back there. Their faces, their voices... It's all as vivid as if they were still alive..."

We sat in silence. The distant, haunting call of an owl filtered through the air.

"You must miss your parents every moment of every day," Kateri said softly.

*Yes, like hell.* But I couldn't talk about it—about them. Not even with Kateri, so I changed the subject.

"I just..." I wrestled with the words. "I do the things I hate, Kateri. The very things I hate about Sparrow, I see raging in myself like a fire that I can't put out. I... I shouldn't have talked to her like that. At dinner."

"No, you shouldn't have."

I blew out an exhale, dragging a hand over my face. "Why am I like this?"

"Like what? A redhead?" she teased. "I'm guessing genetics had something to do with it."

"How will I ever be like Sensei when I act like a—like a foolish child?"

"Shhh. You're going to wake them up." She paused to listen, then lowered her voice. "We are all foolish children sometimes. Sparrow's no better."

"No, she's certainly not."

"But… you know better than anyone that we all have stories, something that we carry… fear, pain… grief. Everyone has something, Keegan," Kateri said, her voice still a whisper. "We don't know what she's fighting."

I knew she was right, but something inside me didn't want to know Sparrow's story. Something inside me didn't even care.

"You could apologize," Kateri said finally, when I didn't respond.

"Apologize? To Sparrow?"

Kateri shrugged her shoulders, moonlight cascading softly over her, reflecting in her eyes. "Why not?"

"Well, because… I… she…" I tapered off. "What she said about me was a lie…"

"So? Why do you care so much about what Sparrow thinks about you?"

"I don't."

"Then it should be easy to let her insults roll off you like water, Keegan."

"You make everything sound so philosophical and easy and… right."

"The things that are right are usually not easy."

"Like apologizing to Sparrow for being an ass."

Kateri chuckled softly. "Like that."

I let go of a long sigh. "Okay, okay. You're right. I'll go talk to her."

"It's a little late. Don't you think you should wait until morning?"

I rose to my feet. "This is Sparrow we're talking about. She's probably still up—trying to light the house on fire or something."

Kateri chuckled. "I'm fairly certain you'll find her asleep in her bunk." She smacked my leg as I made my way past her.

I grinned, but then paused beside her. Her dark hair flowed over her shoulders like two rivers in the pale light.

"Thank you," I said quietly.

"For what?"

My hand brushed her shoulder. "Reminding me who I am."

I felt her fingers close around mine for a brief moment in response; then she let go. I edged my way along the roof until I reached my open bedroom window. Carefully, I slung one leg over the sill and slid into the darkness of the room.

Preston rolled over in the top bunk. "She finally let you go, lover boy?" he quietly teased.

"Shut up." I groaned softly. "You're gonna wake the house up."

"As if you guys didn't already do that with all your talking—right outside the windows."

I strode across the room without replying.

"Where are you going?" Preston whispered. "It's gotta be one o'clock in the morning."

"Yeah, yeah, I know," I said. "There's… there's something I have to do, though."

I slid out into the hallway and walked quietly to the girls' room. The door creaked on its hinges, causing me to hesitate a moment before cautiously peering into the room.

Kateri was still out on the roof, and inside, I could make out the lumpy shapes of Myung and Janna in their respective bunks, peacefully unconscious. The bunk above Kateri's bed was empty.

I stepped inside, scanning the room. Light on my feet, I crossed the moonlit floorboards and paused silently at the bunk. A scrap of paper on the nightstand caught my eye. Picking it up, I squinted to read the messy lines of text. No name, no number, just an address. For somewhere in New York City.

My jaw tightened; my fingers crumpled around the paper, trapping it in a fist.

I walked over to the open window and leaned out. Kateri was still perched out on the black shingles, face tipped up towards the moon.

"Kateri, she's gone," I whispered.

She turned to look at me, stunned. "Gone?"

"Did you notice if she was in her bunk when you got up?"

"I just assumed she was—I wasn't paying attention."

I glanced down at the messy handwriting once again.

"I think she may have transported out."

Kateri crept quietly across the roof to the windowsill. "What makes you think that?"

I held up the scrap of paper. Kateri took it from me and squinted at it in the moonlight. "Keegan, this address is in New York City—you have to tell Sensei that she left."

My throat tightened. "Sensei's been through enough today. I don't want to bother him with something I can handle."

"But, Keegan—"

"This is my fault, Kateri," I told her gravely. "This is *my* fault. She wouldn't have left if I hadn't said what I did. It's my responsibility to find her and bring her back."

"Keegan, you never transport into the city—"

"I know."

"It's crawling with RGM soldiers! What if something—"

"Nothing's going to happen," I interrupted. "There's a greater risk for all of us if I *don't* go after her—she could give us all away now that she knows where we are and what we're doing here. I don't trust her, Kateri."

She looked at me for a moment, worry stirring in her eyes.

"Tell no one," I instructed in a whisper. "Not even Sensei, unless I'm not back by sunrise."

Kateri gave a single nod. "Be careful."

"I will," I said, forcing a smile for her sake. "I promise."

I silently crossed the bedroom and descended the stairs, coming to a halt when I noticed a light in the kitchen. I heard the sound of footsteps and cabinets softly opening and closing. Lara was up.

I trod lightly on my bare feet and slid outside into the darkness. I took the porch steps all at once and sprinted into the woods.

We usually transported using the portal in the broom closet. But spending as much time with my dad as I did, I'd quickly acquired the ability to transport from anywhere, using *myself* as a portal, just as Dad did. I'd learned the technique so quickly that Dad had even taught me how to use my mind-reading ability to lock on someone's thoughts and transport them, even against their will, in case of emergency.

Usually, I made a cognitive lock on a place I knew well and vividly visualized everything. This time, I had no idea where I was transporting myself to, so there was no way for me to create a mental image. I would have to make things up as I went, and it would be easier for me to do that outside, where I had space.

I slowed to a halt in the middle of the glade where Preston and I had been working that morning. Smoothing the scrap of paper over the palm of my hand, I recited the address over and over again, imagining the hovering street sign reading *D147*, the traffic lights, the tall buildings surrounding me. I tried to keep all the imagery loose and generalized.

*Okay… soften your focus… soften…*

I started to tune out the sounds of the breeze caressing the gangly branches overhead. I started to imagine different sounds: traffic, the roar of crowds, music. Suddenly everything felt tight and warm.

My eyes shot open, and I took in a sweeping, panoramic blur of lights and faces at the mouth of a dark alley. I stepped out onto the sidewalk. Pods flowed past like a polluted river, hovering in midair above stainless-steel streets. The sky wasn't even visible beyond what seemed like a shimmering canopy of structures above. Music spilled out of clubs to flood the streets, and everything smelled like smoke.

A vise gripped my stomach; my throat tightened.

*Don't think… just don't think about it…*

I pulled my hood up, concealing my long hair and my face. I melded in among the crowd and let the flow pull me forward, scanning the streets around me and watching for the street sign I'd imagined.

I forced myself to keep walking. Dodging people, I rounded a corner, then slammed to a halt. A cluster of RGM soldiers half-blocked the path. Keeping my head down, I slipped around them, camouflaged by the crowd.

I stopped at a crosswalk as a chime sounded, and the flow of pods dammed up momentarily to let pedestrians cross. I went with the flow, scanning the intersection. Finally, I saw it: *D147*.

The neon-drenched street was narrow and congested. I checked the slip of paper and started searching the buildings for numbers. I had only stopped for a moment when I felt a hand on my arm.

"Looking for something?"

A young woman around my age had stopped beside me. Her face was pale, her lips bright red, and her light purple hair was pulled back into a messy bun. One strap of her tight black dress drooped down her shoulder, and the neckline sliced down to the center of her chest.

"A friend." I held up the piece of paper.

She smiled. "I could be that."

"I don't think so," I said. "But is this address familiar to you?"

She looked at me for a moment with a strange expression.

I thrust the paper towards her. "It's important."

The woman sighed and snatched the scrap of paper from my hands. She bobbed her head, nodding.

"Yep—yep, that's where a lot of the soldiers are being housed." She pointed farther down the street with one long fingernail. "Keep going that way. It'll be on the right."

"Soldiers?" I questioned as she handed the paper back to me.

"The occupation," she replied. "They have to stay somewhere."

I folded the paper into my pocket and gave her a brief nod, a sinking feeling taking over in the pit of my stomach. "Thank you for your help."

I spotted the massive steel building and cut across the street. I stopped beside the steps just as a guy in a black uniform and cap trotted up them himself. I pretended to fumble around in my pockets for a cigarette, all the while watching out of my peripheral vision as the guy halted in front of the door and waved his finger in a swift motion over the clear glass. A glowing blue screen popped up, and he started tapping it.

From here I couldn't see what he was typing, but I didn't need to. I stared at the back of his head, my forehead went numb, and I zeroed in on his thoughts.

*These boots are too tight. I can't wait to sit down; my feet are so sore... oh, shit, where's my...*

He tapped his pockets, then pulled out a small device.

*Okay, good. I thought I forgot it—one new message...*

His hands drifted away from the keypad again as he started typing on his device.

*I can't tonight. Maybe tomorrow... oh my god, just take the hint already. All right, all right, um... entrance code...*

He started typing.

*Five, five... six, one, two... five.*

With a *pssshht*, the doors retracted, and the soldier stepped inside. I sucked in a deep breath, pulling my mind away from his thoughts. I took the steps two at a time, glancing around me before I halted at the door, mimicking the soldier's motions and typing in the appropriate combination of numbers. The doors opened.

Inside, massive high-speed elevators yawned open. There was an empty desk with a massive interactive directory screen. I walked up to it to check the map displayed there. Swiping through a few screens, I found the room I was searching for.

*Okay... floor seventeen.*

"Good evening. How may we help you?" a robotic voice chimed.

I didn't reply or glance up until I heard a soft beep. I looked up to see a tiny camera mounted behind the screen. It was focused on me.

*Shit.*

I backed away, recoiling into my hood, then leaned back into one of the doors and sprinted up the towering flight of cement stairs. When I reached the seventeenth floor, I shouldered the door open and stepped out into the hallway.

A smoky haze hung in the air, and I could hear the muffled pounding of an obvious party on the floor above. I stopped at the door numbered

1765.

I stood there for a moment, debating what to do next, but a loud crash from inside, followed by Sparrow's frantic voice, decided for me.

"No! No... stop it!" A dull thud. "Cal, stop it! *Stop!*"

With adrenaline surging in my veins, I stepped back and locked my arms out at full extension. A quivering yellow orb took form between my palms, spinning. I wound it back and launched it forward.

The orb dispersed in a fluid burst of light, and the door exploded open. I jumped over the debris and landed in the center of a small, cluttered apartment. A scrawny, shirtless guy had Sparrow pinned against the wall.

"Who the hell are you?" he shouted.

I latched onto his shoulders, spinning him around to nail him in the chest with an uppercut. With an agonized gag, he crumpled. He grabbed an empty beer bottle off the floor beside him and launched it at me. I dove to the side, and it smashed into the wall.

With an angry roar, he scrambled to his feet and surged forward, swinging punches that I blocked and used to my advantage. As he reared back for another swing, I kneed him in the gut.

Hacking, he went down again, managing to latch an arm around my legs and take me to the floor with him. Caught off guard, I swiveled around in his grip, snatching a handful of fingers and bending them backwards. Unfortunately, he had another hand.

A sudden jolting pain sizzled through my skull, blurring my vision, as he punched me right in the eye. Going beast, I broke the fingers I still clenched in my grasp and rolled on top of him to return the favor, delivering a vicious jab to his face.

He was done: he curled into the fetal position, screeching raggedly. I leapt to my feet and made it to the door in a single stride, panting. I stabbed a finger at Sparrow, who was still just standing there, stunned. Her eyes were glazed, and her bra was showing out of the top of her shirt.

"Come!" I shouted. "Now!"

She darted across the room and followed. I jumped over the remains of the door and swung out into the hallway. Sparrow stopped abruptly.

"My bag—it's still in there!"

"Leave it!" I shouted back at her.

"I can't!"

"You have to!" I grabbed her by the arm just as the alarms started to blare. I bit back curses.

*Everyone in this building is a soldier. Everyone is armed.*

"Hurry up—this way!"

Each of my footfalls rattled through my body. My mind raced; doors were already swinging open.

"What the hell is going on?" a deep voice bellowed.

"Elevator, quick!" I shouted to Sparrow.

"But what about—"

The chatter of machine-gun fire severed her sentence. I threw myself on top of her. With my arms locked around her waist, we rolled.

The screech of an intercom—heavy boots. "Security, security!"

I leapt to my feet and all but threw Sparrow into the elevator, making sure she went down to the floor. I lunged in after her, slamming the "door close" button, though several rounds hammered the back of the car before the doors had sucked shut. Sparrow struggled to sit up, gaping up at me; her bottom lip was bloodied.

"What the hell are you doing?" Her voice broke as she shouted. "They're going to be waiting down there for us!"

"We won't be here by then."

"But what about—"

"Just shut up, all right?" I staggered forward, wincing as pain rattled through my face. "Stop talking. Stop thinking."

Though she tried to lurch away, I still managed to latch my fingers over her forehead. I closed my eyes and forced my head to clear. I felt her body slowly soften under my grip. I could still hear the blare of the alarm— the countdown of the floors. We were already to the fifth.

*Breathe, Keegan, breathe…*

I imagined the wind. Wind rustling through the branches of the trees above us. *Trees… the forest.*

Pain surged through my face with renewed strength; I felt something rough against my back. Tree bark.

We were back in the woods.

I opened my eyes, and my vision cleared as Sparrow stood up and stumbled forward in the darkness. She didn't turn around. She kept walking in the direction of the cabin, which was visible now in the early purple of dawn. I caught up to her, placing one shaking hand on her shoulder. She whirled around, whipping me in the face with her hair. Her dark eyes were like glinting steel.

"Leave me alone!"

My jaw hardened. "Leave you alone? I just saved your life! You almost got us killed, Sparrow! Do you even care? Do you even care about anyone other than yourself?"

She spat an angry laugh. "I had everything completely under control! I didn't need you."

"Oh, you didn't? You would have rather he forced himself on you?"

"Maybe I wanted him to!"

My teeth clenched as I stared into her eyes, only inches from her face. "Then why were you screaming for him to stop?"

"You should never have come!" she shouted. "You shouldn't have interfered—"

"Why?" I cut her off, shouting back. "Why, because you hate me? Because you hate us, your life—everything?"

Tears welled suddenly in Sparrow's eyes, and she stepped closer.

"It has nothing to do with you—"

"What, then?"

"Because I hate *me*!" Sparrow's voice broke as she cut me off, slamming her hands against her chest. "I hate myself! I hate *myself*..." Her voice faded to a whisper as a tear rolled down her cheek.

Suddenly everything I was about to yell back into her face was gone. We stood there in the middle of the clearing, staring into each other's faces, bruised and bloody.

Finally, she straightened her shirt and headed for the cabin. I let go of the breath I hadn't realized I'd been holding, and watched her go.

# 11

I'D FOLLOWED SPARROW BACK TO THE CABIN. LARA WAS AT the door in a baggy T-shirt and sweatpants. Sparrow stormed past her and ran up the stairs. Lara's eyes went wide when she saw my shiner. She asked me if I was all right. I was fine, I was fine, I assured her and went up the stairs. Preston and Rafael were asleep, thank god. I rolled into bed and lay there, exhausted and petrified, as the dark waves of unconsciousness came, rolling over me like a tide returning to shore. Taking me under.

*Brrrat-tat-tat-tat-tat…*

The growl of the machine gun rang in my ears in the stillness. I tried to focus on my own breathing as I felt myself slipping deeper.

*Brrrat-tat-tat-tat-tat-tat-tat…*

My fingers shook, curling around handfuls of the sheets. Everything spun as I looked around me. Cement: dirty cement. I was sprawled on the sidewalk in New York City. Neon light blurred around me, my heart beginning to pound in my head as a sick feeling clenched my stomach. I tried to get to my feet, but I couldn't move. My limbs felt like lead. I managed to crawl only a few inches before the world pitched beneath me and I collapsed.

*Brrrrat-tat-tat-tat-tat-tat!*

My fingertips dug at the ground, so hard I could feel the little flecks of gravel cutting into my skin.

*I have to wake up… I have to wake up… I have to wake up…*

But it was too late. Her voice came just like it always did. "Keegan!"

I didn't want to look up, but I felt like I couldn't stop myself. New York flickered away to Ireland and an RGM soldier with a rifle in his hands.

My voice splintered out of my throat in a scream that sounded like a child's. "*No!*"

The blare of the machine gun ripped through my eardrums, hammering my skull, sending me flying backwards. I felt myself falling, and then everything flickered away, replaced by pain as it shot through my face. My eyes opened wide. I was on the bedroom floor, my fingernails digging into the floorboards.

"Keegan?"

I writhed in the suffocating grip of the white sheets tangled around my body, shaking uncontrollably. No sooner had I sat up than a dark outline of a body jumped down in front of me. I gasped, shoving myself backward.

"Whoa, whoa, whoa, hey—hey," the voice came again. "Keegan…"

A hand clamped firmly down on my shoulder. Instinctually, my own hand snapped around his arm and yanked him to the ground. I lunged on top of him, panting, and pinned him down.

"Whoa—dude, dude, stop!"

*That voice…*

"Stop it!"

I snapped backward, looking around. Surrounding me were bunk beds.

Preston was on the floor. A light flashed against the darkness as his hands shot up, emanating an orb of white light. For a few moments I sat there, sweat dripping down my face. Preston's face glowed in the light from the orb as he slowly picked himself up off the floor.

"You okay, man?"

"Yeah… yeah, I'm all right."

"You sure?"

"I'm sure." My voice came out a little louder than I expected. I swallowed, pressing my fingertips to my forehead. "I'm sorry about that, man…"

"Keeg…" he said quietly.

"I'm fine," I whispered, shivering. "I'm fine. I-I'm sorry I woke you."

I pulled myself up to my feet, stumbling a little as the room spun around me. I felt like throwing up. Preston reached out a hand to help, but I pushed it away.

"Keegan, seriously—what's going on? You want me to go get Sensei?"

"No," I said firmly, walking to the door. "I don't need anything; I don't need anyone…" I paused at the door. "I… I'm sorry."

Preston didn't say anything. I turned and quietly opened the bedroom door. Closing it behind me, I walked down the hallway to the bathroom. Without turning on the lights, I locked myself in, sliding to the floor and burying my face in my shaking hands.

"What happened to your eye?"

Dad was sitting on the opposite side of the desk; it was covered in flowerpots, soil, and a tray of seedling morning glories. He carefully drilled a small hole in the dirt with his index finger and lowered the seedlings into the pot.

I pushed my hair out of my face. "I'm sure Sparrow has told you what happened."

"I didn't ask for Sparrow's story; I asked for yours."

"I went to apologize to Sparrow last night for… well, for something I said at dinner. But when I checked the girls' room, she wasn't there."

Dad listened intently.

"I found a scrap of paper with a New York address scribbled on it, so

I transported there to track her down." I reached up to touch my eye, where an impressive bruise was blooming. "Things got complicated."

"You transported into the *city*?" he said incredulously. "Was she with someone?"

I grunted. "I could hear her screaming inside. I had to do *something*. I blew the door open with an orb, and after that all hell broke loose—that's how I got the shiner. They got my picture at the desk—and doubtlessly they got Sparrow and me both on security cameras. I broke into an apartment building occupied by the RGM. They're going to be looking for me now." My tone grew more serious. "No human could have done the damage I did—they'll know who I... *what* I am."

Dad didn't say anything, but the expression on his face was grave.

"On top of all that," I continued, "Sparrow left her bag in his room, so whatever was in there is probably in the possession of the RGM by this point."

"Her bag?"

I nodded. "Hopefully her ID wasn't in it."

He didn't respond.

I narrowed my eyes, studying him; I couldn't shake the feeling that he was keeping something back.

"There's no telling how much she's told her soldier boyfriend," I went on. "Our cover could already be blown at this point. The RGM could know exactly where we are and what we're doing here."

Dad rubbed his jaw. "I'll talk to her."

"Talk to her?" I reiterated. "What, you're just going to come out and ask her if she told the guy our location?"

"I know you don't trust her—"

"That's an understatement. I don't think anyone should trust her—especially not you. I don't know what kind of hold she has over you or why, but you cannot simply take her at her word this time, Dad. It's taken us a long time to build this school," I went on earnestly. "A lot of time and effort, and we cannot risk all of that simply to give Sparrow the benefit of the doubt. Because even if she tells you that she didn't divulge any information about us, how can we possibly believe her?"

Dad straightened in his chair. "Everything you say is true. But there's only one alternative."

"And that is?"

"Sending you away," he said bluntly.

"As in—as in Sparrow and me?"

"As in all of you," Dad replied stiffly. "If I can't take Sparrow's word, then that's the only alternative."

My stomach sank. "Where would we go?"

Dad fell thoughtfully silent. "Do you remember when I first brought you here?"

I frowned, trying to recall. "It's all fuzzy memories at this point."

"After I took you in, before we built the Homestead, we lived farther out in Yellowstone for a year. The place is deep in the forest. I can only describe it as… as the closest thing to the Dimension I've ever seen on Earth."

"Was there a waterfall? I seem to remember hearing one… That's one of the few things I do remember about it."

"There was."

"You think we should go out there for a while?" I asked. "Until we're sure that they won't track us down?"

Dad drew a breath, leaned on his desk, and looked me square in the eyes. "I can't risk anything happening to any of you because I brought Sparrow here."

I returned his steady gaze for a moment. "Why *did* you bring her here, Dad?"

"Because I love her," he replied without hesitation. "Just as I love you."

I wasn't expecting this response. Slowly, my eyes lowered from his.

"What about you and Lara?" I asked. "Are you going to come with us?"

"Someone has to stay," he said. "I have other schools and many other students to consider—I can't abandon them to hide from the RGM. The important thing is to get all of you somewhere safe and secluded—just for a few weeks, until we're sure. During the time we lived out there, we never encountered another living soul. There's never been anyone out that far in Section West," he explained. "You would be safe. But you have to promise me something."

"What's that?"

Dad's eyes drilled into mine. "Do everything you can to keep Sparrow safe."

There was something about the way he said it. He sounded almost desperate—almost afraid.

"Dad." I looked him in the eyes. "In case you missed it, Sparrow despises me."

"Keegan, promise me."

"I risked my life for her last night," I told him through gritted teeth.

"Keegan."

"Fine," I said flatly. "I promise."

"Now go and tell the others." He lowered his voice. "I want all of you out of here today."

I started toward the door, the sun-streaked floorboards creaking under my feet.

"Keegan."

I stopped, glancing back at him. His eyes were serious, but there was something I didn't like in them now—something like pity.

"Are you all right? After last night…"

I nodded. "It's nothing."

Dad shook his head slowly, his eyes still locked with my own. "I wasn't talking about your eye."

"I know that. My answer still stands."

Dad seemed to understand. I turned and left, stepping back out into the hallway. I almost bumped into Kateri, who was heading for the back door, a basket of feed for the animals cradled in one arm. Her brown eyes widened when she noticed my face.

"Keegan! What—what happened?"

"Shh, it's nothing." I placed a finger against my lips. "I just haven't had the energy to heal it yet."

"It does not look like nothing."

"Kateri—"

"No, no, no—you're coming with me. No buts."

There was no use in arguing. She already had me by the arm. Surrendering, I let her lead me outside. The June bugs hissed in the hot summer air before the cool, quietness of the barn swallowed us inside.

"Are you going to fill me in, or am I going to have to acquire *your* gift of mind reading?"

I sighed, taking a seat on one of the stools that stood by the door. Rabbits swarmed at my feet, and the fox rubbed up against my shin. The fawn slept quietly in the hay against the opposite wall.

"I found Sparrow," I told her bluntly. "There was a fight."

"A fight?" She sounded a little taken aback. "How bad?"

Light shone through the cracks in the barn walls, casting soft beams of light over Kateri's face, illuminating her brown eyes as she stopped in front of me.

"Bad," I confessed. "Sparrow was with an RGM soldier… There's no way to know how much information she gave away. How much information about *us* she gave away. Sensei's worried about it—he's sending us away for a while in case Sparrow did give them intel. And to make matters worse, they got my picture—and both of us on the security cameras, I'm sure."

Kateri gently touched my face and began to heal the bruise. Her warm fingertips made small circles over my aching flesh.

"But Sparrow may not have breathed a word."

"But she *may have*."

Kateri shrugged one shoulder, leaning a little closer as her fingertips traced along my eyebrow and up over my forehead. "Sometimes you just have to trust people, Keeg."

"Those two words shouldn't be in the same sentence," I muttered. "There's nothing trustworthy about people—nothing consistent. *Nothing.*"

The light shafting through the slats in the walls illuminated her soft brown eyes as she looked at me. For a moment I lost track of what we were talking about.

"Well, I trust you," she said quietly. "And sometimes that feels like a risk—but what's the alternative?" Her eyes moved over my face. "Never trusting—never caring? Never loving?"

I reached up slowly to touch the place where the bruise had been. It didn't hurt anymore.

"If you never love, you'll never be disappointed," I told her, giving a soft, bitter laugh. "You'll never get hurt."

Kateri's lips pressed into a sad smile. She brushed my hair back away from my face before stepping away.

"Can you inform everyone of Sensei's plan?" I asked quietly. "I… I'm just kind of tired. I didn't get much sleep after I got back."

"I know. I heard you up."

"Is there anything I do that escapes your notice?"

Kateri smiled, picking up the basket again. "What do you want me to tell them? We're leaving—for how long?"

I tipped my head back, watching her for a moment, lost in thought. Lost in last night, the ghosts and the guns and the sound of bullets hitting the back of the elevator shaft.

"Indefinitely," I replied.

# 12

I DIDN'T GO BACK TO SLEEP THAT NIGHT. I CRIED UNTIL MY nose ran and my throat ached, but I didn't care. When I heard everyone go downstairs in the morning, I got up and locked myself in the bathroom.

Leaning on the sink, I studied my reflection in the mirror.

With mascara trailing down my cheeks and bloodshot eyes, I looked like an exhausted mess. Yet, looking at myself, I was still reminded of that picture of my mother—the one I'd left in Cal's room. Her long dark hair flowing over her shoulders, just like mine.

"You're wrong, Fin," I muttered beneath my breath, staring into my own hollow eyes. "I'm *nothing* like her."

I turned on the tap and leaned down to splash ice-cold water over my face.

I heard footsteps. Someone rapped on the bathroom door.

"Hello?" The voice was curt and irritable. "Are you alive in there, or should I blast a freaking orb through this thing?"

Drying my face with a towel, I unlocked the door and whipped it open. Janna stood in the hallway, her hair in a sloppy bun and her arms crossed.

"Are… you okay?"

I nodded numbly, stepping out into the hallway.

"It's all yours," I mumbled, starting for the stairs. Janna stopped me.

"You might want to get packed," she told me, a strange tone to her voice.

I turned on my heels to look at her, puzzled. "What are you talking about?"

"We're leaving today."

"Why?"

Janna stared me down for a solid moment before she exploded. "Why do you think? You broke the rules! You ran away! You screwed us over!"

"I didn't screw anyone over," I replied, my voice numb. "I have a life. Is that so bad?"

Janna's large blue eyes narrowed to slits. "When it affects us all and jeopardizes everything we've worked so hard for?" She nodded violently. "Yes, it is bad."

I pounded down the stairs, passing Myung, who offered only a steady glare. I halted when I reached the kitchen, where Preston was standing at the counter, packing things into a bag.

"Where's Fin?" I asked.

Without pausing or looking up, he shrugged. "Figure it out for yourself."

My jaw tightening, I strode down the hallway towards Fin's office. I flung open the door, but found the small, bright room void of human life. I stepped farther in nonetheless, closing the door behind me.

I became aware of the quiet; the deep, golden waves of sunlight shafting in through the windows. I could hear the birds singing outside.

I wiped my damp cheeks once more as I crossed the room, stopping in front of Fin's desk. There were pots of leafy green ferns and seedlings, stacks of notes on faded paper, and a jar of pens and hawk feathers.

I lifted a feather into my palm, exploring it with my fingertips. Blurry visions of the trees from my dream flashed across my mind… the shape of a bird cut out against the sky as it lifted into the air, taking flight.

I could still hear the voice: *"Sparrow."*

Swallowing, I placed the feather back into the jar just as the door to the office creaked open behind me. I turned around, fully expecting to see Lara, but instead my eyes found those familiar green ones I'd grown up with, unblinking in a soft but rugged face, waiting for me to speak first. He stepped in and closed the door behind him.

There was so much I wanted to say, but I didn't know how. I didn't even know where to begin.

When he spoke my name, what little strength I had left crumbled. I pressed my face into my hands, tears burning in my eyes. I sucked in a deep breath and then lowered my hands and looked up at Fin. I barely felt the warmth of his arms as they enveloped my shoulders and pulled me closer. I sobbed against his chest, shaking.

He said nothing; he just stood there and held me until I could finally breathe again. I pulled away, looking up into his face. It was a forest, a mountain. Something vast. Something that offered no sympathy, no help—just an invitation to get back up again.

"If I told you I didn't tell him anything, would you believe me?" My voice slipped out in a cracked whisper. "Because I swear to you, I told Cal nothing."

Fin's thumb came gently across my cheek to wipe away my tears. "Sparrow… Keegan told me that you left something in the soldier's room."

"Y-yes. I… in the confusion…" I dried my eyes with the back of my hand. "My bag got left behind. I wanted to go back for it, but Keegan wouldn't let me."

"And rightly so," Fin said. "You put yourself and Keegan in a very dangerous position."

"Keegan didn't need to be there—I never asked him to be there, and you didn't need to send him after me—"

"I didn't."

I froze. "What?"

"I didn't send him after you," Fin explained quietly, still looking me square in the eyes. "I didn't even know he had left. Going after you was his own decision. A decision he made because he was concerned for you."

Everything I'd been about to argue died in my throat. I lowered my gaze to look down at the floor.

"They may have you on the security recording now, Sparrow. You and Keegan. And whatever was in your bag is in their possession."

"I know. I'm sorry."

"Was there anything important in it—anything that would be cause for concern?"

My mind immediately flashed back to the picture I'd held in my hands only a few short days ago as I stood there in front of the mirror. The picture of the young woman whose face looked so similar to my own. My mother—the alleged "Sunrise," one half of the soul that held the energy of the universe together.

That picture Fin had given me to hold onto had been in my bag.

Surely no one could possibly identify Hawk from a random photo, could they?

"Sparrow?" Fin pried, snapping me out of my thoughts.

I drew a long breath, then shook my head. "No. No, there wasn't."

He remained silent for a moment before folding me back into his arms, gently kissing the top of my head. "I trust you," he whispered.

I felt a pang of guilt, but said nothing more.

"It's time to leave," he continued quietly. "All of you…"

"Because of me?" I whispered, my eyes burning.

"Because you acted as someone you are not," he replied quietly. "Because you were wrong. Because you don't know who Sparrow is."

"No…" I choked, shaking my head as I pulled away. "No… I… I don't."

Later that day, we gathered on the porch with Fin and Lara.

"First, thank you all for making preparations on such short notice," Fin began, looking around at all of us. "As you know, as Keegan has told you… due to an unfortunate incident, your safety has been compromised."

"'Due to Sparrow,' he means," Myung muttered to Preston out of the corner of her mouth.

My gaze drifted to Keegan. His eyes were fixed on Sensei. I lowered my focus to the ground.

"I'm sending you out farther than you've been before," Fin continued, looking around at us all. "To a remote area where Keegan and I lived before the Homestead was built. I am not going to transport you there; you will travel there by foot. It's not only about arriving at the destination; it's about getting there… How you get there makes all the difference. I want you all to work together. To grow together—learn from each other. To be kind to one another, forgiving and understanding."

No one said anything for a moment. Then Myung piped up. "But, Sensei, what about you and Lara?"

"Do not worry about us. We will be fine—we have gone through this many times before. Our top priority is to get all of you somewhere safe— somewhere no one would ever find you," Fin explained gravely. "You must not transport back here—that is of the utmost importance. Does everyone understand?"

I nodded slowly, as did everyone else.

"You must travel there and remain there. I will transport there myself in a few weeks, when I am confident that it's safe for you to return," he concluded. "I would like to make it clear that there may very well be no repercussions… but we cannot take any chances."

I felt the sear of everyone's gaze.

"Sensei, may we heal the woods when we get out there?" Rafael piped up. "I mean, if it's safe for us to be out there to begin with, it must be safe enough to heal at least some of the forest, right?"

"You may heal, but keep it as inconspicuous as possible," Fin answered. "I am not sending you out on a mission; I am sending you into hiding." His voice quieted as he looked around at his students once more. "Treat each other as you would want to be treated. Let this be a time to learn more about yourselves… Rise to the challenge."

A grave silence hung over our small group. I could feel everyone's eyes burning holes in my back. They all knew this was my fault, even though they didn't know the full story. I could have defended myself: could have told them I hadn't even discovered that Cal was a soldier until that night—that I hadn't told him anything. But I knew no one would believe a word I said.

I looked over my shoulder at Fin, who was still standing on the porch as we disappeared into the thick, dark woods.

We trekked forward, single file. I took up the back, and Keegan led in front. All I could see of him from here was occasional snatches of red hair peeking out from underneath his beat-up ball cap.

I focused on the soft blanket of golden needles beneath my feet, clutching the straps of my backpack and steadying my churning thoughts, paying attention to the next step… the next.

"Bummer that we're stuck with walking," Myung muttered under her breath after a while, sidling up next to Kateri, who was keeping an eye on Rafael as he ran ahead. "Just how far out is this place?"

"A ways," Keegan's voice came back. "I barely remember the place, but Sensei's told me everything I need to know about how to get there—I have a feeling I'll remember it when I see it."

I tuned out the conversation. The truth was, I didn't really care where we were going. Every step I took seemed more and more pointless.

*Why did Fin bring me here? Why?*

I could still see that look in his eyes: no anger, no pity. Just searching—but for what, I didn't know.

Why didn't he yell at me—tell me what a screw-up I was? I had run away and dragged Keegan into it, revealing the fact that we were sliders—endangering our lives. And still… Fin didn't say the words that ran on repeat in my head: *screw-up, screw-up, screw-up.*

It really wasn't my fault that Keegan had gotten tangled up in this mess, I told myself; it was his own. There was no reason for him to come find me, at least none that I could fathom.

*Why did he follow me? Why did he risk his neck to get me out of there—*

Fin made no sense to me, but Keegan made even less.

I found myself focusing on the back of his head, where a small braid hung down past his muscled, freckled shoulder blades, feathers at the end of it. I pulled my gaze back down to the ground in front of me.

Hours dragged by like lifetimes.

I twisted my hair back into a messy bun, swallowing the dryness in my mouth. The ground was turning black under my feet, and everything smelled like decay, ash. I pulled the collar of my T-shirt up over my nose.

An elbow nudged my arm, tugging me out of my thoughts. A hand extended a water bottle in my direction. Kateri had fallen back alongside me. Her long black hair hung in a messy braid, a red bandanna was tied around her head, and her legs, like mine, were coated in ash. I hesitantly took the water bottle.

I took a swig and handed it back to her. "Thanks. What the hell is up with the… ash?"

"Fires took most of the forest years ago."

"What were they caused by?"

"Like most problems, there isn't a simple answer…" she explained quietly. "In my family, there are stories passed down through the generations about the Earth, and how we are to care for it because it cares for us. We've lost that connection."

I scanned the clusters of dead trees. Clouds of ashy dust billowed up in the wake of our footsteps.

"We turned our back on Earth, and now she turns her back on us," Kateri went on. "The government claims to be so adept with technology and 'progress,' yet they cannot fix even this." She threw a hand in a wide gesture around us. "We've 'advanced' so much, we now have nothing left to heal ourselves with."

I didn't really know what to say. I just shrugged. "There's some things we can't change."

Kateri stopped and looked at me. "And there are some things we can."

I could tell by the very tone of her voice that this girl actually thought we could save Earth, like we were some freakish versions of superheroes. Inwardly, I sighed. Even this brief conversation with her had acted as a reminder that I wasn't like these people—that I couldn't be, even if I tried.

As darkness set in, we came to a stop in a tucked-away clearing between towering dead pines.

"Clear the ash," Keegan instructed. "We'll spend the night here."

I had no idea where we were or how far we'd gone, but I was tired and sore and not in the mood to follow orders.

I slipped away, ducking into the shadows of the withered trees. My footsteps sent up little clouds of ash as I walked, only slowing to a halt when I was out of earshot of the rest of the group. I let out a long exhale, rubbing the muscles in my neck. I slid one arm out of my backpack straps, rolling the aches away.

Unlike the patch of green forest where the Homestead was tucked away, here the night came in silence: no crickets, no frogs, no screech of bats. But after a moment, I heard the familiar, dry crunching of footsteps.

I stood in silence as I strained to hear, expecting Keegan to lock my arm in a vise at any moment. I scanned the darkening woods around me, searching for any sign of life, but saw no one. Instead, the soft crunching drifted farther away. Then it faded altogether.

"Sparrow…" A gruff, familiar voice echoed distantly from the camp. "Get back here."

Swallowing back a nervous feeling in my gut, I shouldered my load and trekked quickly back toward the group. There was a fire burning now, and everyone was gathered around it. Keegan stepped right in front of me as soon as I'd emerged from the trees. The soft orange glow from the flames glinted in his eyes.

"Where were you?"

"Nowhere," I answered curtly.

His muscled jaw tightened. "Next time you go 'nowhere,' you'd better tell someone."

"I wasn't far away," I snapped. "And I heard something—someone— out there. Was that you who followed me?"

Keegan sighed and shook his head. "No one followed you. We were all here setting up camp… like *you* were supposed to be."

My eyebrows furrowed. "Are you sure? Because I seriously did hear–"

"The wind?" he interrupted bluntly. "Yeah, me too."

"Not the wind; something in the brush."

"There's no one out here, in case you've missed that," Preston piped up from where he sat cross-legged, tending the fire. "It's just us."

I was about to protest, but stopped.

"Look, don't go wandering off again, all right?" Keegan dragged a hand over the back of his neck. "The last thing I want is to have to hunt you down and save your ass again."

"No one's responsible for me. I can take care of myself," I mumbled, reaching back to let my hair down. Keegan looked at me in the low light before he finally stepped closer.

"Out here we take care of *each other*." He lowered his voice. "Don't forget: you're the reason we had to leave…" He leaned in a little closer, his eyes locked on mine, and lowered his tone to an icy whisper. "Better watch your step."

# 13

WE MADE CAMP AS IT GREW DARK, DEEP IN A PART OF THE skeletal forest that I'd never seen before. So far, things had gone without incident, but Sparrow apparently enjoyed bringing my blood to a boil.

"Better watch your step," I told her as I stared into her dark eyes. Maybe that hadn't been the right thing to say. But how are you supposed to talk to a tempest? I wasn't sure.

I lay awake that night, staring up at the night sky and listening to the soft inhales and exhales of the rest of my group sleeping around me. The campfire was fading now, but even in that dim amber glow, I could make out Sparrow's shape stretched out on the ground. Her hands were tucked under her head, and her face was tipped toward the sky, her eyes glossy in the dim, flickering glow.

I jerked my gaze away and rolled over.

I was up with the dawn. Actually, I had never even fallen asleep.

I rose silently and dusted myself off. Beams of lavender light drifted through the trees. I walked a little way into the cool, desolate valley, taking in every charred pine tree, every sticklike figure of what used to be brush. Before me was a scattering of blackened rocks, and I stepped up onto one of the larger ones.

The surface was refreshingly cool against my bare feet as I explored the textured surface before choosing a spot and sitting down. I rolled the tension out of my shoulders and closed my eyes, breathing deeply. Allowing my mind to quiet and settle into a meditative state.

I tried to ignore the strong scent of ash and decay. I listened to the stillness around me, interrupted occasionally by the whoosh of the wind tangling with the clawlike branches. I imagined they were covered in leaves and the ground was coated in moss and creeping ivy vines; imagined the songs of tiny, flitting birds creating percussion for the wind's rhythm.

This took away the tired feeling in my bones like sleep never could. Sleep brought hell, but I was a mind reader… I could read even the Earth's thoughts and dreams, her deepest desires and what she wished to be: utopia.

Sound began to penetrate this vision of grass and trees and flowers.

"Keegan…"

At first it was distant, muted.

"Keegan?"

I opened my eyes, and the vision burned away to ashes. Preston stood before me, at the edge of the rock.

"I figured I would find you out here," he said. "We're packing up."

I rose to my feet, dusting off. "We'd better get a move on, then."

"What are we going to do about Sparrow?" he asked.

He was just as covered in ash as I was; it couldn't be helped. It clung to his plaid shirt and ripped jeans.

"Nothing," I answered. "There's nothing we can do at this point."

"I just wish Sensei hadn't made us take her. She's a bit of a…" He stopped, seeming to choose a different word. "Liability. If you know what I mean."

I stretched my arms overhead and straightened up. "It's not like we're in any danger out here."

"How do you figure that?"

"Because there's no one out here, man—not for a hundred miles."

"I get that," Preston replied, hesitant. "But still."

"This part of the country has been evacuated for decades, Pres. The chances of us encountering anyone out here are slim to none." I jumped down off the rock. "And even if the impossible should happen, and there is someone living out here, I'm pretty sure Sparrow won't be the one to find them."

He nodded like he agreed, but I could still see the gears turning in his mind.

I clapped a hand on his shoulder. "Come on. We've got a lot of ground to cover today."

"One more thing."

"Yeah?"

Preston's face had grown a little more serious. "You okay, after the other night?"

The previous night came pouring back into my mind like floodwater at the very mention: the blaring city, the empty eyes, the gunfire. My stomach flopped. I forced a fake grin.

"Oh, that?" I grunted. "Yeah… yeah, I'm solid."

"You sure?" I could tell by the tone of his voice that he knew I was bullshitting him. "You seemed pretty rattled. Was it because of the city?"

I shook my head and began walking. "Nope. I'm good."

"Because I know you've never gone into a city, not even with Sensei."

"I felt like it this time."

"Because of Sparrow?"

I whirled around to face him. He stopped short.

"I went because…"

Why *did* I go… exactly…?

"Sensei told me she's here for a reason, Preston," I answered, my voice a little hoarse. I cleared my throat. "I wanted to find her and bring her back before Sensei realized she'd run away. I knew how much it would trouble him. He seems to really—" it was hard to say "—think highly of her."

"Why, though?" He sounded puzzled.

"You are asking the wrong guy."

Sparrow was the first one I laid eyes on when Preston and I arrived back at camp. Her face was ash streaked, and her eyes were overcast.

"Keegan?" Kateri raised an eyebrow, stepping in front of me. "Did you hear me?"

"S-sorry, no. What?" I stammered.

"Are we ready?"

I gave a brisk nod. "Ready."

We started out, moving away from camp in a long ragged line, steadily gaining elevation as we hiked deeper and deeper into the forest. We stopped for breaks only when it was absolutely necessary.

Finally, we stopped at the edge of a valley; it rolled out beneath us in rusty gold waves. Half hidden among the swatches of tall, wild grass there was something else: strange, ghostly shapes.

I felt Kateri set a hand on my shoulder.

"Keeg?" she asked softly. "Keeg, what is it?"

I stepped out from the tree line and into the open. Particles of the dusty earth fluttered in my wake, lifting into the sunbeams. Around me, rising from the ground like craggy headstones, were skeletons. Dozens of them. All that was left of the last buffalo on Earth.

I stood in the middle of the field, breathing hard, turning slowly, taking it all in.

"At one time there were millions…" I shook my head slowly as Kateri stood beside me. "How could we have done this?"

Round, arching ribs rose from the dirt where the rest of the bones were embedded. Jaws and horns and gaping sockets where big brown eyes had once been. An entire herd had met its end here. One skeleton in particular caught my eye. Kateri must have noticed it too, because I heard her draw a heavy breath behind me.

Partially swallowed by the earth, a small calf-like skeleton lay beside one of its larger counterparts. A mother and her young, reduced to wind-whipped fragments of what had once been a wonder of the world.

I turned away, disgusted, and trudged forward.

"What are they?" Sparrow asked.

"They were called American bison," I answered solemnly. "They used to live here—by the hundreds of thousands."

She didn't say anything in response. She scanned the meadow, not moving from the patch of dry ground where she stood, while everyone else ventured forward. Out of the corner of my eye, I saw Rafael kneel down beside the skeleton of the calf.

I came up behind him, placing a hand on his shoulder.

"We'd better keep moving, Raf," I told him gently. "Come on."

Rafael's head of dark curls shook back and forth. He squinted up at me. "Why'd this happen?"

I was asking myself the same question. "I don't know, Raf."

He bit his lip and looked back down again. "It's wrong…"

"They're just animals," Sparrow cut in, her voice raspy and fatigued. "It's not the end of the world."

"Just animals?" I whirled around to face her, fuming.

"Don't you realize that's exactly the reason why they're all gone now?" I strode up to her. "Don't you realize this might not even have happened if someone had actually *cared*? If someone had acknowledged the fact that these creatures *mattered*?"

Sparrow shrugged. "I don't care, particularly."

Gritting my teeth, I seized her by the wrist. A satisfying hint of fear flared in her eyes.

"If someone cut off your fingers—your hand—" I jolted it, my eyes boring into hers "—would you say 'it was just my hand'?"

Sparrow stared up at me, wide-eyed, through the strands of dark hair that dangled in her face.

"No," she whispered finally. "No, I wouldn't."

Her dark eyes held onto mine, furious and searching. I let go of her wrist and walked away.

# 14

KEEGAN WAS AN INFERNO, AND IT SEEMED EVERY TIME I got a little close, I got burned. I'd wanted to jerk away when he'd grabbed my wrist, to yell right back in his face—to explode, like I usually did. But his words triggered nothing inside me except a strange and empty feeling as I stood there in that meadow filled with dry, ancient bones.

We didn't hike much farther after that, probably five more miles or so. Still, I wasn't used to so much walking—and through rough terrain. The ground was no longer ashy; it was dry, crumbling and dead. I sat down at the base of a dead oak, sweating and panting for air, watching Rafael absent-mindedly as he hunted around for dead wood to make a fire with. Now and again he accidentally discharged a splash of water from his fingertips, dampening the wood and causing him to kick at the dusty ground.

"Still working on controlling those abilities, huh?" I questioned, untying my filthy sneakers.

Rafael screwed his mouth into an irritated scowl. "I'm getting better every day."

"Didn't say you weren't, did I?"

He trudged over and dumped the armload of wood into a pile beside me, putting his hands on his hips. "What are yours, anyway?"

"My what?"

"Your abilities. You must have something."

I winced, tugging my swollen foot out of my left shoe. "I already told you—I'm nothing special."

Rafael scrutinized me as I took my other shoe off. He sat down, cross-legged. "But you can transport."

"Yeah, but you *all* can do that—that's what portals are for. It's really not a big deal."

"Normal people can't," he pointed out. "So there's *something* special about you."

I gave him a weak smile. "Look, I know you mean well—but I'm not supposed to be here. I don't want any of this like you guys do. I just…" I scanned my fellow classmates, who were scattered around. I dropped my voice. "I just want a life—a normal, everyday life. I don't believe in any of this."

Rafael looked confused. "How can you not believe in it if you're an anomaly yourself?"

"Because, Fin… lied to me," I said, unsure of how to word it.

Rafael shook his head adamantly. "No way. Sensei never lies. Not ever."

My jaw clenched a little. "Rafael, do you have parents?"

The question caught him off guard, but he yielded a nod.

"Then you wouldn't understand what it's like…" I told him. "To be told your whole life that… that they're coming back for you when they're not."

Rafael's blue eyes softened. "Did they… did they die?"

"No, Rafael, they didn't die… It's worse than that."

"What could be worse than them dying?"

I leaned my head back against the trunk of the tree behind me, memories of things I'd said repeating in my mind.

*You don't understand—I don't believe anymore! I never have!*

"Nothing," I said at last, climbing to my feet. "Never mind."

I tried to help with building the fire, but Preston curtly informed me that he could do that on his own. So I stood awkwardly beside him and watched until I noticed Janna clearing away rocks and larger branches. I offered her a hand, but she just gave me a fake smile, shook her head, and said that she had it under control. And the truth of the matter was, they all did.

I went back over to Preston. "I'm walking over there," I told him irritably, tossing a hand in the direction of the thicker part of the woods.

He'd succeeded in starting the fire. He paced around shirtless now, stretching a beam of white light between his palms. He shrugged one muscled shoulder. "Why are you telling me?"

"Because what's-his-name told me I had to tell somebody if I left camp," I grumbled.

"Okay. Why are you leaving camp?"

"I have to pee."

Preston nodded. "Valid."

I turned on my heel and walked off into the thick patches of trees. These trees weren't burned, but they still looked like ghosts, void of color and life. I listened as each of my footsteps crunched against the dusty ground. I couldn't recall the last time I'd gone barefoot. But then I also couldn't recall the last time I'd been outside this long, or hiked this far, or gone days without showering and shaving my legs. My skin was coated with dried sweat and grime. My hair was greasy and felt plastered to my head. I flipped it into a careless bun as I walked.

When I'd trekked far enough to find a secluded place with ample brush cover, I unzipped my shorts. While I relieved myself, I thought about how much I abhorred the outdoors. Then I remembered what Lion Boy had growled at me the night before:

*We're out here because of you…*

No sooner had his words crossed my mind than I heard the plod of distant footsteps. I quickly pulled my shorts up, walked through the brush a little ways, and stopped to listen, holding my breath. I heard nothing.

Then the beat of footsteps came again, but this time they sounded different and came from the opposite direction. I turned and looked over my shoulder to catch a glimpse of a whirring black object—and then heard the dull thud of an impact. I rolled my eyes, trudged over to the large oak, and pulled Keegan's knife free, sending soft bits of decaying wood sprinkling to the ground below.

His tangled mane was tied back in a ponytail. The feathers woven into his braid flopped against his shoulder with each purposeful stride as he walked toward me. His face had reverted to its resting scowl, and sweat patched his dirty green tank top.

"You shouldn't throw these things when there are people around," I said flatly once he was close enough. "You almost hit me last time."

Keegan grunted a laugh, like this was somehow amusing. "I was nowhere close."

"I felt the wind."

"Good." He snatched the blade from my fingers and slid it back into the rough leather holster fastened over his chest, which held three other knives. "Maybe next time you'll think before you do something stupid, like smoke on a blanket of tinder-dry pine needles."

"I didn't notice them."

"You don't notice a lot of things," he shot back. "Why are you so far from camp?"

"I'm not that far—I had to pee. Is that not allowed either?"

Keegan rolled his eyes.

"What are *you* doing all the way out here?" I turned the tables, a bitter edge to my voice.

"I wasn't following you. Kateri and I just got back from checking out the river, which we will be crossing tomorrow," he said, with added emphasis on the last part. "So I suggest you get some rest."

I glanced over my shoulder, squinting back at the part of the woods where I could have sworn I'd heard something else.

"Hey, did you hear me?"

"Yeah, I get it," I snapped. "What is our objective out here anyway? Just to torture me?"

Keegan's lips pressed into a narrow line as he studied me, a look of disgust in his eyes. "You really don't get it, do you? Do you seriously think this is all about you, Sparrow?" His fiery words were harsh in contrast to the silence hanging thick around us. "This isn't about you—beyond the fact that it's your fault."

"Everyone keeps saying that. How the hell is this my fault?"

"Because you blew our cover. Do you know how much effort Dad's put into trying to keep the healers safe—hidden from the people who want to kill us?" he exploded. "You told him where we were, didn't you?"

"Who?"

"That lice-bag you were with that night."

"I told Cal nothing!" I shot back. "He didn't even know I was an anomaly until you came blasting through the door to beat his face in! And *I* didn't know he was a soldier! I told him *nothing* about the school in New York, let alone the school for healers out here—believe me, it was the *last* thing I wanted to talk about."

"You're lying—I can tell."

"Why would I lie?" I forced the words out through gritted teeth. "Haven't I been honest in everything else? Do you really think I would put Fin in danger—after everything he's done?"

A faint hint of surprise flashed in Keegan's eyes. I'd said too much.

"What do you mean?"

"Nothing," I quickly replied, glancing away. "I just meant that... I still love him, even if I don't agree with him on everything. Even if he's not my Sensei. I would never have given information away like that—I would never betray him."

Keegan looked at me hard, his strong arms folded over his broad chest. "Yeah? You think *Sensei* believes that you're loyal to him?"

My words came out in a hoarse whisper. "Of course he does."

I couldn't read Keegan's expression as he scanned my face with his hard green eyes, the freckles on his face blending in with the spattering of dirt.

"He sent us out here because he doesn't trust you," he answered finally, his tone hardening to ice. "He never has. And neither do I."

I stood there as if I'd just been struck.

Words burned in my throat, a chaos of everything I wanted to say but didn't. I shoved past him and walked away, numb.

# 15

*ten years earlier*

YELLOW, YELLOW, YELLOW.

It streamed over the hills beyond the windowpane. I pressed my small face against the cold glass, peering out through tired eyes as the sun made its first appearance. It flooded the swaying grass beyond the window and washed over the roofs of the cement-block buildings that etched the skyline in the distance—what used to be the French countryside. Everything was quiet.

It was early morning. I could hear Fin breathing softly from the couch where he slept so I could have the bed. It was such a tiny house, and we hadn't been there very long. I was finally getting old enough to know that a home felt good. We'd been here long enough to gain a few students, and I was beginning to hope we would stay. I felt safe and secure and had begun to forget about the fact that I was so different from the other kids.

"What's wrong?" Fin had asked me one night. He'd given me that side grin he always did, gently tucking a strand of hair away from my face. "You've been keeping something back all day… Out with it."

"Everyone else can channel so well," I'd whispered. "Everyone else has a power but me…"

"You can transport, Sparr."

"Yes, but anyone can do that."

He'd smiled a little. "You're still a child, my love. You're still growing and learning."

"But not fast enough…" I'd interrupted, my lower lip trembling as I buried my face in the sheets, trying not to cry. "I can't do it… I can't keep up—I don't have a gift like everyone else does… I don't trust myself, Fin… I don't trust who I am."

Fin had just sat there quietly for a long moment before gently tugging back the sheets to look down at me. His tousled blond hair fell into his eyes as he leaned down to softly kiss my forehead.

"I trust you, Sparrow," he'd whispered.

*I trust you…*

"Fin," I'd said quietly after a long moment, "can I ask you something?"

He'd nodded, brushing a strand of hair away from my face.

"Why can't I call you daddy?" I'd whispered.

Fin had looked a little surprised.

"Do you… do you want to?" he'd asked.

I'd hesitated, then nodded. Fin smiled, but something sad welled in his eyes.

"You make me wish I were," he'd whispered gently. "But I know your daddy, little one. And I'm not him."

I'd looked away, tucking my face back into the sheets.

"Then where is he?" My question had come out in a broken whisper.

Fin hadn't answered right away. His eyes were glossy, and he took a deep breath.

"I don't know, my love," he'd said finally. "I don't know. But I know that he loves you… and he's going to come back to you as soon as he can. He and your momma both."

I thought about what he had said as I sat there the next morning, looking out the window while he slept. The sun was over the roofs of the houses by now. I pulled my knees up to my chest, wiping the tears out of my eyes.

I looked over at Fin, who was still sleeping, his tousled blond hair in his eyes and his mouth slightly open. I studied his features for a moment before lifting my gaze to the worn-out mirror across the room, examining my own face, searching for similarities that I couldn't find.

That was when I'd heard the gunshots in the distance. First, they were far away, soft—*pop-pop-pop-pop-pop*. But a moment later they were rattling the glass. *Brrr-rat-tat-tat-tat-tat!*

I heard a startled moan. Fin jumped to his feet, listening for a moment. When the gunshots picked up again, he snapped into action, turning to face me.

"Sparrow, we have to leave—now."

"W-w-why?" I stammered. "W-w-what's happening?"

Without hesitation he scooped me up in his arms.

I was too young to understand what it all meant—the gunshots and the smoke that had begun to billow in the distance. He wrapped me in a blanket, concealing my face, concealing his own beneath the hood of his coat. I saw blurs of the room around me, the worn-out floor and the sturdy furniture washed in morning light. Then I heard the door unlatch, Fin's heartbeat, and more gunshots.

Then we fled.

I was awake before everyone else. I'd never actually fallen asleep.

For a moment I lay there on the ground and tried to feel it beneath me; I tried to feel the dirt under my fingertips. I tried to feel the cool morning air on my face and the stiffness in my shoulders—anything. But all I felt was numb.

I pinched my eyes shut. I could still hear Keegan's hot, angry words: *He sent us out here because he doesn't trust you… He never has.*

*He never has.*

*He never has.*

I gulped back the stinging sensation in my throat. Kateri stirred beside me, taking a deep breath. I waited for everyone to wake up. I kept my eyes shut and pretended to be asleep until I felt Kateri's hand shake me.

"Sparrow, it's time to go." Her voice was gentle, but loud and clear. Kateri stood over me now, extending a hand.

I climbed to my feet, pausing to look her in the face. "We're out here because of me… because I screwed things up," I said quietly. "Is that what everyone thinks?"

Kateri slowly nodded. "Yes."

"I didn't say anything to Cal. I-I didn't tell him anything." I slid my backpack on and straightened up. "I didn't…"

There was no sympathy in Kateri's eyes, but there was no resentment either.

"Trust is earned, Sparrow," she said at last. "You have done nothing to earn it."

Left with nothing to say, I trailed behind her as she started after the others. Eventually, she shot me a glance over her shoulder. "Keep up!"

I picked up my pace. We were coming to the tree line now, to the place where the forest ended and the wide, rushing river began.

"Everyone stick together." Keegan's arms went up over his head for our attention. I lifted a hand to shield my eyes. "It's not too deep, and the water's not toxic, but there's a current, so hold hands and stick together."

Hazy mountains stacked up in the distant smog, steep and gray. The valley rolled out around us to frame the river in a dry, ashy landscape. The other side had burned, but the river had stopped the flames in their tracks. Like a lifeline, it had saved the small portion of the woods we had camped in the night before.

Everyone slid out of their shoes and packed them away. Keegan was the first to wade in, locking arms with Rafael, who grabbed Janna's hand. The chain continued all the way down to Kateri, who stood just in front of me, stepping carefully off the embankment and into the churning, opaque water. She was in up to her knees when she reached for my hand.

"Come on, Sparrow," Kateri ordered. "Take my—"

"No," I blurted, shying away, shaking my head violently. "I-I can't. I... I can't do it."

"Take Kateri's hand. You'll be fine!" Keegan yelled from up ahead. The water was up to his chest now. "We can't stop in the middle like this—the current is too strong. Come on!"

Kateri grabbed me by the wrist and pulled me into the river. I gulped a sharp breath as the icy water rose quickly up to my chest. I staggered forward, trying to keep my balance. The riverbed was covered in algae-coated rocks that were slick under my feet. My fingers latched tightly around Kateri's wrist as I trudged forward after her, fighting my way through the chaotic water. I could hear nothing beyond the deafening *whoosh* the current made as it twisted and turned around the giant boulders jutting out of the water downstream.

My heart was pounding in my chest. I kept my focus up ahead, on the flash of wild red hair. Keegan was almost to the other side—only a few yards away.

*Almost there, almost there, almost there...*

My entire body was shaking as I sloshed forward, sending the dark, icy water all the way up to my throat. My head instantly felt light. I tried to focus on the riverbank ahead.

My foot came down on another slippery rock, and then suddenly, my legs went out from underneath me.

In a flash, the river swallowed me under; I felt the current latch onto my body like teeth around its prey. Kateri's fingernails dug in frantically and then dragged over my skin as the river tore us apart.

I turned end over end, my ears filling with the muffled roar of the water around me. I beat my way to the surface, gasping—screaming. Through the sunlight and splashes of whitewater, the rest of the group were just smudges in the distance. Keegan had stopped just short of the opposite side of the river. The last thing I heard was his distant, frantic voice shouting my name.

Then the back of my head slammed against something hard, and I slipped below the surface. Golden flecks danced in my vision, then disappeared altogether. There was a flickering image like a vision from a dream. Feathers, wings... vanishing and leaving me in darkness.

I LOOKED BACK WHEN KATERI SCREAMED. MY HEART DROPPED when I saw her digging her free hand frantically through the water around her.

Sparrow was gone.

"Sparrow!" I shouted. My gaze skidded rapidly over the water's surface, searching for the familiar head of dark hair bobbing in the whitewater. At first, I saw nothing, then finally Sparrow broke the surface—already a hundred yards downstream. The current threw her against a boulder, and she went under again.

I immediately pulled my other arm out of Rafael's grip.

He stared at me, wide-eyed. "What are you doing?"

"Get them to shore!" I yelled over the roar of the rushing water ahead. "I can't let her drown!"

Before Raf could say another word, I lunged forward into the water. The last thing I heard before I went below the surface was Kateri frantically shouting my name. I tuned out of everything, forcing my eyes open, fighting past the frothing whitewater to come up for air. Sparrow was still a ways ahead, floating on the water's surface, facedown. A sick feeling twisted in the pit of my stomach, my promise to Fin echoing in my mind.

I dug through the angry water with hard, precise strokes, working with the current and maneuvering around the massive boulders that rose from the riverbed. My thighs burned as I fiercely kicked my legs. Another boulder caught Sparrow, and this time the current kept her pinned. It was all I needed to catch up. I was only several yards behind her now; I needed to reach her before the river swept her forward again.

Gasping for air, I fought ahead into the whitewater, swimming harder and faster than I thought possible.

The river grew violent now, throwing me against rocks and shoving my head below the surface. My hands were shaking so much by the time I finally reached Sparrow, I could barely grab hold of her. The river taunted me, tugging her just out of my reach. She rolled in the current, her face stone white.

I was so desperately trying to get far enough ahead, trying to grab hold of her arm or leg, that I hardly noticed that the water had begun to calm and deepen. A distant pounding noise caught my attention.

"Sparrow!"

I knew it was little use calling to her; she was unconscious, barely floating anymore. Her face was slipping below the churning water. Furious white splashes rose around me as I dug forward, faster, faster—

Finally, my fingers locked around her wrist.

I dragged her closer and rolled her onto her back, then slid my arm under hers and across her chest, locking her against me, her back to my chest. I tucked my head in beside hers and began to kick, towing her and keeping us both afloat as I tried to turn and head to the riverbank. Breathing heavily, I glanced up to see what lay ahead of us.

*Nothing.*

I felt my heart sink into my stomach.

*No… no, no, no, no, no…*

There was no way I could fight the current—not with an extra hundred pounds to pull. My mind was racing as the river tugged us farther and farther forward, and the edge began to call my name in loud, raging bellows. Thousands of gallons of water, sliding off into the yawning void. Everything inside me was swirling and burning; I felt sick to my stomach as my entire body shook with adrenaline.

I fought frantically towards the riverbank at a right angle, tearing through the water with my free arm and kicking with every ounce of strength in my body. An agonized growl rattled in my throat; my muscles screamed with the effort of each stroke. The shoreline was a blur of dead grass and ashy trees, hidden behind the water splashing into my face and eyes. Finally, I reached forward and snatched a handful of grass on the embankment only for it to tear out in my hand.

I roared with the barrage of water and clutched Sparrow against me, almost unconsciously keeping her face above the water even as I knew it was over.

For a moment everything was deafening, and then it was silent.

My body felt weightless as we dropped in the blast of water. My arms splayed instinctively outwards, and Sparrow's body separated from mine. My blood was replaced with adrenaline in my veins as I plummeted, down, down, down…

*"Promise me, Keegan… protect her…"*

It was a fleeting thought within the chaos that veils the jaws of death. I wasn't filled with remorse—I was boiling inside. I was angry. Way too angry to die.

Seconds later, I hit what felt like solid iron. Water poured into my lungs, and my bones felt like shattered glass. My vision spiraled into blackness.

I forced my leaden arms out in front of me, pulling myself forward through the bubbles and dark water, scanning frantically above, beneath, all around me for the small shape of Sparrow's body. The water whooshed in my ears as I moved my head back and forth, searching, searching, searching…

*Where are you, where are you, where are you…*

I scanned my surroundings frantically, swimming forward through the cold water, fighting the panic that surged in my chest.

*Don't lose control—don't lose it.*

I forced myself to calm down, detaching from the situation as if I were a mere spectator, backing away from the blistering pain and the fire in my lungs. *Who needs air? Not you... you're an anomaly.*

As my pulse quieted, my thoughts fell away, and my forehead went numb. My mind drifted listlessly, almost sleepily, until finally, it caught on someone else's:

*I'm sorry... I'm sorry... Please don't leave me...*

Sparrow's thoughts passed through my mind like they were my own.

I lurched forward, following the flickering stream of thought, swimming hard through the water around me, down—down, down into the deep until the thought patterns became stronger. Until each word was like a piercing scream rattling through my skull.

*Please don't... don't... leave me...*

I reached out and felt her hand brush against mine. I grabbed it and yanked her up, kicking violently to the surface, which seemed to pull itself farther and farther from my reach with every stroke.

With one last burst of energy, we crashed through the surface.

I sucked air, treading water and holding Sparrow's head above the surface. We were not far from shore. I tucked my arm across Sparrow's chest again, tucked my head up next to hers; she offered no resistance. With no current to fight now, I kicked for shore. Only a few moments later, I felt the gravel riverbed under my feet, then got my legs under me and stood, gathering Sparrow in my arms. I carried her up onto the embankment, collapsed to my knees and lowered her limp body into the dried grass.

"Sparrow!" I shook her by the shoulder and tapped her face with my other hand. She didn't respond.

I quickly centered the heel of my hand on her chest and pressed down hard, over and over and over again. It did nothing more than jolt her lifeless body.

My heart beating faster, I reached up and slid one of my hands underneath her neck, tipping her head back. I opened her jaw and closed my mouth over hers, pushing a deep breath down into her lungs, and then another. I straightened up and went back to pumping the heels of my hands against her chest.

"Come on, Sparrow, come on…" I whispered, water dripping down my face and into my eyes.

I cursed, leaning back down and taking a deep breath. I pressed my mouth over hers again and exhaled. A warm stream of water gushed from Sparrow's mouth and into mine. I quickly rolled her onto her side, and she coughed up mouthfuls of river water and began gasping frantically for air.

Finally, exhausted, Sparrow rolled onto her back again and lay there in the grass, her chest rising and falling at a frantic pace as she drank in the oxygen.

I clambered to my feet and began to assess the situation. My eyes widened as I saw the huge waterfall behind me, like a massive tumbling bride's veil dropping down the mountainside. Incredible sheets of yellow rock rose around us on either side, framing the river as it rolled onward. We were in the belly of a ravine.

"The waterfall…" I barely heard the murmured words leave my mouth. "This… this is it. This must be the place. Come on." I extended a hand down to Sparrow, who was still lying there. "We have to get back to the rest of the group, or we'll be a day behind them—they'll never be able to find this place."

Sparrow squinted up at me. "I almost died."

"Oh wow." I coughed hoarsely into my arm. Water was still making its way out of my own burning lungs. "I wouldn't know how that feels." I started to walk back the way we'd come.

"You're just leaving me?" she called.

I paused at one of the trees. "Yep."

She sputtered and then gagged. "I guess I'll be here." She rolled over on her side and tucked an arm under her head.

"I guess you will."

"You literally don't even care." She closed her eyes.

I shook my head slowly, still breathing heavily as I walked back over to her. I reached down and grabbed her by the wrist, pulling her to her feet. Her dark eyes were wide, and her wet hair hung into her stony white face.

"If I didn't care," I said hoarsely, "I would have let you wash downstream."

"Wait… What happened?" She stared at me in puzzlement. "The rest of the group isn't…?"

"No," I informed her, my voice level. "They're *miles* upstream."

"You left the rest of the group?" Sparrow sounded surprised. "To… to save—"

"I promised Sensei I'd keep you safe," I interrupted. "And my loyalty to him means more than what could have happened to either of us."

Sparrow's dark eyebrows pinched together. "But you could have died… Your loyalty means more to you than that?"

I looked at her steadily. "Yours doesn't?"

Sparrow didn't reply. She stared at me like I was a complete stranger. Finally, I turned back around.

"Come on." I pulled her by the hand. "We've got a lot of ground to cover before nightfall."

We had to hike back up the mountain the river had thrown us over. The climbing was steep—the side of the ravine was a sheer drop in some places. Sparrow, not surprisingly, had almost no experience in climbing. Or hiking, or being outside in general. She'd added several minor injuries to her quiver of complaints by the time we'd made camp for the night among a hilly stretch of trees.

I peeled off my damp shirt and slung it over a tree branch, then knelt on the ground to start building a fire from the handful of sticks and twigs I'd been able to gather.

"How are you going to start a fire with no matches?" Sparrow questioned through chattering teeth, observing me from the base of the tree where she was seated, her knees folded up to her chest.

"No idea," I answered, not taking my focus off my work. "Maybe lightning will strike."

"Your jokes don't amuse me."

"Good." I brought up a hand and took a steady breath, channeling an orb into my palm and watching as it slowly faded from yellow to orange, then from red to pure flame. "Amusing you is fairly low on my list of priorities right now."

I dropped it into the small pile of sticks, satisfied to see them ignite.

"The temperature's dropping." I painstakingly adjusted the sticks and then added a few more from the pile beside me. "We need to get out of these damp clothes."

Sparrow sat shivering violently. "Um, I'm not getting naked with you around."

"No, you're not," I said. "I'm going over there, behind that big oak, and you're staying here and getting warmed up. Then we'll switch."

Sparrow looked at me skeptically, but then yielded a nod as her teeth began to chatter more violently.

I made my way through the scraggly brush and ducked behind the oak tree, undoing my belt. I could hear Sparrow fumbling with her clothes on the other side.

"Where'd you learn to channel fire like that?" She slung her shirt over the branch where mine hung near the fire. "I've only seen Fin do that."

I slid out of my pants and threw them over to her to hang up for me.

"Dad taught me. He said his best friend taught him."

"'Dad'..." Sparrow reiterated. "It's still so... weird to think of you as Fin's son. I mean, I've heard him talk about you and stuff, but..."

I quirked an eyebrow. "But?"

"You're just..." She paused. "Not what I was expecting."

"What were you expecting?"

"I don't know..." Sparrow snorted a laugh. "Anyone but you. Why did he take you in, anyway? As his son, I mean."

I considered the question for a moment and then shrugged. "Because I didn't have anyone."

"You don't have parents?" she questioned, with a refreshing lack of hesitation.

"They died when I was little."

It wasn't the whole truth, but then no one but Dad and Lara knew the whole truth.

"I… I'm sorry…"

"Stop it. I hate sorries, and I hate sympathy in general. Stop."

"Okay, okay—I was trying to be *nice*."

"It doesn't suit you. I've gotten used to how rude and thoughtless you are," I muttered. "Don't become unpredictable now."

The fire crackled, and Sparrow sputtered irritably, fighting with her words. "Well, right back at you. You're the one who said I didn't even belong here!"

"I think I've more than made up for that."

"Oh, have you?"

"I saved you—twice now."

"That doesn't make up for treating me like I'm… like…" To my surprise, Sparrow faltered. "Like I'm… nothing."

A weight sank into my stomach. I didn't know what to say.

"I mean, whatever." She cleared her throat. "I know it's true—I know I'm worthless as an anomaly. And as a human, I can't seem to get either of those roles right. I don't know why Fin brought me here in the first place…" Sparrow's voice tapered off. "I guess I just… I don't know."

*I don't know.* That was where she left it. And honestly, *I* didn't know either.

Why was I risking my life for her? Why had my father asked me to? *Why is she even here?*

I pulled in a shaky breath, shivering a little in the cold shadows. "You know, that night you ran away, I was looking for you to apologize… That's the only reason I even noticed you were gone."

A stunned silence followed. The fire cracked and popped.

"To apologize?"

"For what I said to you earlier that night." My ego writhed as I spoke.

"That you didn't belong at the Homestead—here, with us."

Again, Sparrow went quiet.

"So… you're glad I'm here, then?"

I grumbled a laugh. "Don't jump the gun, okay?"

"It kind of sounded like it."

"Then let me clarify: No. I'm not glad—and I haven't enjoyed almost dying. Twice."

"That's your own fault."

"Oh, *really?*"

"You're the one who *chose* to come after me."

"Would you rather I hadn't?"

I heard Sparrow set a few more sticks on the fire. I could see her silhouette glittering against the trees in the firelight.

"No," Sparrow finally responded. "No, Keegan, I… I'm glad you did."

I listened to the fire and her footsteps and then heard her settling on the ground again.

"Thank you," she added, more quietly this time.

I didn't answer right away. There I was, stranded in the woods with this stubborn renegade of a student, separated from the group of sliders I counted on most, naked and shivering while she absorbed all the heat from the fire I had built. There were a thousand things I could have said in response.

But instead, I just said, "You're welcome."

# 17

*five years earlier*

I BOLTED UPRIGHT, KNOTTED IN SWEAT-SOAKED SHEETS. Everything was dark around me. I didn't know if I was still dreaming, or if I was awake—there was little difference between the two. I was twelve, and the shadows of the trees still turned into monsters on my bedroom walls— silhouettes of RGM soldiers, with their guns and their shouts and the growl of their engines, chasing close behind.

A sob tightened my throat. "Fin! Fin…"

A moment later my bedroom door opened, and I felt his strong arms around my thin, shaking frame. He smoothed my hair again and again, his lips resting at the crown of my head.

"Shhhh," he hummed. "Shhh… it's okay…"

I clung to him, latching my trembling fingers onto his shoulders with no intention of letting go. "I heard something—I heard something." I sobbed against his chest. "I heard the shots of the rifles, Fin. They're coming! They must be!"

He kissed the top of my head and stroked my hair.

"It's okay," he whispered. "You're safe… you're safe."

"But I—"

"It was a nightmare, my love… It was just a nightmare."

"Nightmare? No… no! It was." My chest heaved as I tried to breathe. "It was so loud…"

"I know… I know it was." He drew me tighter into his arms. "But it was as real as those shadows over there—see?"

I could scarcely make out where he was pointing past the tears welling in my eyes. I began to see that they were trees, not soldiers. Not guns.

"Listen," Fin whispered before I could say anything. He nodded toward the open window—one of the only windows in that tiny house in Belfast. "What do you hear now?"

I calmed my breathing and strained to listen, watching the trees sway rhythmically to the sound, drenched in moonlight, their shadows dancing along the empty white walls.

"W-w-wind?"

I felt Fin's nod against my head. "Wind, Sparrow."

Fin leaned back against my headboard and let me lie against his chest.

"Fin?"

"Yes, Sparrow?"

There were thousands of questions gushing up inside me like an underground spring, but I couldn't translate their foreign languages into words he, or I, would understand. I fought with them as I lay there, shaking.

"I miss them…" My voice was a trembling whisper. "And I don't even know who they are…"

Fin was silent. I could hear his heartbeat as he held me close.

"I know who she is… who they both are." His voice softened to a whisper. "I don't know what happened to them, but I know they're coming back for you, Sparrow."

We'd taken turns warming up by the fire until our clothes had dried enough to wear again. Then, without any further conversation, I'd drifted off to sleep for what felt like only a moment.

I started awake, my heart pounding in my chest. My gaze darted up into the treetops overhead, as if expecting to see something I'd been dreaming about only moments before, that voice: *"Sparrow…"* That same smudge against the sky.

I saw nothing beyond inky shades of navy turning dark purple. It would be dawn in an hour or so.

I pressed the heel of my hand to my forehead. The fire was almost out now, reduced to just a few glowing embers between me and where Keegan lay sleeping.

Taking a deep breath, I settled back down on the ground. I willed myself to remain awake, listening for the sound—the voice. But my eyelids were so heavy. They sank shut against my will.

The next thing I felt was something shaking my shoulder.

"Hey, come on, wake up—"

I started awake again, my eyes flying open. Keegan squinted down at me, his freckled face wreathed in sunlight and his feathery braid hanging down over his shoulder.

"Go away," I whined.

"'Fraid that's not gonna happen," he grunted. "We gotta get moving. We've overslept as it is."

I groaned and rolled over onto my side.

"Today," he went on, ignoring my response, "we climb the ravine."

"You say that like it's going to be easy," I grumbled, my eyes still pinched shut.

"No, I don't," he said. "I say it like it's going to be done."

I sighed and pushed myself up off the ground. I rubbed my face in the crook of my arm.

"We have to climb back up the ravine and walk upstream to find the rest of the group." Keegan had rolled up his shirt and tied it around his head, sweatband style. His knife-filled holster was strapped across his bare, muscular chest. "I wish I remembered it well enough to transport…"

"But we don't have a portal."

"I don't need a portal. I can transport without one."

"Oh. Well, I remember it, a little."

He tossed me a dubious look. "I think we'll hike."

"You transported to New York to find me without knowing where you were going," I pointed out, pulling my dirty hair back into a sloppy ponytail. "You could just pull that stunt again."

"It wasn't a stunt, and it wasn't easy—and I had an address to work with." He shook his head. "And that was a bad experience."

"Yeah, I wasn't big into almost getting gunned down, either." I shuddered inwardly.

"No, I just meant the city in general."

I arched an eyebrow. Keegan kicked dirt over the final embers of the fire.

"I don't like cities."

"How come?"

"I just don't like people," he replied bluntly.

"I've noticed."

He jerked his head in the direction of the cliff. "Come on. Let's get moving."

I followed Keegan into the thicker part of the forest that led up to the steep, mountainous ravine. I could hear the rushing of the waterfall that we'd gone over the day before. It was crazy to think we'd actually survived.

"I lost my backpack in the river," I complained aloud as we trekked through the underbrush. "What happened to yours?"

The sunlight blazed a trail down his back as we walked, igniting his freckled, chiseled shoulders, which I hated myself for noticing.

"I never had one," he answered.

"You didn't bring anything?"

"What would I need? Well, other than my knives… But look around you." He gestured towards the nothingness. "There's plenty of firewood for warmth, brush and leaves for bedding, and trees for shade. We don't need food, remember? Was there anything important in yours?"

"Not really…" I replied. "I mean, just a few pictures of Cal and me, and some clean clothes that would have been nice to have right about now."

"You need to forget about it."

"About clean clothes? I'm trying."

Keegan shot me another glance over his shoulder. "About that lice-bag."

"I kind of deserved him, to be honest."

Keegan turned around so abruptly I almost collided with him. I tripped to a stop.

"Don't say that in front of me—not ever." His green eyes locked with mine. "You don't deserve someone who abuses you, Sparrow. No one does," he went on. "You're sacred."

I stared at him. "*Sacred?*" The word felt strange on my tongue. I wasn't sure I knew what it meant, exactly. "There's nothing special about me—well, nothing much. Yeah, I can do some of the things you guys can, just by osmosis, but I mean…" I trailed off. "I don't have any special abilities. I don't… I don't even know where I came from."

*Why did I just tell him that?*

Thankfully, Keegan didn't get stuck on it.

"None of that matters. Every living creature that draws breath carries life in their veins and has a little piece of something divine." He reached up to touch a cluster of crisp, brown leaves on one of the trees. They instantly transformed to a lush shade of green. Keegan jerked his hand away. "I wish I could heal all of it… the whole forest. Each tree has a purpose, every little rock and stream. Every animal."

I bit my bottom lip, turning the idea over in my mind. "Is that what you meant the other day? About the buffalo…"

Keegan ducked below a tree branch and jumped up onto a large boulder. "The Cheyenne view the buffalo as a sacred animal—they used to be dependent on them for food and clothing. They moved with the herds, following their migratory patterns like they were a life source—and they were. Even if we don't depend on animals for food anymore, we still depend on them to keep the Earth alive—to keep *us* alive.”

“Where’d you learn about that?” I huffed as the terrain grew steeper.

“Kateri—and she learned from her grandparents, and they from theirs.”

I thought about it for a moment as I focused on making my way around the rocks and looking for footholds.

“Kateri seems really smart,” I commented finally. “She always does the right thing and knows just what to say… She was the only one who didn’t hate me when I first got here.”

“We don’t hate you,” Keegan corrected me. “We’re just angry with you. But it’s not in Kateri’s nature to be angry.”

“That… seems impossible, somehow.”

Keegan tipped his face to the sky, squinting. “Yeah, sometimes Kateri seems that way to me too. Dad discovered her when he was at a school in Section C. She’d moved out of her parents’ house because she couldn’t conceal her powers—she was basically a hermit for a while.”

“What about Janna? And Myung?”

“Their stories are pretty typical. I’m sure their initiations were a lot like yours.”

“Oh, yeah?”

“Sensei found you, put you through some tests unbeknownst to you, and then revealed your powers without you even realizing it.” Keegan rattled off the scenario like he was some kind of expert. “And so, you trust him, you initiate, you join a school… Am I right?”

I stifled an annoyed laugh. “Oh, yeah. Exactly.”

“I don’t think Sensei had any trouble finding Preston. Channeling light is a hard ability to keep concealed. Then there was Rafael, who accidentally flooded his parents’ house in his sleep…”

“And what about you?” I questioned tersely. “What’s your fairytale conversion story? What brilliant superpower did you have to make Sensei notice you?”

We climbed in silence for a few moments.

“I’m a mind reader,” he said finally, a little quieter. “That’s all.

Nothing fancy, no good story."

"How old were you when Sensei adopted you?"

"Young," he replied bluntly, ducking another branch. "Five. Something like that. I don't remember."

I arched my eyebrows. "How old *are* you, anyway?"

He cast me a sidelong glance. "Is that any of your business?"

The answer was no. So instead of answering, I just waited for him to respond.

"Twenty-two," he answered at length. "What about you?"

"Seventeen."

"No, I mean your story," Keegan clarified. "How *did* Sensei come to find you?"

I felt my throat tighten. "Like you said… Typical initiation story."

*If only you knew…*

Keegan had no idea who I was, and there was honestly something refreshing about that. I was tired of hearing Fin tell me I was born of the Sunrise and the Sunset—the "patriarchs." Out here without Fin, I was just another anomaly. And though I still wasn't a fan of *that* status, it was better than constantly feeling Fin breathing down the back of my neck, watching my every move—expecting the world of me just because he believed I was someone special.

Keegan expected nothing of me—less than nothing.

I was about to say something more when he lifted a hand for silence. We had finally emerged from the trees at the top of the small foothill leading up the side of the sheer-drop cliff beside the waterfall.

I stepped up beside Keegan, squinting at the cliff just ahead, a feeling of dread tangling in the pit of my stomach.

"Is there another way up?" I asked, sounding lame.

Keegan stood there with his hands on his hips for a long moment; his green eyes were narrow slits in the glaring sunlight.

"Nope," he said.

# 18

I SLID ONE OF MY KNIVES OUT OF MY SHOULDER HOLSTER, wound back my arm, and channeled it into the side of the cliff with a mean torrent of illuminated red energy. It impacted with a crack, sending little bits of rubble flying. Sparrow shielded her eyes.

"Hey, watch it," she complained.

Pushing off a large boulder, I lunged up and grabbed hold of the knife's handle. I hung there, a few feet off the ground, using my free hand to grab another one out of my holster. I channeled it forward into the rock, then reached up to grasp it, and hoisted myself higher.

"Okay, so… how am *I* climbing up?" Sparrow called uneasily.

I had to hand it to her—it was a valid question, to which I didn't have an answer. Yet.

"We're going to climb up to that little ledge up there—see it?" I jerked my head in the direction of the place where the sheer incline tapered into a plateau that led to a slope and veered off into the woods. It was about a hundred yards above us.

"Yeah, I see it," Sparrow answered.

I pulled the two remaining knives out of my holster. "Watch yourself."

I dropped them down to her. They clattered against the rocks.

"What the—I don't know how to use these!"

"Just watch what I'm doing and follow," I explained, sending another knife careening into the slab of rock. I heard Sparrow gasp as more rock shrapnel showered down on her. "It's not hard once you get the hang of it."

"Maybe not for you!" she shouted. "I can't do that."

I hoisted myself higher, pulling the lower knife out of the cliff side to throw it again and swinging around to look down at her. She seemed so small from here, glaring angrily up at me with a knife in each hand.

"Only because you keep telling yourself that."

Sparrow growled and stomped over to the base of the sheer wall of rock, where she slammed one blade against it.

"Hey—you have to channel it. You can't just cut into rock with a knife like that. Are you insane?"

Sparrow threw the knife down on the ground. "I'm done—I'm so done. I'm staying down here!"

"All right," I yelled down to her, continuing up the wall. "If that's what you want."

There was a pause. Then she exploded.

"*What?* You can't just—you can't just leave me here!"

I yanked one knife out of the cliff side and slowly channeled it higher, exaggerating my movements so Sparrow could see.

"Look," I shouted down to her. "I can't do it for you. You have to learn to do things for yourself."

Sparrow snorted. "What happened to 'we help each other out here'?"

Levering my legs against the slab of rock, I hoisted myself higher. My arms were beginning to feel heavy in their sockets. "This is helping you—trust me."

"How?" Her voice cracked. I was beginning to sense a little desperation in her tone. Part of me enjoyed it.

"If I did everything for you, I'd be doing you a disservice," I explained through grunts, climbing steadily higher as I continued to channel the knives. "What if I weren't here, and you were out here, facing this cliff alone?"

"I'd sit here until I died."

"Pssh. Unlikely," I returned. "You're too stubborn for that."

Sparrow said nothing else, and after a moment, I heard the sound of her blade clanging against the rock. A growl of effort followed, and then a sharp scream as she fell to the ground below.

"I hate you!" she yelled up to me.

I was almost to the plateau by this point. I heard another blast of steel against rock, and I held my breath. Silence. This time she didn't fall. When I glanced down, I saw her climbing. Her hand shook as she yanked one of the knives out and threw it again, higher.

I focused forward, climbing a little faster until at last I made it to the rocky shelf, hoisting myself up by the trunk of a tree growing at the edge. Flattening to my belly, I leaned over to retrieve my knives, and checked on Sparrow again; she was still quite a distance down.

"How are you doing down there?"

She grunted, yanking at one of the knives. "Just don't talk to me, okay? Oww! Ow! My arms—"

One of the knives clattered down the side of the cliff. Sparrow huffed a few curses, dangling from one hand and clutching the remaining knife.

"Hang on," I yelled down to her.

I scanned my surroundings and spotted a long, thick vine climbing up one of the trees. I unwound it from the scraggly pine branches and tested its strength.

"Hurry up! I can't hold on—"

"Yes, you can." I tied the vine around the tree and threw the excess over the edge. It dropped down to her. "Now grab on and climb up."

I held the vine in place and listened while she struggled and grunted and cursed. But finally, levering her legs against the cliff side, she climbed her way high enough for me to reach down and grab her hand.

I hoisted her up hard. She collapsed into my chest, and we both tumbled backward. Sparrow scrambled off me, breathing hard and brushing the hair out of her face.

"Th-thanks," she stammered. I noticed her arms were shaking.

I responded with a single nod as I climbed to my feet. I quickly began to ascertain that the steep climb turned into a more gradual one from there onward. The ravine side launched up into a steady incline and then looped off into a thickly wooded area. With any luck, we'd be camping there by nightfall.

"Looks easier from here on," I announced, stretching my arms overhead. "Come on."

I looked back at Sparrow; I could tell she wasn't ready to continue yet. She was sitting down, sucking air and pale as a sheet.

"Need a break?" I asked, a little annoyed.

Sparrow shook her head. "I'm fine."

I decided to take her word for it, even though I could tell she wasn't.

"Watch your step," I advised as she got unsteadily to her feet.

The plateau skirted around the steeper part of the cliff and let out at a rocky path. The ground was loose here.

"The rest of the group is still much farther upstream," I announced, wiping the sweat off my face. "We gotta keep moving."

Sparrow leaned back against a tree, breathing heavily.

"We're, like… over a day behind them," she returned, sounding skeptical. "It's not like they just stopped there and waited. For all they know, we both drowned."

I was already starting to contradict her when I stopped. My eyes darted from Sparrow to the trees surrounding us.

"What is it?"

I lifted a finger to my lips, shaking my head, listening.

The pounding of the waterfall was a little more distant now. The wind shushed through the brown leaves and wiry branches overhead.

"Thought I heard something," I said finally.

"Like what?"

I was about to describe it when I heard it again: a distant cry. A scream like something I'd only imagined.

"Shhh." I quietly took a few steps forward into the tree cover. There was still a ledge to my left and a few larger boulders piled after that. "It sounds like… It can't be…"

Sparrow hadn't moved. "It can't be what?"

I listened for the long, shrill scream. It had sounded far off before, but an instant later it came again—alarmingly close.

"Keegan!" My name burst from Sparrow's mouth in a deafening shriek.

I whipped around just in time to catch a glimpse of the several hundred pounds of fur and claws before it lunged forward and latched onto my shoulders, nailing me to the ground.

# 19

"KEEGAN!"

I screamed his name at the top of my lungs, rooted to the ground where I stood, paralyzed with fear.

I saw the cougar a fraction of a second before he did—a mass of tan, matted fur lunging from the top of the boulder above us. That was all I comprehended before Keegan and the gigantic, shrieking animal became a single rolling, writhing mass of red hair, dirty fur, limbs and claws. Rumbling, throaty growls ripped through the air as the two tumbled together, one indistinguishable from the other.

I fell back against the boulder. *I don't know what to do, I don't know what to do, I don't know what to do!* The words juddered through my mind, closing me into a frozen stupor, until Keegan *screamed*. Not a shout for help, not a cry of effort—a pathetic, helpless scream like that of someone who knows they're about to die.

Immediately, I lurched away from the rock. Still shaking, I frantically scanned the ground for something, anything, to throw at it. I grabbed a rock that was a little larger than my hand and pitched it at the blur of cougar and boy, hoping to god it would strike the former. And it did, but the pain seemed only to spur it on.

Shouting frantic curses, I grabbed a larger rock and launched it, this time nailing the cougar in the spine.

With my heart raging in my chest and my stomach churning, I brought my hands up in front of me. I squeezed my eyelids shut and began to feel the veins in my arms heating up, as if my blood had begun to boil. My fingers trembled, and something like electricity buzzed between my palms. I opened my eyes and caught sight of a pulsating blue orb, which quickly turned clear as I wound back my arms and launched it forward.

With a loud *whoosh*, it soared through the air like a heat-seeking missile, vacuuming away the oxygen around it and exploding into the cougar's side. This time it lost its grip on Keegan and stumbled away, dazed. It turned to glare at me, and my eyes stayed locked with its black ones, my hands still shaking in front of me. And then it shook its head, screamed, and bared its teeth as it lunged for Keegan again.

Another orb bolted from my hands, this time only nicking the massive cat before careening farther to nail Keegan in the leg. He gave a pained yell as the impact tossed him backward and into the trunk of a tree, closer to the edge of the rocky plateau.

I had no time to think about it—the cougar launched from its hind feet, flying through the air with its front legs and claws extended.

I stumbled backward, shooting orb after orb, blistering its white underbelly and sending it hurtling back into the woods. I was unable to stop; more orbs rivered from the palms of my hands, peppering the dead trees surrounding us, punching a massive hole right through the trunk of a thin birch. With a loud crack it began to fall to the ground.

"Keegan, look out!" I jumped back to avoid getting hit. Keegan rolled away as the tree crashed to the ground.

The energy channel finally broke, though my hands still shook uncontrollably as I scanned the woods. The cougar struggled to its massive paws a dozen yards away. I lifted my hands, extending them out in front of me once again. I didn't plan on striking unless it came closer—but yellow flickering energy orbs rapidly formed between my palms to continue blitzing the forest.

They impacted first into the cougar's shoulders and then into its side as it twisted around, yowling in pain.

"Sparrow, stop!" Keegan yelled.

Sweat trickling down my forehead, I channeled a handful of fiery orange energy and threw it forward with all my might. It whipped through the trees, cracking through branches and finding the cougar's face. A deafening, agonized scream ripped through the woods as the force sent it careening backward. It collapsed against the rocky ground, and this time it didn't get up.

Wisps of smoke rose from its bloody fur, and crisp brown leaves showered down around it. Broken branches littered the ground.

A sick feeling sank into my belly as I slowly lowered my shaking hands, breathing hard. I quickly turned and found Keegan leaning against the trunk of the tree he'd been able to roll to. I dropped to my knees beside him.

His head was tipped back, his eyes pinched shut as blood trickled from the gash across his forehead. A deep, bloody trail of claw marks tore across his bare chest.

"Oh my god. What can I do?" I asked frantically. "T-t-tell me what to do!"

"Help me up..."

I leaned forward a little so he could wrap an arm around my shoulders. I couldn't help but notice that the skin on his left leg was wrinkled and blistering red, as if it had been boiled, in the place where my orb had struck him.

Keegan's weight shifted to my shoulders as he growled in pain.

"I'm too weak to heal myself." His voice shook through gritted teeth. "We need to get away from here."

I clutched one arm tightly around his torso and supported him as we walked, passing the place where the dead cat lay.

Keegan could barely put any weight on his injured leg, and he was bleeding fast from his face by the time we reached a little glade deeper in the woods.

"*Agggghh!*" Keegan's fists clenched as I helped him lower himself to the ground. "My *god*, it hurts…"

"I know, I know. I'm sorry." I knelt beside him. "Tell me what to do."

Keegan managed to shake his head stiffly. "T-t-there's n-nothing…"

"There has to be something!"

"You can't h-h-heal. There's nothing you can… you can do…" His jaw clenched as he took another labored breath. "I hear a stream, somewhere c-close. Go find it."

"Do you want me to bring you some water?"

He managed a slight nod, writhing with pain and collapsing against the pine tree behind him. He gave another growl of pain as his open wounds made contact with the rough bark.

"Hurry up!"

I jumped to my feet and took off into the woods, pausing for only a moment before I heard the distant trickling sound of water passing over rocks. I found the fingerlike stream only a few yards away, snaking through the trees. I ripped a strip of cloth off the bottom of my T-shirt and soaked it in the stream. The water was ice cold.

The woods were silent around me save for the gurgle of the stream. I tried to calm my own beating heart. Then I heard a soft snapping noise in the distance.

My muscles tensed. My first thought was of the cougar—that maybe there was another.

My eyes darted back and forth between the trees and their long shadows, searching for the source of the noise, but I saw nothing. I could hear Keegan shouting my name.

Balling up the dripping fabric loosely in my hand, I sprinted back through the woods. He was still propped up against the tree, but now he was fumbling with his holster.

"Here, let me." I quickly dropped down beside him. His head lolled back against the tree trunk, his eyes pinching shut painfully as he gasped for air.

I unbuckled the holster and carefully lifted it off him. He lay there for a moment, gathering strength, before finally lifting his fingers to press them into the deep gashes sliced across his chest. I watched in silence as he slowly dragged his fingers down along the bloody claw marks, leaving a trail of clean, completely healed flesh behind his fingertips. When he finished with his chest, he sank back against the tree trunk, cursing in pain. He reached an arm forward.

"Water."

I quickly dropped the cloth into his hand, and he pressed it to his mouth, sucking in the cool liquid.

"Here." I shuffled up next to him and took the rag out of his hand. Trying to be gentle, I mopped the blood off his face and pressed it to the wound.

"Oww!"

"Sorry."

Keegan drew ragged breaths and closed his eyes. "I'm so tired. Just give me a minute…"

"Just try to relax…" I told him, keeping my palm pressed firmly to his forehead.

"We'll be… we'll be two days behind them now." He sighed heavily, swallowing as he closed his eyes again. "I don't think I can go farther today."

I bit my lip, my gaze drifting in the direction of the stream and where I'd heard the snapping sound moments ago.

*It could have been anything,* I told myself firmly. *It could have been anything.*

"It's okay," I said, turning the wet, now-crimson rag and reapplying it to his forehead. "We'll have time to catch up tomorrow."

Keegan didn't look convinced, but he nodded anyway, then placed his hand over mine to tug it away gently. I watched as, wincing, he positioned his fingers at the top of the gash and dragged them firmly downward, healing his forehead.

Dusk faded to twilight. I'd found enough dry wood for a fire. I offered to light it, but he only shot me a wary glance and used one of his own fire orbs to start the blaze.

"I think I've seen enough of your orb-throwing skills," he told me, leaning back against the tree, exhausted. "You just about took my leg off."

Keegan had healed almost all of his wounds by this point. He looked completely drained in the glow from the firelight; he tipped his head back against the tree behind him, and his messy red hair hung over his shoulders.

"I think you're forgetting I saved your life," I said finally, poking at the fire with a stick.

"I'll give you that," Keegan agreed after a moment. "I… yeah. I would be dead right now if it weren't for you. So, thank you."

My gaze shifted back to his glinting green eyes. "No problem," I returned quietly, then smiled. "I guess we're even now."

Keegan looked at me for a long moment. "I guess so." He cleared his throat. "But with that said, we still need to work on your channeling skills, because they completely suck. Who taught you, anyway? I thought you transferred from the school in NYC, not the jungle."

"Um, I *did*, thank you very much. Runner was my main instructor—you've met him, right?"

Keegan nodded. "He's a friend of Dad's. You must not have been the most—" he paused, searching for the right word "—cooperative student, I'm guessing."

I shrugged. "I was never into it—I never wanted to be part of any of this."

"Why'd you initiate, then?" he asked.

There was no way I could tell him the truth—not Keegan, of all people. But I couldn't deny the fact that, sitting there in the darkness of the forest and the glow of the fire, something in me wanted to.

"I, uh, I guess I…" I pressed my lips together, staring into the dancing flames. "I guess I didn't know what I was getting myself into."

I could feel Keegan's gaze. I could tell he wanted to question me further, but instead he left it alone.

"Well, I could teach you," he said finally. "My dad's the best, you know. He taught his best friend how to do it, and she was a legend."

"Oh, yeah?"

Keegan nodded. "She… was someone very, very special to him."

My eyebrow arched a little. "She?"

"Hawk," he clarified. "One of the patriarchs."

*Hawk…*

The name alone was enough to stir a whirlwind of emotions inside me. I'd heard Fin talk about my mother since before I could remember—but he'd never told me she was his best friend.

"What do you mean by special?" I asked.

"Who am I to say… Even knowing my dad as well as I do, I find he's sometimes still completely unreadable." Keegan's eyes narrowed a little as he gazed into the tongues of orange flame. "All I know is that he speaks of Hawk as… as one would imagine the moon would speak of the sun," he said, tipping his head back again. "I think he was in love with her—still is."

I stared at him through the firelight, thunderstruck. "Fin was *in love* with Hawk?"

"He's never come right out and said it like that… He knew he wasn't destined to be with her—that that was Icarus's place…" His words trailed off and he nodded. "But yeah. Yeah, I think so."

My eyebrows came together. "But you just said yourself, they couldn't be together."

Keegan's eyes lifted to meet mine. "So? Just because you can't be with someone doesn't mean that you stop loving them."

For the first time in what felt like ages, I had nothing to say in reply. No good comeback, no sizzling remark. Just a strange, empty, longing feeling in my gut.

"Hawk was a legend at channeling, you say?" I said at last. "You think you're just as good?"

"All I'm saying is, if you'd known what you were doing back there, you wouldn't have had to kill the cougar."

"It tried to *kill* you."

"I know that." Keegan sighed. "But there are so few left. It was hungry… The elk population is down to almost zero—you saw what happened to the buffalo. I was shocked that we even saw a cougar out here. I've never seen one before."

"In all the time you've lived at the Homestead, you've never seen one?"

Keegan shook his head. "I was sure they were all gone by this point. I know there was nothing you could have done, but…"

I frowned a little, swallowing back a dry feeling in my mouth. "But it would have been better to just scare it off and let it live."

Keegan nodded, then huffed a breath. "But, hey, if it came down to us or him… Sorry, cat."

"Yeah. I mean, I wish there had been some way around it… I just have a hard time controlling…" I let out a wry laugh. "*Anything,* these days. I feel like everything I touch spins out of control."

"It only feels that way because that's what you keep telling yourself." His eyes met mine in the firelight. "Since you've been here, I've only known you to be honest once, Sparrow—that night in the woods just beyond the Homestead, when I transported to New York and found you, when you stood beneath the sky and shouted into my face that you hated yourself… You are not at war with the anomalies or Fin or even with us, Sparrow," he finished quietly. "You are at war with *yourself.*"

I wanted to look away but found that I couldn't. I wanted to deny it. I pressed my eyelids shut, trying to push the thoughts away, trying to erase words that were like permanent ink.

"You have more control over your life than you realize." Keegan placed one hand against the rough bark of the pine tree and slowly stood, stepping carefully around the fire and stopping at the place where I sat cross-legged on the ground. Firelight spattered over his face as he reached out a hand. I hesitated a moment, then took it.

Keegan's warm fingers closed over mine as he pulled me up to my feet, and suddenly we were two silhouettes before the dancing flames. One side of his face was illuminated by the orange glow, the other masked in shadow.

For a moment Keegan didn't say anything. His eyes searched my face and then locked with mine. He leaned closer, the stubble on his cheek brushing against my skin as he lowered his voice to whisper into my ear, "Heal me."

For a moment I couldn't stop thinking about how close he was and how the warmth of his breath felt on my skin.

"I… I can't," I whispered back. "I don't know how. I—"

He shook his head and turned his back to me; it was still marred with scratches and, now, blotched black and blue.

I drew a shallow breath, trembling inside. The familiar stories I'd heard of Icarus haunted me: how he'd been a healer. It was something I'd always told myself I could never do. Something I didn't even *believe* in.

"Heal me," Keegan repeated, his voice firm.

I lifted one shaking hand, slowly allowing my fingertips to make contact with his warm, smooth skin just above one of the scratches. The ebb and flow of the flames from light to shadow etched the muscles in his shoulders. I swallowed and tried to focus.

I vividly imagined how the gashes in his chest had dissolved beneath his touch earlier. I thought of how the blood had vanished, leaving only clean flesh.

Tracing my fingertips down over the wound, I heard Keegan draw in a soft breath. I closed my eyes, and my thoughts fell away. First my fingertips were warm, and then they burned.

Streams of what felt like hot water rushed through my arms and into my hands, pouring out through my fingertips as they moved over Keegan's back. For a moment, everything inside me felt weightless.

Abruptly, it stopped. I stumbled forward, losing my balance, but he turned, and his strong arms caught me.

Keegan stood facing me, his hands on my shoulders, steadying me; his face was just a blur in front of me. As I held onto his arms, my vision slowly cleared.

"What just happened?" The question pushed past my lips in a mumbled whisper. "Did I just…?"

I didn't finish. I didn't have to.

Keegan turned around slowly so that I could see his back, which no longer looked like a brutal abstract painting. Where there had been bloody wounds, there was now healed flesh. Where there had been bruises, there was now only a spray of ginger freckles.

My heart began to pound a little faster as he turned to face me again.

"Maybe I was wrong about you." He trailed off, his eyes drifting over my face. "Maybe you do belong here…"

I swallowed, my gaze softening as I searched his face.

He seemed lost for a moment. Then he cleared his throat and stepped away.

"Tomorrow," he began with resolve. "Tomorrow, you learn to channel—*properly*."

# 20

THOUGH I WAS NO LONGER IN PAIN, I STILL FOUND IT difficult to fall asleep that night. In the silence as I lay there, I began to wonder if all of this was actually just an accident: being stranded out there with Sparrow in the ravine. I couldn't help but feel like there was more to this place than I could see. Something seemed to rise from the very ground I lay on to stir my spirit and mind with questions.

Though it had been long ago that Dad and I had lived in this part of Section West, the more time we spent here, the more it was coming back to me. As I lay there listening to the waterfall in the distance, it felt so familiar.

Despite our inability to make it out of the ravine that night, my mind drifted up over the falls and followed the river back to the rest of our group—my anomaly family. I wondered where they were, how they were. I could still hear Kateri's voice echoing in my head, screaming my name as I plunged below the surface and let the river sweep me away.

She probably thought I was dead. They probably all thought I was dead.

*How are we going to find them again?* The river had carried us so far, we were days behind them.

Finally, beneath the weight of all these thoughts, my eyelids closed, and I felt my aching body surrender to unconsciousness.

For a while, I drifted in nothingness. Then…

"Keegan…"

At first, I thought the voice was Sparrow's. Slowly, I opened my eyes to take in blurry snatches of yellow and pink, then white. The woods had fallen away. I was no longer outside and sprawled on the ground, but tangled in sheets and trying to focus on a face bent over me.

Blinking hard, I felt fingers tracing through my hair, soft and familiar.

"Good morning, sweet one."

Spoken in a lilting Irish accent, the words sent shivers down my spine—the voice, the nickname only she called me. I tried to breathe, to close my eyes again and make it all fade away, but my lungs filled with the scent of her perfume, which intensified everything tenfold.

"Keegan, look at me…" she said. "Look at me…"

Her green eyes sparkled in the morning sun, staring down into mine. Her wavy red hair fell around her face, and she smiled.

"Do you miss me?"

I lay there, stiff, my heart pounding in my chest and sweat lacing my skin. Before I could answer, the room went dark, and the deafening blare of machine-gun fire sliced through the room. I started awake with a loud gasp, almost choking.

Icy sweat trickled down my face and chest. My fingernails filled with dirt as they dug into the ground beneath me. The woods surrounded me, drenched in purple predawn. Faded orange coals smoldered in the firepit. Sparrow lay undisturbed on the other side, her head resting on her folded arm. She drew a deeper breath, but didn't wake.

I tried to calm my breathing, wiping the sweat off my face. My hands were shaking.

I felt sick to my stomach, weak limbed, as I slowly stood and walked into the woods a little ways.

I thought of Dad. I remembered what he had said the morning he had poured those seeds into my hands:

*"So… they come from nowhere?"*

*"No… they come from everywhere."*

*Everywhere, everywhere…*

I stopped in my tracks, crumpling against one of the dying trees, pressing my forehead to its rough bark. Hot tears stung in my eyes.

And still… *still* I couldn't leave Ireland behind. Still, I carried with me what had happened there.

*seventeen years earlier*

*Galway, Ireland*

My face pressed against the rocky ground as I shivered, tears streaming down my face. I curled into a ball, willing myself to become smaller, smaller, smaller, until I was nothing at all. I whispered a prayer to a God I no longer trusted, a simple prayer:

*Let me vanish. Let me vanish.*

The sea rose and crashed against the rocks, deluging me. I could still hear gunshots and the wail of sirens as the RGM medics came to collect their dead and leave ours in the street. We were the enemies.

It was a miracle that no soldier found me there first, curled up on the rocks beside the sea, shaking in my tattered clothes as I waited for a wave to come and carry me away. The air was filled with smoke—the sickening fog of war. Galway had fallen, and I was but a remnant of what it had once been. I was debris on the shore, waiting for the ocean to swallow me.

I choked back a sob, my small body shivering uncontrollably as another wave shattered over me. Everything faded away as my eyes squeezed shut. I rolled a little closer to the edge, where the sea met the rocks. The ground grew slicker, and the deep billows of rising, falling water drowned out the guns and the wail of the sirens.

The ocean waited for me, extended her arms. I rolled closer, sniffling back tears, choking on the seawater as it splashed my face. I felt the edge of the rock slab roll beneath me, but two strong arms caught me before I could fall.

"Let me go! Let me go!" My screams were hysterical as I was scooped up and away from the edge. "Let me—let me…"

My garbled words crumbled and collapsed as I sobbed hysterically, pounding a broad chest with my small, curled fists.

"Shhh, now. Shhh." The voice was deep, and the arms were strong as they held me fast, not letting go. "Where did you come from?"

I couldn't breathe; I couldn't speak. My throat was tight and my lungs burned. Hot tears streamed down my face.

The ground bobbed like ocean waves below us as the set of strong arms carried me several paces. He stopped and set me on the ground, squatting down to look me square in the face. Through the blur of tears, I could make out the dark hood of a raincoat and, beneath it, a face. Two green eyes peered out at me, kind but full of urgency.

"Where are your parents?" he asked again.

I gulped mouthfuls of air, my lips trembling.

"Gone." I sobbed. "Gone."

I began to crumple, but he caught me before I collapsed. He tucked me into the flap of his raincoat and lifted me into his arms again.

"I'm going to get you out of here," he said quickly. "I promise."

"I can't leave," I yelled against his chest, unable to see. "I can't leave them…"

"You must, little one."

I shook my head fiercely. "I can't leave Mom and Dad!"

"They're already gone, my son." He gently placed a hand on my head. "The soldiers are seizing the city—we must escape now."

Though I struggled against him, shouting and sobbing, I felt myself being carried again. When I finally blinked my eyes open, I saw the ocean disappear into a cloud of mist.

"You're safe now," he said softly, holding me close. "I promise, you're safe…"

I scrunched my T-shirt up into a ball and soaked it in the stream. I carried it back to camp and wrung it out over Sparrow's head. She bolted upright, gasping and wiping her face furiously.

"What the hell do you think you're doing?" she grumbled, her voice still groggy with sleep.

"Isn't that what I should be asking you?" I gestured toward the sky. "It's gotta be six thirty by now. You should be happy I let you sleep this late."

Sparrow lifted her head slightly to look at me, almost like she was checking to see if I was serious; then she groaned. I picked up my shoulder holster and strapped it on.

For the next few hours we hiked through the woods, following the stream we'd found the day before. We came to a stop where the stream grew wide. Several boulders protruded from the bed of the stream, penetrating the surface and creating a perfect place to build a few cairns.

"Let's take a break," I said, wading into the water, which rose only to my thighs. I reached down to gather a few smooth stones as I made my way over to the boulders.

"What are you doing?" Sparrow yelled from where she stood stubbornly on the bank.

I rolled my eyes, stacking the stones into small towers on the surface of one of the boulders. "You'll see," I yelled back over my shoulder.

I collected a few more handfuls of rocks from the bottom of the stream and waded forward to the other two boulders. The water was sweet and cool in contrast to the heavy, humid air.

"Have you ever channeled at targets?" I asked.

"Only a few times."

"A few?" I quirked an eyebrow. "What did you do with yourself the whole time you were in New York?"

"Tried to get out of as much of the training as I could." Sparrow gave a short, mirthless laugh. "I… never fit in there, and after a little while I had no desire to."

I kept stacking the rocks. "And why is that, exactly?"

"Because I was tired of having an ideal to live up to. I hated the pressure, and I hated being different."

"What pressure? Dad never pressures any of us to be anything except who we really are."

"Exactly." Sparrow sighed. "And what happens if Sensei believes you're someone who you don't believe you are?"

I had to think about it for a second before I answered. I finished with the rocks and waded back over to the embankment.

"It sounds to me like you're the one who needs to change your perspective," I said, stepping back up onto dry ground where Sparrow was waiting, arms crossed. "Not Sensei."

I gestured for Sparrow to turn and face the stream. "Come on, let's give this a shot." I stood beside her, bringing my hands up in front of me to channel an orb and give her an example.

Sparrow glanced from the glowing blue orb to me. "And you don't feel at all uncomfortable doing that?"

I passed the orb off into one palm. "Uncomfortable? Why would I? Look at it… It's beautiful."

"Yeah… I guess." Her nose wrinkled. "But it's… weird."

"Really?" I swirled the energy expertly with my fingers until it gradually faded to a bright, pulsating yellow. "I think people who *don't* channel orbs are weird…"

This got a little smile out of her, though she did her best to hide it. She lifted her hands up in front of her.

"Okay… so…"

"You know how to do this part."

"Yeah, but not very well, obviously."

"Just relax. *Breathe.*" I switched the orb into my opposite hand. "Don't force it. Don't think about it too much. Just let the energy flow with your breath. Let everything else fall away."

"Easier said than done," Sparrow muttered. "When everything else is so loud…"

"You didn't have much trouble with it when that cougar jumped on me."

"Yeah, but I wasn't noticing everything else then—I was just paying attention to you." Sparrow's words tumbled out; then she cleared her throat. "Making sure I hit the cougar, not you, I mean."

Her hands trembled as she tried to force the energy, pressing and clawing at the empty air between her palms. With one quick blast, she channeled the orb forward. It skipped across the calm surface of the stream like a stone. I stepped behind her and eased my hands up over hers, leaning over her shoulder.

"Keep it loose. You're not supposed to be squeezing it." I lowered my voice, pulling her hands gently apart. "Just… let it develop on its own."

Sparrow pulled in a shaky breath and relaxed her shoulders. She slowly began to rotate her palms around an invisible sphere.

Realizing suddenly that my hands were still on her arms, I pulled back. I focused on the orb in her hands, which slowly began to glow pale blue. I held my breath as it flickered for a moment, then began to fade.

With a frustrated sigh, Sparrow started to drop her hands, but I jumped in before she had the chance. Standing behind her, I wrapped my fingers around her wrists and held her hands in place.

"Are you giving up that easily?" I asked, then answered for her as I leaned a little closer. "No, you're not…"

Her hands were still limp in my grasp. "I don't think I can do it on demand like this—the cougar was a totally different situation. I was… I was emotional."

I spaced Sparrow's palms evenly apart and slowly smoothed her fingers out straight, my own filling the spaces between hers. "So that's how it's always going to be, then? You're just going to let your emotions control you?"

I felt her spine tense up against my chest. Immediately she tried to jerk away. "Of course not—"

"Then prove it."

I slowly released my grip, watching her in silence until something began to tug at my thoughts. Almost against my will, I felt my forehead go numb.

*I can't do this… I can't do this… I don't want him to see me fail… I don't want him to see me.*

Pulling in a startled breath, I jarred out of Sparrow's thoughts and took a step back, guilt sinking in my gut. At the same time, the orb in her hands turned red, just as it had the day before when the cougar attacked.

"Aim," I coached her.

Sparrow's dark eyes flickered up to the cairn in the middle of the stream. She opened her palms and sent it sailing forward with a loud whoosh. It impacted loudly and sent half the rocks scattering, skipping into the gently swirling water.

She stood there for a moment before turning to look at me, her jaw slack.

"Did I seriously just do that? Or were you messing with it?"

I shook my head. "That was all you."

"Can I… can I try it again?"

Sparrow started to smile. I caught a glimpse of something in her face that I hadn't noticed there before. Something alive.

"There are two more, aren't there?" I jerked my head toward the stream. "Go for it."

# 21

*I CAN'T DO THIS… I CAN'T DO THIS… I DON'T WANT HIM TO see me fail… I don't want him to see me.*

Thoughts were running wild through my head as I stood there on the bank of the stream, trying desperately to "allow" the energy to channel into my palms. Why did I care whether Keegan saw me fail? He'd already seen that plenty of times, so why did it matter to me now?

I could feel the pulse of his heart against my back as he leaned over my shoulder and guided my hands into place.

*"Are you giving up that easily?"* I'd felt his breath on my neck as he whispered in my ear. *"No, you're not."*

It had felt like slow motion, watching that bright blast of red energy rip through the air and crash into the cairn, sending rocks flying. I couldn't remember the last time I'd done this of my own free will—not just when I was angry and emotional. I did it again and again. Keegan waded back into the stream and stacked more rocks, and I formed more orbs, took aim, and threw them. Some impacted; some didn't. But that didn't matter.

I channeled orbs into cairns, and Keegan tossed knives into the trunks of dead trees across the stream, filling the air with streaks of colorful energy.

By the time we finished, it was midday and blistering hot. Keegan was sprawled on the bank of the stream a few yards away, leaning back on the palms of his hands with his feet in the cool water. He squinted up at the sky.

"Had enough yet?" he asked in a teasing tone.

I shook my head, catching my breath. "Not really, but I'm sweating."

"Me too," Keegan commented, unbuckling his holster.

"What are you doing?"

He rose to his feet and stepped into the stream. The water splashed up against his legs as he waded in deep enough to submerge. He surfaced an instant later, standing and throwing his head back to send a spray of droplets flying from his hair.

"Man, that feels good." He sighed and ducked back into the water up to his neck.

"I'm sure."

He shot me a look. "Why are you still standing there?"

"B-because I'm not going to swim in a gross, probably polluted stream."

"It's not polluted. I drank some of it last night, remember?"

I grunted. "And this is supposed to convince me?"

Keegan rolled his eyes, dunking his head beneath the surface again.

I had to admit, I was tempted. Walking to the edge of the embankment, I stopped there and waited for Keegan to resurface. A moment later, he bobbed up again, and his muscular arms rose out of the water to rake back his unruly mane.

"What?" he asked.

I drew a narrow breath and scanned the trees around us. "Yesterday when I came out here to get water for you, I thought I…" I trailed off, twisting my lips as I considered whether or not I should make anything of it. Whether I should risk looking like a wimp.

"You thought you…?" Keegan's green eyes were curious, his forehead crinkling as he waited for me to go on.

I drew a breath and shook my head, pressing my lips into a narrow smile. "Nothing," I said finally.

I splashed in before he had a chance to question me any further, dropping to submerge as soon as I was in up to my waist. I closed my eyes and listened to the gentle pulse of the stream, so unlike the angry roar of the river when we'd nearly drowned.

I resurfaced and gulped in a breath, pushing my hair back away from my face. "I still can't believe I was clumsy enough to slip and fall and almost drown…" I leaned back against one of the boulders. "It's a little pathetic."

Keegan nodded, tipping his head back toward the sky. "I thought you *had* drowned—you were unconscious."

I shuddered inwardly in remembrance of the ordeal. "How did you revive me, anyway?"

"Just because I'm an anomaly doesn't mean I don't know CPR."

For a moment my mind lingered on the small fact that Keegan's lips had been on mine. "You mean you weren't hoping you were rid of me?" I asked, a self-deprecating grin forming on my lips.

Keegan shot me a look as I hoisted myself up to perch on the edge of the large, flat boulder, looking down at him now.

"We may be different, you and I," he began slowly, his voice unusually soft. "But I would never want to lose you. I would never want to lose any one of us…"

I swallowed, focusing on my hands. "But we *have* lost them…" I returned quietly. "Because of me…"

Keegan didn't respond. When I looked up, I found him listening intently, his green eyes scanning the forest.

"What is it?" I asked when a grin broke over his face.

"Maybe we didn't lose them after all." His voice filled with excitement as he quickly rose to his feet, torrents of water rushing off him, and splashed for shore.

"What do you mean?"

He gestured wildly for me to follow. "Come on!"

"Keegan?"

At first the figures among the trees were just blurs; then Kateri's voice cut through the quiet air and laughter burst from her lungs as she ran the rest of the way to meet Keegan. He sprinted past the brush to the tree line, open-armed.

"*Keegan!*" she gasped, relieved, as he closed her into his arms. "Oh, I've been so worried about you! I thought you'd—"

"Drowned?" he questioned, pulling away from her. "What an idea. We've been trying to get out of this ravine to catch up with you."

Kateri's lips twisted as she tried not to smile. Everyone else emerged from the brush into the clearing, as tattered and dirty as we had been before the swim. Preston was the first to notice me.

"And Sparrow lives," he said, announcing the obvious. "I'm starting to think your natural ability is possessing nine lives."

"Sparrow." Kateri's attention turned from Keegan, and she dashed over to me, placing her hands warmly on my shoulders. "Thank God."

"Actually, Keegan did most of the work," I joked halfheartedly. "I… definitely wasn't expecting him to jump in after me."

"He would do it for anyone," Kateri said finally, more to herself than to me. "It is part of him. Of who he is."

A strange feeling tweaked in my gut, but I brushed it away, forcing my lips into a tight smile and nodding.

Kateri smiled, turning towards the rest of our now-reunited group. Preston slapped Keegan on the back, and the air filled with chatter. Rafael latched his skinny arms around Keegan's torso.

"And in spite of it all, you guys still found this spot before we did…" Kateri gestured in the direction of the ravine through the woods. "I can't believe it."

"I can't believe you guys found *us,*" Keegan cut in, turning to Kateri. "This is it—this is the ravine where we lived by the river when I was a kid.

I remember it now. How did you guys find it?"

"We just followed the river." Janna combed her fingers back through her curly blonde hair. "And prayed we'd find you alive."

"Well, Sensei definitely chose wisely." Myung stopped in the middle of the clearing with her hands on her hips. "Who the heck would ever find us all the way out here? We're in the middle of nowhere."

"Sensei obviously thinks we're really in deep because of…" Janna shot me a sidelong glance.

I stepped forward when she didn't finish.

"Because of what?" I piped up, looking her in the face.

"Because you told," she shot back. "You divulged our location—at least own up to that!"

The chatter died down within the group as I took a narrow breath.

"I didn't tell anyone *anything*," I emphasized icily. "I met someone that night, but we spoke of nothing regarding any missions or our locations."

Janna's expression grew mocking as she stared steadily into my face. "From what I've heard, you weren't *talking* much at all."

Anger flared up inside me. Kateri stepped up next to me.

"Janna, you can't say things like that." She began to defend me, but I put up a hand to stop her, my heart beginning to beat in my throat.

"Haven't I done anything to prove that I am sorry?" I asked, turning to face everyone. No one said a word.

Preston's arms were crossed over his chest, and Myung looked at me scrutinizingly. Rafael's lips were curved into a confused frown, and Kateri remained silent.

I turned to Keegan. His hair was still wet from the swim; his skin still sparkled with water droplets in the sunlight. His ginger eyebrows were crushed together over his turbulent green eyes.

"Have I done anything to redeem myself?" My voice dropped, cracking. "Have I done *anything* to make you trust me?"

To anyone else, it must have seemed I was asking everyone—pleading with the group of sliders to believe and trust me, just this once. Part of that was true—I was asking for trust. But I wasn't asking everyone. Just one person.

Keegan stood there for a moment, his eyes narrowing, searching mine. His lips slowly parted as if to speak, but after a moment he just lowered his gaze to the ground. Not saying a word.

# 22

SPARROW SAVED MY LIFE.

When that cougar attacked, she could have run—left me there. We were closer to being enemies than we were to being friends, she and I. But Sparrow had stayed, she had fought, and in doing so, she had saved my life.

Those were all the things I should have said as she stood there in front of everyone, feeling condemned. I should have said:

*She saved my life.*

But then something stopped me. Maybe it was the feeling of Preston's eyes, Myung's, Kateri's—everyone's. So I lowered my gaze to the ground, and I said nothing.

"See?" Janna sighed. "She runs from her own guilt—which is what she's done since she arrived."

I lifted my gaze only to glimpse Sparrow's back and flowing hair as she walked away. A cold, heavy feeling settled inside me as I watched her go.

"Keeg?" Preston waved a hand in front of my face. "You okay?"

I nodded, refocusing.

"I guess it's getting a little too late to go farther tonight… What do you think?" Preston asked.

Kateri stood at the edge of the clearing, talking to Janna and Myung, a frown on her face. The trees stood empty beyond them. I didn't see Sparrow anywhere.

"Keeg?"

My attention snapped back to Preston, who quirked an eyebrow.

"Are you even listening?"

"Yeah—yeah, I'm listening…" I trailed off, dragging a hand over my face. I forced myself to think over what he had said. "I say we go a little farther—there's a few hours until it gets too dark."

Preston stroked his chin with his thumb, and then he turned. "What do you think, Kateri?"

Kateri stepped away from the girls and walked over to us, crossing her arms over her dirty T-shirt. "What's that?"

"Should we keep going?" I asked.

Kateri pushed her long jet-black braid over her shoulder and nodded. "I agree—now that we know we're where Sensei wants us, let's follow the river a little ways."

She gave me a smile. I tried to return it.

"Okay, guys." Preston spoke more loudly now, to include the rest of our small group. "We're moving out!"

Myung groaned, shouldering her backpack. Kateri stepped back into the clearing. "Where'd Sparrow go?"

"She walked off that way." Rafael pointed toward the forest.

Kateri frowned. "I'll go see if I can—"

"No," I blurted, interrupting her. "I'll go—I'll be right back."

Kateri asked no questions, giving me a single nod as I started for the woods, brushing past Janna, who was still wearing that same hard expression.

The earth was spongelike beneath my feet as I picked up my pace, scanning the trees around me. Cupping my hands, I called her name.

"Sparrow!"

My voice echoed, then faded. I slowed to a halt, listening. Silence encompassed me. I walked deeper into the woods; the air was filled with the scent of rotting wood.

"Sparrow," I yelled again. "Sparrow, come on—we have to leave!"

Still, no answer came. A snapping sound to my left caught my attention, but when I turned to look, I saw nothing there. A few leaves danced in the breeze before floating to the dirt once again. I listened; a crunching sound like footsteps came again—still to my left, but now, farther away. This time I followed, taking quiet, steady steps as I scanned the trees.

"Keegan?"

A familiar smoky voice grabbed my attention. I turned to find Sparrow leaning back against a tree just several feet away. Her wet, dark brown hair was twisted over her shoulder, and her arms were crossed.

"Sparrow." I took a steady breath. "I-I thought I heard you over…" I glanced back over my shoulder in the direction of where I thought I'd heard her footsteps. "The sides of the ravine must make sound echo…"

Sparrow's eyebrows were raised when I looked back at her.

"You heard it too, didn't you?" she asked, her voice quiet but urgent. "The footsteps?"

I shrugged my shoulders. "I don't know. I heard something. I thought I did, anyway."

Sparrow stepped away from the tree and began to close the distance between us. She stopped a few feet away, her eyes flashing up to meet mine.

Words tangled in my throat as I looked at her. "Sparrow," I finally managed, "back there, I… I didn't mean…"

*You didn't mean what? To take what little trust you had built with her and dash it against the rocks?*

"I-I wanted to tell them—"

"Then why didn't you?" Sparrow cut in.

It was a question I didn't know how to answer. Maybe I was too afraid to answer.

Everything I wanted to say died in my throat. Sparrow's lips pressed into a thin line, and she shoved past me and began walking back to the rest of the group. I stood there in the quiet and listened to her footsteps.

Then I turned and followed her.

As soon as we started hiking, I took the opportunity to explain to everyone that I had been attacked and that Sparrow had saved my life. Sparrow added nothing to the story; she kept her eyes on the ground and walked in silence. No one but Kateri seemed to believe my account.

"Sparrow doesn't channel, Keeg. Come on," Preston teased, brushing my words off as an exaggeration. "I think you're completely capable of saving your own skin—you're a great channeler."

I shook my head, starting to protest, but Janna cut in before I had a chance to say anything.

"Yeah, Keegan, that's a little…" She looked for the right word. "Far-fetched."

I kicked myself for not having told them right away—for being a coward. I couldn't even look Sparrow in the face now without a sinking sense of shame.

I stayed on high alert the entire time we hiked. Every shadow, every rustling branch, every scattering of leaves caught my attention. Preston led the way, and Kateri hiked alongside me.

Sparrow lagged in the back. Rafael talked to her the entire time, filling her in on everything that had happened since the river had washed us away, which wasn't much at all. But Sparrow listened to all of it and asked him questions in return.

By the time we stopped, it was twilight. The rocky ground had completely leveled out. The dark sides of the ravine rose around us like giants. The river had calmed considerably.

Everyone was busy figuring out where we should make camp. I tuned out of the conversation, focusing on Sparrow. She stood beside Rafael, her face tipped back toward the sky. She looked miles away.

"Keegan?"

My gaze snapped to Kateri, who was now beside me, an inquiring expression on her face. Her eyes were like black pools in the shadows.

"We'd better build a fire."

"Right." I shook out of my thoughts. "Uh, dry wood."

She chuckled a little, then nodded. "Naturally. Where were you just then?"

I felt my ears heat up slightly. "Just thinking."

"About?" She rubbed a hand over my back, shepherding me along with her in the direction of the woods.

I shrugged a shoulder, falling into step beside her. "Everything." I sucked in a deep breath, trying to ignore the strange feeling in the pit of my stomach. "It's been a long couple of days."

Kateri ducked below a branch, swiping a few sticks off the ground. "Mm, that's for sure."

A short time later, we reached a little clearing where some branches had fallen.

"You and Preston must have had your hands full," I commented. "I know how much Janna and Myung appreciate roughing it."

Kateri laughed quietly. "We all managed. That wasn't even the hard part."

I snapped some smaller branches off a larger one, tossing them into a pile on the ground. "Rafael's teenage antics, then?"

She laughed again. "No, not that either."

"No?" I straightened up and stepped closer, lifting an eyebrow. "What, then?"

For a moment Kateri said nothing, her eyes searching mine.

"The hardest part was being without you," she said quietly. "I guess I'm just…" She trailed off, her gaze floating gradually down over my face, then shifting back to my eyes. "I guess I'm just used to you being there."

I looked down, my clammy fingers wrapping a little more tightly around the wood in my hands.

"And I'm used to being there," I replied, lowering my voice. "That's how it's always been, hasn't it?" I breathed a sigh, shaking my head.

"What is it?" she asked.

I was beginning to wonder if *she* were the mind reader.

"Nothing, except that… I'm not used to the feeling of letting someone down…" I confessed. "Someone I've unexpectedly grown to trust more than I ever thought I would. Someone who deserves to be defended."

In my mind, I could still see Sparrow. I could still see the fire in her eyes.

*She saved my life.*

"You can't think like that, Keegan," she answered quietly. "You did what was right—there was nothing else you could do."

Confused, I felt my eyebrows come together.

"You had to jump in after her—you let no one down. Least of all me."

At first, I didn't understand what she meant; then it finally hit me. My stomach sank a little more.

"And honestly," Kateri continued on the edge of a shaky breath, "I… I trust you more than I ever thought I would, too, and I…"

A numbness tingled in my forehead as my mind drifted against my will. It was barely there—like a whisper on the edge of the cool night air.

*I think of you as so much more than just… than just a friend. I wish I could just tell you that… How much I wish—*

I squeezed my eyes shut, warmth springing to my face.

"Keegan." Her voice slipped out quietly. "What is it? What's wrong?"

My heartbeat faster now. I felt frozen as I stared into her eyes, only a few inches away. The more she said, the more I didn't know what to say, or how to say it. My thoughts were a tangled mess, but before I could get a word out, a crashing sound came from the brush just behind us. Rafael stumbled out into the clearing.

"There you guys are—"

Kateri took a step back, a little startled.

"Oh, sorry if I'm interrupting," he said, then chuckled. "Not really—hurry up! It's getting dark."

Kateri brushed her braid aside, shouldering the bundle she held in her arm. "We were just—"

"Making out?" Rafael offered coyly.

"Getting firewood," I corrected him, clearing my throat, my cheeks still burning. "We were about to head back."

"*Suuuure.*"

"Lead the way." Kateri shooed the lanky boy back toward camp. "And please stop sneaking up on people like that."

I forced myself to follow, my palms sweating and that cold weight still lingering in the pit of my stomach. Kateri's words rang in my ears:

*"I trust you more than I ever thought I would, too…"*

*She'd thought I was talking about…* I kicked myself. *Shit, I am so stupid.*

But her thoughts echoed even louder: *I think of you as so much more than just a friend…*

God, I wished I hadn't seen that in her mind. I wished… Dammit, I didn't even know what I wished.

When we arrived back at camp, everyone seemed to have something to say about the place we'd chosen to stop for the night—everyone but Sparrow. Chatter and complaints filled the air as I built the fire.

Thoughts churned in my mind as I stared into the flames.

Kateri had been there for so long—since we were both young kids. We were cut from the same cloth, she and I—misfits with so much in common, chasing the dawn, bringing the trees back to life, healing the wild things we could relate to more than we could relate to people. I'd grown so used to her always being there. I barely thought of her as a separate person; it was like she was just part of me.

Kateri sat across from me, bathed in the warm glow of the fire, laughing and talking with Preston and Myung. I just studied her in silence, a storm churning inside me of feelings I hardly knew how to decipher.

She thought of me as more than just a friend. Did she… did she *love* me?

Somehow, the idea had never seriously crossed my mind. Sure, Preston had teased me about it before, but I'd always just shrugged it off, knowing Kateri would never…

I watched the light and shadow of the flames dance over her face.

*Did I feel more for her, too?*

Earlier that day, when I'd seen her coming toward me from the woods, when she'd embraced me… it had felt like coming home again.

Yet something inside me was uneasy.

My gaze drifted away from the flames to the edge of the river. Alone, a figure sat, lit only by a pale gibbous moon.

Sparrow.

# 23

I opened my eyes to the soft purple blurs of predawn. I sat up, passing my fingertips over my eyelids.

Smoke feathered up from the dying remains of the fire. The rocky ground beneath us was sheathed in dew, and sleep blanketed our group. Keegan's slumbering form wavered in the heat wafting up with the smoke, but even from the other side of the fire, I could see his back arching and falling with each inhale and exhale.

"*Sparrow…*" It came again like a whisper on the edge of the breeze.

I sat there for a moment, my hands pressed against the stony ground. Stillness fell over the camp once again, silence ringing in my ears.

"*Sparrow…*"

I wanted to whisper back—to ask who was there, but I was afraid of waking anyone. Getting quietly to my feet, I crept farther from camp. I trod softly into the woods, damp moss pressing against my bare feet.

"*Sparrow.*"

There was a soft rustle among the foliage far above, and a flapping of wings caught my attention.

I stared up into the pine boughs stretching out against the sky above me. In a flash of movement, a grayish black chaos of feathers lunged from the treetop and spread its wings, soaring up above the trees.

For a moment I felt frozen, every muscle in my body stiff.

Then I bolted after it, my feet pounding against the soft, damp earth.

Brush tore at my bare legs, and rocks blistered my feet, but I didn't care. I stumbled, fell to my knees, and picked myself back up, biting back curses as I felt the warmth of blood. I could still see the wings overhead. I chased them, and the blurry woods around me seemed to chant with the rhythm of my footsteps, taunting me and at the same time thrusting me forward:

*Who are you, who are you, who are you?*

I ran harder and faster, following the looping circles the hawk made above me, racing it along the river, farther and farther downstream, where the trees grew healthier and the ground became a little less rocky. I swung to a halt, collapsing against the trunk of a tree.

Panting, I scanned the sky for the hawk, but it was gone. The voices in my head were replaced by silence. I reached up with shaking hands to wipe the sweat off my forehead, trying to catch my breath. Every inhale was loud in the silence. The river sounded far off now, muted by the thick brush and trees. I began to see the forest around me for the first time—and it was like nothing I'd ever seen.

The ground beneath my feet was soft, carpeted with light green moss. The trees, their bark thick and reddish brown, bristled with tiny leaves. Flecks of pollen drifted through the air in the wide shafts of dawn light.

The voice breathed down the back of my neck, brushing aside my hair to whisper first in my ear and then through the trees. "*Who are you, Sparrow?*" The words bent and reverberated. "*Who are you that the Earth…*"

I tripped over my feet as I stepped backwards, the stirring pines spinning over my head as I regained my balance.

"*That the Earth groans for you to awaken?*"

The voice was haunting. I tried to speak, but I couldn't.

Slowly I leveled my gaze, squinting through the light as the ground beneath me stilled. In the distance there were two jagged rocks collapsed against each other, standing guard over what looked like an entrance to a cave burrowed into the hillside. For a moment I stood there, dizzy and attempting to get my bearings; I couldn't distinguish what direction I'd come from.

I stepped cautiously around the trees, listening to the soft padding of my feet. A thin trail of blood trickled from the scrape on my knee. I made my way to the gap in the hillside and stopped in the shadows of the rocks, staring into the dark interior.

It was a cavern.

Swallowing hard, I ducked inside. Extending my arms in front of me, into the inky blackness, my fingers met with the cool stone sides of the cave, trickling with condensation. My breathing quickened and began to echo in the void around me, which grew narrower and narrower until, suddenly, darkness seemed to encompass me no matter which way I turned.

Gasping, I pressed my hands against the rough stone walls on either side of me. My heart pounded in my throat as I twisted around, trying desperately to move within the tiny space. I thrashed away from the wall and staggered back. The air rushed out of my lungs as I fell back against something hard but hollow. A dull thud echoed in the tiny space.

I turned, feeling around in the darkness. My fingertips brushed against damp wood.

I swept my hand back and forth until, finally, my skin came in contact with something damp and cold like iron.

A handle.

With a grinding *click*, I twisted it and pushed the door open.

Like a flash from a bolt of lightning, the cavern filled with blinding, white light; I shielded my eyes, startled, as a wave of warm, sweet air whooshed in, whipping my hair into a whirlwind. A low roar filled my ears.

The door stood open, and beyond it, a passage stretched out before me, lined with tall glass windows. Dust particles sparkled and danced in the rose-gold sunlight. Beyond the window, a rocky cliff rose, spilling thick carpets of emerald green.

A strange, warm feeling swirled inside me.

I walked quietly to the window, staring down, down, down into the steep ravine billowing with clouds of mist. My breath fogged the glass in front of me, and I was about to touch it when someone spoke my name. This time, the voice was not like the wind; it was not like a distant voice from a memory of a dream.

It was close and crystal clear. *Human.*

I quickly turned and caught a blurry glimpse of a long hallway lined with windows. I caught snatches of a figure, of long dark hair like my own, eyes as black as the night sky. Her lips formed my name:

*"Sparrow…"*

I bolted upright, gasping. My eyes darted frantically back and forth, taking in my surroundings.

I was back at camp. Kateri lay sleeping to my right, and beyond her lay the other girls. The boys slept on the other side of the fire, washed in that same purple light.

I pressed a hand to my eyes, trying to steady my breathing, trying to pull myself back down to earth.

*It had been a dream? It had all been a dream?*

Lifting to my feet, I crept quietly from camp and walked down to the riverbed. Kneeling, I dipped my hands in and splashed water over my face and neck.

The ravine looked so different in the faint daylight. You could see the places where its cliff sides had eroded away over time, carving out the flat, rocky shore on which we were camped.

The two sides of the ravine seemed to swell up like massive ocean waves to brush against the sky. Squinting up at the carpets of faded brown trees only made the images of the green cliff sides I'd seen in my dream all the more vivid. When I closed my eyes, I could almost still feel the warmth of the sunlight on my face; I could almost taste the sweet air.

I glanced in the direction of the woods behind me. My thoughts raced.

*The cavern hadn't been far from here, had it?*

I walked quietly across the rocks, making my way along the river until I reached the thick tree line leading deeper into the woods. I wound around the trees and boulders, thinking back to the dream and trying to remember every step, every turn, and the way the landscape had looked as it transformed to lush woodland around me.

Finally, in the distance, I glimpsed something darker among the pines. I was about to quicken my pace, thinking of the two jagged stones that framed the cavern's entrance in my dream. But then it moved.

Every muscle in my body tightened, and I froze.

I folded myself behind one of the thick pines, holding my breath. I heard the snapping of twigs. *Footsteps.*

Cautiously, I gripped the rough bark with my fingertips and peeked around the trunk of the tree. I heard the muted crunch of footfalls—then a sharp breath.

A slender shape wove in and out among the trees, camouflaged. It reached out a hand and steadied itself against a tree trunk; I saw a tattooed arm sleeved in a sage-colored shirt.

I felt my eyes go wide. I pulled back behind the tree, pressing myself flat against it and listening intently over the pounding of my pulse. After a moment, I carefully stole another glance.

The forest was still around me, and there was no sign of life.

I stepped slowly away from the tree, making my way cautiously backward until finally I whirled around and ran. I sprinted through the forest, back the way I'd come, until at last the woods spat me out onto the rocky riverbank near our camp.

Everyone was up now. Preston was hunched by the fire, and Myung and Janna sat nearby, chatting in low voices. I spotted Kateri, Rafael, and Keegan down by the river's edge. I observed all of this in a glimpse as I ran the rest of the way there and skidded to a stop in front of the fire, where coffee was percolating over the flames.

Preston's head shot up, his copper eyes scrutinizing me curiously. "What's wrong?"

I leaned forward on my knees, gulping in air. "There's—there's someone out there," I panted, extending one shaking arm toward the forest.

"Someone?" Preston looked alarmed. "Where? In the woods?"

I nodded, still gasping.

Preston squinted, shielding his eyes as he rose to his feet, glancing toward the woods.

"Are you sure?" Myung spoke up, skeptical. "Section West was evacuated ages ago."

"I know that." I straightened, turning my attention back to Preston. "But I saw someone! There was someone out in the woods, not far from here!"

Preston's eyes flashed to mine, then back to the woods again, his brow wrinkling as he crossed his arms over his broad chest.

"An animal, maybe?" he muttered. "Keegan mentioned about the cougar—maybe it was another one."

I shook my head adamantly. "It was a human—I saw!"

Preston didn't seem convinced.

"What's going on?"

I whirled around to find Keegan approaching, a stern expression beneath his mess of ginger hair. His eyes met mine immediately.

"Sparrow thinks there's someone running around in the woods," Janna chimed in before I could get a word out. She glanced down at her fingernails. "We're trying to decide whether we believe her or not."

"I don't *think*, I *know* I saw someone out there," I insisted. "I think it was a guy, but I couldn't really tell for sure. There were tattoos on his arm, and he looked like maybe he was wearing some kind of uniform."

Keegan's expression didn't change. He stared out toward the woods.

"You saw someone?" Kateri questioned, coming up behind Keegan.

I nodded violently. "I-I couldn't sleep, so I went for a walk," I fibbed. "At first, I didn't know what it was. It looked like a rock, but then it moved. I saw someone, I swear! We have to go out and check—what if it's the RGM?"

"You mean your boyfriend?" Janna interjected mockingly. "Your directions must have been helpful."

I gritted my teeth. Something inside me was reaching a boiling point. "You're not listening."

"Sparrow." Preston sighed, bending down to take the coffee off the fire. "Are you sure you weren't dreaming?"

"I'm sure."

"There's no one out in those woods. We hiked through them all day yesterday—"

"Please believe me. I know what I saw," I pleaded. "Why would I lie? What would be my purpose in lying to you?"

For a second everyone was silent.

"There couldn't possibly be anyone else out this far," Kateri began quietly. "Could there?"

Keegan slowly shook his head. "I don't know… but we're going to find out."

Something inside me lifted. I let go of the breath I hadn't even realized I'd been holding.

"Keeg." Preston huffed a sigh. "It's not pos—"

"Yeah, the cougar wasn't possible, either," Keegan interrupted, already stepping forward and around the fire. He stopped in front of me, his eyes serious. "Lead the way."

"I'll come too," Rafael piped up.

"No, stay," Kateri said. "Stay here with Janna, Myung and me."

"But I want to go help!"

"There's nothing to help with," Keegan assured him as Preston followed reluctantly. "We'll be back in a few minutes."

It didn't take long for the three of us to make it across the rocks and into the shadows of the trees. Keegan walked close behind me.

"What were you doing out here, anyway?" he asked, keeping his voice low enough for only me to hear. "I thought I told you not to go out by your—"

"No one trusts me anyway." I cut him off, shooting him a look over my shoulder. "Why bother trying to explain?"

Keegan's jaw hardened. He trekked after me in silence. Preston was right behind him, grumbling about how this was a waste of time. By the time we finally reached the place where I'd seen the figure, I was determined to prove him wrong.

Keegan dropped to a crouch, searching the ground for footprints. I dropped down beside him.

"This it?" he leaned in to ask.

"Yes," I answered softly, pointing through the scraggly branches. "See those birches?"

Just over my shoulder, his chin brushed against my hair as he nodded.

"That's where I saw him."

Preston stepped up behind us just as Keegan moved forward again, wading through the brush. I followed him without hesitation.

"Guys, there's no one out here," Preston hissed, remaining behind the tree.

I emerged from the brush beside Keegan, into what I could now see was a small clearing. Keegan bent down to pick up a twig.

"Snapped," he muttered, examining it. "But it could have been from anything."

"There was *someone*," I insisted, circling around him, my gaze glued to the ground. "I swear it…"

Keegan tossed the stick to the ground and rubbed his chin thoughtfully. "The ground is too rocky for any evidence of footprints to be left…"

Preston thrashed through the brush grudgingly, coming to a stop beside us. He glanced around the silent woods. "Can we accept that there's no one out here and go back to camp now?" He rolled his shoulders back. "We have a lot to accomplish today, and we're wasting time."

Keegan remained silent for a moment, his lips pressed together and a distant look in his eyes. I didn't realize I was staring at him until his gaze returned to mine. He began to say something, then stopped. "Sparrow, what happened to your leg?" he asked suddenly.

Confused, I glanced down. Blood dribbled from my left knee, which was scraped and streaked with dirt from the forest floor.

Keegan squinted, still waiting for an answer. "Did you fall?"

I could feel the color draining from my face, my thoughts immediately flashing back to when I had started awake to the sound of my own name, to the wings soaring high above me, to when I had slipped away from camp to follow them through the forest where I ran, heart in my throat—where I slipped and…

I pressed my hand to my forehead, feeling dizzy all of a sudden.

But it had been a dream… *hadn't it?*

"Yes," I answered quietly. "I fell."

# 24

WE SPLIT UP INTO GROUPS THAT DAY AND SPLINTERED OFF into different sections of the forest to explore the area. I still felt dazed. I couldn't stop thinking about what had happened—I couldn't stop trying to untangle whether it had been a dream or reality.

*If it had been a dream, how on earth did I have the scrape on my leg?*

"Up ahead!" Rafael's excited tone jarred me out of my thoughts. I picked my way around large boulders that jutted up from the ground. His shirt was off and tied around his head, mimicking Keegan and exposing his skin to the sun. He was all ribs and energy. He stabbed a finger through the air and looked back at Kateri. "There's a stream!"

We were about a mile from camp and trudging through a thicker part of the woods. "We" meaning Kateri, Rafael, and I. Janna and Myung had gone in a different direction, as had Keegan and Preston—neither of whom had said another word about our fruitless search for the figure I'd seen in the woods. Preston didn't believe me, and I didn't care, but I couldn't help but wonder if Keegan did.

"Lead the way," Kateri called back to him, ducking below a branch. Her long hair was tied back in double braids.

We followed Rafael through the woods and came to a stop beside the narrow creek. I dropped down to my knees beside Rafael. His mop of dark hair hung down in his face as he bent closer as if to examine something I couldn't see. But what I *could* see was alarming enough.

The water was sludgy and brown, almost completely opaque as it rolled over the rocks stained black beneath the surface. I had to resist the urge to cover my nose.

"What happened to the water?"

Rafael looked intently into the stream for a moment longer before he stretched out his arm and lowered the palm of his hand to the water's surface. "We did," he answered.

I felt my brow furrow, sitting back on my heels. "How do you mean?"

"Not us specifically," Kateri added from where she stood behind us. "But all of us—humankind. The Earth is more like us than we realize… She has lungs and veins and a heartbeat, just as Lara described it. She can only take so much smoke and waste and chemicals."

"But we're out in the middle of nowhere," I came back skeptically. "Isn't most of the pollution in the cities?"

Kateri nodded. "But a disease in one part of the body, left to fester, soon spreads to the rest…" She trailed off, turning her gaze back to Rafael, who was still leaning out over the riverbed, his hand dunked below the surface now.

I traced Kateri's gaze back to Rafael and felt my eyes widen a little as I noticed the spidery fingers of clear water bursting from his touch. For a moment it merely mixed and contrasted with the murky brown, but then gradually began to absorb it.

"How are you doing that?" I asked, wonderstruck.

"What, this?" Rafael grinned a little but maintained his focus. "This is just fledgling stuff."

I grunted. "Then I must seem pretty infantile."

"It takes time to find your gift," Kateri assured me.

I didn't say anything. I sat there for a moment, watching the small, polluted stream slowly transform to crystal clarity. I got to my feet and brushed myself off.

"Fin told us not to waste this time that we spend in hiding—to use it to heal the forest. But I'm pretty much powerless to help." I poked at the ground with the toe of my Converse. "I've healed very few times—I have little to offer."

Kateri turned to shoot me a dubious look. "Little to offer? Sparrow, you *saved Keegan.* Even if the others don't acknowledge the story he told us, I hope you know that I do." She tipped her face back and looked up into the trees. "I was so worried that we had lost him to the river… Knowing he survived and then losing him to the cougar—it would have been more than my spirit could bear."

"Mm, well, did he tell you I blasted him with an energy orb by accident?" My shoulders slumped. "I'm so far beneath all of you—so far behind."

"Yet no one else could have saved Keegan in that moment except *you.*" Kateri's eyes were serious. "You judge yourself too harshly, Sparrow."

I fell silent for a moment as I watched Rafael.

"Not as harshly as everyone else, apparently," I said finally. "Or else they would believe that I saw someone out there this morning."

Kateri only sighed.

"You and Keegan." I changed the subject. "You guys must be really close."

Kateri nodded. "I was the second student to come to the Homestead. For quite some time it was just Sensei, Lara, Keegan, and me. We worked together quite a bit… He's a great healer, and my gift is the ability to communicate with animals, so we made a good team. We still do. We are friends, yes. But…"

She trailed off, blushing, almost as though she had said too much.

"But?" I asked.

She glanced toward Rafael, who was still solely focused on the stream, then took a few steps back, away from his earshot. I followed. When she

stopped, she drew a breath and turned to look at me again. "Keegan is…
so much more to me than just that."

My chest tightened. I cleared my throat. "You guys are—"

"No," she interrupted quietly, shaking her head. "No, he doesn't
know. I've…" She drew an unsteady breath, gazing up at the treetops again
for a moment. "I've never told him how I feel about him."

I tried to think of something to say in response, but my heart was
pounding. A strange feeling tangled in the pit of my stomach.

It was nothing I hadn't already suspected—I'd seen the way she
looked at him. But I wasn't sure why hearing it confirmed had me feeling
so thrown off my axis.

"Keegan is an ocean," Kateri continued at last, sparing me the need
to respond. "I can see the waves, rising and crashing—I can see the surface,
but I can't see the depths." She bit her lip, pausing. "There's a part of him
no one sees but Sensei."

"He mentioned he lost his parents when he was very young," I said as
Rafael got to his feet and walked over to us. "That's hard."

She nodded. "None of us knows how hard."

A chill washed over me. *If only she knew…*

"He has dreams, but he never talks about them," Kateri went on. "I
see that his heart still grieves."

My mind reeled back to the dreams that had begun to plague me since
that night I'd returned to the school in New York City to find Fin waiting
up for me.

"Dreams?" I asked. "Like, nightmares?"

Kateri looked uncertain. Her fingertips wove along the trees, leaving
streaks of healthy new bark.

"I believe so," she answered, lowering her voice a little. "As I said, I
know little beyond how much they seem to trouble him."

I fell into a thoughtful silence, glancing down at the waves of green
that now washed over the ground in Kateri's wake. A twisting vine crept
up around my ankle. I brushed it gently away.

"My father always told me that what we see in our dreams often has a deeper meaning," Kateri continued, hopping out onto a small, flat stone peeking above the now-clear stream's surface. "Hidden guides, he called them. Teachers, if we choose to be taught."

"What do you mean?"

Stepping from stone to stone, she crossed the stream to the opposite embankment. I stepped carefully out onto the first stone.

"I mean that we believe all things—even the animals and plants—have purpose and meaning," she explained, gesturing to the woods around us. "They teach us and guide us—warn us."

She lifted a hand into the air as I hopped onto the embankment, rubbing her thumb over the pads of her fingertips. I watched, bewildered, and Rafael stopped, straightening to attention.

"Are you calling the—"

"Shhh." She placed a finger to her lips. "They won't come if you're not quiet."

My eyebrows pressed together, I watched closely. For a moment nothing happened; the air was thick and quiet around us, interrupted only by the gurgling stream.

Then I caught a glimpse of something pink, like a rose-colored petal, flitting through the air, then another. Kateri began to loop her hand gently through the air, still rubbing her fingers together. More delicate, pink, flitting petals appeared in the atmosphere around her hand. As I drew closer, I realized they weren't petals at all.

They were *butterflies*.

Swooping down, one landed on Rafael's forehead. His blue eyes went wide, and he bit his lower lip in an attempt not to laugh.

"Butterflies are the guardians of transformation," Kateri explained, slowly opening her hand. "They speak of our lives changing and growing…" Fluttering velveteen wings hovered and then gracefully landed in the palm of Kateri's hand. She carefully lowered it for me to see, smiling. "Creativity, romance, joy," she went on softly. "A raven is a symbol of healing; a deer of gratitude; an otter—laughter."

I leaned closer, studying the soft shades of pink as the delicate creature shivered against Kateri's palm before it lifted into the sky. Shielding my eyes, I stared after it. I had never seen a butterfly before.

"What about the warnings?" I asked.

"Crows, coyotes," she offered, watching the butterflies in stillness now. "They warn us of the darker parts of our selves—our selfish intent. Or of deception and weakness."

I squinted for a moment in silence, then lowered my gaze. "What about a hawk?"

"A hawk?" she asked curiously. "A hawk is a messenger."

"A messenger of what?"

"I couldn't say." She gestured for Rafael and me to follow as she began walking again. "I've never seen one."

# 25

"YOU BELIEVE HER, DON'T YOU?"

I looked up, my hand still pressed to the rough bark of a pine. Preston stood just behind me, a glowing orb of white light between his palms.

"You believe she saw someone out here." He dipped his head and gestured around us. "You think she's telling the truth."

I felt my fingertips twitch against the trunk of the tree. "Sparrow has never lied to us, has she?" Bursts of fresh life rolled from my fingertips and up the trunk. "I know you think I was just joshing about it, but if it weren't for her, that cougar would have *killed* me."

I could feel Preston's gaze burning the back of my neck. "Keeg, you hate her."

"I hate no one."

"Yeah, but you know what I mean." He channeled the light up into the treetops. "You guys have been like oil and water from day one."

"I know," I replied. "But she's never lied—she's always said exactly what she thinks, regardless of what people think of her."

I watched the tree in front of me slowly burst back to life, letting out a puff of what looked like sweet, pure air as light green leaves flourished at the top. Preston watched in thoughtful silence.

"You know, if I didn't know better, I'd think you were sticking up for her."

"I'm sticking up for the *truth*, Preston. I can't go against my own conscience." I moved on to the next tree. "That's why I think we should get out of this area."

"Why? Just because Sparrow was freaked out by a few snapped twigs?"

Preston clenched his fists, and the beam of light vanished with a soft *vvwoomm*.

"Because what if it's more than a few snapped twigs?" I asked, lowering my voice. "What if it *is* something dangerous?"

Preston's expression was dubious, then concerned. "Keeg, come on…"

"Don't give me that, Pres."

"Keeg!" he groaned. "There's no one out here! There hasn't been for ages."

And that was exactly what he told everyone when we all reconvened at camp as dusk fell.

"I think Sensei wants us to be *here*," Preston continued adamantly. "I mean, didn't we all agree that this is the place he was telling us about? That he thinks we'll be safe here in the ravine?"

"I agree with Preston—I'm sick of wandering around aimlessly," Janna agreed, pulling her frizzy hair back into a ponytail. "We found the place Sensei told us to find, and we're safe here. That's why he sent us out here—so that we would be safe. I vote we lie low for a while."

I felt my jaw tighten. Dad had told us to stay here—yes. But he also hadn't known we would encounter anyone out here—in fact, that was exactly why he had sent us this far out: so that we wouldn't be detected.

Rafael kept shooting me puzzled glances from where he was seated beside me. Finally, he spoke up, barely able to sit still.

"Where's arguing like this going to get us?" His question cut through the bickering. "Can't you guys see how this is ripping us apart? Sensei told us to work together—that this journey would be a test for us. Well, we're failing! We can't just keep fighting about everything—"

"No one is fighting. We're just trying to figure things out." Janna shushed him irritably. "Now chill, Raf."

I could practically feel his blood boiling. I listened in silence, my eyes shifting to Sparrow, who sat next to Kateri but stared into the fire, seeming completely detached from the heated discussion.

"Sensei told us to stay here no matter what." Myung spoke up now, her tone steely. "If you all want to move on, fine—but the forest is dying, and we're finally out far enough that the RGM won't detect the revival." She glanced around the small circle of us. "Let's do what we've trained for all these years!"

Murmurs arose from the rest of the group. Even Kateri seemed to agree.

"And what if something happens to one of us?" I shot back. "How can we stay here, knowing full well there's something or someone out there, and completely ignore the warning signs?"

Myung snorted. "You guys went out there and looked around—did you see anything, Keegan?"

Everyone was quiet, leaving only the soft murmur of the fire as Myung waited for me to respond.

"No," I replied at last. "I saw nothing."

Myung shrugged her shoulders. "I rest my case."

"But I believe Sparrow," I added firmly.

Sparrow's eyes met mine for a moment. At first no one said anything; then everyone burst into disagreement once more.

Sparrow took the opportunity to rise to her feet, stepping back from the fire and retreating into the darkness. I watched her go, the turbulence around me muting gradually to white noise.

Unable to sit still any longer, I left the group and the fire behind, taking off after Sparrow. Jogging quietly over the stony ground, I found her at the riverbank, seated at the edge with her head tipped back and her fingers in her hair. For a moment I hesitated.

The moon glowed in an overcast sky, creating a silver halo around the edges of the clouds. The pale white light reflected off her skin and hair.

"Are you too scared to sit beside me?" she asked dryly after I'd stood there a moment. "I don't bite. Often."

I walked over to the slab of cold rock and sat next to her.

"Why'd you leave?" I asked, for lack of anything better to say.

Sparrow only shook her head, staring down at the dark, glistening water ahead of us, rushing onward and away.

"I guess I'd just heard enough," she told me finally. "I'm sick of it… I'm sick of being here."

I decided to take a shot at making her smile. "You don't like camping?"

Her lips twitched just a little. "I mean everyone doubting every word that comes out of my mouth. Not that I've given them much reason to trust me… Not that I've done anything worthy of their respect."

"Except save me."

"No one seems to believe that except Kateri."

"That's because they'd hoped to be rid of the rogue redhead." I turned and gave her a teasing grin.

Her smile increased, but she brushed it away with her fingertips, clearing her throat.

"Kateri could have done a much better job anyway. She probably would have coaxed it into gentle submission," Sparrow mused. "Whereas I, on the other hand, blast everything until it's dead."

I knew she was being serious, so I withheld a smile.

"Hey, I'm not dead yet," I pointed out.

"Keyword *yet*."

She turned to face me for the first time since I'd sat down beside her. The moonlight looked the same in her eyes as it did in the rushing water. But beyond the light, there was something darker—an urgency—as she stared into my face.

"I sometimes feel as if I was born only to destroy everything I touch, Keegan—that's all I ever seem to do." Her eyelids dropped beneath the weight of her words, her voice soft and defenseless. "Why do you think I make myself keep you at arm's length?"

"Make yourself?" Restless waves stirred inside me. My voice quieted to a whisper. "Do you... do you want me closer than that?"

Something in Sparrow's eyes softened. The moon bathed her face in light and shadows. "I don't know," she answered softly.

There was something about the way she said it. Something that made me want to question it further. But instead, I just kept listening.

"Keegan, I'm afraid," she said, her words coming out in a rush. "I don't think I can stand to stay here even one more night."

"Why?" I asked quietly. "What do you think is going to happen?"

Sparrow bit her lip, shaking her head furiously. "I don't know—that's just it. But I have such a horrible feeling..."

"I believe that you saw someone, Sparrow."

"I know. I know you do." She nodded, though her face was still sheet white. "But that doesn't change anything—they're not going to leave because they don't believe we're in danger." Her eyes stayed fixed on the water. "But I have these dreams, Keegan..." She paused, pursing her lips. "Someone speaking my name... I always see this hawk soaring above me..."

"A hawk?"

Sparrow nodded. "Kateri told me that the Cheyenne believe the hawk is a messenger."

"What happened with the hawk, in your dream?"

"I followed it—I fell down in my dream and scraped my knee. And then when I awoke, I went and found that same place where it had led me." Her eyes were intense as they flickered to mine. "That's where I saw the... That's where I..."

"That's where you saw someone," I finished for her, the hairs on the back of my neck rising. "And... and you actually had a scrape..."

Sparrow nodded, her fingertips brushing the wound. "I've heard sounds in the woods like footsteps since the first night we set out, but this is the first time I've *seen* something. Why hasn't anyone else seen or heard the things I have? Why haven't you or Preston or Kateri?" Sparrow paused, tipping her head back, pain on her face. "What if I'm just making this all up in my head? What if they're right to not trust me? *I* don't even trust myself…"

Sparrow trailed off, pinching her eyes shut.

"Well," I whispered back, "maybe you should start trusting yourself. Maybe you have to."

"Kateri told me that you have nightmares sometimes."

The statement was so abrupt and unexpected, it caught me off guard.

"Kateri shouldn't have told you that," I replied stiffly. "She doesn't know anything about them—"

"I know," Sparrow interrupted gently. "She said as much. I knew you would get angry if I said anything, but I thought maybe if I talked to you about them, I would learn how to escape my own." There was an undertone of desperation in her voice. "Maybe I wouldn't be so… terrified."

I took a slow breath, trying not to think about what she was saying— trying to brush away the memories of the nightmares, the familiar sounds and smells and sensations that plagued my sleeping hours.

"Sparrow." Her name rolled quietly off my lips. "Do you know what will happen if you swim out to a drowning man to help him?"

Sparrow looked at me curiously for a moment before slowly shaking her head.

"He will pull you down, and you will both drown," I finished bluntly. "So it's best to watch from shore."

Her gaze softened and flicked over my face. "Is that so?"

I felt frozen, noticing how close she was, but I managed a nod.

Sparrow leaned a little closer. "And what if they're both drowning?" Her voice dropped to a whisper. "What then?"

I lay awake for a long time that night, staring up at the sky, for once not fearing what would come when I fell asleep. I thought of everything

Sparrow had said. I thought of the way the moon had reflected in her dark eyes, along with the glimpses of fear and pain.

Sparrow had made such a mess of me—a few days ago everything had been so clear. So black and white. But now everything was a tangled, confusing explosion of color. Sparrow was so irritating, so strange, yet so hard to stop thinking about.

I squeezed my eyes shut. But she was beneath my lids.

I cursed a little under my breath and rolled over on the hard ground, suddenly angry with myself and everything else for no reason. Rafael lay snoring softly beside me. I could see the vague outline of Sparrow on the other side of the fire.

I rolled to my opposite side and closed my eyes again, focusing on the soft sizzle of the flames and the distant whoosh of the river.

Finally, I felt the thick presence of unconsciousness roll over me like steady ocean waves, pulling me farther away from my thoughts and senses until I was lost in the disembodying depths of a dream.

I was back at the Homestead, hunched over the kitchen table with my face in my palm and glossy light pouring in through the windows. Dad sat across from me, elbows on the table and wearing a white T-shirt. There was something intense about the look on his face, something urgent in his green eyes, as if he could see right through me, as if he were dumping the contents of my soul out on the table for both of us to sort through.

"Why are we here, Dad?" My words came out in a rush, as if I'd been longing for this moment. "Why did you send us here to hide?"

Dad waited for me to go on as I began shaking my head.

"I can't believe the only reason we're here is to hide..." I answered my own doubts, still looking at him steadily. "Or even to heal the forest... I feel like there's more..."

"Do you trust those feelings? Do you trust your feelings towards Sparrow?"

I felt something inside me freeze, my thoughts running from me. Slowly, I yielded a nod.

"Yes, I do," I answered quietly.

Dad's eyes were still focused earnestly on mine. "Then you don't need to ask me. Trust yourself, Keegan. Trust who you really are, and you will find out why you are here."

I thought this through carefully; then I remembered something else: Rafael's question at the campfire.

"Dad, is this a test?" I asked quietly. "Being here... Sparrow... everything?"

"Do I give you fear, Keegan? Or pain? Or suffering?" He shook his head slowly, his gaze still locked with mine. "You told Sparrow she is at war with herself, and you were right; we all have a battle, Keegan. With every breath, every heartbeat, we are indeed tested... tested by ourselves."

I squinted, trying to focus on every word, though the room around us was beginning to spin and fade.

"There is a wolf inside each of us, my son," Dad went on, though his voice bent and began to echo. "But there is also a warrior."

*A warrior... a warrior...*

*A warrior.*

The words clanged in my head like clashes of thunder as everything dissolved to blackness, and then the blackness gave way to slits of pale light as I slowly opened my eyes.

Dawn was just breaking, and the woods around me were still and drenched in the early light. Pressing the heels of my hands into my eyelids, I sat up. Kateri was just waking up, too, standing to stretch her arms overhead.

"Morning," I said quietly.

She glanced my way, sweeping her long hair over her shoulder. "Good mor—" She froze, her expression instantly transformed to one of panic and her eyes going wide.

"What's wrong?" I asked, alarmed.

"Where's Raf?" Her voice cracked, sounding terrified.

"He's right—"

My gaze shot to my left, where Rafael had been curled up, sleeping soundly between Preston and me. He was gone. There was just a rumpled blanket, a rolled-up T-shirt he'd been using as a pillow... and blood smeared in the dirt.

# 26

"EVERYONE UP—NOW!"

The urgent shout startled me from the darkness of unconsciousness and into the light of day. I scrambled to my feet.

"What's going on?" Preston jumped to his feet.

"Rafael's gone!" Kateri shouted, looking around at the rest of us. "Has anyone—"

"My god…" Preston stared down at the stretch of rock where Rafael had been sleeping.

Rounding the hot coals in the middle of our camp, I ran over to see what they were looking at. I halted beside Keegan and felt my stomach churn when I saw the streak of blood across the rocky ground.

"What happened?" I choked.

Keegan shook his head; his face was drained of color. "There's no time for questions—come on, we have to split up and find him!"

Snatching his holster off the ground, he ran for the forest's edge. I was right behind him when he stopped at the tree line, pointing at the ground.

"More blood," he panted, examining the ground. "Scuff marks."

I instantly saw what he was talking about: drag marks in the dirt, along with more droplets of blood. Keegan waved for me to follow as he turned to look over his shoulder at the others, who were just emerging into the woods behind us. "Split up!"

I ran ahead of Keegan, searching the ground for more droplets of blood or drag marks in the dirt.

"Over here," Keegan called, halting alongside a dead pine. "The brush is bent back…"

I chased after him through the brush as he took off at a sprint.

"Rafael!" he shouted, cupping his hands to his mouth. "Rafael, where are you?"

Echoes of our voices filled the forest, along with the thwacking of leaves and branches as we beat our way through the brush and deeper into the woods, splitting off in different directions.

"Look for blood," Keegan shouted to me, frantic. "Keep looking!"

I scanned the forest floor as best I could while we ran, our feet pounding over the soft earth. The farther into the forest we wandered, the faster Keegan ran.

"Keegan!" I shouted ahead between breaths. "Keegan, slow down!"

"We can't!"

"We have to!"

I slowed to a stop as we came to a glade.

Keegan ran several yards more before he stopped at the edge and looked hurriedly back at me, his pale face dripping with sweat.

"Come on!" he shouted at me hoarsely. "We have to keep going!"

"We can't just blindly run through the forest, Keegan!" I yelled back breathlessly. "I don't know about you, but I lost the trail a ways back—there's no footprints, no scuff marks, no blood! I'm no tracker, but I do know that we're obviously off track. Otherwise, we would have seen more signs of him by now!"

Keegan's expression was melting from one of urgency to one of fury. He stabbed a finger at the woods ahead.

"You don't know anything!" His voice rang harshly through the quiet trees. "Those tracks were headed in this direction! He could be just ahead—he could be bleeding or worse! We have to find him!"

I stared at him from across the clearing, dumbfounded. "I understand that! And we're going to keep looking, but we have to backtrack—"

He was already shaking his head. "No!"

"Keegan, please."

"I said *no*!" This time, he strode across the glade, closing the distance until he stood right in front of me; his furious green eyes drilled down into mine. "You don't understand." I could feel his hot, frantic breath on my face. "I can't let Rafael die—"

"He's not going to—"

"You don't know that!" he burst out, yelling right into my face. "You don't know what it's like to just stand by and watch while someone you love is killed right in front of you, Sparrow!" Beads of sweat rolled down his face. "I can't let that happen again—I *can't* let that happen!"

Everything I'd been about to say dissolved in my throat. I stared at him, frozen, inches away, with no idea what to say. He stayed still, gasping in narrow, shaky breaths until finally he pressed his hands to his face.

"I'm sorry," he whispered hoarsely. "I—I'm sorry."

I grabbed him by the wrists and lowered his hands. His eyes were damp as I stared up into them, suddenly full of resolve.

"We are *going to find him*," I stated firmly. "I promise."

For a second Keegan just stared at me, his eyes glistening. Then, slowly, he gave a heavy nod. I released his hands and motioned for him to follow me back in the direction we had come.

We searched for hours. We found nothing: no snapped twigs, no disturbed brush, no blood on the ground. We backtracked to the first signs we had seen at the edge of the woods. Kateri and Preston were already there, reexamining them. We trekked back into the woods and covered as much ground as we could until we finally all bumped into each other, reconvening among the thick swatches of trees.

"We have to get out of here." Janna was the first one to speak up, her tone panicked. "Whether the RGM knows about the Homestead or not, we need to go back."

"And leave Raf behind?" Preston shook his head. "No. No one's going back."

"Preston's right. We can't leave until we find Rafael," Kateri agreed. "We have to keep searching."

"We can't stay here. It's not safe!" Janna protested.

"We decide these things as a *group*, not on our own." Preston's voice hardened. "I can't believe you—wanting to abandon Raf and run back home! I thought you were a bigger person than that!"

Janna looked on the brink of tears. Keegan stood a little ways off from the rest of us, staring blankly at the woods. I wished more than anything that everyone else would just vanish—that I could have just a moment to talk to him alone.

"We stay together, and no one leaves." Preston abruptly ended the debate. "From the traces we did find, it looked like they headed downstream."

"*They?*" My attention snapped back to him. "So you admit there's someone out there, then?"

Preston rubbed the back of his neck, looking reluctant. "It could be an animal—you and Keegan can obviously attest to the fact that—"

"If it's an animal, Raf's already dead." Keegan spoke up numbly. He didn't move from where he stood, staring through the trees. "And no one heard anything. He would have screamed if an animal had attacked him in his sleep."

"Whatever it was, it went downstream," Preston insisted. "That's the direction we need to be heading."

"No!" Janna finally burst out. "I'm not going."

Myung sighed. "Janna…"

"I'm *not going*!"

"What do you want us to do, then?" Preston barked, frustrated. "Leave you here?"

"I want to go home!"

"Why not just let her?" Myung muttered, shrugging her shoulders. "It's not like she's going to be much help to us anyway."

Preston shot her a look. "And blatantly disobey Sensei?"

"I don't care about Sensei's orders; I care about staying alive!" Janna erupted. "What if something bad happens to all of us?"

Preston stepped up to Janna, placing his hands on her shoulders. "Something bad already *has* happened."

I heard a rustling over my shoulder and turned to see Keegan walking away. His arms hung limply at his sides, and his steps were heavy. I turned to look at Kateri and noticed her eyes were following him too.

We walked back to camp and found that Keegan had already packed everything up. He shouldered two packs and jerked his head in the direction the river flowed.

"Let's go." His tone was commanding though his face was still sheet white. "We've wasted enough time as it is."

Something inside me ached as I looked at him. His eyes flashed to mine as he turned and started walking. As I began to follow, I couldn't help but turn and look back at the towering walls of the ravine rising on either side of us. I couldn't help but remember my dream. The hawk I'd seen, the wings I'd followed into the woods, the place where I'd found the cavern in the hillside. I couldn't help but look down at the dried, bloody scab on my leg where I'd fallen.

*I was dreaming... or was I?*

We walked a few miles, weaving through the woods. Finally, we stopped in a clearing and ditched our gear to head back out and search for any sign of Rafael.

The sun was high in the sky when we set out, and dwindling below the horizon by the time we returned. None of us had much to say.

Kateri brushed off her hands after building the fire, looking around at the rest of us.

"We should all try to get some sleep." Her voice was as numb and hollow as the look in her eyes. "We need to get an early start tomorrow.

We should take turns keeping watch…"

Preston volunteered to be first. He walked a little ways from our group, settling down near a tree just beyond the glade. Everyone else mutely followed Kateri's advice, seemingly devoid of anything to say.

I lay on the ground and stared up at the sky, listening to the others toss and turn restlessly until unconsciousness had swept over our now smaller group.

Between the wiry arms of the trees overhead, I caught glimpses of blurry silver pinpricks stuck against the dark satin of space. In New York, the smog had been so thick, I could never see the stars.

Fin's words echoed in my mind as I lay there, staring up at them.

*"It's time to leave."*

*"Because of me?"*

*"Because you acted as someone you are not… Because you were wrong. Because you don't know who Sparrow is."*

*You don't know who Sparrow is…*

*You don't know.*

I squeezed my eyes shut, rolling to my left. When I opened them again, I saw Keegan's face in the low, flickering light.

He lay several feet away, firelight casting him partly in shadow. His face rested on his folded arm; tears glistened on his cheeks. I glanced over at Preston. He was far enough away to be out of earshot.

"Keegan?" I whispered finally, my voice so soft I could barely hear it myself.

There was a long pause.

"Yeah?" he whispered back.

Sitting up, I quietly slid closer and lay back down beside him. Keegan didn't move, didn't shift his gaze from the fire. I watched the shadows flicker over his face, igniting the streaks of tears.

Finally, he took a shaky breath, squeezing his eyes shut. "I remember fires like this as a boy," he whispered. "Dad and I would lie out under the sky… watching the stars for hours until I couldn't keep my eyes open. The sky was a little clearer back then, in Galway."

"Do you remember living there?"

"Only a little, in snatches. And only at night—when it all resurrects…" He was quiet for a moment. "You asked about my nightmares—"

"It was wrong of me to ask," I whispered. "You don't have to—"

Keegan shook his head, blinking back tears. "I want to tell you, Sparrow…"

I waited in silence for him to go on. His eyes met mine, heavy and sparkling.

"I was young. About five when the RGM took Galway," he began. "They raided the neighborhoods for supplies and recruits."

"Recruits?"

"They're always looking for kids—the young ones who will be easy to indoctrinate. Fragments don't work anymore, so now they just brainwash the young ones as best they can. My parents tried to hide me, but the soldiers found me easily," Keegan went on, his voice strained. "They wanted to take me. My parents tried to stop them, but they… the soldiers… they…"

Keegan's voice splintered, and my heart sank.

"I couldn't save them, Sparrow—I could do *nothing*," he went on in a broken whisper. "I stood by and watched… I escaped while they…" Keegan squeezed his eyes shut, a hot tear rolling down his cheek. "I escape every night while they die," he finished, his voice barely audible. "And every time, I can do nothing to stop it—every time I feel just as helpless, just as…" He swallowed, shaking his head. "I can't lose Raf… I can't stand by and let it happen all over again…"

I didn't know what to say. I could barely see past the tears that were welling in my own eyes.

"Keegan." I finally managed to whisper his name. "I wish I could take your pain away… I wish I could… I wish I could promise you that we'll find Rafael. I wish… oh, god, I wish so many things, Keegan…"

I trailed off, my voice cracking.

"But I will promise you this," I continued at last. "I'm going to do everything I can to help find him… *We're* going to do everything we can."

His lips trembled as he began to nod. He tried to whisper back, but his voice crumbled. Something inside me overflowed; leaning in, I wrapped my arms around his shivering body. For a moment he only stiffened, shaking with silent sobs. Then, like a dam holding back a river, he broke.

Sinking into my arms, he pressed his face into the curve of my neck. Keegan's arms encompassed me, and his tears fell against my skin.

I didn't let go.

# 27

I AWOKE TO A SCENT LIKE PINES AND SOIL AFTER A SPRING rain. Slowly, I opened my eyes.

Sparrow was the first thing I saw. Strands of her long dark brown hair ventured into my face. My arm was wrapped underneath and around her, numb, tingling, but still holding her.

Sparrow's face was soft and expressionless as she slept. Her dark eyelashes contrasted against her skin. Her lips were slightly parted as she gently breathed.

It was so hard to believe that she was the same girl I'd tackled that day in the woods beyond the Homestead. The girl I'd rescued that night in New York. It was hard to believe that this same girl now slept in my arms.

It was hard to believe I'd let my guard down. No… no, it wasn't hard—it was scary. I'd told her something I'd never told anyone before: I'd told her that I'd seen my parents murdered in front of me. For the first time, I'd let myself cry—and in front of Sparrow, grasping handfuls of her hair and sobbing silently against her neck.

She'd held me all night, and I'd held onto her. And now I lay there in the silence while everyone else slept, and I studied her every feature as if I'd never seen her before. Frustrating, stubborn, headstrong, impossible, fierce, *beautiful…* I knew she was all of these. But somehow, staring into her face, I still didn't know Sparrow.

Yet, more than ever, I *wanted* to.

I couldn't put out the fire in my chest. I wanted to know who she really was and where she had really come from. I wanted to know *everything*.

Carefully, I slid my arm out from under her, leaving her asleep on the ground. I got to my feet and stretched my arms overhead. Slowly, yesterday trickled back into my consciousness, and my heart sank into my gut.

Soon everyone was awake—including Preston, whom I'd found reclining against a tree, sound asleep. No one had much to say.

"Let's get a move on." Preston clapped a hand on my shoulder as he walked past, heading for the woods. "We splitting up again?"

"I don't think that's a good idea." Kateri shouldered her backpack, her long black hair draping loose and bedraggled over her shoulders. "We need to stick together. Who knows what might happen?"

"Agreed." I nodded.

Myung slung her backpack over her shoulder. "I say we keep following the river."

"We don't know if they followed the river," Preston countered.

"We don't know *anything*," Myung stated firmly. "But it's worth a try. It's not like we have anything else to go on."

Janna hung back, her arms folded over her chest and an empty look in her large blue eyes. She added nothing to the discussion.

Preston seemed to think it all through for a long moment before he finally turned and glanced between Kateri and me. "What do you guys think?"

I gave a solemn nod. "I think we have to try everything, and we can start with this."

Kateri agreed. I kicked dirt over the remains of the coals, and the group filed forward into the woods. I waved almost everyone past me and then fell into step beside Sparrow. Janna reluctantly trailed behind us.

Sparrow glanced up at me, her hair a mess and her eyes bleary.

"What good will following the river do?" she asked only loud enough for me to hear. "We don't know that he's anywhere near the river."

"What would you suggest?"

"Nothing." She dragged a hand over her face. "I don't know what to do. I have no idea how to help—I hate it. I hate *this*."

"You're not alone there," I answered grimly, focusing on the ground ahead.

For a long time after that we didn't talk—no one did. We walked in silence, listening to the soft hush of the stirring trees overhead. Heavy gray clouds crowded the sky, blotting out the hazy sun. Myung hummed along to the rhythm of the wind, most likely trying to keep her mind occupied. Though I tried my best not to, I kept staring at the rivers of Sparrow's hair. I kept stepping in the tracks her feet left in the dirt.

Rain had begun to fall in large, rust-colored drops. We'd reached the mouth of the ravine now—the opposite end, where it rolled open into a valley thickly forested in pines.

Around noon, the rain came down like fallout, fast and heavy, pelting our skin and staining us all the color of the ground we walked on. Sparrow tipped her head back and let it drizzle down her face like she didn't care. It soaked her hair.

My head felt like a storm at sea—I couldn't focus. My heart felt torn in two, one half full of pain and determination to find our missing brother, and the other half brimming with questions: *Who is she, who is she, who is she?* In a way I resented myself for even being able to think about anything other than finding Rafael, but in the confusion and despair, I couldn't seem to help myself.

Everyone's head was down as we searched the forest floor for any signs of disturbance. The hours dragged on.

Preston took up the back with Janna for a while, walking beside her. Finally, he sidled up next to me, putting a hand on my shoulder. "What's going on?" he muttered as inconspicuously as possible into my ear.

I shot him a glance. "What do you mean?"

Preston jerked his head towards Sparrow. "I mean, what is up with you guys?"

"Nothing," I said.

"Then why do you keep staring at her?"

Preston squinted over my shoulder at Janna, who was lagging far behind in spite of our slow pace. "Hey, keep up!" he shouted to her. She didn't respond, but I could hear the reluctant scuffing of her boots.

"Why do *you* keep staring at Janna?" I tossed the question back.

Preston grunted. "Hey, stay on subject. Did Sparrow do something the rest of us don't know about?"

"No. Nothing like that…"

Preston looked confused as we continued, ducking beneath low tree limbs and climbing over rotting logs in our path.

"Keeg, you would tell me if there was something going on with her, wouldn't you?" he questioned. "If she had done something—"

"She has done *nothing* wrong," I cut in firmly. "And of course I would tell you if that were the case, but it isn't. I just…" I trailed off, shaking my head again.

"Just what?"

"Don't you ever wonder why Sensei brought her here?" I asked him, keeping my voice down. "It obviously wasn't because she earned it—"

"Obviously."

I cast him a pointed glance before shifting my eyes back to Sparrow, who was far ahead of us by now.

"Doesn't it make you wonder why she's really here? What Sensei's real reason was in bringing her here?"

Preston's brow furrowed as he went thoughtfully silent.

"I'm guessing you must have your own suspicions already?" he asked finally.

My mind wandered as I thought back over everything that had happened over the past week. Finally, I drew a deeper breath. "No," I replied. "I have no idea."

"So… maybe you just like her, then?"

"I like her better than that first day, anyway."

"Yeah, yeah, but that's not what I mean, and you know it," he insisted.

I swung below a branch and wove my way around the boulders that lay ahead. "Can we move on to the next topic, please?"

"Whatever you say, man, but—" He cut himself off with a curse, his footsteps halting behind me. I glanced over my shoulder to find him staring into the empty woods behind us.

"What is it?"

His gaze shot back to mine. "Where's Janna? She's not behind us anymore."

I quickly scanned the surrounding trees. Preston was already retracing our steps, jogging back over our tracks.

I turned back toward the rest of the group farther ahead, cupping my hands over my mouth. "Wait up!"

Sparrow was the first to whip around and look at me. "What is it?"

"We lost Janna," I called. "Preston and I are going to backtrack."

"We'll wait here," Kateri shouted back, stopping up front.

But Sparrow disregarded the order, sprinting back towards me through the brush. She slowed when she reached me.

"I want to come with you," she panted, breathless.

I replied with nothing more than a nod, and we ran to catch up with Preston, who was about twelve yards up ahead now. He had stopped in the middle of a group of pines, scanning the forest around him. He cupped his hands over his mouth and yelled Janna's name into the woods. It echoed emptily through the trees.

He cursed as we skidded to a stop alongside him. "She was behind us just a second ago."

I glanced at Sparrow. Her face was pale, and her eyes were wide as they searched the forest floor. She staggered back so suddenly she crashed right into me.

"Oh my god—get down!"

Tensing, I dropped to the damp ground. Preston followed. Sparrow's eyes were wide, and her breathing was frantic as she lifted herself just slightly. She pointed frantically. "Do you see them? Keegan—look!"

My heart lifting to my throat, I quickly followed her gaze, my eyes darting back and forth through the trees.

"Where?" Preston hissed.

"Right there!" Sparrow clutched onto my arm with one hand. "Between the two…"

My gaze darted back and forth as I strained to see whatever it was Sparrow was staring at. But now her grip loosened. Slowly, her expression changed. She rose to stand, then staggered to the edge of the small clearing.

"There was someone between those two pines over there…" She trailed off, sounding thunderstruck.

"Over there?" Preston glanced from me to her, getting to his knees. "The ones with most of the bark worn off?"

Sparrow nodded.

"What was it you saw?" he asked.

"A person! How could you not see them? They were—they were right over—"

"A person?" Preston cut her off. "You saw a *person* right there?"

Sparrow whirled around to face us. "Didn't you see them?"

Preston shot me another glance as he got to his feet. "I… saw nothing."

"What?" A look of shock washed over Sparrow's face.

"I said I didn't see anything," Preston repeated. "Look—there's nothing over there!"

"There *was* a second ago!" Sparrow argued hoarsely. "How could you not see them?"

Preston opened his mouth to protest, but I intervened before he could say anything.

"What did they look like?" I asked.

"You didn't see them either?" Sparrow's dark eyes were desperate.

"Just tell me what you saw," I reiterated firmly. "*Exactly.*"

"A person—I couldn't see much of them; their back was to me."

"Did they look anything like the person you saw before?" I questioned.

Sparrow shook her head, still sheet white. "I couldn't tell. They were too far away."

"Did you see which way they went?" I asked, my head still on a swivel.

"When I looked up, they were gone."

"Well, either way—" Preston cleared his throat "—we'd better keep looking for Janna."

"I did see someone; you've got to believe me!" Sparrow stormed after him. "I saw someone there, just like—"

"Just like last time?" he sliced in to finish for her. "Sparrow, look…"

I didn't hear the rest of what he said. Their argument became muffled as I scanned the trees. Suddenly I spied something sprawled on the forest floor a little ways off. I swiftly but carefully approached the lumpy shape on the ground. As I got closer, I realized what it was.

"Hey!" I shouted hoarsely over my shoulder. "Come quick!"

The distant sound of Preston and Sparrow's arguing stopped abruptly, replaced by the pounding of their footsteps approaching me.

"What is it?" Sparrow said, stopping beside me. Preston was just behind her.

I lifted the light green and gray backpack. It was unzipped, and most of its contents were scattered over the ground. My eyes met Preston's gravely.

His eyes were wide with terror. "Oh god… that's Janna's."

# 28

"WHAT ARE WE SUPPOSED TO DO? KEEP GOING LIKE THIS? Keep blindly marching forward and getting picked off one by one by a predator we can't even see?" Urgency flared in Kateri's eyes as she looked at me. "Sensei needs to know what's happening—he needs to be told!"

The rain stopped as we regrouped in the clearing where we'd found Janna's torn-apart backpack. My jaw tightened as I considered the few facts we knew, which only seemed to add to the blood-curdling mystery this was turning out to be.

Kateri and I stood off to the side, talking in low voices. The others whispered among themselves, their faces grave and frightened—all except for Sparrow, who stood alone and silent.

"Even if we go back now, even if we tell Sensei everything, what can he do?" I whispered, turning back to Kateri. "Send us out to look for them? We're already here."

"We don't know that's what he would do."

"What, then? Do you think he would just leave Raf and Janna out there?" I asked dubiously. "You think he wouldn't send us out to find them?"

"I don't know, Keegan! I don't know…" She pinched her eyelids shut. "I'm afraid."

"I'm pretty sure we all share that feeling."

By this point I'd heard Preston numbly mutter, "I should have let her go back," at least half a dozen times. His face was blank, and he looked badly shaken, just like the rest of us.

"What are we going to do?" Kateri said.

"We have to figure out what's out there," Sparrow said, striding purposefully over to the place where we stood. "How can we stop something we haven't even identified?"

Kateri turned to look at her. "Who's to say we *can* stop it?"

"We're anomalies, aren't we?" Sparrow shrugged her shoulders. "We have freakish abilities for a reason."

No one could argue there.

"But so far, you're the only one who has claimed to see anything out there," Kateri reminded her. "How are we supposed to go off that?"

"By trust," Sparrow answered, her voice tired and tinged with desperation. "Have I still not convinced even you to believe me on this, Kateri?"

"It's not that I don't believe you, Sparrow," Kateri hastily assured her. "It's just that… we've all been out here, we've all been paying attention, yet you've been the only one to hear or see anything."

"Just because I'm the only one who—"

"We were standing *right there* with you, Sparrow." Preston came up behind me. "Keegan and I aren't blind, you know."

"I never said you were." Sparrow's voice rose. "You just weren't paying attention, apparently."

"Uh, pretty sure I was literally straining my eyes trying to see whatever it is you were pointing to, Sparr," Preston shot back, frustrated. "I saw no person in the shadows, no RGM soldier. Did you, Keegan?"

I shook my head. "But I believe Sparrow saw it."

"She saw *something*, but that doesn't mean there's an RGM soldier out here picking us off one by one," Preston huffed. "What would be the purpose? Why would the RGM be all the way out here in the middle of nowhere?"

"Look, I don't know *who's* out there, okay?" Sparrow exploded, scanning the half circle of us desperately. "But I've been seeing and hearing something—*someone*!"

No one said a word. My eyes didn't leave her.

"If it were a wild animal, there would be traces—we would have found something by now, but we haven't! Someone is… someone is *taking* us, one by one. And we have to figure out who."

Preston crossed his arms. "How?"

"By wandering around in these woods until we all disappear?" Myung added, joining our little group.

From there, the discussion ignited into panic again until Sparrow finally raised her arms.

"Listen! Listen…" She waited for everyone to stop talking. "Please, just—just hear me out on this one: whoever is out there is interested in us."

"That's one way to put it," Myung grumbled.

"So much so, they're following us—I've been hearing footsteps in the woods since the day we left the Homestead."

"You don't know for sure they were footsteps, though," Preston argued. "It could have been just an animal in the brush. You can't just connect all of those occurrences and assume—"

Sparrow lifted her hands defensively. "Even so, we lost Rafael *miles* upstream. Whoever kidnapped him obviously tracked us in order to take Janna, too."

"What makes you think it was the same person?" Kateri asked, genuinely curious.

Sparrow began to pace. "Because of the similarities between the disappearances…"

"What similarities?" I questioned, my interest piqued. "What did you notice?"

"Rafael was the youngest, smallest—easy prey," Sparrow explained. "Janna was straggling far behind the rest of us. Once again, easy prey."

Our small group went silent. Myung's face twisted. "And how on earth will this information help us find them?"

Her question was somewhat sarcastic, I could tell. But Sparrow took it completely seriously.

"It helps us because it means we can trap them. Stage the next attack," Sparrow answered. "Catch them in the act. Someone needs to put themselves in a vulnerable situation on purpose, and this time we need to be paying attention."

A stunned silence followed.

"Are you insane?" Preston exploded. "We can't just—we can't—"

"We can't just sacrifice ourselves to some probably flesh-eating mutant hiding out in the woods," Myung said bluntly. "Sorry to break it to you."

"Isn't it enough that we've lost Raf?" Kateri spoke up. "And Janna? We can't possibly risk losing another—"

"I'm not asking anyone to sacrifice themselves," Sparrow interrupted, her expression grave once more. "I can't and won't ask any such thing… But I *know* what I saw. And I think it could be a clue—the key to understanding what's happening to us, and how to stop it before we all end up…" She sighed.

I looked at her steadily. "So what exactly are you suggesting?"

Sparrow stepped a little closer, folding her arms over her chest to mirror me; there was no fighting the determination in her eyes.

"I'm not suggesting," she answered firmly. "I'm volunteering to be victim number three."

"Sparrow—Sparrow, stop walking."

"Why?" she called over her shoulder. "I already know what you're going to say."

"You can't just run off like that." I fell into step beside her. "Not before we've discussed it all through, as a—"

"As a group?" Sparrow quipped, giving me a searing look. "Let them discuss it—the three of them who are left. Let them argue and reason and come to their own conclusion about what should happen. It doesn't matter to me; don't you see that?"

"I've seen that since day one."

Sparrow jerked her head in an angry nod. "You even said so yourself, once—that I didn't belong here with all of you."

"I took that back," I reminded her.

Sparrow took a few more angry strides before coming to a halt, panting for breath as she scanned the forest around us.

"Yet sometimes I think you shouldn't have," she commented, breathless. "Sometimes I think it was the truest thing anyone has said to me since I've come here."

"Sparrow."

"Don't… please don't try to convince me, Keegan."

"I will if I want to." My words came out hard. "You don't control what I think—"

"No. Only you can read minds, unfortunately."

My muscles tightened as she held my gaze for a moment before turning, grabbing a low branch with both hands and swinging below it.

"I think you're feeling sorry for yourself now," I announced bluntly, following suit. "You feel 'out of place,' and you've put forth no effort to make anyone like you, so no one does—and now, you'll play martyr so we can all feel sorry for you."

Sparrow gave a mirthless laugh. "How little you know me."

I couldn't help but think back to the day I had read her mind, by accident—that day on the bank of the creek where I'd taught her to channel. So recent, yet it felt like a year had flown past since then.

"Where are you going, anyway?" I finally asked. "How many times have I told you not to just wander away from camp without a word to anyone. Especially now, with…"

"I didn't 'just wander off,' Keegan. I have you with me," she countered, glancing back. "Don't I?"

They were just lightly spoken words on the surface, but I sensed something deeper underneath.

"Yes." My voice came out a little softer. "I'm with you, Sparrow."

She paused, resting one hand against a slouching birch, all its papery bark peeling away. Her big brown eyes studied me for a moment, and then she pulled herself away again as soon as I got close.

"But anyway, to answer your question: I thought I saw water over here when we were hiking," she explained.

We took a few more steps and, sure enough, the thick trees suddenly yawned open and revealed a lake. Actually, it was too small to be a lake. It was more like a pond: round and glossy and painted with soft streaks of the sunset now that the rain had stopped and the clouds had dispersed.

"Have you ever seen a sunset like this?" she asked, breathless.

"Many times," I answered, still watching her. "The air is still a little smoggy out here, but not anywhere near as much as that cesspit of yours—New York."

"It's not mine." Sparrow's voice sounded far off. "It may have been once… but not anymore."

I slowly followed her over to the shore of the pond.

"I've never really been anywhere long enough for it to feel like home," she said quietly. "I thought France was home when I was little, but then… we had to leave…"

"We?"

"It's not important," she said quickly, her expression faltering a little. "Then when I was older, Ireland for a bit, then New York. I felt so lost in its lights and rhythm; it was easy to forget who I was… who Fin thought I was, and everything he expected of me…" She paused, glancing up at the sky again. "There were never sunsets like this."

"And who *does* Sensei think you are?" I asked, looking up at the sky. "And what makes you think he expects anything of you?"

Sparrow hesitated. "I won't lie to you… I can't…" She forced a little smile and tossed me a pointed glance. "You are a mind reader, after all." The expression on her face slowly faded, and a heaviness entered her eyes. "But, Keegan, if I told you everything, you would never believe me," she whispered. "How can I expect you to believe something I doubt every day?"

I looked at her steadily for a moment. "Do you seriously think you're the only anomaly student who has ever doubted, Sparrow?"

She seemed a little surprised. "You? Solid as a rock, and unwavering in faith?"

"Dad has always said that 'both doubt and belief are the way of the student,'" I began. "I doubted everything when I lost my parents... I doubted that I could ever be a healer—I felt like an impostor; I knew I was only at the school for healers because I was Dad's son, not because I'd earned it."

"But you *can* heal."

"Yes, now." I nodded. "But I didn't know I was an anomaly until Sensei showed me who I was... My initiation wasn't like the others'. Sometimes I feel like a cheat, to be honest."

Sparrow listened, waiting for me to go on.

"But then I remind myself that to every sunset, there is a sunrise to put to death the darkness," I went on quietly. "And we *are* that Sunrise. Sensei expects nothing more of us than to realize that this is so..." My voice faded in my throat as I looked back down at her. "And to fall in love with the light."

Sparrow's eyes were soft and lost in mine. She said nothing as I stepped closer.

"I don't know who you are, Sparrow, not really." My words softened to whispers. "But I don't have to know where you come from, what's happened to you, or what you've done, to know that my dad *loves you* just the same as he loves all of us. He didn't save you because he expected anything of you... anything more than that you awaken to the Sparrow he sees in you." My voice faded a little as I looked into her face. "And when he looks at you, he doesn't see someone who doesn't belong: he sees a warrior."

Sparrow's eyes searched mine. I gently reached down to brush her hair away from her face. My fingers grazed her skin, and it felt like I'd touched fire. I heard a soft sigh push past her lips... They were so close to mine, I could feel the warmth of her breath.

"If you really don't want me to know who you are, you shouldn't be this close," I whispered almost inaudibly. "I already read your mind once, by accident."

"You read my mind?" she asked softly, sounding surprised.

"I didn't mean to."

"And what did you find there?"

"That… that you didn't want me to see you," I answered softly. "Who you really are."

Sparrow nodded, her dark eyes probing mine. "And what do you think you would find there now?"

I took a slow breath, frozen for a moment as I studied her face, feeling something in me ignite. Unable to hold it back anymore, I took her face in both my hands and pressed my lips softly against hers, drinking her in like the warm sunlight. Pulling her close, closer.

My fingers wrapped around a handful of her soft hair. My lips melted into hers as her fingertips pulled me closer. The waves inside me crashed to a silence; stillness. I felt like we were slipping beneath them, sinking. But for a moment, we weren't drowning anymore.

# 29

"IT'S SOMETHING I HAVE TO DO," I SAID BY THE FIRE THAT night, with everyone else listening somberly. "It's something I started, in a way."

"Sparrow, you can't blame yourself for everything." Kateri looked at me from across the flames, from where she sat beside Keegan. "No one could have foreseen that this would happen."

"Yeah, but Sparrow *is* the reason Sensei sent us into hiding in the first place," Preston added carefully, catching my glance. "I mean, if Sparrow hadn't…"

"See?" I gestured in his direction. "For once I agree with Preston. Let me go."

"We can't just let you go," Myung interjected. "We don't *know* what's out there. We don't know what happened to…"

She didn't finish.

"Look," I began. "I don't pretend to be the most likable person. I know I'm not anyone's favorite—and I know that I've done nothing to deserve that privilege. I've done nothing in my life worthy of anyone's respect. I've done nothing to help anyone but myself." I paused, my voice shaking a little as I studied the flames dancing in front of me. "I'm nothing like what I should be. I know that now."

"Sparrow," Kateri began, taking a sympathetic tone, but I lifted a hand to stop her before she could say anything else.

"I don't want sympathy—I don't deserve it, and that's not why I'm saying any of this. I want you to let me go. And honestly… I don't even know why I'm asking permission from any of you, it's my decision, and I've already made up my mind."

In the shadows and light, I saw the muscles in Keegan's jaw tighten. "What's the battle plan, then?"

"At first light, I'll wake you guys," I explained, piecing it together in my mind as I went. "Keegan and Preston can trail behind me a little ways, and Kateri and Myung—you guys could stay here at camp in case we're being observed. I want whoever's watching us to think I've separated from the rest of the group, making myself vulnerable."

"I should be beside you, Sparrow," Keegan cut in, sounding strained. I shook my head.

"It would be dangerous for our group to get any smaller than it already is," I argued. "You have so much to offer the group, Keegan. I have very little. Besides, I'm the only one who ever seems to see anything—I think you and Preston can both attest to that."

Preston rubbed his jaw thoughtfully. "So you basically want us to watch from a distance?"

I nodded. "And snap into action as soon as you see anything," I affirmed with emphasis. "We have to capture them… It's the only possible way we'll ever find out what happened to Raf and Janna."

No one said anything for a long moment.

"We'll leave at first light," I announced finally, breaking the silence. "I'll wake the two of you." I tipped my head toward Keegan and Preston. "And I'll go out into the woods to wait there and see what comes."

Keegan didn't say anything. He just stared at me from across the flames, searching my face—possibly reading my thoughts. In a way, I hoped he was: he would quickly realize there was nothing he could say or do to make me change my mind. Even so, when I looked in his eyes, I saw that he trusted me; I'd felt it when we'd kissed.

*He kissed me; I kissed him.* I had stood at the edge of the pond, drenched in the colors of the sunset, and kissed the lion boy. I'd felt a stirring like the wind inside me, shaking everything I'd worked so hard to build, tearing down the guards and shattering the walls. It had been so long since I'd felt anything, and now I felt everything, all at once.

After everyone had dispersed to their respective sleeping areas—except Myung, who had lookout duty—I trekked a little deeper into the woods to relieve myself. On the walk back, I found Keegan waiting at the edge of the trees. He latched onto my wrist and pulled me into the concealing shadows of a massive pine.

"Sparrow, please let me come with you." Even in the low light, I could see his eyes brimming with urgency. "There's something more to this. I know there is—I know I told you I don't need to know, and I don't…" His words trailed off, and he squinted at me as he studied my face. "But there's something you're not telling me, something that's making you do all this—making you play martyr."

I let go of a narrow sigh. "No, Keegan, it's not that."

"What, then?" His question came out almost frantic now. "Why won't you at least let me come with you?"

"You *will* be with me. I told you and Preston that—"

"Yeah, watching from a distance. What if something happens to you? What if you disappear, just like Rafael and Janna? Sparrow—"

"I saved you from the cougar, didn't I?"

Keegan nodded reluctantly.

"Then trust that I'll be able to defend myself—and besides, I'll have you guys for backup."

Keegan was still staring at me, searching my eyes. "You're the most infuriatingly stubborn being that ever walked the earth."

"Oh, and I could say the exact same thing about you."

Sighing, he leaned his forehead against mine. "You make me so angry, Sparrow." I felt his warm breath on my lips as he whispered, "It's so frustrating…"

Goose bumps rose over my skin as he spoke. I wanted to kiss him so badly.

"They need you," I tried to explain, breathless. "I have to do this… We have to find them…"

His forehead caressed mine as he shook his head. "*I* need *you*, Sparrow."

I felt the warmth of Keegan's words on my face. My fingertips slowly found him in the darkness, the skin on my palm brushing against the stubble on his jaw. Lifting onto my toes, I pressed my lips against his. He leaned into my kiss, lingering there.

Everything faded, falling away. I felt lost and dizzy and so many other things I had no words to describe. His warm fingertips brushed back my hair, caressing my neck to pull me closer.

For a moment, everything melted away.

"I *will* come back to you," I whispered, breathless, as I pulled away. "I promise."

"Let me at least come with you," he pleaded again. "I'll keep myself hidden."

"What if you're seen?" I protested. "What if something happens to you?"

Keegan shook his head, then leaned in again to let his lips brush against mine once more. "Nothing will happen." He tasted my lips in another slow kiss. "Nothing."

"I can take care of myself, you know."

"Believe me, I'm aware of that." He kissed me once more before finally drawing back just enough so that I could see into his eyes. "But I love you, Sparrow."

Everything I was about to say came stumbling to a halt. I could hardly believe what he'd just spoken. For a second, I wondered whether I'd just imagined it.

"What?" he asked softly. "You don't believe me?"

I shook my head, looking down. "No, it's not that… It's just… you don't know me, Keegan. Not really. We've only just met, really."

"I know everything I need to," he whispered, placing a soft kiss on my forehead.

"Not everything." I pulled in a slow, shaky breath. "Keegan… I can't… *we* can't be this way."

Keegan's eyes probed mine. "Because you don't feel the same way?"

"No, it's not that—"

"So what is it, then?"

I hesitated, the words sticking in my throat. "Because… I'm not that simple, Keegan," I answered quietly. "I wish I were, but I'm not."

"What do you mean?"

I gently kissed his lips one last time, pausing inches from his face.

"I mean that if you knew the truth, it would change everything," I said softly. "It would change the way you think of me."

"Nothing could."

"This would."

"Sparrow." His eyes glimmered. "What are you saying?"

I stopped him, taking a step back, becoming aware once again of the tired, dark shapes of the trees, the cool night air, and the distant chatter of voices lingering around the campfire.

"Ask the man you call father," I answered.

Keegan looked at me for a long moment, saying nothing. I forced myself to walk away, to leave him standing there and return to camp. I slowed to a halt when I reached the fire. Preston was already sprawled out on his back, gazing up at the sky. Myung and Kateri were talking in low voices by the fire. They looked up when I approached.

"I'm going to try to get some sleep," I told them quietly. "I'll start out at dawn."

The expression on Kateri's face was grave, her dark eyebrows pressed together over her large brown eyes. "Sparrow, are you sure—"

"Yes," I cut in before she could finish. "I'm sure."

I heard Keegan's footsteps come up quietly behind me. Kateri's eyes switched to him. Something restless churned in my chest as she immediately rose to her feet to talk to him.

I took my usual place on the ground, tucking an arm under my head. I tried to concentrate on the stars flickering above, almost completely eclipsed now by the light of the rising moon. When I closed my eyes, I could still see the blurs of wings soaring and circling over my head. I still couldn't tell if they were calling me closer or warning me to stay away.

Slowly, unconsciousness smoothed away all these thoughts until finally it carried me away in its dark folds.

I awoke to the sound of a snap. I sat up slowly. Like always, everyone slept around me—including Myung, who had dozed off at her post. The firelight had dwindled, and all was quiet. I pinched myself, checking to see if I was dreaming—if I had just "awoken" within a dream like I so often did.

Slowly, I rose to my feet, straining to listen. I glanced over at the dark shape I knew was Keegan, then stepped across the soft ground, pausing again as a gentle breeze began to brush the boughs of the trees aside.

*"Sparrow…"*

I whirled around, scanning the bodies lying unconscious around me, searching for who had spoken, but no one else was awake.

The hairs on the backs of my arms rose as another snap came from the edge of the forest. My gaze darted to the rows of pines. I caught a fleeting glimpse of a blurred, dark shape against the moonlit forest.

Squinting to see, I trod silently on my bare feet across the soft ground, moving carefully closer to the tree line where I'd seen the shadow and deeper into the semidarkness. The moonlight bathed the woods around me in milky light as I walked, quietly weaving my way around the brush and trees. I listened carefully… and then I heard it:

*"Sparrow."*

I drew a sharp breath. Whipping around to face the opposite direction, I searched the darkness.

*"Sparrow…"* The soft whisper came again, this time from another

direction, paired with the sound of a footstep and a twig snapping.

A shadow moved to my left, vanishing as soon as I turned to look. I swallowed back my heart, moving more quickly now through the dizzying rows of pines. Breaking into a run, I emerged from the woods onto the shore of the lake, which was glossy with the reflection of the moon. The wind began to stir the trees, swishing them back and forth in a lulling dance as I too spun, searching for the source of the sound. The shadow I'd seen among the trees.

*Should I go back and wake Keegan?*

I listened, struggling to detect anything beyond the pounding of my own heartbeat.

I was about to take another wary step forward when a hand closed over my mouth from behind.

Every muscle in my body went instantly into paralysis. I tried to focus on channeling—to swing my arms up in defense—but my body was frozen stiff. A strong arm wrapped around my waist and yanked me backward into the darkness.

With every ounce of strength I had, I writhed and spun around in the vise grip, and my eyes locked with two deep brown ones. That was all I could see of him. Something was pulled up over the lower half of his face.

Grabbing me hard by the throat, he pulled my face into his, filling my ear with hot breath. "Hush."

I felt a prickle in my shoulder blade, and everything began to spin.

Suddenly a soft whipping sound penetrated the air—followed by a dull, fleshy thud. The arms around me loosened slightly as a throaty growl jerked from my attacker's chest. It was just enough for me to duck out of his grasp, staggering forward as the world heaved beneath me.

Turning, I could see him now—the dark outline of my attacker's frame. My thoughts blended and rolled. I heard the thunder of frantic footsteps, the *whoosh* of another blade whirring through the air.

My assailant lurched after me, grabbing hold of my legs and sending me sprawling to the ground—dragging me backward. The blade of a knife protruded from his shoulder.

"Sparrow!" Keegan's frantic shout cut through the night.

The powerful arms yanked me backward, and I heard a whoosh as fabric swept over my head and tumbled down my body, swallowing me into blackness. I felt myself being lifted; I heard the sound of a gunshot. Then everything went black.

# 30

I COULDN'T SLEEP. I CURSED INSOMNIA AS I LAY THERE, listening to the silence ring in my ears.

I needed to know what Dad would do; I needed to know what he thought of all this... I wondered what his reaction would be when he finally did find out. And Lara... I craved her advice, her soldier way of fighting the demons our brains liked to breed in the early morning hours. She knew how to use weapons like faith, which she fired like a sniper would. Me? I was still trying to find the trigger.

The trees above me seemed to whisper, taunting me as I tossed and turned on the ground.

*Faith... Where was mine?*

Lying on my side, I turned my gaze on Sparrow sleeping several yards away. Her back was to me. All I could see in the glow from the fire were wild rivers of dark hair and the pale-yellow flickers of firelight ebbing over her shoulder. Our conversation reverberated in my thoughts, echoing.

*"I'm not that simple, Keegan... If you knew the truth, it would change everything."*

She didn't understand that nothing could change the way I felt—how *much* I felt. What could possibly be so different about her that she believed it would reverse the storm inside me? She said I didn't know the truth about her… *but what is the truth?*

Sighing, I reached up and rubbed my eyes, pushing myself up to a seated position, pulling my gaze away from Sparrow. I kept thinking about how her lips had tasted and how much I wanted to kiss her again. It wasn't helpful.

"You're awake too?"

I glanced over at Preston, who was hunched by the fire several feet away, his head in his hands and his gaze on the flames.

I nodded. "Can't sleep."

"Yeah?" Preston looked over at me. "Nightmares?"

I lifted a finger to my lips. "What nightmares?"

Preston gave a weary laugh, stroking his forehead.

"What's eating you?" I tipped my chin back a little.

"Nothing," Preston insisted.

"Pssh. I know you."

He sighed, still rubbing his forehead. "I just can't stop thinking about them… Janna especially. If I hadn't stopped her from leaving… I should have just listened to Myung. We should have let her go—you could have transported her back there easily. But I was stubborn…"

"It was the group's decision," I reminded him, keeping my voice down. "Not just yours. Besides, Sensei told us not to return until he comes for us. He was insistent about it."

"I know, but… but maybe it was selfish on my part," he whispered, resting his forehead on his fist. "Maybe I just… wanted her to stay."

"There's nothing wrong with that."

Preston's mouth curved into a somber frown. "There is when it costs someone their…"

We both went silent for a moment. I followed Preston's gaze to the fire.

"Love is a frustrating thing," I said finally. "It's… the center of the universe, in a way. Yet I despise it because it feels like crap half the time. When they don't love you back or when something happens…" I blew out a long sigh.

He glanced over at me. "Sparrow?"

"What are you talking about?"

"I was out getting some dry wood, and I saw you guys by the lake."

I cursed inwardly, but he put up a hand before I could speak.

"Like I would ever say anything."

"I know you wouldn't…"

"So you're really gonna let her go off by herself and try to figure this out, then?" He picked up a slender stick to poke at the fire. "You're not worried about the woods eating her alive?"

I blew out a tired sigh, watching the tiny sparks dancing into the air. "More than that—I'm terrified. But it's not like I can stop her… and on top of that, she's right: she's the only one who ever sees them."

"Maybe she really will find Raf and Janna… if they're still alive." Preston's voice came out jagged. "Maybe she knows something the rest of us don't… We're like oil and water, she and I, but I'll admit that there is something…" He trailed off, lowering his voice as he stole a glance at the place where she was lying. "… strange… *different* about her."

"Yeah, I know what you mean," I agreed quietly. "I see it too. We've talked about it, a bit."

"And?"

"She won't tell me. I told her she didn't have to… that I didn't need to know about her past because it didn't matter."

"Because… you love her, apparently?"

I nodded without even thinking about it. Preston laughed under his breath.

"We'd better try to get some sleep if we're going to keep up with her tomorrow." He set down the stick and leaned back on his elbows.

I chuckled quietly before collapsing back onto the ground, feeling a little lighter somehow now that the weight of everything I'd been swallowing back was out in the open. I turned to look at Preston as he, too, stretched out on his back.

"Maybe Sparrow will find them," I whispered. "Find them *both*."

Preston stared up at the sky for a long moment before finally drawing a deep breath. "I hope so, Keeg."

My eyes flew open. I was expecting to find early dawn settling in, but it was still night. The moon was high and rinsing the surrounding woods in white light, illuminating our campsite in place of the fire that had long since dwindled to glowing embers. I sat up stiffly, reaching up to wipe away the sweat that was trickling down my forehead. Then I froze.

Our small group of anomalies lay around me, all asleep and all accounted for. All except one.

Sparrow was gone.

*Shit.*

I jumped to my feet, glancing around.

"Sparrow?" I whispered into the darkness.

No response came, but the quiet sound of footsteps in the distance grabbed my attention.

I snatched my holster off the ground and fastened it on over my bare chest as I skirted the edge of camp and slipped silently into the woods. I wound around the tall pines, slipping in and out of the brush. A crashing sound jerked my senses wide awake. In between the trees up ahead, a blur of movement caught my eye—someone was sprinting. *Sparrow.* Rivers of dark hair flowed out behind her in the low light.

*Why the hell did she leave camp this early?*

A thousand questions raced through my mind all at once as I kept low and quickly followed, dodging the dark shapes of rocks and fallen trees.

I halted at the place where the tree line yawned open to the glittering, moonlit lake. There was enough light to see Sparrow in the distance, walking toward the edge of the water. Suddenly, she stopped, stiffened— and then began wildly struggling and writhing as something dragged her backward.

Sparrow fought against the force, her heels dragging trails in the dirt, until finally she whipped around to face the nothingness behind her and then wrenched her head back as if something was trying to grab her by the face.

For a second I stared, stunned. *Why can't I see it?*

Fire in my veins, I sprinted forward through the brush, quickly unsheathing one of the two remaining knives in my holster with my focus. With a blast of dusty red energy, I channeled it forward, sending it hurtling through the air. With a muted *thwack*, it impacted, freezing in midair as if it had actually hit something. Sparrow wrenched away, falling backward, staggering away from the place where the knife hung, suspended in space. I sprinted through the brush and into the clearing—grabbing another knife and preparing to blast it forward. But this time I missed. The blade spun through the air—and into oblivion. I watched in horror as the invisible force attacked Sparrow once again, dragging and lifting her crumpling body.

I surged forward, keeping my focus on where the blade hung suspended in midair, shouting her name. I heard a sound like the whip of fabric, and then Sparrow vanished.

The suspended knife jolted and bobbed through the air, moving rapidly until, abruptly, it stopped. Before I could get any closer, a soft click broke the silence. A sound so familiar, I didn't even question what it was. I heard it every night in my sleep.

A shot rippled through the silent atmosphere. Bright orange sparks exploded out of thin air. A burst of white-hot pain surged through my body as the bullet found me.

# 31

MY BODY DRIFTED AWAY FROM ITS SENSES, AND DARKNESS gave way to a deeper kind. My nostrils filled with a scent like lavender. Sweat trickled down my forehead.

"Keegan." A hand touched my shoulder.

I gritted my teeth, tears burning in my eyes. I didn't move.

"Keegan, please…" She guided me by the shoulders, turning me around to face her, though I never saw her face; my eyes were shut tight. A tear escaped to roll down my cheek as her arms folded around me, and I shook, crumpling. "My sweet one," she whispered.

I tried to pull away from her, tried to force some words out of my throat, but nothing would come. Everything began to fade and bleed together. The feeling of her warm arms still encompassed me.

Then machine gunfire filled my ears, and it all swept away to darkness again.

I tossed and turned, feeling unable to breathe. I felt two hands close firmly around my arms. I writhed in their grip, still struggling to suck air, feeling as though my lungs were turning in on themselves.

"Keegan, shh—stop. It's okay…"

The voice was distant and distorted. The words didn't make sense within the fog hanging over my brain.

I felt my lips moving, but nothing intelligible came out. Finally, I swung my body to the left, rolling onto my side. No sooner had I done this than a fiery surge of pain rippled through my shoulder and chest. Gasping, I collapsed onto my back again, and my eyes flew open. The sky spun overhead, along with blurry snatches of faces.

"Keeg, can you hear us? Keeg…"

My brain scrambled to piece everything together. Steadying my breathing, I reached my shaking hand out over the ground. It brushed against a softer one. My fingers closed around it, and it grasped mine in return. The hand was warm and familiar.

I sucked in a deep breath. "Kateri?"

"Yes, Keegan, it's me—it's both of us. Preston and I are with you. It's going to be all right…"

I swallowed, feeling droplets of sweat trickling down my face, hot tears draining from my eyes.

"Preston, there was a stream back there—go get some water, quickly," Kateri directed.

"Kateri…" I murmured, my voice hot and garbled in my throat. "I lost her…"

"Shhh…" she hushed me. "Lie still. I need to take this bullet out of your shoulder."

In my mind's eye I could still see the sparks flying in thin air, a shot bursting out of an invisible gun. I squeezed my eyes shut.

"They got her," I murmured feverishly. "I tried to stop them, but they got her, Kateri…"

"Keegan, we'll figure it out—I promise." I heard the sound of ripping fabric. Kateri tore part of her shirt and pressed it to the bloody hole in my shoulder. "Right now, I need to focus on healing you."

I clenched my teeth, biting back the pain.

"What can I do?" Myung's voice.

"Nothing right now... Just make sure nothing happens to Preston."

"Follow him," I mumbled. "Don't let him go by himself. It's too danger—"

"Shhh, don't talk—you're making the bleeding worse."

The cloth felt like sandpaper against the open wound. After a moment, she took it away and replaced it with her hand. Her fingertips burned against my icy skin. I felt warm energy flow into the bullet hole, soaking into my skin and pulling at what felt like a massive piece of shrapnel lodged in my chest. I gripped the dirt, stiffening, as Kateri drew the bullet to the surface of my skin. I felt a painful release as it left my body. She placed both hands on the wound now, pressing with the heels of her hands as if kneading my flesh. Warmth spread over me, and gradually I could no longer feel the trickle of blood. Then the warmth faded and everything stilled.

Breathing hard, I opened my eyes, straining to look down at my shoulder. The wound was healed now, the blood and pain gone. The ripped piece of Kateri's shirt was splotched crimson, and on top of that was the blood-coated bullet.

"How do you feel?" Kateri asked. Her urgent brown eyes scanned my face and chest, examining me. "Are you dizzy?"

I slowly shook my head, reaching over to pick up the bullet. I studied it, turning it over in my hand before finally wiping away the blood with my fingertips. The deep red smudges gave way to nothing at all: invisible matter. Rubbing the bullet against my pants, I wiped it clean. I could feel the weight of it resting in the palm of my hand, but it was invisible.

Kateri shook her head, reaching out to feel it with her own fingers. I could see the indents on the pads of her fingers where the invisible bullet pressed against them.

"But... how..." she murmured, more to herself than to me. "How is this possible?"

"I heard Sparrow leave camp early this morning. I followed her, and I saw someone grab her and drag her away—but I didn't see anyone."

"What do you mean?"

"I mean it looked like someone grabbed her, but I could see *nothing* there. It dragged her backward, and she fought it. I channeled my last knives at it. That was the only way I really knew it was *there*. I could see the knife stuck there, in midair. I tried to attack, but they shot me," I finished through gritted teeth, looking down at the place where the wound had been. "And by then, it was too late—she'd already vanished."

Kateri's eyebrows furrowed. "What do you mean she had already vanished?"

"I'm not sure what I mean," I whispered finally, my voice as numb as the rest of me. "I just know that it took her and that we have to find her— *I* have to find her."

"*We* will find her," she responded quietly, her fingers closing around the bullet in the palm of her hand. "There is no alternative."

Preston's and Myung's footsteps came into earshot. Preston dropped down beside us, handing me a tin mug of water. He helped me to sit up, and I drained it, leaning back against the tree behind me.

"We have to go look for her," I began. "They could still be nearby. There's still tracks."

"There won't be for long," Preston pointed out, blinking up at the opaque sky. "It looks like some rain might be rolling in."

I was already struggling to get to my feet. Kateri reached out her hands to help me, but I made it all right on my own. Still a little dizzy, I glanced around at the three of them.

"We have to head out—now. Before the rain washes away whatever traces we might find."

Preston nodded in agreement, already looping one arm around my torso to help steady me. The creases in Kateri's forehead only deepened as she watched me.

"Keeg, you're not strong enough."

"Bull." I winced back the fatigue, taking a few careful steps with Preston's help. "I've never been better."

The truth was, I felt like I'd been run over by a bus. But that was just a minor detail. I would have gone to look for Sparrow even if the bullet was still in my shoulder.

Kateri and Myung led the way, since they could move faster than I could at the moment. I limped along behind them, calling up directions, my arm looped over Preston's shoulder. The lake was still a ways off, and the going was slow.

"So," Preston muttered in my ear when Kateri and Myung were far enough away not to overhear. "You took a bullet for her. That's kind of next level."

"Not really. I just got shot, that's all."

"Oh, that's all, huh?"

"It's not like they were going to shoot her. They *took* her…" I trailed off, squinting up at the darkening clouds that were beginning to roll in now. "They took her and left me… Why couldn't it have been the other way around?"

Preston fell silent for a moment, focusing on the ground ahead. "I know how you feel," he said hoarsely. "I know."

When we reached the edge of the lake, large icy raindrops began to fall, pelting the dirt and summoning blankets of warm, wispy fog from the mountaintops to cascade over the carpets of trees.

Sometimes it was easy to forget that I was a healer. That I'd grown up glued to Dad's side, hanging on his every word, peering over his shoulder. I had wanted to know everything, had wanted to be like him: healing trees and people, and bringing things back to life.

"Footprints!"

Myung's voice jolted me out of my thoughts. I broke away from Preston and stumbled forward. Kateri stood by Myung, who was squatting on the ground. I could see the indents of footprints in the grass as soon as I had halted alongside them.

"They headed east," I announced immediately, sizing them up. "Let's see how far we can track them before the rain erases everything."

"Shouldn't we be thinking about finding shelter?" Myung objected, pushing back up to her feet. "Can't you hear the thunder in the distance? The wind is picking up."

"If we head east now, we'll be fairly out in the open for a while," Preston said as he scouted around. "Maybe we should just—"

"We can't stop now." I cut him off. "We'll be even farther behind them."

"We might not have a choice," Myung shot back, throwing a hand at the sky just as the clouds sizzled with electricity. "Do you want to get killed?"

I was willing to risk it. It was better than standing by when I knew Sparrow was already miles ahead and god only knew where. My stomach was in knots as the thunder rolled, pounding through my chest and shaking the ground underneath us.

"Let *me* go, then," I said finally. "I'll start east, and you guys can find shelter."

Kateri's eyes went wide behind the wet wisps of hair that hung down into her face now. "Are you out of your mind? There's going to be a storm!"

"I've dealt with storms before."

I thought of Sparrow.

"No—no, no, no, no! You can't just leave on your own like that!" Kateri strode up to me, anger flaring up in her eyes. "You can't just walk off into the storm while we go find shelter. You've said this whole time that we all need to stick together!"

"We do! And if you guys stay together, you'll be—"

"And what about you?" she sliced in, now almost nose to nose with me. "You will have no one. We will lose you too!"

Another low rumble of thunder made the ground pulsate beneath us. The wind was swirling around us now.

"I'm not stopping," I said, resolute. "I'm going to find Sparrow."

Kateri's expression didn't alter. In fact, she looked almost like she'd been expecting me to say this.

"Fine," she answered firmly, her own voice equally decided. "I'm coming with you."

# 32

KATERI AND I HAD JUST BEGUN OUR HIKE ALONG THE shore of the pond, and the larger lake beyond it, when the sky opened.

Rain poured down in buckets, deluging us. The turbulent black and blue sky was illuminated in shades of white and green; deafening claps of thunder split the air. I kicked myself for letting Kateri come, but who was I kidding? She would have come regardless of my arguments.

"Stay close!" I shouted to her from a few yards ahead, though I could barely see her.

"Right behind you!" she yelled back over the roar of the wind.

I felt her fingertips sweep across my arm as she reached for my hand. I grabbed hold of it and didn't let go, squinting desperately to try to see ahead.

*Just keep the lake to your left… As long as you can see the lake, you'll be fine.*

Lies. I was already frantic. I'd been going off the assumption that Sparrow's captor had probably stuck to the shoreline, but the boot prints had disappeared a good ten minutes ago when the heavy rain had begun to fall, washing away the tracks.

A red flag rose in the back of my mind as the land began to slope downward, guiding us farther to the right where the eroded ground dipped and then rose again into the woods on a steeper incline. I slipped and fell as the earth turned to mud under my feet. I heard Kateri gasp as I slid the rest of the way down the slope.

"Keegan!"

I dug my heel into the mushy ground, steadying myself and squinting at her through the rain. "I'm fine!" I called up to her. "Be careful!"

Kateri edged her way down the slope, sloshing through the muddy water that was collecting around our ankles. "Should we keep going?"

"There's woods up ahead," I shouted back. "It shouldn't be long."

Kateri nodded, taking my hand again as we pressed forward, the mud sucking at our feet with every step we took. The trench offered us a little shelter from the whipping wind.

We trudged on uneventfully. Then Kateri's fingers froze tightly around my wrist, and she halted.

"Listen!"

I slowed to a stop. After a second, something began to replace the howl of the wind. Something strangely louder.

My mind immediately flashed back to when I'd gone over the waterfall. I feverishly started scanning the sopping ground around us. Even in the rain I could see the scattering of rocks and tiny bits of debris embedded into the dirt.

The rushing sound rose to a roar. In the distance I could just make out what looked like a rolling wall of brown, churning water.

We had been hiking down the middle of a wash.

"Quick!" I shouted hoarsely, grabbing Kateri by the arm. "We have to climb up!"

"It's too steep!" she screamed back over the noise.

We frantically scanned the steep hillside and began clawing our way up the muddy slope, gaining little ground for our efforts. I glanced back over my shoulder, peering farther down the wash. I could see the approaching floodwater. It was a hell of a lot closer.

"It's all mud!" Kateri cried, panicked. "There are no footholds!"

"Just keep trying! There's no time!"

We pushed off and tried the opposite side.

I scrabbled up the incline a little ways only to slide back almost to where I'd started. Straining and scrambling, I forced my way back up again and latched onto a jagged piece of rock sticking out of the muddy hillside, but it started to come loose as soon as my weight tagged on. I cursed as it came free, rolling down and bouncing against my right leg with crushing force.

"*Keegan!*"

An electrifying *vvvvmmm* followed the sound of my name. Before I could even process what was happening, the rock dissipated into pieces, the shards rocketing through the air with a burst of bright white energy and leaving my leg completely untouched. I flattened myself against the hillside, digging in with my toes. I whipped around to look back at Kateri, who was still farther down the slope, a white-hot orb pulsating in the palm of her hand.

"Stay where you are!" she shouted back hoarsely—I could barely hear her over the roar of the approaching water. My stomach knotted. It was almost on us.

"Keep your head down!"

I obeyed without question, dropping my face to the mud just as a crackling *tssshhww* blistered the air, followed by an earsplitting thud. Then I heard the sound of cracking, splintering wood above the chaos of the storm. A massive dead pine crashed down the slope into the mud, sending waves of spray over the two of us.

"Grab on, quick!"

Kateri latched onto the dead branches, using them like the rungs of a ladder to climb up the slope just as the roaring wall of water smashed through, wiping away the hillside from beneath us.

"Hurry!" I yelled at the top of my lungs. Kateri was on the other side of the tree, still a little lower. The trunk was beginning to totter as the earth beneath it eroded away.

"Just keep climbing!" she shouted back.

I didn't obey this time. I waited until she was just opposite me, close enough for me to reach out and grab her if I needed to. Together we grappled our way up the slope until finally we clawed our way frantically onto the level ground, stumbled to our feet, and lunged into the forest. We fell to our knees, soaked and shivering and covered in mud, and looked back at where we'd been climbing.

The tree balanced on the edge for a moment as the ground melted away beneath it. Then, with a groan like a dying animal, it reared upright, then rolled and crashed, end over end, down into the gushing rapids.

I scrambled a few feet farther back, then jumped to my feet. Kateri was right beside me.

We ran out of the danger of the eroding hillside, into the safety of the thick, dark woods.

Ducking under the shelter of a tree, Kateri bent forward, clutching her knees and gasping for air. Her clothes were covered in mud, and her face was sprayed with it. I probably didn't look much different. I wiped my face off in the crook of my elbow, breathing heavily. The sound of the rushing water was distant now, and the thunder had rolled on with the black clouds, echoing farther down the valley.

"That was some fast thinking," I panted, throwing my arms around her as she straightened up. "I don't know what I would have done without you."

She laughed a little, still breathless, as she embraced me, resting her forehead on my shoulder, exhausted. "Probably drowned."

"Probably."

We both just stood there, panting for a moment, listening to the quiet rain that seemed a freakish contrast to the hell we'd just survived.

Finally, Kateri separated herself to arm's length, giving me a little smile.

"And you wonder why I didn't want you wandering off alone." She jabbed a playful punch into my abs and turned to stalk farther into the woods. "Come on. Let's find a place to rest for the night. It'll be dark soon."

I stood there a moment, watching her, still a little breathless. Then I pushed myself forward and followed her into the woods.

As we hiked deeper into the woods, my thoughts drifted back to Sparrow. What I felt for her was like the floodwater, the kind of love that could destroy a person, sweeping them away, pulling them under, and demolishing everything in its path. It was dangerous, it was a warning sign, but still every one of my thoughts seemed to be consumed with her. Her lips, her hair, the tones of her voice. Her deep, dark eyes, pulling me in— pulling me *under* and holding me down.

*Does she even realize what she is doing to me?*

"What are you thinking about?" Kateri's voice pulled me back down to earth.

I rubbed my eyes. "Hmm?"

She smiled a little. "You seem miles away."

We'd walked probably a mile more to find an area of the woods that was sheltered and dry enough to build a fire and crash for the night. Kateri had managed to keep her small backpack on through our scramble up the wash, so she had dry clothes and a towel for me to wrap around myself while my own clothes dried over the fire with hers. We were camped beneath what remained of a dead willow tree. Its long, wiry branches reached down around us, almost like a thatched roof.

It was dark now. Kateri had let her hair down to dry. Mine was tied back and caked with the dried mud that had also settled into the stubble on my face.

"Just the past few days," I answered her finally. "Everything that's happened—Raf, Janna, Sparrow."

Kateri nodded, a heavy look in her eyes. "I can't stop thinking about them either." She paused, letting out a long sigh as she combed her fingers through her hair. "I can't stop thinking about the invisible bullet I took out of you."

"I don't understand it," I said, looking at her from across the fire. "How is it possible…?"

"Your guess is as good as mine," Kateri answered gravely. "But I think we were wrong to mistrust Sparrow after she warned us about the things she had seen and heard in the woods. *I* was wrong not to trust her. Because it wasn't nothing… Nothing can't fire a gun."

"Or abduct three people," I added.

Kateri stared at me for a long moment, a distant look in her eyes.

My thoughts traced back to the moments after Janna's disappearance, when Preston and I had run back through the woods looking for her, and Sparrow had followed. When she had shouted that she saw someone beyond the trees—asking us if we could see them too. Neither Preston nor I had been able to answer yes. But whoever or whatever had been out there now had Sparrow in their grasp. And maybe Raf and Janna too.

I shivered, trying to push the thought out of my head.

"Why do you think only Sparrow could see them?" I asked. "Why not you or me—Preston, anyone? Why was it always her?"

Kateri bit her lip. "I have no idea."

Silence swelled between us. Leftover drops of rain dripped down from the branches above to sizzle in the hot tongues of flame.

"Maybe it's like how Myung can hear things the rest of us can't… or how you can read things in people's minds that are locked away to everyone else," Kateri began quietly. "Maybe she sees things the rest of us can't."

"What do you mean?"

"It's obvious she was picking up on something we weren't able to," Kateri went on, her voice quiet and grave. "Something that's been costing us dearly."

"She thought she saw a soldier," I whispered finally. "But why on earth would there be a soldier all the way out here in the middle of abandoned country? The RGM hasn't been in these parts for ages, and even if there were soldiers out here for some… insane reason, we would all be able to see them."

Kateri didn't say anything. She stared into the fire, and I could see the gears turning behind her dark eyes.

"My father used to tell me I was impatient when I was young," she began quietly. "Even when I was little, I would feel the tingling in my fingertips when I saw an injured bird, a limping stray cat—I wanted to know what it was… this strange longing I felt within me, yet couldn't see. My father would smile and say he didn't know what it was, but that if I believed, the teachers would appear. They would show me the things I couldn't see. And he was right… I found Sensei. I found out what that desire inside me was," she went on softly. "I finally saw the things I couldn't see before, and everything fell into place."

Kateri's eyes shifted curiously up to mine. "How old did you say you were when you first realized that you were an anomaly?"

I grunted a laugh and got up to check on my clothes. They were dry. "When I was twelve or so; that's when I began to accidentally read Sensei's thoughts—Lara's. I couldn't control myself. Sensei taught me to harness the ability, to use it only for missions, only when I had to."

I pulled my clothes off the low branch, stepping behind the thick trunk of the tree to take off the towel and change.

"Mm. I'm glad you got that under control before I arrived."

I swallowed back a pang of guilt. I glanced up at the clouds passing over the moon as I dressed. "That so?"

"Everyone has thoughts they wouldn't want to speak aloud," Kateri said. "Dreams, desires. Things they would never tell another living soul."

This did nothing to quell the feeling that tangled inside me—the feeling that I'd done something wrong. Without meaning to, yes, but still… that was the trouble with my ability. Once I read someone's mind, I couldn't unread it. I zipped up my pants and stepped out from behind the tree again to toss the damp towel over one of the branches.

Part of me wanted to just admit it. To tell her what I had done, because this was the first time I'd ever really kept something back from Kateri. But at the same time, I knew I couldn't. If I told her I'd read her mind, I'd have to tell her what I'd seen. And if I told her that—if I told her that I knew she had feelings for me—it would force me into a discussion I wasn't ready to have.

*Do I love her too?*

Before Sparrow had arrived, I'd begun to ask myself that question. I couldn't blame the others for teasing us sometimes—Kateri and I were so much alike. We understood each other so well. If Sparrow hadn't come, maybe I would have been able to answer that question with a yes.

But now… Now I was lost at sea. Lost because Sparrow had come and flipped my world on its head, and now, just like that, she was gone.

I couldn't have this conversation, not now. Not when I knew it would divide Kateri and me. She was all I had left.

"Kateri?" My voice came so quiet I almost didn't hear it.

"Yeah?"

I turned to face her once more. The shadows and flickering of the flames danced in her eyes.

"I don't know what I would do without you." The words were honest, raw, and slow in coming. I wanted to get them right. "I… I hope you know that."

She looked at me for a long moment without saying a word, just staring at me over the flames.

"I don't know what I would do without you either, Keeg," she said quietly.

We sat in silence for a long moment. It seemed like neither of us knew where to go from there.

"We should try to get some rest so we can get an early start," I said finally, my voice quiet. "We can figure out where to go from here when dawn comes."

# 33

FOR THE FIRST TIME IN A WHILE, THE NIGHTMARES DIDN'T come. I didn't dream about Galway or my parents or the gunshots. I didn't even dream of Sparrow. Sleep was cold and deep and all-encompassing. I sank into it like ocean water until I hit the bottom. When I opened my eyes, it was already morning. Kateri was still sleeping on the other side of the feathery pillar of smoke rising from the dying fire.

I rolled onto my side and got to my feet, gently shaking Kateri awake. "Come on," I said gently. "We have to get moving."

She stirred, rubbing her eyes, then slowly got to her feet.

I started pacing the perimeter of the clearing, scouting the woods, while Kateri pulled her muddy clothes down from the tree and tossed them into her backpack. My thoughts raced as I searched between the trees and in the clearing, looking for signs of disturbance. Everything seemed still and untouched. Until the brush up ahead began to rustle.

Staying low, I remained where I was. The dry brush swayed to stillness again. I glanced back through the trees, craning my neck to see Kateri, who was kicking dirt over the remaining coals. When she finally glanced my way, I rapidly gestured her over.

"What is it?" she whispered, dropping down beside me.

Tipping my head in the direction of the brush, I placed a finger to my lips. "Listen."

For a long moment there was nothing but thick silence and the occasional brush of the wind through the trees. Then the stirring came again, and this time a strange, high-pitched screech followed it.

I quirked my eyebrows as I turned and looked at Kateri. She was staring ahead at the brush, continuing to listen intently.

The soft shriek came again, paired with a rumble, almost like a purr.

Kateri smiled a little, placing a finger to her lips. She stood to take a few quiet steps closer, then squatted down a couple of yards from the wobbling bushes and extended her hand. She made soft clicking sounds with her tongue, waggling her fingers.

"What is it?" I asked, my patience exhausted.

"Shhh. You'll scare it."

Confused, I watched and waited. The mass of dead grass and bushes wavered a little more, and then something small and furry and tan parted them, tumbling out onto the damp earth. As it stumbled to its feet, I realized, unmistakably, what it was.

No bigger than a small dog, it was tan and marked like the larger version that had attempted to kill me. It had huge blue eyes and splotches of black across its soft coat. I rolled my eyes.

"Hey, love…" Kateri hushed her voice. "It's okay…"

"We should probably leave it alone. The mom might be around." I was already scanning the forest, bracing myself for an uncomfortable repercussion.

It chirped and squeaked like cubs do, sauntering over to sniff Kateri's fingers.

"I don't think so," Kateri answered, maintaining her quiet tone. "It… sounds like she's an orphan."

"Sure. That's what they all say," I replied, sounding a little bitter as I continued scoping our surroundings.

Then it hit me.

My eyes lowered to the tiny cub now pressing its forehead into the palm of Kateri's hand. Sighing, I moved a bit closer and then stooped down, squinting at it. It lifted its head weakly to gape up into my eyes with its own, which were like large sapphires confined to a skull. Its ribs pressed up against its skin, its coat was dull, and its paws trembled under its own weight.

My heart sank a little. I reached out a hand to let it sniff me.

"Pretty sure I know how it became an orphan," I said finally, looking at Kateri knowingly. She seemed confused for a second; then understanding washed over her face.

"Oh…"

"Yeah."

The cub sneezed on my hand and fell over. Rising to my feet, I dusted my hands off on my pants and frowned.

"It's going to slow us down."

"But you know full well we can't just leave it here. We have a responsibility to it as healers," Kateri reminded me. She scooped the cub gently into her arms; it did not resist.

"Speaking of leaving, I have no idea what direction we should go from here," I said, deftly changing the subject. "The rain would have washed away any evidence they left behind."

"What about Preston and Myung?"

I shook my head. "They'll be fine as long as they stick together. I'm not ready to go back."

Kateri's brow creased as she thought, shifting the lanky cub to her opposite arm, where it settled against her shoulder. "Neither am I. Not until we find some trace of them."

The thought was overwhelming. "Some trace…" There was something so dark and final about those words.

We trekked our way back to the lake, finding a new path on dry ground to follow.

Time seemed to drag slowly and aimlessly as we hiked for miles, searching the ground and the trees for anything out of the ordinary. Hours felt like days. Each step felt more and more futile in this vast and barren wilderness.

I kept wishing I would wake up, that this would all just be some kind of awful dream.

We stopped at a stream for water. The cub lapped the cold, clear liquid while I splashed it over my face. Straightening, I turned and walked to the edge of the forest and then froze. Almost under my nose was a set of watery, smudged, staggering footprints. I called to Kateri as I carefully scoped the ground, studying the tracks.

"What is it?"

"Boot prints—the same ones."

Kateri jogged over, the cub following at her heels, and examined the prints. We stared at each other for a moment, and then without a word, set off in the direction they were leading.

As we followed the tracks, I found myself holding my breath. I felt like we were close—to what, I wasn't sure. But with each footstep, Sparrow's name seemed to echo in my brain.

I picked up the pace, following the tracks until, abruptly, the trail came to an end. We were standing at the edge of the woods, looking out over a desolate valley. Steam sprang up from the ground in the distance, and closer, a bright blue pool churned as if boiling. I'd only ever heard about places like this from Dad… This was the first time I'd seen anything like it with my own eyes. Out in the center of the open area was a rocky mound that rose a few feet from the ground to form a wide cone shape.

"What do you think that is?" I pointed it out, squinting through the sunlight.

Kateri lifted her free hand to shield her eyes from the sun. "Geyser, maybe?"

I took a few more steps forward, staying just inside the tree line. "This is definitely geothermal ground. They must have headed out into it."

"The ground's too hard and crusty to tell, though, and it's way too volatile to walk out on. But this is where the boot prints end," Kateri reasoned, squinting out at the hissing, steaming valley ahead. "But why would they head out into the open? It doesn't make sense. There's nothing out there for miles."

We both fell silent for a long moment as we stared out at the hissing, gurgling geothermal valley ahead. "Let's skirt around it and see if we find anything," I suggested.

Dirty steam lifted from the ground in puffs, and distantly I could hear the choked gurgle of thick, boiling mud. Towards the horizon, the earth flattened out to whitish-yellow crusty ground. Rotting splinters of wood spread out over the ground where pathways had once been back in the day when this wasteland had been a park.

"Watch your step," I warned as Kateri scooped up the cub. "There might be hidden hot springs." I took a few steps along the tree line, scanning the ground as I went, but Kateri didn't move from where she stood. For a moment she just gazed out into the open valley, holding the scruffy cub against her chest. I was about to ask if she was coming when a loud blast roared through the silence. Startled, I turned back to the geyser. The cone-like formation in the distance remained static, though a sound like roaring water still resounded through the atmosphere.

*Where on earth is the sound coming from?* It sounded like it had emanated from the geyser across the valley ahead, yet I could see nothing. The callused, sulfur-rich ground remained unaltered.

"What the…" I muttered, squinting ahead. "Where do you think it is?"

"No idea…"

"But doesn't it sound like it's coming from that geyser across the valley?"

Kateri pursed her lips. "Maybe there's another geyser over that ridge, and it just sounds closer than it is," she reasoned, absently stroking the cub's head. "I can't imagine any other explanation."

Neither could I, but I couldn't ignore the sirens inside me, almost screaming that there was something strange about this place.

"Come on." Kateri stepped past me now as the sound of rushing water slowly diminished to nothing. "Let's see what we can find this way."

Now I was the one lagging behind, standing there at the edge of the woods, gazing out into the white and rust and red barrens of the valley. The sound of rushing water faded now, and everything went back to normal. Mud pots gulped and gurgled in the distance, steam howled up from cracks and crevasses in the earth, and a gentle breeze stirred the trees.

I couldn't shake the feeling: there *was* something strange about this place. The valley seemed to be beckoning me, whispering that I should step closer. Something inside me still hummed, and her name still echoed in my thoughts:

*Sparrow. Sparrow. Sparrow.*

"Keeg?" Kateri called from several yards away; she was nearly invisible, camouflaged among the trunks of naked birches and pines. "You coming?"

Swiftly, I nodded, forcing myself to focus on the mission at hand. I quickly jogged after her, following the trail she had begun to blaze.

"Right behind you."

# 34

WE TREKKED FOR MILES THROUGH THE BUBBLING LANDSCAPE, avoiding clearings where the trees splayed out to encompass simmering turquoise pools and gurgling mud pots boiling violently and spitting scalding wet clay. The sun was hot and golden, beating down on us as we hiked. After a time, the hissing of steam faded out of earshot. We had yet to relocate the tracks, and the sun was lowering in the sky.

Kateri had set the cub down to let it walk freely on its own, and now it frolicked around my legs, butting me with its head when I finally halted to take off my T-shirt, roll it up, and tie it around my head. I shooed it away absentmindedly, but it didn't seem to get the message.

"What do you think we should do?" Kateri asked, breathless, as she came up beside me. "We haven't seen tracks since the valley."

"I know, I know." I wiped the sweat off my face, frustrated. "It doesn't make sense. There were no prints leading into the valley. They just stopped. Nothing makes sense except that they must have gone this way."

"Well, there must be another explanation, because we would have found *something* by now."

I kicked at the ground, leaning back against one of the trees to press my eyelids shut, trying to think.

"We should think about heading back towards Preston and Myung, Keeg," Kateri suggested finally. "It's been a day…"

"And what?" I snapped. "Just—just leave them out here? Sparrow, Raf, Janna—what about *them*, Kateri?"

Kateri's expression hardened. "Keegan, I care about them just as much as you do. I've thought of nothing else but them, and…" Her voice splintered as she pressed a hand to her mouth. "But I also know that we can't just wander around forever, separated—do you want to lose Myung and Preston too?"

I didn't know what to do. I didn't know what the right choice was anymore.

"Kateri." I spoke her name quietly. "Tell me what you think we should do."

"It's not just my decision to make."

"It has to be," I replied numbly. "It has to be, this time."

"Why, Keegan? What's going on with you?" She studied me with worried eyes.

"Nothing." My voice cracked. "Nothing is going on with me. I just…"

Kateri waited patiently, but I couldn't finish. I couldn't tell her the real reason—that I couldn't be the one to make these calls because my judgment was clouded by my feelings for Sparrow. So instead, I just shook my head and repeated, "Nothing."

The searchlights didn't fade from Kateri's eyes. Even when my gaze lowered to the ground, I could still feel them. Then a crashing in the brush interrupted the conversation. My head jerked up.

Kateri glanced around. "Where's the cub?"

She got her answer when some bushes ahead, between a cluster of pines, stirred with motion.

I cursed and took off after it, Kateri just behind me. Sprinting up over a large rock, I leapt from the top to grab a low branch growing out from one of the pine trees, swinging myself over the mass of thorny brush and landing in a crouch on clear ground. Immediately I spied a snatch of speckled fur up ahead, racing through the undergrowth. Kateri landed beside me.

"Told you it was a mistake to take him."

"*Her.*"

"*Whatever.*"

Kateri shielded her eyes from the sunlight. "Look—she's stopped."

I followed her gaze, and sure enough, the cub had scampered to a halt, turning to gape at us with its wide blue eyes. It made cub noises, leaning its paws up against the massive protruding root that carved the forest floor like a vein in a hand. Kateri studied it intently for a moment, then made a few soft clucking noises with her tongue. The cub lowered its head and backed off, turning back to stumble forward over its own paws.

"She's caught scent of something," Kateri concluded finally, getting to her feet. "Come on."

I quirked an eyebrow. "*Come on?* Kateri, it's not a bloodhound."

"Shhh. Just trust me."

Though skeptical, I ran after her, winding through the trees and dodging rocks. The small cub raced ahead, obviously having regained some of its strength as it leapt over logs and landed silently on all fours. We swung a sharp left, following the cub's trail until it began to slow down. I started to become aware of a sound other than our own footsteps or the sharp intermittent yelping of the cub. A sound like water trickling over rocks.

"Listen." I slid to a halt, putting up a hand for Kateri to stop.

The patter of the cub's paws, the crunching of dead brush, and then, beyond it—water. I looked over at Kateri.

"Did you see a stream on the way in?"

Kateri was thoughtfully silent; then her narrow eyes grew wider as she turned to stare back at me. She shook her head. She strode quickly ahead after the cub, then halted to point at the ground. I followed her gaze down to the thin trickle of water that was winding its way through the forest. Starkly contrasted against the dead landscape, bright green moss sprouted up from every place the water touched.

I felt the muscles in my jaw slacken as we stood there, watching the lush growth spread farther and farther out. The cub was several yards ahead, lapping up water with its tongue. I watched, stunned, as a healthy sheen returned to its fur. I turned to Kateri. I could tell she was thinking the same thing I was:

*This is no ordinary water.*

Taking off at a sprint again, I splashed through the water and followed it through the forest, Kateri just behind me. Several hundred paces on, the ground began to slope downward; the moss was damp and slick under my feet. Suddenly my legs went out from beneath me, and I fell down the embankment, landing hard. The craterlike clearing was filled with thick green grass and surrounded by dark pines through which the bright sunlight bled, igniting the freckled air, which was alive with pollen and moths.

In the middle of this tangled green cauldron, a body lay, vines looping through his hair and trailing down his arms. His hands lay open, and water drizzled from his fingertips.

"Rafael!" I scrambled to get up and ran to his side. "Rafael, can you hear me?"

His eyes were clamped shut, his lips parted, and his head tipped back. I leaned over him, pressing my ear to his chest just as Kateri slid down the embankment and rushed to my side.

"Rafael! Oh my god…"

"He's still breathing." I continued to listen to the faint sound of his heartbeat, reaching for his wrist.

"His pulse?"

I pressed my fingertips to his carotid artery, saying nothing. I straightened up again after a moment. "Weak."

Kateri repositioned herself behind Rafael, gently lifting his shoulders to rest his head in her lap. His neck bent back listlessly, and he made no sound.

"He's so cold." Kateri brushed the hair away from his bruised and dirt-streaked face. "We have to get him off this wet ground—do you think we should move him?"

"Not any more than we already have. We need to heal him as quickly as possible."

Kateri slid her backpack off her shoulders and unzipped the top. Rifling through it, she pulled out a towel and spread it out over Rafael, covering his limp body up to his chin. Before I could move closer, the cub nudged my arm, bringing my attention up to the forest just as voices rang out from somewhere close by. For a split second everything inside me tensed like a vise, and I felt Kateri stiffen next to me. But an instant later I recognized the voices.

Jumping to my feet, I ran ahead to the edge of the clearing and squinted through the trees. Two smudges of red and green backpacks stood out in the dense forest. I could see Preston's pack bobbing among the undergrowth.

I waved my arms overhead. "We're over here! We found Raf!"

"Keeg?" Preston hollered back.

Myung appeared beside him, and the two of them rushed over to me. I led them to Kateri and Rafael and dropped back to my knees beside them. Rafael still hadn't moved a muscle.

"Keep him still," I told Kateri breathlessly as I folded back the towel enough to position my hands on his rib cage. "I'm not sure what's wrong…"

I felt around his ribs, then, with Kateri's help, turned him over onto his side. His back was soaking wet, and moss grew over the wet underside of his T-shirt. I peeled it back to reveal blotches of purple and blue stretched across his skin. Kateri pulled in a sharp breath.

"Oh my god. What happened?" Myung fell to her knees beside us.

"Is he alive?" Preston said.

"He's alive," I answered quietly, placing a hand gently on Rafael's spine. "I just haven't figured out what's wrong… He's been beaten, but nothing seems to be broken…"

Everyone was silent as I felt for any possible fractures and then moved on to his head, staring emptily as I focused on feeling every inch of his skull. My heart was beginning to beat faster in the back of my throat. I couldn't figure out what was wrong.

Finally, I looked at Kateri. I didn't have to say a word—I could see in her eyes after a moment that she knew what I was about to do.

Taking a deep breath, I closed my eyes, keeping my hand on Rafael's forehead and stroking my thumb over his third eye point. I felt my own forehead begin to go numb, warmth radiating through my arms and legs.

Darkness… darkness… nothing. Raf's subconscious was like a void. Like a dark room. I was feeling my way around in the darkness, searching for the light.

*I have to…*

I stopped, stumbling—listening. I squinted through the darkness.

*I have to get back to them… I have… to tell them…*

A faint thought flickered in the emptiness. I raced forward before I lost it, circling my thumb faster over his forehead.

*I have to tell Keegan…*

The thought was as soft as a whisper, a breeze blowing past and then fading away, plunging me once again into darkness. I pulled in a deep breath and quickly wrenched myself out of his thoughts.

"Keeg." I felt Preston put a hand on my shoulder behind me.

I stayed bent over Raf's body, my lungs burning as if I'd just emerged from deep water. Slowly, I straightened back up, looking at Kateri.

"We have to…" I began, breathless. "We have to go back. We have to get him back to the Homestead."

"What?" Preston burst out. "Keeg—no. No, no, no—we can't just do that! What about Janna? What about—"

"I can't figure out what's wrong with him, Preston! His mind is giving me *nothing*!" My voice splintered. "I can't heal him when there's nothing physically wrong… It's not his body that's broken!"

Preston's eyes were hollow and damp. His jaw clenched, and he backed away a few paces, dragging a hand over his face.

Myung cleared her throat hesitantly. "What do you mean by that,

Keeg?"

My eyes were still focused on Kateri's, but now I looked down at Rafael again, first to his face and then to his hands still listlessly channeling water. I felt a lump form in my throat as I gently lifted his cold, open palm. I swallowed and shook my head.

"Keegan's right. We have to get him back to the Homestead," Kateri finally answered for me. "We have to transport back and tell Sensei…" Her voice faded, sounding choked. "We have to tell him everything."

"And leave Janna behind?" Preston asked, his voice crumbling.

I pulled my gaze away from Rafael to look back up at Kateri. Her face was drained, and a tear rolled down her cheek.

"And Sparrow." She bowed her head in a grave nod, her voice barely above a whisper. "Yes… for now."

# 35

*two days earlier*

IN THE DISTANT, INKY BLACKNESS, I HEARD A LONG, SHRILL call. It was so muffled I couldn't identify it. I strained to listen, trying to speak, trying to breathe. Like clouds, the darkness began to slowly clear around the familiar shape of a doorknob.

My body felt strangely weightless, my thoughts incoherent. I was numb.

Reaching out, I grasped the knob and felt cold iron against my skin. I turned it, pushed. The hinges groaned loudly as the door slowly swung open, letting in shafts of blinding light. My heart began to palpitate as I stepped forward, squinting and shielding my eyes with my hands. Blinking, I staggered forward, over to the tall glass windows lining that same long hallway.

*Where is this place?*

Though all of my movements felt sluggish, I managed to lift my hand to touch the glass; it felt cool against the pads of my fingers. Beyond the glass there were billows of churning white mist, and beyond the mist, thick, green carpets of trees, and towering cliffsides. The pastel sky was drenched in the colors of a sunrise.

The same shrill cry exploded through the air. I started awake, bolting upright. My fingers clutched at the ground. But the ground was no longer ground; it was cement.

My fingers were torn and bleeding against it. I looked down at myself, feeling droplets of sweat slipping down my forehead.

My clothes were tattered, and my knees were scraped and bloodied. I squirmed backward, glancing around, but my back slammed up against one of the tiny cell's cement walls, three of which were tall and white. The fourth was made of steel bars stretching from ceiling to floor and facing out at what looked like a mirror reflection: more steel bars, more white walls. The air stank of disinfectant.

I clapped my fingers down over my left shoulder as a stinging pain sizzled through it, as if I'd been pricked by a needle there. I squeezed my eyes shut, feeling sick, as I tipped my head back against the wall, my thoughts spiraling out of control. Fluorescent lights droned above me, filling the room with sterile white light.

My mind raced as I began to recall everything that had happened the night before, and I began to vaguely remember the prickle I'd felt in my back right before I'd blacked out. Then I remembered everything else: the noises, the whispers of my name, wandering from camp, the soldier…

*Keegan.*

Keegan's voice filled my mind. I remembered the sound of my name as he had shouted it hoarsely into the darkness, followed by the sound of a gunshot and then silence.

A sob rose in my throat. I clapped a hand over my mouth, breathing hard, as a thousand possible outcomes twisted through my mind. After a few moments, I wiped the tears from my eyes and took an even breath.

I forced myself to stand up, clutching at the walls with both hands as I got to my feet. I stood still for a moment, steadying myself, then walked across the tiny room to grab hold of the steel bars with both hands, leaning my face through one of the gaps.

From this vantage point, I could finally see who was in the cell across from me. The figure was crumpled on the floor in the fetal position, facing away from me, but I still recognized his mop of curly black hair, his skinny frame, and the clothes he was wearing.

"Raf!" I called. I shot a quick glance around, then lowered my voice. "Raf! Raf, it's me!"

Rafael didn't move. My heart started beating faster.

"Raf… Raf, can you hear me?" I pleaded in a hoarse whisper. "It's me—it's—it's Sparrow."

For another long moment he didn't move, and then he began to stir. Shivering, he rolled onto his back and then onto his other side, facing me now. My fingers tightened around the two bars as I held my breath.

"*Sparrow?*" he managed.

I nodded my head, the cool steel grazing my cheek. "Yes—it's me."

Slowly he eased up off the ground to a seated position, rubbing a dripping hand over his face. "Sparrow, how did you… What happened?"

The question alone was enough to cause the gunshot to ricochet through my head again, sending chills down my spine.

"They found me," I explained, my voice hoarse. "I… I went out into the woods after dark, and I wandered too far from camp…"

Rafael stared at me with large, empty eyes. His face was like stone, and a thin trail of water channeled listlessly from his fingertips.

"What happened to you?" I asked urgently. "We've been searching for you for days. Did they take you from camp? We heard nothing, but there was blood. Did they hurt you?"

"I smashed my elbow on the rocks when I tried to get away." He lifted it for me to see. There was a bloodied gash on his right elbow. "Something grabbed me—clamped something down over my mouth. I couldn't see it. I could smell sweat and hear breathing, but I couldn't see anything…"

Rafael began to stand slowly, extending his arms until the palms of his hands were pressed against the bars. He trembled as he began to cautiously search around him as if looking for something.

"Rafael, what is this place?" I asked urgently, pressing closer up against the bars. "Who kidnapped you and brought you here? Have you seen them yet?"

Raf's eyes slowly returned to my own, still bearing that same eerie hollowness.

"I haven't seen anything," he began, his voice an unsteady whisper. "I haven't seen anyone."

My brow furrowed with confusion. "Someone must come in here and check on you from time to time."

"In here?" he repeated, his eyes glossy, as he shook his head back and forth again. "In here, Sparrow? Are we in some sort of building?"

I stared at him, thunderstruck.

"Raf, can't you see any of it?" I whispered. "The walls, the hallway— the cells?"

Rafael blinked and squinted, extending his arms again to take a few careful steps around his cell. He started slightly when his hands hit the wall to his right.

"This is a wall?"

My throat was tight with a lump that was forming there. "Raf, can you see *me*?"

He staggered carefully back in my direction until his fingertips finally grazed the bars, and he gripped them. He leaned his cheek to the cold metal, tears welling in his eyes.

"Sparrow, you are the first thing I have seen in days."

"You can't see the rest?"

"I see darkness, Sparrow," he answered softly. "Darkness, and now you. That is all I see."

A strange, sinking feeling settled into my gut. I backed away from the bars, beginning to pace.

"And Janna?" I asked. "What about her?"

"Janna?" Raf's voice trembled. "How many of us have been taken?"

*He didn't even know about her...*

"Three," I said finally. "You, me, and Janna."

"The others aren't safe." His voice rose, cracking. "They're going to go back for them! They're picking us off one by one, Sparr. Do you really think they'll stop now? Do you really think they'll let the others get away?" Raf slowly shook his head. "They know where we are. They're watching us all the time."

"And who are *they*?"

"I don't know." Rafael swallowed, blinking back tears. "You're the one who can see them, Sparrow…" He trailed off, seemingly lost in thought. Then his eyes locked on mine again with a sense of urgency. "You can't let them know, Sparrow," he whispered. "You can't ever let them know that you can see them."

I thought back to the night before—to the soldier I'd stared right in the eyes and tried desperately to escape from.

"What do you think would happen if they knew I could see them?" My voice was almost inaudible. "What do you think they would do?"

Before he could respond, a loud groaning sound echoed down the concrete hallway. Rafael lurched back, stumbling to the floor. I sat down against the wall, staring blankly ahead.

Damp, sticky thuds of footsteps drew nearer. I held my breath, tipping my head back to pinch my eyes shut.

*Click… click… click…*

And then suddenly they stopped. I heard a soft bleeping and then a dull grinding as the door retracted and the steel bars rolled aside. Slowly, I opened my eyes, forcing myself to just keep staring straight ahead. In my peripheral vision I could see a pair of boots, caked in powdery white dust, stride steadily over and halt in front of me. I could see only the lower parts of his arms. He extended a club and firmly placed the end of it under my chin, tipping my face upward. Now I could see his face.

He was short, hunched, and missing several teeth. Keys jangled on his belt.

"Another stupid kid. My god," he muttered, more to himself than to me. Reaching down, he grabbed me by the back of the neck and yanked me to my feet. I let out a yelp of pain, writhing in his grasp.

"Be still, or I'll beat you as hard as I beat him." He jerked his head towards Rafael's cell. "I will have silence."

My teeth clenched; my stomach lurched as though I might throw up.

"What the hell is *wrong* with you?" I exploded. "He's a *child*."

The guard pressed the end of his club more tightly under my chin and leaned into my face. I felt his hot breath on my skin.

"You will soon learn that every word you speak comes with consequences."

For a moment he held me there on my tiptoes, club to my throat. Then he jerked me forward, dragging me out of the cell and down the hallway after him.

"Sparrow!" Rafael cried, clutching the bars of his cell. "No! No, you can't take her! *Sparrow!*"

The guard tightened his grip, his fingers tangling in my hair as he dragged me forward, sending me stumbling over my own feet. The hallway ended at a large metal door. The guard swiped a hand through the air, and a keypad appeared. I watched out of the corner of my eye as he typed. A second later I heard a deadbolt retract, and the door swung open. I squinted against the harsh morning sunlight.

He moved the club to the back of my neck and forced my head down. As I stumbled along, the crusty ground passed beneath my feet in a blur and then changed abruptly to a wooden walking path—and I soon saw why. The strange white rocky ground was now freckled with pockets of boiling mud and pools of iridescent, teal-colored water. The guard kept marching me along; it was a while before I dared to even look up, but when I did, I felt my eyes widen in spite of myself.

All around me were thick concrete walls crowned with barbed wire, encompassing several square miles of rocky, almost volcanic-looking terrain. A long dirt road ran down the center of the area, winding around sections of bubbling ground that were closed off by makeshift fences. On either side of the dirt road were small, dilapidated cinderblock shacks, sprayed with mud and caked with dust.

Far in the distance I could see a structure that had been built around what looked like a cone-shaped geyser. A huge funnel-shaped roof connected it to the looming structure, which boasted three tall smokestacks, all of which seemed to be pumping steam into the air. A smell like rotting eggs hung thickly around us as we trudged forward. The guard lowered my head again with the club.

Engulfed in anger and fear, I was beginning to feel my fingertips heating up, trembling slightly with the will to channel an orb and blast it into his face. I started silently coaching myself: *Don't lose it, don't lose it, don't lose it.* Yet it wasn't my own voice I heard in my head; it was Keegan's.

We stepped off the boardwalk and onto the dirt road, where my captor shoved me in front of him, still keeping a hand clamped down on my shoulder. I kept my gaze soft and empty as we walked. Several equally muddy figures stepped out of a few of the shacks, watching silently as I passed. They were all dressed in gray uniforms, and I could feel their eyes burning right through me.

The guard jerked me to the left just before we reached the giant factory-like structure with the smokestacks, stopping at a cement building that stood out among the long row of shacks. This one had bars on the windows and a lock on the door.

I swallowed as we stopped in front of it, and my stomach filled with dread as my captor twisted keys in multiple locks. When all the bolts had retracted, he eased the door open.

In contrast to the daylight, it was dark inside the building, which was lit only by the shafts of light coming in through the two small dirty windows on either side of it. The guard shoved me hard into the dank interior, and I fell to the floor, landing on my hands and knees. The guard stomped in after me, halting.

"I have Sparrow," he announced. "Per your request."

I kept my eyes down. I began to feel warm blood rising to the surfaces of my scuffed palms.

"Leave us, Mooney," a deep, husky voice replied.

My throat tightened as the guard marched back over the threshold, slamming the door shut behind him. I kept my eyes fixed on the floor, still breathing hard.

The sound of a chair scuffing back over the floor cut through the quiet. Then footsteps; heavy boots came into my line of sight. I tensed, expecting to be grabbed and dragged to my feet again. But this time, a hand extended into the space in front of me; I saw smooth, dark skin washed in the vague traces of dusty sunlight.

"It's all right," he assured me when I flinched. "I'm not going to hurt you."

Swallowing hard, I reached out, pretending to feel around before my hand clasped his. He helped me to my feet, and finally, I lifted my face. I looked past him, as if I couldn't see. But I *could* see him, and I recognized those dark eyes immediately. He leaned a little closer.

"There's no need to pretend." His voice softened to a whisper. "I know you can see me... *Sparrow.*"

# 36

SLOWLY MY EYES LOCKED WITH HIS. HE WAS BLACK, WITH A craggy jawline and a crew cut, lips that were like hewn stone. Tall and handsome, he couldn't have been more than twenty-five. He was dressed differently from the rest—no uniform. Just black pants and a sage green shirt. A tattoo peeked out from the underside of one of his large, muscled biceps.

"Who are you, and what is this place?" I kept my voice steady.

For a long moment, he didn't answer. He just stared at me like I was the first person he'd ever seen in his life. Stepping back a few paces, he yanked the chair out from under the table, two of the only items in the sparsely furnished room. He nodded for me to have a seat. When I didn't budge, he pulled the chair closer and sat down himself, folding his hands on his knees.

He looked at me for a moment longer, that same, almost shocked expression still on his face.

"My name is Corporal Price." He cleared his throat, seeming to snap out of it. "And you're in District Firehole, an RGM prison camp."

My jaw tensed, and a cold feeling settled in my gut. "And you work here?" I asked.

He rendered a slow nod.

"Why are there bars over the windows, then?"

He leaned forward a little, still staring at me, stupefied. "Before I answer that, I have a question for you: how the hell are you seeing me right now?"

"I don't know," I answered flatly. "I don't know how I can see you—how I can see any of it…"

My voice splintered, and I stopped, placing a hand to my lips. The corporal stared at me long and hard, the muscles in his jaw twitching.

"Does…" he began, then trailed off. "Does anyone else know that you can see us?"

I swallowed, slowly shaking my head.

The corporal seemed to consider the fact for a long moment. "Good," he announced at last. "Keep it that way. Bask will kill you if he finds out."

"Bask?"

"My commander."

"And you won't?" I inquired.

He was quiet for a moment as he studied me; then he shook his head. "No. Not yet."

"And why's that?"

His expression hardened. "Reasons you wouldn't understand."

I tipped my chin up slightly, looking down at him. "You do realize I could leave at any time, don't you? I can see—I could blast an orb through that wall over there, obliterate you, and leave all this behind."

"But you wouldn't," he countered. "Because then we would kill your friends."

"I'm pretty sure that's what you're planning to do anyway."

Fire flaring in his eyes, Corporal Price stood, closing the gap between us. My heart hammered in my chest as the gears in my head spun wildly.

"I have something you want," I began slowly. "I have the ability to see you, to see this place. You want to know why. You want to understand me.

And the only way that will ever happen is if I talk."

After a hesitation, the corporal nodded.

"I'll make a deal with you," I said softly.

I felt him tense; he was still staring into my face. For a moment I thought he would punch me, but instead he just drew a narrow breath. "What is your requirement?"

"Rafael and Janna's release," I replied. "Or I'll break out of this place, and you'll never see me again."

It was total bullshit—I could barely channel at will, never mind use my abilities to break out of a prison camp. But he didn't need to know that.

"Don't try to escape, Sparrow," he said finally, in a low voice. There was something sincere in his tone this time. "You won't succeed in anything beyond getting yourself killed."

"I guess that's the risk I'm willing to take," I replied, still watching him closely. "Not that it would be any skin off your nose, would it, Corporal?"

His eyes hardened, but I held my ground, and after a moment I could tell he was thinking.

"I don't have to comply with your demands," he said finally.

"You do if you want me to put up no resistance."

He chuckled. "As if I would take you at your word."

"I swear," I insisted, my voice going hoarse. "I'll do whatever you ask if you let them both go."

The corporal slowly walked the length of the room to the window, where he stopped and looked out. The distant grumble of machinery and engines filled the gap in the discussion.

"The boy probably won't live for much longer…" he said to himself, thinking aloud. "It would be no great loss to turn him out into the woods to die. But not the girl—we still have a lot to gain from her."

He turned back to me. "And if I do this for you, you will be indebted to me." His words were tense and quiet. "Not to the RGM, not to Bask, but to me personally."

The hairs on the back of my neck rose as I stood there in silence.

He narrowed his eyes. "Do you understand?"

I hesitated a moment longer before answering, "Yes." My voice came out strained. "Yes, I understand."

The corporal gave a stiff nod, folding his hands together behind his back.

"Good," he said flatly. "You can leave the boy to me, then."

My fingers trembled as they curled into fists. "How will you—"

"There's nothing you need to know about it." Price cut me off coldly. "Only that the boy will be gone when the sun rises."

The guard, Mooney, held a fistful of my hair as he dragged me down the echoing halls of the containment lab—that was what had been printed on the sign outside the door. He pushed me in front of him, past numerous empty cells. I was beginning to realize, given Price's words, that Rafael and I were the only ones incarcerated in this particular facility. I couldn't help but wonder where they had Janna locked up.

I began to hear Rafael stumbling around in his cell, calling out and slamming up against the bars as we drew closer. His blue eyes were bloodshot and welling with tears, but a glimmer of hope still flashed in them when he saw me.

"Sparrow!" he yelled, his voice cracking. "Sparrow, are you all right?"

"Yes," I said through gritted teeth, then urged him with my eyes to be silent. I deliberately stumbled over my own feet as we passed his cell, as if I couldn't see where we were going.

Mooney opened the door of my cell and shoved me inside. I stumbled forward, falling to my hands and knees. I heard the bars rattle shut behind me.

When I was sure he was gone, I scrambled across the floor and pressed my face through the bars.

"Rafael, listen to me," I hissed, shooting a glance down the hallway. "You're leaving."

Rafael stared at me, looking thunderstruck. "W-w-what?"

"You're leaving," I repeated.

"How is that possible?"

"That's not important," I whispered. "What's important is that I'm getting you out of this place, Raf—I'm getting you back to them. And I need…" I trailed off, shooting another quick glance around. "I need you to find Keegan and tell him something for me, okay?"

He nodded despondently.

"I need you to tell him that I'm all right… that everything will be all right." My throat tightened around the words. "I need you to tell him that I found a cavern in the forest, where we camped before you disappeared. Do you remember?"

He nodded, but looked puzzled.

"I'm not sure if I was awake or dreaming, but I… I found something there. Something I can't explain… I need to know if Keegan can find it too."

Rafael looked at me intently. "What did you find there?"

I thought back to the day, the dream… the door in the cave and the ravine beyond it. With my face still pressed against the cold bars, I shook my head slowly. "I don't have the words to describe it…" I whispered back. "But there was something about it… something important."

He didn't say a word; he just kept staring at me with that same puzzled look on his pale face.

"Promise me you'll tell him," I urged.

Rafael's eyes welled with tears. "I don't want to leave you, Sparrow," he whispered. "I don't want to leave you here."

Though a lump was forming in my throat, I forced a brave smile.

"Don't worry about me. I'll find a way out of here, Raf." My voice cracked a little. "I promise."

# 37

WHEN I CLOSED MY EYES, I FELT KATERI'S HAND CLOSE around mine. The dark woods around us faded. There was no sight or sound, just us, huddled around Rafael. Being the only one able to transport without a portal, I led the transportation, I forced myself to focus on the Homestead. On the barn tucked away behind it. On the gardens and the sprawling green acres of pines, oaks and birches. On the birds that filled them with chorusing song.

It was home. It was all I'd ever known. Yet the fact that we were returning early, against orders—without Raf and Janna and, most of all, without Sparrow, whom I'd sworn to Dad I would protect—was unbearable.

My eyes stung when I finally opened them again. The air warmed around us, and the texture of the ground had shifted beneath our feet. I let go of Kateri's hand to lift Rafael from the ground and into my arms. The air was thick, and gray clouds crowded the sky.

"Keeg?" Kateri's voice pulled me out of my thoughts.

I'd yet to step forward. Preston and Myung were already running ahead, but I felt frozen as I stood there with Rafael hanging lifelessly in my arms. My eyes were burning as I stared at the Homestead from the edge of the woods; the woods were now alive and awake around us. They seemed loud in comparison to the silence of the dead forests we'd spent so many days wandering.

The house stood among the trees as peacefully as ever, seemingly unchanged. How different I felt in contrast.

I pushed myself forward, following Kateri to the house. By the time we reached the porch, the screen door swung open, and Lara met us there. Her eyes were full of fear, widening as she took us in and then freezing on Rafael.

"My god," she breathed, stumbling aside and holding the door wide for us. "What happened? Where are Sparrow and Janna?"

My voice having already vanished, I let Kateri do the talking; I couldn't think straight. With one last glance over my shoulder as the screen door swung shut, I could only think of one thing: Sparrow was still out there.

Dad emerged from the hallway just as I walked in. When he saw Rafael in my arms, he rushed over.

"Did you heal him?" was the first question out of his mouth.

I shook my head. "I don't know what's wrong with him."

Dad slid his arms under Rafael's body and lifted him into his arms, his eyes connecting briefly with my own as he turned and started for the staircase. I began to follow him, but Lara grabbed me by the arm before I could get very far, pulling me aside. She held onto my shoulders and looked me in the eyes.

"Are *you* okay?"

I forced a nod, closing my eyes to evade hers. "I'm better off than some of us."

Lara leaned in closer, her wide eyes full of terror. "What happened?"

"We don't know—none of us saw anything," I said, and then forced out a miserable sigh. "Except for Sparrow, but now she's gone too, she and Janna both. We searched everywhere for both of them and found nothing…”

Lara staggered back a step, catching herself on the kitchen counter. “My god… and Raf?”

“We found him lying in the woods, left for dead.”

“And you have no idea what happened to him?”

“None.”

Lara’s face drained of color. Kateri came up behind me, setting a hand on my shoulder.

“Our only hope is that Rafael recovers, and that he can tell us what happened and where the others are.”

“He will recover.” Kateri spoke up gently. “I know he will.”

I said nothing, and neither did Lara. She remained leaning against the counter with her fingers wrapped tightly around the edge. I could hear the muffled sounds of Dad’s footsteps on the floor above.

“I can’t believe it…” Lara whispered. “I just can’t believe something like this could have happened…”

I backed away from Kateri’s touch, unable to stand there any longer. I bolted up the stairs, quickly striding down the hallway and bursting into the bedroom Preston, Raf, and I shared. The doorknob slipped from my fingertips, and the door hit the wall with a bang.

Dad was kneeling on the floor beside Rafael, whom he’d laid on the lower bunk. He brushed back Raf’s curly black hair and laid a hand on his forehead. He lifted a hand, focusing open one of the windows to let the fresh forest air waft in.

“I’m so sorry, Dad,” I said at last, unable to keep it in any longer. “I’ve failed you.”

Dad continued stroking Raf’s forehead for a moment. “This has nothing to do with you.”

“It has everything to do with me,” I argued. “I know the woods better than he does; I should have protected him.”

“You cannot blame yourself,” Dad responded softly.

I stepped over the threshold and into the room, quietly closing the door behind me and leaning against it for a moment. He didn’t know about Sparrow or Janna yet; he'd left with Rafael before any of us had had a chance to explain.

"You were right," Dad said again after a moment. "There's nothing broken. This is trauma… He's been beaten. Who did this?"

"We have no idea. We saw nothing. He was taken in the night. We found him in the woods like this, days later…" I trailed off. "Sparrow… Sparrow saw something—someone—out in the woods." I choked on my own words, shaking my head. "But we… but we didn't believe her, Dad. We didn't trust her until it was too late."

Dad stayed frozen, crouched on the floor by Rafael's bed, staring at me.

"Can you please go downstairs and ask Sparrow to come up?" he asked, his voice heavy but even. "I want to speak with her."

My sweat-slicked hands trembled as I tried to force the words out.

Dad got to his feet and crossed the room to me. "Keegan?"

The familiar, craggy features of Dad's face began to waver behind the blur of tears.

"Keegan," Dad repeated, his voice firm now, "what is it?"

I shook my head slowly, swallowing hard. "Sparrow's not downstairs, Dad."

"Where is she, then?" Dad clamped a hand down on my shoulder, his gaze drilling into my own. "Keegan, *where is she?*"

A hot tear rolled down my cheek. "I don't know, Dad," I whispered, my voice splitting. "We… we lost her—whoever took Raf took her too. Her and Janna both, but we… we never found them."

Dad looked as if he'd just been punched. He sucked in a breath and staggered backward.

"We don't know what happened to them—we searched for them everywhere. Kateri and I searched the woods all day. We tried to…"

My father didn't reply. His back was to me now; he lifted his hands to clutch his head between them. He said nothing for a long time—so long, in fact, that for a moment I began to wonder if he was going to respond at all.

Finally, he did. And when he did, his voice was just as shredded as mine.

"Not Sparrow…"

"Yes." I swallowed hard. "And Janna too."

Dad said nothing, but when he finally turned around, his face was ghostly white and his expression hadn't changed.

"Both of them?" he questioned, sounding winded.

"What *is it* about Sparrow, Dad?" I prodded. "Since the day you brought her here, I have asked myself that question over and over and over again—and I've yet to be able to answer it…" I trailed off and looked him in the eyes. "I know she's not a healer—but I know she's not just an ordinary student, either. What is it about Sparrow that you're not telling me—that you're not telling any of us?"

For a moment Dad just stood there, holding his head in his hands as if frozen.

Finally, he began to speak again. "Everything I have told you, and everything I have kept back," he began, strained, "has been to protect her… because you are right about one thing, Keegan: she is no ordinary student."

"Who is she, then?"

Dad's eyes rested wearily on mine.

"Sparrow is Hawk and Icarus's daughter, Keegan," Dad answered quietly. "She is the daughter of the Sunrise and the Sunset."

# 38

MY EYES SLOWLY PEELED OPEN. I WAS ONCE AGAIN IN A cell, but this one was different. They had moved me; I was below ground now, in what seemed like a dungeon. The ceiling and walls dripped with condensation; the ground jolted beneath me, shaking as a distant roar like water ripped through the air, pounding through the walls—and through my head, which was splitting.

I wrestled myself up to my hands and knees, squinting to see in the dim light that filtered down from a narrow slot close to the ceiling. My conversation with Corporal Price wove through my thoughts. All I could think about was Rafael and whether or not he'd escaped with his life. I had to know whether he'd escaped—whether Price had kept his word.

Cautiously getting to my feet, I made my way over to the barred door. My fingers wrapped once again around cold iron as I leaned my face through, peering into the darkness.

"Hello?" I called into what looked like a tunnel. "Hello, is anyone there? Hello!"

For a few seconds the only replies were the ghostly echoes of my own voice, ricocheting off the walls and fading away. There was a stiff silence and then, finally, the jangle of keys. I held my breath and my ground, leaning farther through the gap between the bars. After a moment, the shadows cleared around the form of a soldier, a small man with a shaved head and a round face. He strode down the corridor, halted in front of me, and studied me through eyes like ice. I stared straight ahead, pretending I couldn't see.

"You shouldn't be talking," he muttered.

"I have to talk to the corporal," I blurted, then stopped. "That is, Corporal Price."

The man's face remained steady for a moment; then he snorted a laugh, his lips curling back slightly to reveal rotted teeth.

"*Corporal* Price, is it? Well, well." He chuckled mirthlessly and then lowered his voice to a grumble. "What do you want with him?"

"Something I can only discuss with him," I answered firmly. "It's urgent."

He grunted. "Not much is urgent down here."

"*Please,*" I pleaded with him. "I *have* to talk to him."

The guard stared at me, then finally yielded a nod. "I'll see what I can do."

He was already beginning to walk away when I stopped him again.

"W-w-what is that sound?"

"Sound?"

"That horrible roaring. The ground started shaking, and—"

He broke into heinous laughter before I'd even finished, then coughed into his elbow.

"It's just the geyser," he said. "Don't worry."

Before I could say another word, he turned on his heels and walked away, vanishing once more into the shadows. My hands shook as my fingers wound more tightly around the iron bars. I stood there with my cheek pressed to the metal as the floor continued to tremble beneath me. I waited and waited, unsure of how much time was passing. Finally, I heard the sound of keys jangling and heavy boots once more in the passageway.

I straightened as Corporal Price emerged from the darkness. His shoulders were back and his jaw was set. I waited a moment to see if the guard was following him.

"I'm alone," he said, as if reading my thoughts.

My fingers gripped the bars tightly. "Rafael…"

He placed a finger to his lips, stepping closer and waiting a moment before lowering his voice to answer.

"It's done," he whispered.

"Was he all right?"

"Far from," he answered quietly. "As I said, I doubt he'll last the night."

I swallowed hard, lowering my gaze. "What are they going to do with me?"

"What the RGM does with every slider we get our hands on—squeeze them for what we can and then dispose of them," he said flatly, then lowered his voice. "Though freeing Rafael is of little consequence to me, I can assure you that you will be made to pay for it."

"Me?"

He scanned my face dubiously. "What, do you think they would suspect *me*, Sparrow?" His eyes didn't move from mine as he slowly shook his head. "You are the one they will suspect. I'm not a sympathizer."

My throat tightened as I leaned closer to him. "Then why are you helping me?"

"There are some things you could never understand, Sparrow. Things you would never believe if I told you."

I swallowed hard, staring into his eyes as he studied my face.

"For now, cooperate with them as best you can," he went on quietly. "Let them think you're just as blind as the others we've captured."

"Cooperate with them?" I repeated hoarsely. "How?"

He reached into the breast pocket of the black jacket he was wearing and pulled out a tattered piece of paper. Unfolding it carefully, he slid it through the bars and into my hands.

"By helping us find what we're looking for."

My throat ran dry as I looked down at the printed page in my hand, a grid of numerous grainy, black-and-white photos of anomalies. My heart began to beat a little faster as I scanned the page and then finally stopped on one photo in particular.

My mouth ran dry.

It was of a young woman with long dark hair. Brown, arching eyebrows, and eyes as deep as the night sky. It wasn't just any photograph. It was *mine*. The photograph of my mother—the one I'd left in my bag that night. The bag that had been left behind in Cal's room. The room of an RGM soldier.

Swallowing hard, I looked down at the name: *Hawk*.

Beneath her name was a price. A reward, *a bounty*.

I couldn't believe it… It was like all my worst nightmares were coming true.

They had her face now—my mother's. And it was all *my* fault.

It was *all* my fault.

I scanned the rest of the photos. My heart sank when I noticed Keegan's: his wild mane of hair, his braid, the feathers. I recognized the lobby of the apartment building in the background. Cal's lodgings.

*The night Keegan rescued me.*

Under his picture were printed the words *Identity unknown. Assailant.* A hefty bounty was printed below his picture, too.

I quickly shook my head, scanning the rest of the page. "No… No— I can't. I won't!"

I closed my eyes, feeling sick. I folded the page and drew a sharp breath, shoving it back through the bars to Corporal Price, whom I could feel watching me closely.

"I don't know any of them," I said, handing the paper back.

When I opened my eyes, he was still regarding me steadily. He took my hand in his own and pushed the slip of paper back into my palm, then closed my fingers around it. "Prove to be useful, Sparrow," he whispered, something strange in his eyes as he took a few steps back. "Give them a reason."

"A reason?" I repeated.

Corporal Price nodded gravely. "To keep you alive."

My stomach sank. Without another word, Corporal Price turned and walked away. Tears welled in my eyes as I listened to his footsteps fade.

The paper shook in my hands as I looked down at it through the tears welling in my eyes. I could take only a few steps before I crumpled against the wall, sliding down to my knees and burying my face in my hands. The tiny cell filled with the echoes of my sobs. My face burned, and pain surged through my head. I gasped for air and lowered my face to the cold, wet floor, resting it there, my tears trickling to the floor to mix with the condensation.

Minutes passed like hours. I had no idea how much time had gone by, but finally I couldn't cry anymore. There was nothing left inside me. The roar of the geyser had died away, leaving the room washed in silence.

Within that silence, however, something else began to stir. Slowly I lifted my face from the floor, straining to see through the one narrow shaft of sunlight that separated me from the shadows on the other side of the cell.

At first, there was a soft sound like breathing, then movement. Then finally, a voice. "Why are you crying?"

I started a little, realizing, even through the clouds of grief, that I was not alone in the cell.

"Because I… I have lost everything," I whispered hoarsely, blinking. "Everything I didn't even know I had… Everything I didn't even know I was…" I trailed off, my voice splintering. I pressed my fingers to my mouth, my eyes welling with tears again.

There was a long silence from the shadows. For a moment I began to question whether someone had actually spoken or whether it had just been a figment of my imagination. But then it came again.

"You have lost hope, then?"

I swallowed, wiping at my tears again and climbing to my feet.

"W-who are you?" My jaw trembled as I stood there in the blade of dusty light, staring into the shadows before me. "S-s-show yourself."

"Answer my question first," came the steady, deep voice again, rising and echoing as powerfully as the raging water had. It filled the cell and rattled in my chest. "Have you lost hope?"

I stood there, breathless, shaking, straining my eyes to see.

"Yes…" I finally whispered, my voice small and broken. "Yes… I have."

A wave of silence washed over the cell again. The shadows were empty and quiet. But then, slowly, something moved forward, seeming to take form even as it stepped closer: a figure—a man. Quietly, gently, he stepped into the light. An old Asian man. His face was wrinkled and weathered, but it shone like the sun.

I stared at him, and he stared back at me through gentle, shining eyes.

"Well then, young one," he said softly, "we must find it again."

# PART TWO

# 39

I CAN STILL REMEMBER THE DAY I GRADUATED FROM RGM training like it happened yesterday. I can still remember the electricity in the air—my heart beating so fast it threatened to burst through my uniform.

We were lined up in formation, and our families and friends surrounded us. The band played, and black confetti showered down on us. I can still remember the roar of the crowd and the beat of the drums as we marched. It was late spring, overcast and drizzling tainted rain, yet the dismal backdrop couldn't dampen the fire inside me.

I was finally an RGM soldier. It was all I'd ever dreamed of, all I'd ever wanted.

As we halted in the middle of the pavement in front of the stadium, my eyes scanned the thousands of faces, searching for one in particular. When I found my mother's face in the crowd, a tide of emotions flooded my chest.

She was afraid. I could see the fear in her eyes. Like so many of the other parents, whose Frags no longer functioned, they could think and feel outside the RGM's influence now, and therefore they were afraid: afraid of what could happen to us. Because of the system's collapse, newborns were no longer Fragged—I didn't have a Frag, but I wasn't afraid. I wished I could tell my mother not to worry, that everything would be fine, even if it wasn't in the end. Even if I died, it would be for that supreme purpose to which I had already pledged myself.

And so I stood tall with my shoulders back as I listened intently to my commander's voice.

"Soldiers." He addressed us by our newly appointed title. "Though it may seem that you have, at last, reached the end of your training—that you have finally crossed the finish line and emerged into the promised land—do not be deceived. For you have only just begun. This is not the end of your training. This is, in fact, the very beginning of what will be the hardest next few years of your life…"

He paused, scrutinizing the young men and women in front of him with an expression of stone.

"We live in a time of war—a war that you have inherited. Anomalies have dismantled what our founders spent decades trying to establish—a system of equality. A level playing field, with equal knowledge for all. The anomalies have destroyed this." Our commander gazed steadily out at all of us. "They have disrupted a delicate balance and have destroyed many of us in the process…"

My teeth clenched, a fire sparking in my chest. My mother was still looking at me, and this time I knew we were both thinking about the same thing: the empty seat next to her, the seat where Dad should have been.

The clear, strong voice of my commander seemed suddenly to mute as my thoughts ebbed away from the graduation, transporting me back one year ago to the day.

The gray sky had wept as it did now. The quiet knock on the door had echoed through the house like a siren. I'd been the one to answer it, to find the officer standing there, holding my dad's black RGM helmet under one arm.

I can still remember how my mother cried when she came down the stairs and saw the officer standing there. How she had cried again the next day when I'd signed up.

Tears filled my own eyes as I stood there, back straight and shoulders square, listening intently to my commander speak of the hellfire we would be heading into.

"… and so we send you to reestablish order, peace, and sanctity." My commander's voice clasped my attention once more. "We send you out into chaos to make sense of it—to cleanse Earth of parasites that jeopardize its progress. We have equipped and groomed you for everything you are going to encounter out there. We've done our part, and now you must do yours."

A unified, uproarious shout went up from all of us. My body trembled as the battle cry rattled in my throat.

I imagined my dad sitting there, watching me graduate, stern eyes fixed on mine, rich black skin, a perfectly starched uniform, and a stony brow. I thought of what I would have told him if he were there that day: that I would kill as many of them as I could. My fingers stiffened and curled into fists as I stood there, angry and burning and determined.

The confetti showered down around me, and the crowd roared as we once again began to march. When I looked back to my mother, I noticed that a man had sat down in the seat next to her, an old black man with weathered skin, white hair and a wiry beard. His eyes met mine from across the pavement. I hadn't seen him arrive, and I had no idea who he was, but as I marched, a strange feeling filled my gut. I turned away from him and focused on my comrades as we proceeded around the stadium one final time and came to a halt to be dismissed by our commander. When I looked back up, the man was gone. The seat beside my mother was once again empty.

After the ceremony, I immediately headed for the reception area, scanning the crowd until my eyes caught on my mother. She was wearing a dark blue dress, and her sandy hair flowed over her shoulders. When I strode up to her, she planted a kiss on my cheek.

"Private Aaron Price." She smiled proudly.

"Who was that man?" I asked her before she could even congratulate me. "The old man sitting in the seat next to you?"

She stared at me for a moment, confused. "What man?"

"The old man in the seat next to you," I insisted, glancing around to see if I could find him among the crowd. "He came in about halfway through."

My mother thought about it and then shook her head. "There was no one sitting next to me."

"Yes, there was."

The puzzled expression on her face remained. She shook her head. "No, there was no one."

"No one?" I reiterated, an uneasy feeling rising in my stomach. "No one, the whole time?"

My mother nodded, looking up into my eyes, concerned. "Why, Aaron?" she asked. "Did you see someone?"

Yes. I had. And little did I know it would not be the last time. Little did I know that the strange face I had seen in the crowd would haunt and, eventually, *destroy* me. Little did I know he would turn me into that which I despised.

"No," I had finally answered. "No, I didn't see anyone."

# 40

RAIN DRIZZLED FROM THE DARK GRAY SKY. ITS EARTHY scent mingled with the aroma of freshly split cedar as I positioned another log on the old stump in front of me. Drops of water rolled down my face as I raised the ax over my shoulder and swung it down. The log split and fell to the ground. I picked up the pieces, threw them into the pile of chopped wood, and grabbed another. I lifted the ax again and slammed it down, chopping the log in half. Again and again and again.

The cool rain felt good on my face. I heard the kitchen window creak open.

"Keeg?"

Lara waited until I turned to look at her. Her blonde hair hung messily around her face, and her eyes were filled with concern. She rested her elbows on the windowsill, leaning there as she looked out at me.

She didn't say anything else; she didn't have to. I knew that look.

"I'm fine, Lara," I said, looking back down at the log. "I'm fine."

I could still feel her watching me as I carried an armload of wood over to the stack. I dumped it there, resting my hands on the rough, wet wood as I stared out at the fog-blanketed forest for a moment. I walked back to the front of the house, making my way through the garden.

I peeled off my soaked shirt and rolled it into a ball under my arm, swinging the screen door open and stepping into the cabin. I pulled off my wet moccasin boots and ditched them at the door. My bare, damp feet clung to the floor as I walked across the quiet, empty room and down the hallway. I paused at the door to Dad's office, grasped the cold doorknob, turned it, and eased the door open. White light rinsed through the windows and over Dad's desk; papers and plants and other things were scattered across it. Dad was nowhere to be seen.

I emerged from the hallway just as Kateri descended the steps. "Keegan, there you are. I was just about to head out into the woods." She came to a stop in front of me, her soft eyes focused on mine. Her brown arms were folded over her long tunic shirt, and her hair hung over her shoulders in double braids. "You want to come? I could really use you."

I lowered my gaze to the floor as I shook my head. "Is Preston free? I'm sure he'd be happy to go."

"Preston's been going out there with me almost every day for the past two weeks, Keeg," she responded, quieting her voice as she stepped closer, looking up into my eyes with a serious expression. "When am I going to get *you* back?"

Before I could respond, Preston descended the stairs, calling Kateri's name. He stopped when he saw us standing there.

"Hey," he said. "Are we heading out?"

His gaze switched back and forth between Kateri and me.

"*We* are," she answered, starting for the door. "Keegan has other things to do."

Preston stared after her until the screen door shut. Then his gaze returned to me.

I put up a hand before he could say anything.

"Don't," I said numbly. "Please don't."

Preston frowned and then turned and followed Kateri out the door. I started for the stairs.

When I reached the door to the room I shared with Preston and Rafael, it was closed. Standing there for a moment, listening, I could hear the quiet tones of Dad's voice as he read to Rafael.

A door creaked open farther down the hallway. I glanced over just as Lara stepped out of the girls' room.

"Any change?" I asked as she came up to me.

Lara brushed her hair back off her forehead and sighed. "No, not really."

The sinking feeling in my gut only increased.

"Your dad's in there with him now," she continued when I didn't say anything. "You're welcome to go in, if you want to spend some time with Raf."

"No, that's okay," I answered quickly. "I was actually going to ask what else I could do to help you."

"I was actually hoping you'd gone out with Kateri."

I shot her a look. "Did you put her up to that?"

Lara hesitated, then sighed, nodding. "Someone had to."

I rubbed a hand over my face, not sure what to say.

"Keegan, it's been two weeks," Lara said quietly. "Why don't you move back inside?"

I shook my head fiercely, gesturing toward the door.

"Do you think I can handle seeing him like this?" I asked, my voice a broken whisper. "Do you think I can handle it—knowing that it's my fault?"

"How is it your fault?"

"I was supposed to be the leader, wasn't I?" I said, more to myself than to her. "I was supposed to keep everyone safe and together. I failed miserably."

Lara placed a hand on my shoulder. "Keegan, look at me. Look…"

Finally, I dragged my gaze up to meet hers.

"You did *everything* you could. But sometimes things happen, things that are beyond our control. Things that aren't our fault or anyone else's."

"But some things *are* our fault." My voice rose a little and cracked. "And we *are* the ones to blame."

Lara didn't reply. I turned and walked back downstairs.

I could feel my arms around her, the warmth of her body against my own, and when I inhaled, her scent filled my lungs. Her eyelashes were like butterfly wings against her cheeks, her hair like rivers as dark as night. Her head rested on my shoulder and her hand on my chest. I didn't dare breathe.

Her name filled my thoughts and tingled in my throat. There was so much I wanted to say—so much I wanted to tell her. In that moment there was nothing but her soft, warm skin under my fingertips. Her body against mine.

When I woke up, she was gone.

I opened my eyes to find the roof of the barn stretched out above me. My fingers clenched around fistfuls of hay, and my heart sank as reality hit me. It was just another dream.

I hadn't meant to fall asleep in the hay. I'd just shut my eyes for a moment, exhausted.

I rolled onto my side, reaching over to run a hand through the soft lump of fur stretched out beside me. Cub stirred a little and rolled over onto her back, inviting me to rub her belly. She'd apparently decided that I was her soul mate, sleeping by my side each night and typically waking me each morning with a startling pounce. But right now, she still lay slumbering—not surprising given that it wasn't morning: it was afternoon.

I brushed the hay off my clothing as I got to my feet, stepping carefully around grazing rabbits and the foxes playing rough and tumble in the piles of straw. Grabbing a rake from the corner, I started cleaning up, trying to brush off the haunting dream.

I'd been the last one to see Sparrow, to catch a glimpse of the invisible force that had taken her. Dad, Lara, Kateri, and I had transported back to the place where she'd disappeared, searching everywhere for any trace of her or Janna. But our efforts had yielded nothing new; there was no trace of either one of them.

And so we'd come back to the Homestead, hoping that Rafael had awakened and could tell us where Janna and Sparrow were. But when we had returned, we'd found him just as we'd left him: still unconscious and in the grip of an illness none of us could seem to heal. Dad spent his days taking care of Rafael, and I spent mine trying to drown out the regret that haunted me day and night, along with Dad's words:

*"Sparrow is the daughter of the Sunrise and the Sunset."*

I had poured my heart and soul out to Sparrow, things I'd never before revealed to anyone. I felt like I knew her, yet I now realized that all that time, she'd still been a closed book. I'd just been too blinded by the fire that ignited inside me every time we were together to see it. Dad had made her swear not to reveal her identity, but something in me still wrestled with the fact that she hadn't trusted me enough to tell me the truth.

Sparrow knew me, but I didn't know her at all. Yet, every time I closed my eyes, she was there.

I'd started sleeping in the barn with the animals. I couldn't bear to see Raf lying there, day after day after day—reduced to a frail body trapped in a coma. I couldn't bear to hear the silence that came when I was alone in the bedroom with him, watching the sheets rise and fall as he lay there, a bucket underneath his hand to catch the water that drizzled from his fingertips.

As bad off as he was, he was better off than Sparrow and Janna— wherever they were. There was no way for us to know until Rafael woke up… *if* Rafael…

I shoved the thoughts out of my head, focusing on the rake in my hands as I swept it back and forth over the barn floor, sweeping the scattered straw into a pile.

*Where is she? What happened to her?*

Finishing with one more violent stroke of the rake, I stopped, clasping my hands over the top of the handle and resting my forehead there. I could feel the cool shape of the invisible bullet in my pocket. I carried it with me every day. No one could figure it out—not Dad, or Lara, or any of us.

But then, *no one* could see invisible things. No one except Sparrow, it seemed… though no one had believed her.

The door creaked softly open behind me, and I started.

"Thought you might be in here." Preston closed the door behind him.

I started moving the rake across the floor again. "Did you need something?"

"Yeah, I do need something." He was standing there with his arms folded firmly over his sweatshirt. "I need *you* back."

I dropped my gaze to the ground and started raking again, harder this time.

"Listen to me." He took a step closer. "It's not like I don't know, okay? I know what it feels like—hell. *I know.* I lost Janna, Keeg… I mean, we all did, but…"

"I know what you mean," I said, saving him from having to explain. "But it wasn't your fault that she…" I swallowed the rest, shaking my head. "It wasn't your fault."

"Yeah? Well, I'm the one who told her she had to stay, even when she begged to go back."

"You were just trying to keep us together."

"Well, so were you," he said sternly. "Now, you have to stop beating yourself up over this, Keeg. We need you here, *now*—you might not be able to go back in time and change what happened, but you can sure as hell change what's happening *right now*."

Squeezing the handle of the rake in my hands, I straightened up to look at Preston, my jaw square. "I can't heal Rafael! I *have* tried—everyone has tried!"

"Keegan, if you think Rafael is the only one who needs healing…" Preston studied me for a moment, then slowly shook his head. "Think again."

# 41

DISTRICT FIREHOLE LAY BLANKETED IN THE PURPLES OF predawn, speckled with the yellow lights of the lamps hanging outside the doors of the lodging shacks. In the distance, clouds of steam rose against the darkness. Like clockwork, the ground below began to rumble and shake. A few minutes later, the sounds of rushing water and hissing steam erupted from the direction of the factory.

I heard the old man stir in the corner of our cell where he slept, seated and cross-legged. When I looked over, he lifted his head from his chest and blinked his eyes.

Even from here I could see the corporal's shack at the far end of the road. I lowered my head a little as the door to the guard shack on the opposite side of the road burst open. Squinting to see, I recognized the hobbling gait of the toothless guard, Mooney. He wore only suspenders over his bare chest, his belly sagging over his belt. He fumbled in his pockets as he walked.

"What do you see?" the old man asked.

I stared intently past the bars. "Not sure yet."

A tiny flicker of orange illuminated as Toothless lit himself a cigarette and relished a sip of smoke. I ducked behind the window frame as he scanned the dirty shacks, equipment, and tactical vehicles scattered around him. When I looked again a moment later, he was walking away, heading for the corporal's lodgings.

I straightened a little, clutching the bars as I watched.

"Corporal Price told me that Bask would blame me for Rafael's disappearance," I mumbled softly. "Yet he hasn't done anything."

"Bask breaks prisoners before he questions them. It is his way."

"Pfft. He's going to be disappointed, then." I kept my voice low. "What about the corporal—do you know Corporal Price?"

The old man was quiet for a moment before slowly nodding. "Yes, I do," he replied. "But he does not know me."

Puzzled, I turned and shot him a glance. "I've spent weeks in confinement with you, and you still haven't even told me who you are," I reminded him. "Why are you even here? You don't exactly seem like a threat."

"Perhaps not to you, but not everyone sees me the way you do," he replied calmly. "Why were you captured? Because you can see?"

"Shhh!" I hissed.

"You needn't worry," he assured me in that same calm tone. "They cannot hear my voice."

"I think they probably would if you talked a little louder," I countered, which only made him smile.

"I never raise my voice."

"I could teach you how."

"You only ever need to raise your voice to those who do not wish to listen," he explained. "And they will not hear you anyway."

The quiet jangling of keys caught my attention. I turned back to the window. Halting in front of Corporal Price's lodgings, Mooney reached into his pocket with his free hand and pulled out a clanking key ring. Using a series of keys, he unlocked the door, which was bolted in several places. Thinking back, I remembered seeing the locks on the door, though they'd all been undone at the time. *Weird.*

Other doors to other dirty shacks opened now, spitting out shapes of men pulling on shirts and stepping into boots. A few moments later, a shrill whistle blew, and the camp instantly burst to life. The men flowed toward the factory, flanked by overseers who seemed to have been roused by the same signal.

I looked back at the corporal's lodgings. The door had not opened. *Hmm.*

Releasing my grip on the window bars, I dropped back down to the floor. Pressing my hands against the wall, I stood there for a moment, my thoughts racing with questions.

"It makes no sense…" I said to myself. "He's an RGM soldier, yet he's locked into his own lodgings."

"People are not always what they seem to us at first," he said after a moment.

"What do you mean?" I asked.

Old Man was still seated cross-legged on the floor, watching me intently. "I mean that you yourself are evidence of that."

I opened my mouth to speak, but the loud grinding of a door opening cut the silence before I could get a word out.

Instantly I dropped to my hands and knees on the floor, pressing my fingertips to the wall as if to orient myself. The loud clop of boots drew nearer until finally they scuffed to a stop. The cell door creaked open, and the heavy footfalls continued inside until they stopped beside me. Mooney's rough, damp hand seized me by the back of the neck and yanked me to my feet, dragging me out of the cell.

I stumbled in the darkness, pretending I couldn't see a thing. Outside, little orbs of rusty lamplight bobbed and swayed in the purple darkness as if choreographed by the gurgles and bellows of the restless ground. Mooney shoved me wordlessly forward until we reached a particular cement-block building. The door was illuminated by two lamps hanging on either side of the frame.

My toothless captor opened the door and shoved me inside. The interior was dimly lit but lavishly furnished. Burning logs snapped and sparked in the fireplace at the far end of the room beneath a massive mounted bison head. In front of all this was a thick, wood-slab desk. Commander Bask was seated behind it. He had dark, combed-over hair and looked like he was in his forties. His mouth was a stern line beneath his mustache, and his eyes were hard.

"Sparrow, sir, per your request," Mooney announced. Bask lifted a hand, and the guard hastily released me and stepped back outside, closing the door behind him and leaving me alone with the commander.

I stared blankly ahead and waited for him to speak.

"Have a seat," he said finally, closing the book in front of him.

"Where?" I asked.

"Where, *sir*?" he corrected me firmly.

"Where, sir?"

"Exactly where you are."

Slowly, I lowered myself to the floor, settling on my folded legs.

"I presume Corporal Price has told you what we're looking for," Bask began, his voice like steel. "The names and the whereabouts of the other sliders in your group."

My gut twisted. "I believe you think I know more than I do."

He chuckled under his breath. "I believe you *want* me to think that. But know this: your lack of cooperation will result in the execution of your friend."

I was silent.

"Where are the others?" he asked. "How many others are there?"

I drew a narrow breath. "I do not know."

In one swift motion, Bask launched a book across the room. Pain surged through my head as it struck me. I clamped my arms over my head, my gaze fixed on the floor and my heart hammering in my chest.

"How many others?"

"Several," I blurted. "There are… there are seven of us."

"What about the boy? The sick one with the wet hands?"

I didn't respond.

"Do you know how he escaped?"

"I… I cannot see anything… sir," I replied, my voice shaking. "I don't know what happened to him."

Bask said nothing for a long moment.

"Did you hear anything that night?"

"No, sir."

"Are you sure?"

"I was asleep, sir."

I braced a little, expecting him to throw something else.

"Think of your friend Janna, Sparrow," he said finally, leaning back in his leather chair to fold his hands over his stomach. "Consider carefully how much you value her existence."

My thoughts raced along with the adrenaline in my veins. "Where is she?"

"That's none of your concern." Bask's tone was cold and unrelenting. "All you need to do is tell me who leads you, and where your group is located."

I kept my gaze leveled at the floor. "I won't tell you a damn thing."

There was an instant of calm before Bask's angry boots carried him swiftly over the floor. He grabbed me by the jaw and wrenched my face toward him, staring down into my eyes.

"If you don't tell me, so help me, I will *kill* her," he growled into my face. "And then I will take *great* pleasure in killing *you.*"

Everything inside me was shaking as I stared blankly ahead, as if I couldn't see his dark eyes piercing mine, his face reddening as his angry fingers tightened around my jaw.

"Where is the rest of your group?" His voice trembled as he sharply enunciated each word. "Who leads you?"

I clenched my teeth, holding back words I refused to let out.

Grabbing me by the throat, Bask jerked me to my feet and slammed me back into the wall. His eyes were blades piercing my own, seeming to slice right through my facade. I writhed in his grasp, but the vise only tightened.

"Where is the rest of your group?" I felt his spit on my face. "I will stand here and strangle you until you either yield or die," he whispered hoarsely. "Now, which will it be?"

My brain was as chaotic as the pounding of my heart in my chest. I couldn't speak; I couldn't think; I couldn't breathe. The more Bask shouted, the fainter his voice became. A moment later, I faintly heard the door burst open. Muffled sounds of footfalls over the wooden floor.

"Bask! Bask, *let go*…"

The voice ebbed in and out of my hearing as I began to feel my consciousness slipping away.

"Get out of my office—now! This is no concern of—"

"She's worth nothing to us dead—neither of them is. Now *let her go*."

There was a moment of delay; then I was released.

I stumbled and felt myself falling forward, but two arms caught me before I could hit the floor. I was conscious of them only for a moment before everything slipped beneath the surface of blackwater darkness.

# 42

SLEEP WOULDN'T COME. I COULDN'T STOP THINKING about Sparrow.

*I should be out there. I should be looking for her…*

My thoughts tormented me, whispering in my ears as I tossed and turned in the hay. Finally, I could take it no longer. It was the middle of the night when I crept out of the barn for a breath of fresh air.

Walking out to the garden, I found myself scanning the cabin roof. My eyes immediately caught on a familiar figure in the soft folds of the waning moonlight. For a long moment, I didn't move. I just stood there watching her, feeling strangely out of place. I wanted to slip noiselessly back into the barn, but Kateri spotted me before I could retreat.

"Keegan?" she asked the darkness softly. "Is that you?"

I didn't say anything. Instead, I walked over to one of the cabin windows and climbed up on the sill. Grabbing hold of the edge of the porch roof, I pulled myself up and onto the rough wood shingles. Kateri placed a finger to her lips as I made my way over to her, passing the bedroom windows, which were open to let in the summer air.

I sat down beside her. Neither of us said a word for a moment.

"Were you going to just stand there watching me?" she asked finally, her voice a whisper.

I shrugged a little, gazing up at the moon. "I was thinking about it, yeah."

She was quiet for a long moment. "You never used to be afraid to talk to me. Lately, I feel like I hardly know you…"

"Don't say that." I pressed my eyelids shut. "You know me better than anyone. You know that."

"Do I?" she asked quietly.

I could feel her looking at me. I turned to face her. Her soft brown eyes searched mine in the moonlight.

"Why do you think I'm here, Kateri?"

"Because you are afraid."

"Afraid?"

Kateri reached over and placed her hand over mine. Though her fingers were warm, I felt chills race over my skin.

"Afraid that the blame rests on your shoulders," she replied quietly. "There is no fault in this, Keegan. But searching for blame is a waste of your energy at a time when we need you more than ever. Do you not think you were given so much for a reason?"

I swallowed back a tight feeling in my throat, unable to answer.

"Rafael will awaken," she whispered. "And when he awakens, I hope you are the first person he sees."

I swallowed hard, closing my eyes. "And Sparrow?"

"We will find Sparrow—and Janna. We *will* find them, Keegan."

"How can you know that?" I dropped my voice. "We've searched everywhere, Kateri, and there's… there's no trace of them. How could there be…" I reached into my pocket and took out the invisible bullet. I could feel it between my thumb and forefinger, but all I could see was moonlight streaming through the space between my fingers. "How can we fight something we cannot see?"

"The things we cannot see are the things we all must battle, Keegan.

Finding Sparrow is no different… It has little to do with your eyes…" Taking my hand in hers, she lifted it to press it to my chest.

"You have looked with your eyes—fought with your hands, reasoned with your mind," she whispered. "But what does your spirit tell you, Keeg?"

I drew a breath, thinking of how to reply, but Kateri shook her head before I could say anything.

"You don't need to tell me," she said. "No one needs to know but you."

I looked at her questioningly for a moment.

"What you *can* tell me, though, is that you'll come out to the woods with me in the morning and stop this sleeping-in-the-barn thing."

"I've gotten used to sleeping in the barn," I countered stubbornly. "But I'll come out to the woods with you tomorrow if you want me to."

A smile tugged at the corners of Kateri's mouth. "Of course I want you to."

"It's just so hard to stop thinking about her." I let out a long sigh. "Them."

"They fill my thoughts too, Keegan."

"If only Rafael would just wake up." A note of desperation bled into my voice as I looked up at the deep sky again. "He was the first one to disappear… What he saw, what he knows… it could lead us to the others—help us find them."

"Yes, it could," Kateri agreed. "But right now… just focus on being there for him."

I drew a long breath. "I know. You're right."

"So you'll read to him tomorrow? Instead of Sensei?"

"Well, I…"

Kateri gave me a look, one dark eyebrow raised.

"All right," I said, surrendering. "I'll give it a shot."

Kateri smiled, climbing to her feet. "Good. Now try to get some sleep. I'll see you in the morning."

"All right…" I trailed off. "Kateri?"

She stopped at the windowsill, turning to look at me over her shoulder. "Mmm?"

"I… I'm sorry I didn't come to you sooner. I don't really know why I didn't just talk to you about… well, about everything."

"You don't need to apologize to me, Keeg," she whispered back. "I understand."

For a moment she stood there, her gaze locked with my own. Then, giving me a little smile, she turned and slipped back through her bedroom window again, leaving me alone with the moon.

*I'll give it a shot*—that was what I'd promised Kateri, but it was easier said than done, easier than it felt, the next morning when I found myself standing there in front of that familiar door. I could hear the hushed, gentle tones of Dad's voice on the other side as he read aloud, accented by the steady drip, drip, drip of water.

I took a deep breath.

*Okay… okay, you can do this…*

Forcing myself to grasp the doorknob, I twisted it and stepped inside. Dad was seated at the end of Rafael's bed with a book in his lap. He didn't stop reading as I entered. Fresh air and sunlight tumbled in through the window at the far end of the room, spilling over Rafael. His face was drained, his chest rising and falling to the rhythm of his shallow breathing.

Closing the door gently, I stood there for a moment in silence, listening to Dad read; sunlight washed over his broad shoulders to illuminate the pages of the book in front of him.

"…Of all the creatures that had been made, the wolves were the fiercest, the wolves could run faster than any living thing, and their eyes, being the sharpest, pierced the darkness of the night. They were the phantoms, the hunters, those who ruled the night." Dad turned the page. "The boy could not run faster than the wolves, and the boy was afraid of the darkness, for he had not eyes which could see beyond it. He saw only the blackness of the night and could not find his way…"

The steady drip, drip, drip continued as water drizzled from Rafael's fingertips into the bucket on the floor beside him. I forced myself to walk steadily forward.

"The boy, alone and lost in the darkness, found himself surrounded by the wolves—from every side he heard their howls. They circled closer and closer until the boy could almost see their dark fur against even the blackness of the night," Dad continued. "Until he could feel their breath. 'Surely,' he thought, 'this must be the end.' For the boy did not run fast like the wolves, nor claws did he possess… but there in the darkness, there in the night, the boy began to see not with his eyes but with his spirit. No, claws and teeth he had not, but fire he did possess—a great and burning fire within his heart, so that when he opened his mouth, a light like the first flash of dawn came forth from his throat. It rose into the night sky like fire; it spun round and round until it became a bright ball of flame, creating our sun. And so, the boy created day…" Dad finally lifted his eyes from the page, looking over at Rafael. "And the wolves scattered, afraid of the fire in the boy's heart."

The room swelled with silence for a moment. Then, gently, Dad closed the cover of the book.

I knelt down beside Rafael's bed, reaching over to gently brush the hair out of his face. He didn't stir.

Biting my lip, I shook my head, scanning his face. I cursed. "Everything is so wrong," I whispered.

Dad reached over and smoothed the blankets over Rafael, tucking him in.

"To dwell on everything that is wrong, Keegan, is to deny your own power," Dad answered, his voice soft but firm. "He can hear you, you know."

Swallowing hard, I looked up at Dad. "I hate that I'm so afraid." My voice came out in a choked whisper.

Dad remained where he was, seated on the edge of Rafael's bed, his emerald eyes probing mine. "Afraid for Rafael, Sparrow, and Janna?" he asked quietly.

I looked back down at Rafael, taking his damp hand between my own.

"Afraid because I feel helpless," I answered quietly. "Afraid because I feel as though I can't stop life from slipping through my fingertips and spinning into chaos."

"Do you think I never feel that, Keegan?" he asked. "That horrible, restless feeling of something—someone—slipping away from you, that feeling like there's nothing you can..." Dad's voice faded in his throat, and he stopped, pressing his eyes closed. A long pause elapsed between us. "Yet it still stands true that when we find ourselves surrounded by wolves, it is futile to speak unless our words be of fire."

Droplets of water rolled over my own palms now; Rafael's hand was still between my own. "Dad, why didn't you tell me?" My eyes shifted up to lock with his. "Why didn't you tell me who Sparrow was?"

Dad smoothed his hands over the book's worn cover.

"Would it have made you treat her differently?"

The question caught me by surprise. I gently placed Rafael's hand back down on the edge of the bed, positioning his fingers carefully over the bucket, and rose to my feet.

"I guess in some ways," I began slowly. "Yeah, it would have."

"That's exactly why I didn't tell you—or anyone."

"But why? Shouldn't the daughter of the Sunrise and the Sunset be treated differently?"

"It's the very last thing her mother would have wanted for her..."

I glanced over at him as he trailed off. His eyes remained fixed on the cover of the book.

"Hawk and Icarus... left her with me so that she would be safe. I vowed to protect her and love her as my own daughter, and that is what I've done."

I walked slowly to the window, lost in thought as I paused to look out over the yard. "What happened to them?"

The room fell silent for a moment.

"I don't know," he answered finally, as though the words were heavy and hard to speak. "But I know that as long as the universe exists, so do they.”

“So… you raised her like she was one of your own, like how you raised me?” I could hardly believe the words as I spoke them. “How did I never know?”

“Because I told no one—no one but Lara. I moved her, all the time, to keep her safe,” he explained. “You stayed here, with Lara. We built this place together, and you didn’t have a desire to leave.”

“But still…”

“But still what?”

I turned away from the window, looking at my father. “You never told me.”

“Because I had to do what was best for her—and for you.”

I turned to face the window again, pressing my hand to my forehead. “What was best for me was Sparrow,” I whispered, my throat aching with the words. “And now she’s gone. And it’s killing me.”

I heard Dad rise, his footsteps on the floor. A moment later I felt the warmth of his hand on my shoulder.

“Keegan.”

My eyes stung as I pressed them shut. I couldn’t answer.

Dad tugged my shoulder and slowly turned me around to face him. I sucked in a breath to speak, but instead my voice crumbled beneath its own weight. I folded against his chest, wrapping my arms around him as I let the tears come, unable to hold them back any longer.

# 43

"YOU COULD HAVE KILLED HER; DO YOU REALIZE THAT?"

Bask stood behind his fortress of a desk. He pulled open one of the drawers and took out a cigarette. He held it between his lips while he lit it.

"You've talked to her, haven't you?" he said, ignoring my question.

Embers glowed at the end of his cigarette. He took a long drag.

"Yes, sir." My voice was level. "I spoke with her when she first arrived, per your request."

Bask grunted, sitting down at his desk now. He shuffled papers around for a moment. "What did you do with her after your unnecessary interference last night?"

"She's asleep in my room," I answered.

"She was to be brought back to her cell in the basement of the experimentation lab."

"Well, she wasn't; I took her to my room," I said. "She was unconscious. I wanted to make sure she was all right."

"I'm sure," Bask grumbled through the side of his mouth. "I hope you enjoyed her."

"It was nothing like that." I parted the shade to look outside. I could see the door to my lodgings from here. I'd had Mooney lock it for me. It had been strange to be standing on the other side with him, watching him take out his jangling set of keys and twist seven of them into their respective locks. "Explain to me how we can get information out of a dead prisoner and I'll start treating her just as brutally as we did the others," I went on. "Until then, I'll work on keeping her alive."

The room went quiet for a moment. Then Bask gave a dry, rumbling chuckle.

"If you were anyone else, Price," he muttered, "I'd have nailed you to the floor and beaten your head in for that."

"But I'm not anyone else, am I?"

When I turned around, I found Bask reclining in his large leather chair, his muddy boots poised on the edge of the desk and a scowl resting on his mouth. With one hand he fingered the binding of a hardcover book.

"You've never cared about any of the prisoners before, Price," Bask commented, exhaling a stream of smoke. "What's different about this one?"

The question was enough to raise the hairs on the back of my neck and arms.

*Everything*, I thought.

"Nothing," I replied. "She's not even on the bounty list."

Bask scratched his meaty nose. "No, but there is something strange about the girl, and no mistake. She bothers me—something about her."

"If Sparrow bothers you, sir, leave her to me," I offered, walking slowly back across the room. "I'll question her."

Bask lifted one thick eyebrow. "You? *You'll* question the prisoner?"

"Why not?"

His lips curved. "I could give a thousand reasons."

"You sent me out there to track them down, didn't you?"

"And you failed to get them all," he replied dryly, staring straight ahead. "According to Sparrow, there were seven. You only got three—now, minus one. The little lice-bag who got out somehow."

"It wasn't on my watch that the boy escaped," I replied flatly. "I'm as pissed about it as you are."

"Are you, though?" He picked up the book. "I work with you, Price—I oblige you more than you deserve."

"By locking me in each night as if I'm a prisoner?"

"By *refraining* from locking you away *permanently*." His voice hardened. "Which is exactly what I would do if things were different."

"Yes, if things were different…" I crossed the creaking, grime-coated floor and stopped at his desk, leaning forward on my fists. "But as it is, I'm the greatest asset the RGM has ever possessed… I'm the only reason you've gotten to where you are."

The tortured expression on Bask's face didn't change as I reached over his desk and picked up the silver flask that he'd set down among the papers. The book he was holding crumpled in his grasp; his knuckles whitened.

"I may not have my uniform anymore, Bask, but I've still got my brain." He stared hollowly as I untwisted the cap. "And I still have something you want… something the RGM depends on."

I threw back my head, taking a shot of whiskey from the flask. I swallowed and slammed it back down on his desk.

"I'll work with you if you work with me… *sir*." I had to force myself not to sneer the last word. "You know I hate the anomalies every bit as much as you do—and you know all the reasons why."

Bask sat stiffly for a long moment before lowering his boots to the floor and drawing a narrow breath.

"If you're willing to stick your neck out to run to this girl's defense, why wouldn't you have helped the boy escape?" he shot back callously. "You obviously sympathize."

I leaned in a little closer. "I'm the furthest thing from a sympathizer, but unlike you, I understand that not everything can be obtained by brute force." I dropped my tone. "I'm the one who watched her out there—who studied her, who learned all her little movements. She won't come around by force, trust me. She'd sooner die."

"So what do you recommend?"

"Giving me time with—"

He cut me off. "Don't waste your breath, Price—it will not happen." He shook his head absently. "I may not be able to abuse you, Price, but so help me god, I will make Sparrow wish she'd never been born if you don't return her to her cell within the hour." His voice lowered to a growl. "She will remain there for three days: without food or water."

"It won't work with her," I replied stiffly. "Believe me. I know."

Bask lifted the cigarette to his mouth again, concealing a smile with his hand. "Return her to her cell, Price." He exhaled the words with the smoke. "And don't let me see you anywhere near her, understand?"

I remained there a moment longer before straightening up, breathing in his smoke.

"What if I want to see her?"

Bask reached over to extinguish his cigarette on the edge of his desk. "If you go to her, it will be the last time you see her alive, Price."

"Fine," I replied, forcing my voice to remain neutral. "Fine. Do it your way, but it won't work. I'm telling you that right now: it won't work."

I slammed the door to Bask's office on my way out just because I could. I began walking down the road toward the factory; its tall smokestacks heaved clouds of soot into the already smoggy atmosphere. I breathed it in, closing my eyes as I walked, stepping out of the way of teams of dirty men carrying massive logs. They marched forward in groups of five, hollow eyed, their toes protruding from their tattered boots.

I ducked just as a log swung towards my head. I didn't bother saying anything. The prisoner clomped numbly onward.

A deep grumble filled the air as the crusty ground began to shake and lurch. I picked up my pace to a brisk walk, weaving around the stream of prisoners. Like clockwork, the tallest stack, protruding up from the center of the massive structure, began to rattle as the geyser blew. The factory had been built over the top of the massive geyser, capping it to capture the power of its steam. Here, ninety percent of our artillery was forged, built on the backs of those who could no longer serve anywhere else. Those who had committed what we called "crimes of weakness"—the ones who had failed to make the cut in one way or another. There were more of them than ever now that we no longer had Fragments—a system that had failed in my father's time, thanks to the resurgence of anomalies.

At least my father wasn't alive to see what the RGM had degraded to since the fall of Fragmenting. At least he wasn't there to see what *I'd* degraded to.

I jogged through the clouds of billowing smoke as it spilled from vents and rolled over the well-trodden dirt road. I skirted the factory, gazing up at the tall stacks and the rows of windows on the second and third floors. Though the glass was coated in a thick layer of dirt and grime, I could still make out the thin faces that occasionally peered out from behind it as they worked. The panes were broken in places, and through the holes I could hear the striking of metal on metal, the crackle of welding, and the shouts of the men.

I kept jogging, rounding the building and making my way to the outer limits of the district, where clusters of dead pines stood like an army of skeletons reaching over the towering cement wall, which was topped with razor wire. I jumped out of the way of a vehicle as it barreled down the road toward me. A thick cloud of chalky dust rose behind it.

As I reached the perimeter, I turned and ran parallel to the wall, the only barrier standing between that which was visible and that which was not. The district was about five miles all the way around, encompassing the rows of shabby buildings. Prisoners lived in the small ones that all looked the same. The larger buildings were the offices and barracks for the soldiers who were in charge of running and maintaining District Firehole.

I slowed down only when I had circled back around to where the lodging shacks were, completing my loop. I stopped alongside one in particular. It was shabbier than the rest, and one of the windows had rotted out. A figure stood hunched by the open front door, his mud-caked suspenders holding a dirty unbuttoned shirt against his malnourished frame. He fumbled in the deep front pocket of his pants with one hand, a puzzled expression on his thin, craggy face as he stared hollowly into space.

I spotted the pack of cigarettes lying on the ground a few yards from where he stood. I strode over and stooped down to pick it up.

"Damn, did I drop it again, Aaron?" he asked as I approached the place where he stood. He extended a pale hand as I placed the pack into his open palm. "Much obliged."

I looked steadily into his face, into his light blue eyes that stared hollowly ahead. "How the hell do you always know it's me, Viner?"

His parched lips formed a little grin. "I recognize your overconfident stride."

I grunted. "Are you going to offer me one, or am I going to pry it from you?"

He held out the torn-open pack, and I snatched a cigarette and pinched it between my lips.

"I hear there's a new one in the pit." Viner slid the pack back into his pocket, switching it out for a lighter. "Another female."

"Yes. Yes, there is," I replied, wiping the sweat off my face with the crook of my arm and taking the lighter from him.

"Heard she's pretty hot."

"When the hell have people seen her?" I asked. "She's been in solitary confinement for—"

"When she first got here."

"I see."

"And I *can't*, so I expect you to fill me in."

I rolled my eyes, but as much as I wanted to brush the question off, I couldn't deny that it filled my stomach with a tingling sensation. I shot a quick glance in the direction of my lodgings: the dirty shack that looked like all the rest, yet was different because of who was inside it.

"She looks all right," I replied absently.

"All right?"

"Dark hair. Dark eyes. Hell of a temper."

"Just your type."

"She's a *slider*," I said icily, and took another drag.

Viner shrugged, tipping his head back against the side of the building. His light brown curls hung into his eyes. "Desperate times call for desperate measures, Price."

"Yeah, well, I'm not *that* desperate yet." I pulled my gaze away from the shack again and stared at the ground. "I'll never be desperate enough for their kind." I tossed the cigarette onto the dirt and crushed it with the heel of my boot. "And you wouldn't be either if they'd…"

I didn't need to finish. Viner nodded slowly as wisps of gray rolled past his lips.

"No," he said finally. "No, maybe I wouldn't. Has Bask questioned her yet?"

"Last night, yeah. It didn't go well."

"For whom?"

"Either of them," I replied wryly. "I had to drag her out before Bask killed her along with any chance we have of getting information out of her."

Viner looked in my general direction. Though he couldn't see me or anything else, something about his stare was chillingly penetrating.

"What about the other one?"

"They're still working on her," I explained. "Trying to get her to talk."

Viner nodded slowly. "And when she does…" He cocked a finger gun at his temple and made a quiet *pow* sound. "Just like every other piece-of-shit slider."

My throat tightened, and I looked down. "Yeah. Yeah, of course."

# 44

I CAUGHT GLIMPSES OF GRAY WALLS AND SPARSE furnishings around me. There was a coat hanging on a hook by the door. I was no longer in a cell. I was lying on a soft mattress with warm blankets spread out over me.

Dawn filtered through the window, filling the room with cool, blue light. I could hear the cold wind whipping outside, howling through the cracks around the windows. I lay there for a moment, listening. After a while, I became aware of the folded piece of paper through the fabric of my jeans. The list Corporal Price had given me. The list of sliders, with bounties printed out beneath each of their names.

I tugged it out and unfolded it, holding it up to the light to study the faces once more. Each of them, even the many I didn't recognize, seemed familiar to me at this point. As I studied their eyes through the grainy photographs, three stood out among the rest. One of those three faces in particular captured my attention. A face so much like my own, I couldn't help but feel almost like I was staring into my own reflection.

Deep eyes in a face crowned by rivers of dark hair. She stared out from the photograph like she knew me, and something inside me felt like I knew her, too… from a dream, from another world.

The face beside hers was Icarus; his features were handsome, almost chiseled. Eyes like crystal and dark tousled hair.

They looked so… right, side by side like that, almost too perfect to be real. *Could it be possible? Are they my parents?*

My gaze slipped to the bottom of the page, where I found Keegan's picture. His mane of hair ventured out from under his hood, a tiny braid hanging over his shoulder. Freckles were sprayed across his nose. A boy with the heart of a lion beating in his chest.

*Keegan.*

Weeks had passed. Weeks that felt like an eternity, yet I could still see him in my head, standing by the lake, drenched in the colors of the sunset. I could still see his eyes. His soft, whispered words still haunted my memory: *I love you, I love you, I love you.*

And now I held his picture, wondering if I would ever see him again. Wondering who I really was. Wondering if I would make it out of this place alive, or if they would kill both Janna and me. It seemed that no matter which way I looked, there was darkness; no matter which way I turned, the light slipped away.

I gently lowered the paper to my chest, holding it there for a moment, listening to the low roar of the ground as it began to shake and tremble.

I slid the paper back into my pocket as the heavy clomp of boots came into earshot. I quickly sat up and slid my legs over the side of the mattress, brushing my hair out of my face as the sound of deadbolts retracting interrupted the silence. My gaze swept to the door as a few more clicks rang through the air. The knob slowly turned, and the door swung open.

I sat in silence, my heart hammering in my ears, as Corporal Price stepped into the room, closing the door softly behind him. For a moment he remained there, his bright, coppery eyes studying me from where he stood. He wore RGM combat boots, black joggers, and a sweat-soaked sage green tee.

I gave him a swift once-over before clearing my throat. "Why am I here?"

The corporal stood there for a moment, studying me like he'd never seen me before. He crossed the room to the small, weathered table with two wooden chairs tucked underneath. In the middle of the table was a steaming tin jug on a small burner. He took a mug out of the cabinet mounted to the wall above, lifted the jug, and filled the mug with what looked and smelled like strong coffee. He carried it over to me.

For a second I was shocked; then I shook my head.

Corporal Price held the mug extended for a moment longer before he finally withdrew it. He walked back to the table, draining it himself. As he lifted the cup to his mouth, I caught a glimpse of the ink curling around the underside of his left bicep. He slammed the cup down on the table and dragged one of the chairs across the floorboards to the bed where I was sitting. He pulled it up close and sat down to face me.

"Why is it that you're keeping the fact that I can see a secret from Bask? You clearly work together, yet you act as if he is the enemy—"

"Bask is neither an enemy nor a friend," Price interrupted. "He's just another piece in the game."

"Game?" I repeated. "And is that what I am, too? A piece in a game?"

Price only continued to study me with that same, searing gaze.

"Why do you keep staring at me?" I narrowed my eyes. "Haven't you ever seen a slider before?"

"You're different, Sparrow," he answered, getting to his feet and crossing the room. He leaned against the wall and crossed his arms, staring at me. "Your ability to see makes you different."

"So no one has been able to see this place?"

"No one."

"But you can see each other…"

Corporal Price hesitated, then nodded. "The prisoners and personnel are invisible to everyone but themselves. They can see each other and everything inside the walls of the district."

"So am I invisible too?"

"No, you're simply inside something that is; therefore, no one outside the district can see you."

"How is it that this place is invisible?" I asked, confused. "How is it that *you* are?"

"You ask a lot of questions."

I studied the back of him as he walked over to one of the barred windows and looked out.

"You're not going to tell me," I concluded.

He turned to glance at me over his shoulder. "Why would I? You're a slider—a prisoner. You're entitled to *nothing*."

"Yet you released a prisoner upon my request," I shot back. "Which means I obviously have something you want—"

In a heartbeat he was across the room. Lunging forward, he pinned me down on the bed and clamped a hand over my mouth, looking down into my face. My heart hammered in my chest as every muscle in my body tightened.

"Never speak another word on the subject," he whispered, his voice level. "I did *nothing*, and you know *nothing* about that boy's escape. Do you understand? *You know nothing.*"

I struggled to nod my head under the pressure of his grasp. He jerked back, releasing me and straightening up to stand.

"You're living in a lion's den now, Sparrow. It's just a matter of time until you slip up and they devour you." He cursed and started pacing the room again.

Finally, he halted, turning to stare at me again with that same almost haunted look in his eyes. When he spoke, it was under his breath. "We have to get you out of here..."

"*What?*"

This time Corporal Price didn't respond. He paced from one end of the room to the other.

I pushed myself up to a seated position on the mattress. "I don't understand. You hate me because I'm a slider, yet you want to help me?"

"The reason I'm helping you has nothing to do with the fact that you're a slider—I hate that you're a slider because it makes me hate myself for helping you. I am *not* a sympathizer."

I reached up to rub my forehead. "Then why would you—"

"Because if they kill you, I'm right back to where I was before!" Price whirled around to face me. "Don't you see that?"

His voice was like an explosion in the quiet room. His eyes were wide, and perspiration sheathed his face. I studied him through narrowed eyes, trying to make some sense of his contradictory speech.

"You wouldn't understand," he went on quietly. "And you don't need to—you don't need to understand *anything*. You just need to trust me…" He paused. "Especially over the next three days."

"The next three days?" Fresh anxiety flooded my veins. "What do you mean?"

"I mean that Bask has ordered that you be taken back to the pit and left there with no food or water for three days," he answered gravely. "But you'll survive."

I tipped my chin, meeting his gaze. "He won't break me, Corporal— I'll die before I tell them anything."

"I've told him as much."

"You never even came to see me when I was down there," I said. "And now you want me to trust you? Well, I don't. Not at all. Why would I *ever* trust you? *Why should I?*"

The corporal's expression hardened for a moment, then melted away.

"It's not all black and white, Sparrow," he said quietly. "I was forbidden to see you while you were down there. I'm forbidden to see you for the next three days…"

My stomach turned as I considered the prospect of being dragged back down to that suffocating dungeon, dead to the rest of the world.

"But I promise I won't let Bask execute you." He stopped in front of me, speaking quietly as he looked down into my face. "I promise I'll get you out of here before anything happens."

I said nothing as I stood there, looking up into his eyes, trying and failing to read them. Wishing I could catch just a glimpse of something behind them, something that would give me a clue as to what this RGM soldier's true motivation was—why he even cared whether I lived or died. Yes, I could see while the other sliders hadn't been able to… But so what? *Why the hell does it mean so much to him, and why is he keeping it a secret from the RGM?* If anything, I would have thought it would increase his eagerness to dispose of me.

Before I could speak, someone pounded on the door. Startled, I sucked in a breath.

"That will be the guard," Price informed me quietly. "You have to go."

Wordlessly, I followed the corporal across the room, the cold floor stinging my feet.

When we reached the door, I turned and looked at him. In his eyes there was conflict, though I couldn't understand why. Lowering his voice, he leaned a little closer.

"Are you afraid?" he asked, his voice low.

I didn't answer. There was no need; my eyes had already confirmed it.

"I won't leave you there," he assured me. "I promise."

I turned my face away, scanning the long row of deadbolts.

"Why do they lock you in?" My voice faltered. "Are you… are you a prisoner too?"

Corporal Price's gaze shifted over my face for a moment before, finally, a ghost of a smile passed over his mouth.

"If only I were," he answered quietly. "If only it were that simple."

# 45

I SAT ON THE EDGE OF RAFAEL'S BED AND OPENED THE SOFT leather book, quietly bringing each word to life as though it were a tonic that would cure him. I didn't know if it could, but I poured myself into it, forgetting everything else. Kateri often came to listen, kneeling beside Rafael's bed and stroking her fingers through his hair.

Kateri had finally convinced me to go back into the woods with her. Sometimes Preston joined us, but today it was just the two of us.

I followed at a distance as she hiked ahead, craning my neck to peer up at the pines swaying gently in the quiet northerly wind. We were under strict orders from Dad not to venture out too far; we only went out to maintain the trees we had already healed. They needed light and water and insects to keep them pollinated—all the things we provided.

Kateri paused at a tree with faded bark and wilted leaves. I watched as she placed her palms against its rough, textured trunk and closed her eyes, slowly breathing fresh streams of color back into it. The branches danced and swayed as the leaves overhead trembled and returned to their original bright green state. She then lifted a fist to the sky, flicking her fingers open to release a cloud of what looked like yellow dust—like pollen. It swirled in the air, lifting and bending until it morphed into a swarm of honeybees. They hummed and drifted, murmuring among the trees.

The moss was soft under my bare feet as I stepped forward, coming to a stop at her side.

"The trees seem well today," she said quietly. "Just a little thirsty."

"With no water channelers to quench them," I answered quietly, gazing up into the treetops once more.

The corners of Kateri's lips turned down. "We'll get them back."

In my mind I could still see Sparrow standing there between the trees, as clearly as the day I'd met her, with a cigarette poised between her lips and her eyes searching for an escape.

It was so hard to stop thinking about her…

It was so hard to stop *thinking*.

"I just can't understand what's wrong with him." I spoke quietly. "I can't grasp why he's not getting better. I'm a healer, so why can't I *heal* him? Every time I try to read his thoughts, there's nothing there," I continued, my voice ragged. "There's just emptiness… darkness that I can't pull apart no matter how hard I try…"

Kateri studied me with the same heaviness in her eyes that I felt inside.

"What could possibly be wrong with him?" I whispered.

I could still hear the quiet humming of Kateri's bees. She brought her palms together in front of her after a moment, clasping her fingers together, save a bit of space between her thumbs.

"I think sometimes questions are like signs, appearing to us for a reason," she answered. "I think this question comes to you for a reason, Keeg… You are the tree where it has made its nest."

I watched in silence as Kateri lifted her hands to her mouth, took a deep breath, and blew into the space between her thumbs as if making a bird call, though no sound passed through her fingers.

"I don't get what the hell that means." I exhaled, slumping back against a tree.

The corners of her lips twitched a little. "It means that maybe *you* have the answer."

"Answers seem to be one thing I'm fresh out of."

She took a deep breath and blew into her hands once more before finally unfolding her fingers to reveal a small, soft butterfly. Its tender metallic-green wings twitched as it crawled to the tips of her fingers.

"Stop thinking so much… Quiet all those voices and listen to the one that matters." Kateri's voice was hushed as she stepped closer, lifting her hand so that the butterfly could climb nimbly into the tangles of my hair. Kateri smiled, watching it for a moment before her eyes drifted down to meet mine. "The butterfly's."

I quirked an eyebrow. "Are you serious?"

Kateri gave my face a thoughtful once-over and then shook her head, biting back a grin. "No. But you're *too* serious."

In spite of everything, I felt the ghost of a smile on my lips. Kateri walked away, back to her trees, back to letting bees slip from her fingers and into the air.

"You'll know its voice when you hear it, Keeg," she called. She flipped her long braid over one shoulder and lifted her hands to rub them together. "I cannot tell you how to listen to your own voice."

I frowned as the butterfly climbed down my forehead to rest between my eyes.

*Why does she always have to speak in riddles?* Sometimes it was harder to understand her than it was to understand Dad.

Still, I turned her words over in my mind for the rest of the day, thinking about our conversation as I chopped the wood and cleaned up the barn and helped harvest enough vegetables for Lara to make dinner with. Myung and I had kitchen duty that night. It was the last thing I was in the mood for—I didn't want to eat or be with anyone. I wanted to hide away in the barn and be alone with my thoughts.

But Lara had other plans. Like the mushrooms piled in front of me and the large knife in my hands. The house was washed in a strange and gloomy silence.

Clouds had filled the sky since Kateri and I had returned, and now rain pattered on the roof, accompanying the snapping of the fire, the only sounds to interrupt the silence that ran thick between us.

I chopped the mushrooms. Myung stirred something over the fire, more and more violently until finally she spoke up.

"Is this ever going to end?" she erupted. "Hiding away like this—not knowing if the RGM will show up any day and kill us all."

Lara turned to look at her.

"We all know deep down that Janna and Sparrow are as good as dead. Why can't we just accept that and move on to trying to find a way to defend ourselves from future attacks?" she went on bitterly. "How long does Sensei expect us to hold out for something that's not going to happen?"

She looked between Lara and me, as if expecting us to agree with her.

"Myung, we have to keep our faith," Lara answered quietly. "When we have nothing left, we still have that."

"No..." she shot back. "No, I *don't*."

"Myung—"

"I can't anymore, Lara! I can't." Myung's voice became watery. "I can't deal with it anymore..."

"Myung, it's hard for everyone," Kateri said from the living area, where she was curled up on a large floor cushion with a rabbit. "But it won't always be this way."

Myung sniffled, starting to cry. I looked from Kateri to Preston, who was sitting on another cushion nearby, his head tipped back against the wall and a heavy look in his eyes as he stared up at the ceiling.

"Sometimes I think our faith is just..." Myung's voice tattered and faded. "A blindfold... a drug to help us cope with the pain. But it doesn't mean the pain isn't still there."

I said nothing in response. My eyes drifted to the stairs as I listened for the scraps of Dad's voice; he was reading to Rafael... the story of the boy and the wolves again.

"I don't want to be here anymore," Myung whispered, her voice weak. "I don't want to watch Rafael die... *I* don't want to die..."

Inside me, the words of the story still echoed: *The boy, alone and lost*

I felt my fingers clench more tightly around the knife, trembling slightly as I listened to Myung sniffle.

"Maybe we were wrong about the world." Her voice trembled as she went on, tears drizzling down her cheeks. "Maybe we were… maybe we were wrong about *us*."

My jaw tightened. I spun around before she could say another word, unable to control it any longer. Involuntarily, my palm spread open, throwing the knife into a levitation and sending it hurtling across the room to nail into the wall with a thud. Everyone fell quiet.

"If you're going to speak darkness…" My voice came out hard and level as I stared down into her eyes. "Don't speak."

Myung stared at me in stunned silence. Then she slapped me across the face, fled the kitchen, and pounded up the stairs.

"You know, when we found Rafael unconscious out there in the woods, I couldn't figure out what was wrong with him," I began breathlessly before Lara could get a word in. "I couldn't read his thoughts, I couldn't find an injury, and I couldn't heal him. I couldn't figure out what was wrong with him, but now, finally, I know!"

Lara waited for me to finish, the expression on her face fading along with the color. I turned around to look at Preston and then at Kateri, locking eyes with her from across the room.

"*We* are what's wrong," I said finally. "Us and *every word we speak*."

# 46

THREE DAYS PASSED.

I could no longer remember what it felt like to be outside. It seemed as though I'd forgotten how to breathe—breathe the way I had when I'd first arrived at the Homestead: deep, eager breaths like someone who's just beginning to realize they're alive.

I'd had no food or water. I could barely get up off the floor. I lay there and listened to Old Man speak to me, but his voice grew fainter and fainter until sometimes I couldn't tell if he was really there at all.

The sun dropped and then swelled and then dropped again. The ground seemed feverish, trembling, rattling my bones and making my teeth chatter. I heard the sounds of the factory. I heard shouting and footsteps and engines churning, but I could no longer hear the old man.

My eyes were too heavy to keep open. My bones felt as though they were sinking into the ground where I lay, as though the earth itself were trying to pull me under, to help me vanish forever, leaving behind the solitude and the cold and the confusion that I felt within myself.

I trailed my fingers across the cold, crusty ground and reached out my hand. The old man clasped it, encompassing it in his own. I felt my head being lifted gently from the ground and placed on soft knees. Hands that were like swatches of well-worn leather caressed my face and my hair, as Fin's had, what felt like a lifetime ago. I felt myself crumbling inside from the mere weight of it all, like a star pulling in on itself. I wept.

I lay there on the ground with my arms wrapped around the old man's waist and allowed myself to empty until I shook like the raging ground below.

Quietly, he held me in his arms. He no longer felt like a stranger. It was as if I'd known him all my life.

"They'll never find me here." My voice came out in a broken whisper. "No one can see this place but me… How could they find me?"

Faintly, I heard the old man draw a breath. "You are not the only one who can see, young one."

Sniffling, I sat up to look into his worn face, my eyes meeting his lively blue ones.

"You?" I inquired softly. "Y-y-you can… see?"

Old Man bowed his head in a slow nod.

"B-b-but how? How is that possible, when none of the others could see?" I asked. "To Rafael, this place was darkness."

"But you see light in the darkness, Sparrow," he said softly. "You are different from the others. You were *born* different."

The statement caught me by surprise. I stared at him, frozen. "H-how do you know my name?" I whispered. "I never told you."

"Did you not?" he asked.

I studied his face. "Am I imagining you?" I questioned after a moment. "Am I going out of my mind?"

"Those who wish to see me can always find me beside them," Old Man replied. "You see me because you desire to, and your desire creates space for truth to fill."

"Truth is something I've never been good at. I've always been the one to get right and wrong mixed up—the problem, the screw-up." I wiped my damp cheeks with the backs of my hands. "And now I'm a prisoner."

Old Man smiled. "You are only a prisoner if that is how you see yourself, Sparrow."

A strange feeling settled over me as I gazed into the blueness of his eyes. There seemed to be an expanse as vast as the ocean within them.

"The corporal says he keeps my secret because… Well, I don't really even understand why he does," I confessed, keeping my voice down. "I don't trust the corporal… yet there is something about him… something I can't put my finger on."

Old Man listened, looking at me intently, wrinkles forming around the corners of his sharp eyes.

"You said that you knew Corporal Price, but he didn't know you," I went on. "Would you, knowing him, advise me to trust him even the slightest bit?"

His forehead creased a little as he looked at me. "Your answer is already within your question, Sparrow. The very fact that you doubt him…"

"Means that I shouldn't trust him," I finished for him, sighing. "Yet…"

"Yet?"

"Going along with him may be my only means of escape—and of finding Janna," I answered, smoothing my forehead with my fingertips. "Wherever she is… God, I don't even know how I'll find her. Or if she's even still here—or alive at all."

A quiet filled the cell, interrupted only by the low rumbling from the belly of the earth below. The ground began to tremble.

"What other choice do I have?" I pushed my back up to the wall, leaning there. "I have no other option: Price is my only escape—the only way I can possibly get out of this hellhole. I have to get out of here before they figure out that I can see. The corporal said they'll kill me if they find out," I whispered. "So far, he's been protecting me."

The old man's expression remained calm, but his eyes grew serious. "One must wonder why."

I didn't say anything for a moment. The unsettled feeling in my gut remained, and my head was beginning to ache, pounding with so many questions I felt like it would burst.

"But if it comes down to trusting Price or being locked away down here forever… I'll take my chances."

Before the sun had even peeked over the horizon, I heard the heavy clomp of boots in the passage. I pretended to be startled when the door to the cell creaked open. I scrambled back against the wall, wide-eyed and staring straight ahead.

"Come." Mooney laid a hand on my shoulder. He pulled me up, then shoved me forward, out through the door and down the long, narrow hallway. I stumbled over my feet and up the staircase into the dim light of dawn.

Zombie-eyed prisoners were just beginning to emerge from their shacks. They wore tool belts and overalls and plodded listlessly toward the factory. Mooney marched me forward, right through the middle of them.

"Move!"

He struck me hard in the back, and I fell forward onto my hands and knees. A yelp of pain burst from my throat as I hit the ground. Before I could get to my feet, I felt Mooney kick me in the thigh.

"I said move!" he roared, spit flying out of his mouth. "Get up!"

Shaking, I tried to climb to my feet, but he only struck me again. Pain rattled down my spine, and I instantly felt my hands start to heat up.

By this point, several of the prisoners around us had slowed their mindless progression toward the factory. A few stopped and looked at us.

"Get up!" my captor raged, gesturing wildly for me to stand. "Get up now!"

The air seemed to become still as I climbed to my feet. He waited until I had turned to face him, looking at the ground. Then he slapped my face. I staggered backward and landed hard on my knees again, gasping for air, my jaw throbbing. The dirty men laughed, beginning to gather around us.

My hands were still hot, and now my fingertips were starting to tremble.

"Get up! Get on your feet before I kick you again!" Mooney yelled, his voice going hoarse.

Pain wrung through my weak, aching body. My fingertips trembled as I clutched at the dirt, trying to catch my breath. I tasted blood on my lip.

"I said get up, you lice-bag!"

I stayed on the ground, my eyes fixed on the dirt and my entire body trembling. My fingertips felt like they were on fire.

Mooney lurched forward, fuming. "I said—"

I caught a glimpse of a blur in my peripheral vision and heard the impact of a punch. A familiar figure appeared, contrasted against the hazy sky. Mooney staggered backward, clutching his stomach. Corporal Price stepped forward, towering over him for a moment before lunging forward and tackling the gasping, toothless guard to the dirt. Pinning him down with one hand, Price curled the other into a fist and decked Mooney in the jaw. Then he wound back his arm and did it again and again.

More prisoners stopped in their tracks to gape at the unfolding spectacle, swarming like vultures around a fresh kill. I forced my head back down, afraid someone would catch me *looking*.

Mooney wailed like an injured animal, writhing on the ground and flailing as if he didn't know where the next blow would come from. Cheering, chortling prisoners closed in, drowning out the sound of the fight and quickly overrunning me.

I felt heat pulsating between my hands and the ground, and could see a glow emanating from under them. I tried to crawl through the crowd, but it was too thick. I could barely move.

A large hand reached down and grabbed me by the hair, dragging me up to stand. A tall, muddy-faced prisoner with slate-gray eyes stared me in the face, clenching his yellowed teeth as he tightened his grasp.

"You must be the new one," he snarled above the chaos around us, his face inches from mine. "Why don't you come with me and I'll show you what sliders are good for?"

Trying to twist away from his vise grip on my scalp, I kept staring straight ahead. "Let go of me!"

Grabbing my waist with his free hand, he jolted my body against his own, yanking my head back. He stared down into my face with hollow, hard eyes. He leaned in, pressing his mouth against my face to whisper into my ear, "Sliders don't tell me what to do."

My fingers felt on fire as he raced his hands over my body. Wrenching one arm free, I clamped a hand over his face and dug my nails in. In a flash, bright orange energy exploded out of my palm.

A blood-curdling scream pealed out of his throat as he flew backward through the crowd like a rag doll, knocking other prisoners to the ground. I staggered backward—and felt a hand clamp down on my shoulder.

Corporal Price shot me a look, panting for breath. His left eye was puffy and bruised, and his shirt was ripped open at the sleeve.

"Come on." He guided me forward, shoving prisoners out of the way. Startled and confused, they stumbled aside.

The corporal heaved heavy breaths and marched forward until we reached Bask's office door. There, he stopped and turned to look at me, leaning closer to lower his voice. "For god's *sake*, keep yourself under *control*."

I swallowed and nodded. Price pounded the door with his fist.

"Come," a voice ordered from within.

Price swung the door open and pushed me inside, stepping in after me.

Bask looked up from his desk.

"Sparrow, per your request," Price announced wearily, then gritted his teeth, "sir."

Bask pursed his lips and straightened the papers in front of him, making no comment about the corporal's disheveled state.

"You may leave us," Bask replied coldly.

Corporal Price stiffened. I felt his hand slip away from my shoulder and then heard his footsteps retreating. A moment later the door slammed shut. My stomach sank as I lowered my gaze to the floor and waited for

Bask to speak.

He rummaged around for something, and a moment later I heard the click of a lighter.

"Sit," he said.

I lowered myself carefully to the floor, keeping my gaze fixed in front of me.

He took a long sip of smoke, leaning back in his chair.

"Well, here we are again." He blew out a long stream of ashy gray. "Are you ready to talk?"

"About what?" I asked dryly.

There was a long pause, then after a moment I heard the sound of his boots on the floorboards. He stopped in front of me and knelt down, suddenly at my eye level.

"Tell me where your group is based," he whispered. "Tell me the name of the one who leads you."

Silence swelled in the room. I swore he could hear my heart beating.

"Tell me his name and tell me the names of the others," he continued, his narrow eyes scanning my face. "And I won't kill you yet."

My back stiffened, and I slowly shook my head. "I will tell you *nothing*."

His rough fingers wrapped around my jaw, and he jerked my face towards his. His eyes glinted, and his skin had gone red.

"You will." I felt the heat of his breath on my skin. "*You will.*"

My body trembled, frozen in place, as I forced myself to just keep staring. To stay calm. To not say a word.

Bask's hand shook and so did his face. A moment later he erupted. He lurched to his feet, dragging me with him.

"Your chances are up," he bellowed into my face. Grasping me by the back of the neck, he lifted me onto my tiptoes and got right in my face. "Tomorrow," he whispered, "you swing."

I gulped breathlessly, barely able to touch the ground. Bask spun me around, then dropped me and shoved me forward. I stumbled over my feet, straightened—and then halted in my tracks.

Corporal Price stood beside the door, leaning back against the wall with his arms folded over his chest, staring straight at me. He said nothing—only lifted a finger to his lips.

"Move!" Bask flung the door open. Pushing me forward, he shoved me past Corporal Price, as if he didn't even see him standing there.

# 47

1 STOOD IN THE MIDDLE OF THE DIRT ROAD WITH MY hands clasped loosely behind my back, watching the dusk as it came and settled, hazy brown and warmer than usual.

The factory whistles had blown about a half hour earlier. The prisoners had scurried back into their holes, and the streets had once more calmed to the stillness of a ghost town, patrolled only by armed soldiers.

Behind me, the factory pumped out listless wisps of steam. In front of me was the experimentation lab. I could see the basement ventilation window from here and the window to Sparrow's cell.

"Quite a show you put on earlier. I heard all about it."

I turned and found Viner sitting on the doorstep of his shack, his shirt unbuttoned and his suspenders hanging at his waist. He fumbled in his breast pocket for his pack of cigarettes.

"You broke Mooney's nose," he went on, pulling a cigarette out of the pack and pinching it between his lips. "No doubt he went crying to Bask."

"No doubt," I agreed, shifting my gaze back to the barred window farther down the road. "But Bask never liked him anyway. He won't punish me for it."

"You speak like you own him—like it's not the other way around."

"It's fifty-fifty," I replied, though I could tell Viner thought I was joking.

"Seems kinda strange, though," he mused after a long drag.

"What does?"

"You sticking up for a lice-bag slider."

"I wasn't sticking up for her. I was simply ensuring that she remained alive," I explained. "How the hell do you interrogate a corpse? It may be Bask's way to beat someone within an inch of their life, but it's not mine."

"What does it matter? Everyone will be watching her dangle through the trapdoor in the morning, myself included." He paused, smoke seeping from his grin. "Well, not *watching*, but… you know, I'll be there."

My stomach sank at the thought of the execution. I pressed my eyelids shut, taking a steady breath.

"Not everything can turn out how we hope." My voice came out sounding hollow and absent. "Sometimes everything goes to hell, and there's nothing you can do about it."

"You say that like you don't want her to be executed… Was there something between you?"

My jaw tensed as I stared straight ahead at the experimentation lab. "Like you said, she's a slider. Why should I care?" I lied. "I just… I was hoping my efforts to get her here hadn't been in vain."

"Bullshit, Price," he concluded at length, lifting the cigarette to his lips again. "Bullshit."

It was a provocation and I knew it, but I wasn't about to spill my guts.

Leaving Viner standing there, I made my way to the lab. I took the steps all at once and swung the door open.

The room was small, sterile and white. The medic at the desk across the room didn't even look up.

"You're late," he said.

Making no response, I took a seat on the stiff wooden examination table. I watched as he gathered his equipment and placed it all on a metal tray. He carried it over and set it down on the table beside me.

He extended a hand for me to take. For a moment I just sat there staring at him.

"Price." It was a gentle command. "Your hand."

I hesitated a moment before reaching my hand out and grasping his.

The medic was younger than me, but not by much. His eyes were gray and hardened by life in a post-Frag RGM, but they'd yet to see real combat, I could tell. He was nothing more than a fixture shuffled from base to base.

Fastening a tourniquet around my arm, he stared straight ahead as he traced his fingers along my superficial veins. He paused, marking the spot with his thumb and picking up a syringe. I felt a faint prick and then watched as he pulled back the plunger, filling the barrel with my thick, clear blood.

When it was full, he detached the vial, capped it and set it aside, leaving the needle in place. He took a second vial from the tray, uncapped it, and attached it to the needle.

"I heard you were in a tussle this morning," he said as he watched the vial fill with more of my blood. He cleared his throat. "Any injuries from that?"

"I don't know. Why don't you check?"

He rolled his eyes and removed the second vial of blood, capping it and repeating the process with a third and final vial.

"Just hurry the hell up, would you?"

He finished and put the needle back on the tray. He pulled a piece of gauze off a roll and handed it to me to bandage myself up with. I wrapped it around my bleeding arm and slid off the table.

The medic walked back to his desk, tray in hand. "I'll see you in three days."

Crossing the room, I flung the door open and stepped back outside, slamming it behind me. I scanned the fading purple sky, trying to ignore the pounding of my heart.

Bask's words to Sparrow echoed viciously through my thoughts.

I took a deep breath, scanning the sprawling, grime-coated district around me. Steam lingered and faded in the air; mud pots gurgled and fumaroles hissed.

It was only a matter of hours before Bask had Sparrow executed.

I cursed, descending the steps and stroking a hand back over the stubble of my hair. I circled around the building to the place where the small barred window let air into the pit. I slowed to a stop, my heart rate picking up as I looked down through the bars.

There was just enough light left to make out Sparrow's shape far below. She lay on the floor in the fetal position, her long dark hair flowing out around her. She was asleep, her chest rising and falling softly, her lips parted and streaked with dried blood.

I couldn't help but wonder what had gone through her head when she'd turned around and saw me standing there, still inside Bask's office—Bask totally unaware of my presence. Her dark eyes had widened, and I'd placed a finger to my lips before she'd had a chance to blurt out a word.

I stood there a moment longer, watching her sleep, then tore myself away and proceeded to the gates.

The two guards posted there went on talking obliviously as I slipped past them.

For the first time in what felt like ages, I breathed. I hadn't left the base in a while—not since I'd captured Sparrow. The air was still a little smoggy, but it was free air.

When I was far enough away from the base, I stopped, tipping my head back to stare up into the opaque navy sky. I could see dim pinpricks of stars trying to cut through the faint wisps of smog overhead. Dad had taught me the constellations, constellations no one could find anymore.

I walked through the trees, hiking steadily up the incline. I knew this place by heart; it was my refuge. The shack was built into the hillside, so surrounded by trees and grown over with brush that it was almost not there at all. I opened the door and stepped inside, turning in the threshold to stare down at the district in the distance, sprawling far below the ridge.

I closed the door behind me and stood there for a moment.

God, sometimes I wondered why I didn't just leave: freedom was right there in front of me, whispering seductively. But I was in lust with something better—something I could only get if I stayed the course; Bask understood that. That was why he let me come and go, locking me in at night only to exercise his authority over me. He knew I would never really leave.

Feeling sick, I stumbled forward through the darkness, sprawled out on the bed pushed off to one side, and stretched out.

Building the shack—my little tucked-away place of refuge—had been an ongoing project of mine for years, and every moment had been worthwhile. I finally had a place to go that Bask didn't know about. I had to be back by the time they came to lock me in for the night—which would be soon.

I couldn't stand the thought of Sparrow being executed, but I couldn't stand the thought of saving her, either. She was a *slider*—and I'd already stooped to saving one just to get her on my side. Sparrow was an embodiment of everything I despised. She was one of *them*. The ones who had taken everything from me.

In my mind I could see her face as clearly as if she were standing in front of me. Arching dark eyebrows with curtains of long flowing hair to match it. Eyes so full of questions, of an eagerness to understand things that weren't meant to be understood. With the dawn would come her death; Bask would not relent this time.

I had to get her out of there.

# 48

"WHAT ON *EARTH* ARE YOU DOING?" PRESTON STARED AT me from the barn door, bewildered.

"What does it look like?" I gestured towards my backpack. "I'm leaving. And I'm taking Rafael with me."

"You cannot be serious."

"Yeah?" I continued gathering my things, working around Cub as she nuzzled against my arm. "Why not?"

"Keegan, Rafael can't be moved. In case you haven't noticed—he's sick," Preston continued. "He could even be—"

"Don't." I turned around to jab a finger at him. "Don't you say it, Pres! Not you."

His eyes narrowed a little, and he seemed to be pondering my words.

"You carry light in your veins, Pres," I went on, my voice rising. "We need to stop acting like the roar of the wind scares us—we need to fly into the storm and roar right back in its face! I'm tired of the silence I hear inside myself…" I zipped my backpack shut and slung it over my shoulder. "It's our silence, our complacency, our willingness to simply embrace the storm that's keeping him sick," I finished, my voice raw. "Raf's not going to get better here, surrounded by doubt and unbelief."

"So what the hell are you going to do, Keeg?" Preston asked, his voice sharp. "Transport somewhere else with him?"

"Not transport, no," I explained. "I'm going to take him into the woods with me."

Preston dragged a hand over his face, going silent for a moment before he exploded.

"That's how he got sick in the first place! That's how we lost them!" His voice cracked as he shouted. "What the hell, man—what are you thinking? You can't—"

"Not to that part of the woods, not beyond the river," I said defensively, cutting in. "The only way Raf's going to get well again is to get away from all of this… this death. He needs to be outside. He… he needs to hear the rush of the stream, the songs of the birds, the wind in the grass—he needs to *feel it* on his face, not be shut away, listening to us all despair! He can hear us, Pres!" My voice became jagged as my throat tightened. "I know he can… I know he can hear me when I read to him."

Preston bit his lip, looking down at the ground.

"Why don't you come with me?" I went on, my voice a little calmer. "Get away from all of this for a while…"

"Get away from thinking about Janna, you mean? I can't, Keeg… I think you know that better than anyone." Preston stepped closer. "Is that what you're *really* trying to do?" he asked. "Forget Sparrow?"

The question was like a punch in the gut.

"I could sooner forget myself," I whispered.

He pressed his lips together. "Keeg, maybe you should just try to—"

"No—"

"Accept that—"

"*No.*" My voice hardened as my eyes locked with his. "Will you ever accept that *Janna* is gone, Pres? That you'll never see her again? That she's lost to us?"

I saw a twinge of pain in Preston's brown eyes. "I think I've already begun to, Keeg… as hard as that is to say.”

I studied him in disbelief until he turned and opened the barn door, holding it open as he stepped outside.

“You go, Keegan,” he said. “Get away from everything and everyone—go look for whatever it is you obviously need to find,” he finished, giving me a small, sad smile. “You know where to find me.”

I stood in the middle of the barn for a moment, trying to figure him out. Wishing there was something I could say that would make him change his mind, that would make him come with me. But I could tell from the look on his face that his mind was made up.

I followed him outside, my backpack slung over my shoulder and Cub at my heels.

“Is Sensei upstairs?” I asked.

Pres nodded. We walked around to the front of the cabin and up the steps. Cub put her paws up on the door as it closed in her face.

Heading upstairs, I bumped into Lara.

She raised an eyebrow as soon as she saw the pack. “And where do you think you’re going?”

“Anywhere but here,” I answered, continuing up the stairs.

“Keegan, what are you talking about?”

I didn’t answer her. I pounded up the stairs and halted in the hallway just as Kateri emerged from the girls’ room at the opposite end. Her hair was wet, and she was drying it with a towel. Our eyes connected as I shouldered open the door to Rafael’s room.

I found Dad seated at the end of Rafael’s bed. This time he wasn’t reading; he was just sitting there, looking into Rafael’s face as he stroked back his messy dark hair. He looked up when I closed the door behind me. His face was drawn and tired, and a heaviness clouded his normally bright green eyes. He straightened a little and drew a deep breath.

“Keegan.”

“Dad, I have to talk to you,” I answered quickly. “And I hope you’ll be on my side because I’m sure Lara won’t be.”

Dad’s eyebrows arched curiously. “What is it?”

Sliding off my pack, I walked across the room and knelt down beside Rafael's bed.

"Dad," I began softly, "you can't stay at the Homestead forever. There are too many other students depending on you. You are *their* Sensei too. They need you just as much as we do. You've done everything you can for Rafael."

Dad shook his head. "I cannot give up."

"No, you can't," I agreed. "But… you can let me step in."

"What do you mean?"

I turned to look back at Rafael. His eyelids were tinged purple, and his lips were dry. I reached over and placed a hand on his forehead, letting the warmth of my hand soak into his cool skin.

"Dad, there is a restlessness inside me… I don't know how to describe it, but…" I trailed off, shaking my head. "It hit me like a lightning bolt today why Rafael isn't getting better here. He can't get well because doubt is like…" I searched for the right words. "It's like a cloud hanging over this house. Dad, I want to leave and take Rafael with me."

"Leave?" he repeated, sounding surprised.

"Not forever, but for a while. I feel like I've lost something, and I'm not just talking about…" I didn't finish. "I need to find the center of things again. To feel Earth breathing under me again. To remember why *I* breathe again."

As I spoke, Dad watched me without judgment in his eyes. He didn't protest or shut me down. He listened.

"You promised Hawk that you would take care of Sparrow, and I promised you the exact same thing." I quieted my voice. "I failed. And now, the only key we might have to finding out what happened to Sparrow and Janna is Raf… He has to wake up. And I… I feel like I may know how to heal him…" I trailed off, then corrected myself. "How to give him the space he needs to heal himself, really. Let me take him… Let me redeem myself."

He pulled in a deep breath, rubbing a hand over his face. "Into the woods?"

"Just the woods we know. The forest we have healed and not beyond it," I assured him. "We won't be in any danger."

"I thought the same when I sent you out the first time," Dad said, strained. "Yet here we are…"

"This is different. Dad. You know he can't get better here. I think that's why you wanted me to hear that story about the boy and the wolves," I answered quietly. "I *am* that boy in the story. I think you know that."

Dad looked down at Rafael. Droplets of water continued to trickle from his fingertips and into the bucket on the floor.

"How long will you be gone?" Dad asked finally, his soft voice breaking the silence.

For the first time since Sparrow had been taken, something inside me felt alive.

"Probably two weeks," I managed. "We won't go beyond the river."

Dad nodded. He stood and put his hand on my shoulder, clasping it like someone who was hanging on, hanging on like I was. For a moment I felt like I understood him better than I'd ever understood anyone before. And he understood me too. Or maybe he always had, but the momentary connection between us made me realize it more deeply now.

Dad turned and slipped out of the room. I heard his footsteps on the stairs and then voices—his and Lara's. They began to argue, and Lara made all the protests I knew she would. I knew no one would understand but Dad.

I was still kneeling on the floor, watching Raf's chest gently rise and fall, when Kateri came in and knelt on the floor beside me. She looked into my face, her warm brown eyes seeming to reflect my unspoken thoughts.

"You're leaving," she whispered. It was more of a statement than a question.

I nodded.

"To be alone?" she asked.

I thought about it, tilting my head slightly to one side. "I don't know, really."

Kateri nodded slowly, looking down at her knees folded in front of her. "Because if you're all right with it, I'd love to come with you."

"Would you?" I asked quietly. "Really?"

Kateri's eyes searched mine. "Unless you wanted to be alone…"

I slowly shook my head. "I can be alone better when I'm with you."

# 49

I LAY ON THE FLOOR BELOW THE WINDOW, WATCHING THE sunset drizzle in to paint the dirt in hues of red and gold. I pulled the familiar paper out of my pocket. The corners were folded and the edges tattered now.

I closed my eyes and pressed the photograph of Keegan to my mouth. I thought of how my lips had once touched his. I remembered how I had once fallen asleep in his arms, listening to his heart pounding in his chest.

I swallowed hard, blinking back the hot stinging in my eyes as I slid the paper back into my pocket, sighing out a shaky breath.

Twilight rolled out like a blanket, welcoming the night and plunging the small cell once again into darkness. I rolled onto my side, pulling my legs up to my chest. I shivered as I listened to the earth grumbling beneath me. I listened for the old man's breathing and movements above the noise, but I couldn't hear him. I lifted my head a little, squinting through the darkness, and could just barely make out the outline of his figure hunched against the wall opposite.

I lay back down, pressing my ear to the earth. Suddenly the walls of the cell began to shake; the steel bars rattled. My body tensed as a loud, groaning rumble, louder than the one before it, sent tremors surging over the length of the floor. I scrambled to my feet, pushing my back to the wall, as I struggled to see what was happening. An explosive bang penetrated the air, followed by a thick *pffttttt* and then the sound of gushing water. The ground continued to shake violently.

"What's happening?" I yelled to Old Man, clinging to the wall.

No response came.

"Old Man!" I shouted hoarsely. "Wake up!"

A moment later, water sloshed against my feet, causing me to gasp and stagger along the wall to escape it. But I couldn't—water covered the floor now. In an instant it was almost to my knees.

"Old Man!" I screamed, sloshing forward. "Wake up, wake up!"

I stopped in the middle of the cell, looking up toward the tiny, barred window at the top. I cupped my hands to my mouth and screamed at the top of my lungs.

"Help! Someone help us!"

I couldn't hear anything over the rush of the water. It was up to my waist now as I sloshed back and forth, frantically searching for the old man, trying to save him before he drowned.

"Can you hear me?" I shouted. "Old Man, can you—"

I was cut off by a mouthful of water as I slipped and fell, submerging. I tumbled in the rushing turbulence, upside down one moment and thrown against the wall the next. My vision wavered as pain shot down my spine. Swinging my arms and kicking my legs, I swam in the direction of what I thought must be the surface. I broke through, gasping for air. I could no longer touch bottom.

"Help!" My voice rattled in my throat as I trod water, fighting to keep my head up. "Help me! Please, someone!"

I kicked, spinning around in the water, straining my eyes as I searched for another body in the water. "Old Man, can you hear me?"

No answer came.

Sucking in a deep breath, I plunged back below the surface,

swimming downward, extending my arms in front of me as I felt around frantically.

Finally, I swam up again, gulping air. This time I extended one arm overhead and felt the ceiling above me. Fear filled my chest, tightening every muscle in my body and making it even harder to keep myself above water.

I screamed for help over and over again. I yelled until my throat burned. But we were underground, and everyone else was above, tucked away in their lodgings and presumably sleeping.

Soon the ceiling was only a foot overhead. I pressed against it with the heels of my hands as I kicked my legs furiously to keep myself above the surface. Water gushed out the small window. Stroking furiously through the water, I bumped up against the cold steel bars and wrapped my fingers around them, thrusting my face into the spaces between them and gasping for air to shout one more time. "Somebody help me!"

Water continued to pour out the window, but it was too small to vent it fast enough to offset its rising inside my cell. I tried to pull myself as close to the bars as I could, but in an instant I was submerged in the thick exiting torrents. I couldn't breathe. I felt my fingers loosen and then slip, my arms bursting out between the bars. My hands grasped at thin air even as the torrent of water shoved against my back, nearly crushing me. It ebbed for a moment, and then, with a renewed surge, threw me forward against the bars again, knocking the wind out of me. Instinctively, I gasped, and my lungs filled with cold, gritty water. My body convulsed as I choked.

Suddenly I felt warmth at my fingertips. A hand seized mine, pulling. I grasped the hand with every ounce of strength I had left in my body. I could hear a loud groan like buckling steel over the roar of the rushing water. The warm hands gave a violent tug, and like a cork blown out of a bottle, I surged forward in the flow of water and spilled out onto the ground, gasping and choking.

"S-s-someone's still down there!" I choked, scrambling to my feet, splashing through the water and lunging for the window. Two hands seized me by the waist.

"Stop! Stop, you can't go back down there—come on!" said a man's voice. It was familiar somehow, yet...

There was no time to think. He pulled me by the arm and began to run. I stumbled into step beside him, unsure of what was happening or who had my arm in a vise grip. Alarms began to blare. A flashing red strobe swept the camp and reached up into the sky.

"Come on!" he urged.

We tore across the district to the wall, where a rope was hung. He scaled up the wall, and though I was exhausted, I grabbed onto it and hauled myself up after him, staying close on his heels. Landing hard on the other side, I tried to catch my breath as he jerked the rope down, looped it over his shoulder, and surged away into the darkness. From there onward, everything was a blur, but I could feel brush scraping against my legs and low-hanging tree branches whipping against my arms. I stumbled over the rocky ground, but each time I almost fell, the same strong arms caught me.

Finally, we stopped. I heard a door open. I was pulled forward, and suddenly I felt the solid planks of a wood floor beneath me.

I crumpled to my knees, gasping for air. A match hissed, igniting the darkness with a dim golden glow that illuminated only vague shapes lingering around me like ghosts.

"Here... here, come on." The hands lifted me to my feet, guiding me forward. "Listen, I need to get back before they suspect anything—I will come back as soon as I can. Do *not* go outside."

As the adrenaline coursing through me began to taper off, I began to recognize the deep, smooth voice.

"But there was someone..." I mumbled, my voice fading. "There was someone else down there..."

"Shhh," he hushed. "Keep as silent as possible—I will be back as soon as I can."

The half-consumed match illuminated the dark eyes and stony features of Corporal Price's face in faint, flickering amber.

"Where are we—what about Bask?" I whispered. "He's going to be looking for me. What if he—"

"Bask will not find you." Corporal Price blew out the match, submerging us in darkness. I felt his breath on me as he leaned closer. "If you want to make it out of this place alive," he whispered in my ear, "you'll keep your mouth shut, and you'll stay here until I come for you."

I was too exhausted to ask questions. Words simply wouldn't form. I sank back onto what felt like a stiff mattress. I heard the corporal's footsteps pass over the floorboards. I heard the door open and shut.

I collapsed back, drinking in the oxygen. My eyelids sank shut.

# 50

LARA SAID NO.

She didn't see what I saw when I looked at Rafael. No one did but Dad and Kateri. Everyone argued about it, but later that day I gathered Rafael's wasted form in my arms and headed into the forest with Kateri beside me. Cub frolicked just ahead of us as we listened to the sounds of the cabin grow more and more distant. Finally, we were far enough away that only birdsongs and the chirrup of summer crickets filled our ears.

"I thought Lara would understand." I sighed heavily. "We're usually on the same page about so many things, she and I."

Kateri seemed thoughtful for a moment, her steps in sync with mine. A pack was slung over her shoulder, and a bandanna was wrapped around her head. "Some things take time."

"Yeah… and I hate that because I have literally no patience."

"I've noticed."

I glanced over at her, and she grinned. I surrendered a little laugh, shifting Raf's weight in my arms. His head rested on my shoulder.

"I guess it's just that sometimes we're patient, and time goes by only to reveal to us that we've screwed up and should have done something differently," I went on. "Sometimes I just want to fast-forward time and find out what the results of my choices will be, and then rewind and do it all right."

"And what about all the space in between the means and the end?" Kateri inquired. "The sunrises, meals, chores, target practices, nights on the rooftop—what about all the cricket songs and shooting stars? The good, tired feelings from working hard, and the cool of the rainy afternoons?" She looked at me intently. "Wouldn't you miss all of that, Keeg?"

"I wouldn't have until you mentioned it all." I passed her a fatigued smile. "But yeah. Yeah, I would. I guess it's just… that I want so badly to know whether I'm doing the right thing."

A gap slipped into our conversation. A pair of sparrows swooped low overhead, singing. I lowered my eyes to the ground in front of me.

"Do you think I did the right thing, Kateri?" I asked quietly.

"Would I be here if I didn't think you were doing the right thing?" she responded.

A small smile passed over my lips.

We walked for hours until we came to a small clearing, soft with moss and sheltered by tall, swaying pines. I laid Rafael gently on a bed of moss. Kateri stayed with him, and I went a little deeper into the woods to find sticks to start a fire with.

The air was still, void of even a slight breeze to stir the trees overhead. The occasional scurry of a squirrel or the quiet flitting of tiny wings were the only sounds to disturb the otherwise silent atmosphere.

I gathered sticks as I walked, scanning the lush woods around me. The last time I'd been out here, Sparrow had been with me. It had been among these same trees that I'd yelled at her, suspecting her of informing on us to her military boyfriend. I'd told her that Dad didn't trust her and neither did I. I'd been hard on her, and she'd given it right back to me.

I picked up another stick, trying to ignore the memories, but it was impossible. With each step that I took, the same question echoed louder and louder in my thoughts: *Where is she, where is she, where is she?*

I could feel her everywhere, yet she was nowhere.

Clutching the pile of twigs and dry, broken branches, I circled back through the woods and emerged into the clearing just as the dim brown hues of dusk were beginning to settle. Kateri cradled Rafael's head in her lap, her back to one of the thick trees. Cub was curled up next to her; her ears pricked back and her head lifted as I walked into the clearing. I knelt down, choosing a spot for the fire. I stacked the wood and dried bits of bark carefully. Cupping my hands together, I channeled an orb, letting it evolve slowly; first clear, then fading to orange and finally red. Then fire. I let it roll off my fingertips and into the kindling, sending it up into flames with a soft *whoosh*.

Sitting back on my heels, I watched the fire take form. It crackled and popped, interrupting the silence.

"What are you thinking about?" Kateri asked.

*Sparrow.*

I got up and walked over to take a seat beside her. I placed a hand on Rafael's forehead, stroking his messy dark curls out of his eyes.

"I just wish I could read him," I said softly, staring down into his face. "I wish I knew what was going on inside his head…"

I carefully placed my first three fingers on Raf's forehead in a triangular shape to create a point of focus. I pulled in a breath and closed my eyes. My surroundings and Kateri's presence faded away, along with the warmth of the fire at our feet. My forehead went numb, and I dove into the darkness.

I felt like I was submerged in water. I floated there, moved by the rhythm of the waves. I listened carefully for any sounds. A faint whisper whipped past me like a spinning blade. It seemed to flit around me, slicing through the darkness, so soft I could hardly distinguish the words.

"You're leaving… you're leaving… you're…" it said. It was interrupted by another disembodied whisper.

"They're letting you… they're… tell Keegan… promise…"

The voice became clear and familiar—so familiar it sent my head spinning. I dropped out of Rafael's mind and back into my own. I jumped to my feet, my heart in my throat. For a moment everything was still black.

"Keeg? Keeg, are you all right?" Kateri asked, alarmed.

I took a few steadying breaths. "I saw something this time."

"Really?"

"I *heard* something. I heard Sparrow's voice."

"Sparrow's? Why Sparrow's?"

I began to pace in front of the fire. "They must have seen each other. He keeps replaying it in his thoughts: 'You're leaving… they're letting you…' and 'tell Keegan…'"

Kateri held Raf a little closer, cradling his head in the crook of her arm. "Tell you what?"

"I have no idea."

"But it proves that Sparrow *found* Rafael after all…" Kateri concluded.

"But why would they have let him go?" I said, thinking out loud. "Or did he escape?"

"Maybe Sparrow helped him?" Kateri offered softly.

My mind drifted as I studied the flames.

"Maybe… but he seems to think that they let him go…" I muttered. "But that makes no sense. The RGM would never release anyone. They would have just killed him. It's almost like…"

I traced my fingertips over my forehead, thinking back over what I'd read in Rafael's thoughts.

"Almost like what?"

I shook my head slowly, reliving the night Sparrow had been taken, the things we'd said before. How she'd told me that she wanted to redeem herself by finding Raf, by finding both of them.

*God, why the hell did I let her go?*

Swallowing hard, I turned to look at Kateri. "It's almost like they let him go because they finally had what they really wanted."

"Meaning *Sparrow*?" Kateri said. "But—but why would they want Sparrow specifically?"

*Could they possibly have figured out who she really is?* That was exactly what I dreaded, but I didn't share this with Kateri.

"Sparrow could see them—she was the *only* one who could see them. That was her ability, and she didn't even know it. None of us did."

"So… you think that's why they took her?"

"I don't know what to think, Kateri," I replied. "Except that Sparrow must have been able to accomplish exactly what she told me she would."

"Which was?"

"To find them—to free them," I said quietly. "Even if it was in exchange for herself."

"Do you think it's possible that she found Janna too, then?"

Shrugging my shoulders, I gave a frustrated sigh. "Raf is the only way we're going to find out."

"But his mind is full of darkness, you said." She looked down into Rafael's face. "Nothing can be known in the darkness. No one awakens until the dawn. If darkness is what's keeping him asleep… then we will fill his mind with light."

I watched her as she leaned closer to place a gentle kiss on Raf's forehead. The gears in my head started turning.

"Light…?" I repeated slowly. "I think I know just the place."

# 51

MY EYELIDS FLEW OPEN AS I BOLTED UPRIGHT ON THE STIFF mattress. The floor creaked as I stood, everything blurring as I spun around. I was in some kind of shack, but I couldn't make anything out in the darkness.

Suddenly, everything came rushing back: the flood, Corporal Price rescuing me… Old Man, and how I hadn't been able to find him in the rising water.

Stumbling to one of the walls, I pressed my hands against it, running my fingertips frantically over the wood.

*There has to be a way out. There has to be a way out…*

My heart began to pound in my chest as I crossed the room and tried the opposite wall, slamming the palms of my hands against it again and again. My fingernails dragged over the slats, searching for a break, a latch, anything.

The dull thud of boots grabbed my attention. I held my breath as I backed away from the wall, chills rising over my skin.

I braced inwardly, bringing my hands up in front of me to channel an orb of bright, flickering energy. It wavered and pulsed between my fingers as I waited in the middle of the room, my toes digging into the floor. My eyes remained locked on the place where the footsteps had stopped.

The wall rattled, then slid aside. My next breath caught in my throat as cold night air swept in, along with a figure, its face illuminated by the glow from the orb in my hands.

Though Corporal Price's voice was quiet, it seemed to fill the tiny room as he stepped inside, closing the sliding panel behind him. "Don't look so surprised. I told you I would be back."

Breathing a sigh of relief, I clenched my fingers to fists, dissolving the pulsating orb.

Price made his way through the darkness and to a small table, striking a match to light an oil lamp. I gave his tall frame a once-over. He was wearing civilian clothes: gray joggers and a sand-colored T-shirt. His dark brown skin was washed in the golden reflections of the lamp on the table.

"You scared the shit out of me." My voice was icy. "What happened last night? You said you would get me out of there, Price—you never came."

"I got you out, didn't I?"

"Seconds before I drowned!"

He shrugged his broad, muscled shoulders. "Better late than never."

My stomach sank as I looked down at the floor. "Did they get him out?"

"Who?"

I swallowed hard, reaching for words but finding none.

I already knew the answer.

Finally, I shook my head. "No one. Never mind." I sighed. "You said you would get me out of there, you said you would come, and you never did."

"I couldn't let Bask suspect me of being a sympathizer." Price's tone remained flat.

"Which is *exactly* what you are."

"As far as anyone knows, you got out of there on your own, because you're a slider and because you can see—they *know* that now, Sparrow. How else would you have been able to escape?"

"So in helping me get away, you've also blown my cover?"

"In a sense, but it won't matter," Price answered, his tone strangely calm. "I could very well be the one they put in charge of searching for you—I'm going to make sure of that, actually."

"How do I know you won't lead them straight to me, Corporal?" I asked, narrowing my eyes at him. "I don't understand why you're even helping me—"

"But I *did* help you, didn't I?" His question sliced through my words. "I could have let you drown down there, but I didn't. I saved you and brought you here."

"So you expect me to just trust you and wait here while you lead the RGM on a wild-goose chase until they give up on finding me?"

"Exactly."

"That sounds… insane."

"What's the alternative?" He looked up at me. "Bask was going to execute you, Sparrow. He wants nothing more than to watch you *hang*. Is that what you want? I took advantage of the chaos—and that just happened to be the first opportunity that presented itself for me to help you."

"*Help* me?" My voice was steely. "It's clear you're *not* helping me escape. You would have let me go by now."

"Didn't I help the boy escape?" Price continued to look at me, his gaze unfaltering. "Didn't I tell you that you would be in my debt because of that?"

A heavy, sinking feeling filled the pit of my stomach.

"What is it you want from me?"

"Nothing yet," he answered flatly. "Only that you stay here."

"What the hell makes you think I will?"

"If you leave, I can't guarantee that the search teams won't find you. If you stay here, I'll know exactly where you are and be able to lead them away from you." His explanation was as stern as his tone. "You're *safe here*. But as soon as you step outside, I can no longer protect you. Bask will be more eager for your demise than ever."

"Because I can see?"

"Because you *saw*," Price corrected me firmly. "You saw *everything*, Sparrow. You're a walking liability."

"A walking liability that *you're* sheltering." I lowered my voice. "What happens if the RGM finds out?"

"They will never find out."

For a moment we both stood there, looking at each other in tense silence.

"I have to get back," he said, though he didn't make a move to leave. He remained where he was, studying me. "Please… stay inside if you value self-preservation at all."

I didn't reply. I felt stiff as my fingers clamped around the edge of the table. I watched him walk over to the wall, open the sliding panel, and slip back outside again.

# 52

*My dear sweet boy,*

*The day you became an RGM soldier was both the saddest and the proudest day of my life. I cannot tell you what I felt as I sat there watching you. There aren't enough beautiful words to express what can only be conveyed in tears.*

*They told me today. They told me what's happened to you. I find myself with that same lack of propensity for words, but this time there is no longer pride in my heart, only sorrow. Grief.*

*Aaron, they have told me I can never speak to you again. That I can never attempt to make contact with you again. I hope to god they will spare you.*

*The sergeant said he will put this letter into your hand, and that it will be my last communication with you. So I want you to know that I love you. Even though part of me feels as if I do not know you at all.*

*Your loving mother*


I sat on the edge of my bed, staring down at the worn, yellowed page. Why I'd kept it all these years I couldn't explain even to myself. Maybe it was just the normal thing to do. Maybe it signified that I still had emotions, which I hated to acknowledge. Even so, I don't know why I kept it. It did nothing but make me hate my mother and the RGM at the same time, when in reality I loved them both and hated *myself.*

Still, I would never—*could* never—forget that face in the crowd, the old man who had sat beside my mother at the graduation. The man only *I* had seen. Everything had been so perfect until that moment. He'd taken the happiest day of my life and transformed it into a nightmare, a nightmare that I'd yet to wake up from.

I could still see him when I closed my eyes. Some days I would see him walking in crowds or turning a corner. For a while I thought I was being stalked; then I began to wonder if I was hallucinating, until finally, on that last night, he appeared… and I met him face-to-face…

The sound of deadbolts retracting startled me out of my thoughts. I folded the letter back up and tucked it beneath my thin mattress, getting to my feet just as the door burst open and Bask stepped inside. The whole structure trembled as he slammed the door shut behind him.

His face was a deep, angry red. His hands were clenched to fists, and he was breathing heavily.

"Where is she?" he growled.

"Who?"

"You know full well."

"No, actually, I don't. I've been locked in here all night," I replied through gritted teeth.

Without warning, Bask wound back one arm and punched a hole in the wall, cursing.

"Has something happened?" I asked flatly.

"Sparrow has escaped." He spat the words out like venom. "There was a flood in the pit from an underground spring, and she escaped through the window. She bent the bars and escaped." The wind hissed through the hole he'd made in the wall, accentuated by Bask's angry gasps.

"Bent the bars? How?"

Bask clamped his eyelids shut, looking about ready to explode. "How do you *think?* She's a lice-bag *slider*—who can apparently *see!* How the hell could she have gotten out if she couldn't see?"

"Has the district been searched?"

Bask nodded. "And the process continues."

"She's a slider who's obviously capable of bending steel, but that doesn't mean she can see," I said, hoping to throw him off track. "She could have felt her way out. She could be hiding somewhere."

"Bullshit. She's not within the wire anymore; I can feel it," he muttered under his breath, rubbing his jaw. "Did she say anything to you? Anything at all?"

"How could she have? You forbade me from seeing her."

"I wasn't convinced you'd obey me."

"Well, I *did* obey you, and I know nothing. But if she has escaped and she can in fact see..."

"... then we have a massive liability on our hands."

"To put it lightly."

Bask clenched his teeth, squeezing his fingers into tighter fists. "Did you get any information out of her that night you spent with her?"

"We didn't spend the night together," I corrected him. "I brought her here after your fit of rage, yes. But she just slept, and I learned no new information from her."

He cursed again, pacing across the room and back again.

"She must have been the one who helped the boy escape. She *had* to have been. Who else could have done it?" he snapped. "*She can see,* Price."

"Why wouldn't she have just escaped herself, then?"

He shook his head. I was surprised to see a lost, terrified look in his eyes. "No damn clue. But if this goes up the chain of command..."

I folded my arms over my chest and tipped my head back as I watched him walk his tortured walk, pulling at his face.

"I have to go," he said abruptly. He sucked in a large breath, coming to a halt in the middle of the floor. "I only came to see if she was here, or if you knew anything."

"Maybe I would have if I hadn't been locked in all night, but we all know I can't be trusted, don't we?"

Bask said nothing in response to this. He turned on his heels and strode to the door, slamming it again as he left.

I sank back on my mattress, letting go of a sigh of relief.

The previous night felt like a dream—rescuing Sparrow from the flooded cell, getting her over the wall and up into the woods. I'd helped another slider escape, which felt so wrong… and *so right* at the same time.

I had to keep reminding myself that I hadn't really helped her *escape*. No, escape was when someone got away, and that was the last thing Sparrow had done. I'd saved her from inevitable death one way or another, but she hadn't gotten away—not from me.

She said she didn't trust me. Maybe she didn't think she did, but behind her angry words I could sense that for her, I was the rock in the rapids; I was all she had to hang on to for the time being. Something inside me didn't mind it. Something inside me felt the same way about her, even though it would be impossible for her to understand why.

This time I knocked softly. She didn't answer. I slid the door open, stepped inside, and found her sleeping. She was sprawled on her back on the mattress, her hair spread out around her, one arm tucked under her head. She looked just like she had when I'd stood outside her cell and watched her from the window. Except now she was right in front of me.

I closed the door behind me. She stirred a little, rolling over, murmuring inaudibly.

I walked across the room, taking a cloth sack out from under my jacket and setting it on the table. For a moment I stood there, listening. Behind me I could hear the soft sounds of her inhales and exhales.

After a moment she stirred again, drawing a deep breath.

"Corporal," she mumbled, then sat up, startled, as I turned around to face her. "What's happened?"

"Nothing," I said, picking up one of the rickety chairs and spinning it around to face her. "I just… brought you something to eat."

Sparrow sat there stiffly for a moment. Dried blood still creased her lower lip.

"I'm not hungry," she said finally. "Do they suspect anything?"

I shook my head. "Only what I assumed they would."

"So Bask knows I can see?"

"I tried to confuse him on that point, but yes, he knows. Bask is no fool."

Sparrow cursed and dragged a hand over her face.

"Price, look—"

"I think it's time for you to start calling me Aaron."

Sparrow's eyes narrowed a little; her mouth seemed frozen open. She recovered herself. "Fine. *Aaron*. When will the search team start looking for me? Have you heard?"

"They've already begun looking for you."

"Is it night now?"

"Close to sunset."

She nodded slowly, seeming to think. "When do you think they'll give up?"

"Bask isn't going to let you slip through his fingers that easily."

"And you're not going to help me get away, are you?"

I looked at her for a long moment, thinking about it.

"Not yet. It's too risky. Besides, I want to get to know you better."

Her eyebrows lifted.

"Not like that," I assured her. "I just… I'm just interested in you. I haven't been interested in anything for a very long time."

"And why's that?"

"The district has a way of beating the life out of the people it swallows."

"How the hell did you end up here, anyway?"

"They sent me here to help manage the district."

Her piercing eyes slowly narrowed. "Bullshit."

"You're very honest."

"While you are the exact opposite," she shot back. "You ask me to trust you, yet you've given me no reason to. I can't trust someone who never tells me the truth."

"So, it's truth you want, then?"

"Isn't that what we all want?"

"No. No, not really. I can think of a lot of things that I would rank higher on the list, actually."

She swung her legs over the side of the mattress and stared at me. "You're an asshole, you know that?"

"I know. So let's talk about you, then."

"So you can go report it all to the RGM?" she snorted. "I don't think so."

"How could I? Then they would know that *I know* where you are," I pointed out. "As hard as it might be for you to believe, I have no intention of telling the RGM anything about you. This isn't an interrogation, Sparrow. I didn't even mean that you should tell me about yourself as a slider." I faltered over the word, but then glanced back to her eyes. "I meant… tell me about *you*. The young woman named Sparrow."

"You're not just… pumping me for information?"

I shook my head slowly. "No."

"Tell me about you first, then. Starting with why Bask couldn't see you."

I stiffened, taken aback.

"Did you really think I wouldn't notice?" she asked. "When Bask told you to leave his office that day, you didn't. You slammed the door like you had left, but when I turned around, you were still standing there, and Bask was none the wiser."

I thought for a moment, running a hand over the back of my neck.

"Do you remember when I told you that even though no one can see invisible RGM personnel and prisoners, *they* can see *each other*?" I asked.

Sparrow nodded. "Yes, I remember."

"Well, I'm the exception to that rule," I said simply. My voice suddenly sounded small in my ears. "None of them can see me."

"Holy shit," she murmured. "*No one* can see you? How is that possible?"

"I received an accidental overdose of the invisibility inoculation," I lied. "It was supposed to wear off over time, but… mine didn't."

"Wouldn't the rest of the RGM soldiers still be able to see you, then?"

"The dose I received was much stronger."

"Where do these inoculations come from?"

"A classified source."

"And why is the RGM making its units of troops invisible?"

"Think of all the things you can do when no one can see you. The RGM has mastered the formula to the point of being able to make not only its troops invisible, but also objects, structures, entire bases. The district supplies artillery to the rest of the militia. Being invisible is the perfect way to keep out unwanted guests."

Sparrow rested her elbows on her knees, leaning forward to look at me. Her dark eyes probed mine.

"You talk like a soldier through and through."

"Because I *am* a soldier."

"Then why *the hell* are you helping me?"

I scanned her face for a moment. "I've been invisible for so long, I'd forgotten what it felt like to be seen… It's something so simple, no one ever even thinks about it. Yet years of being invisible has made me realize how intoxicating it is just to have someone look into my eyes… and actually see me."

Sparrow stood, her hair flowing over her shoulders and spilling down her back as she began to pace.

"So… no one can see you…" she began, then trailed off. "Except for me?"

I pulled in a breath to answer, but she kicked the wall before I could get a word out, cursing.

I jumped to my feet, striding forward to grab her by the arm. "Sparrow—"

She struck my hand away, whirling around to face me. Her nostrils flared, and her cheeks flushed.

"Is that the only reason you saved me?" she shouted right into my face. "So you could keep me for yourself—lock me away like an animal?"

I opened my mouth to speak, but she grabbed me by the collar of my shirt and jerked me closer before I could say anything, her lips trembling.

"Would you have saved me if I were just a normal slider?" Her voice shook as she spoke. "If I was blind to you just like everyone else—would you have saved me then?"

It had been so long since a woman had touched me—had been this close. I could feel Sparrow's breath on my face, the warmth of her hand on my chest.

"Probably not," I whispered.

Sparrow stared me in the eyes, her fingers trembling as she clenched my shirt in her fist. Then, with all her strength, she slapped me.

# 53

I WAS UP LONG BEFORE KATERI AWOKE. THE SKY WAS DARK and overcast as I lifted Rafael gently from the ground, cradling him in my arms. Treading softly, I carried him to the edge of the clearing where a large, flat rock stood. I lowered him carefully onto it, then took a seat beside him, resting his head in my lap. Water drizzled from his fingertips and rolled over the surface of the stone, leaving moss to bloom in its wake.

I took a deep breath and closed my eyes, trying to ignore the sinking weight in my chest.

Everything seemed like it was breaking apart. If this was reality, I wanted to kick it in the face. I was a slider—I was supposed to be *above* the circumstances, not under them. I sat there in the silence, listening to Rafael's shallow inhales and exhales. It was hard to imagine a different reality.

I gently stroked Rafael's forehead with my thumb and began to imagine him as he had been before: so awake and alive and full of energy. He was like rocket fuel. He always had been. I could see his sparkling eyes. I could hear his voice, his laughter.

*Wake up… wake up… wake up…*

I couldn't tell if I'd spoken the words or merely thought them, but they burned inside me like fire.

I could still see him in my head, trailing behind the rest of the group to talk to Sparrow. I think he'd been the first to make her smile.

"Keeg?"

A familiar voice tugged me back down to earth. I felt a soft hand on my shoulder as Kateri came up behind me.

"How's he doing?"

I opened my eyes. "He seems all right."

Kateri reached over my shoulder to gently touch Raf's face. "We should get moving," she said quietly.

I nodded slowly, getting to my feet. I lifted Raf into my arms again. "Fire out?"

Kateri nodded. "And everything's packed."

"You're always two steps ahead, aren't you?"

A grin was her only response.

The sky was still overcast but turning pink now as we journeyed deeper into the woods. The ground was soft with dew, and the air was thick and warm. Kateri took the blanket off Rafael and stuffed it into my backpack. She hummed softly as we walked, winding around trees and ducking low branches. Kateri walked ahead as I lagged behind. Cub followed at my heels, lunging after leaves that swirled in the wind.

"You were up early this morning," Kateri said, breaking the silence. "Were you meditating?"

"Trying to." I sighed. "Sometimes I just… show up. And fight with myself."

She hummed a laugh. "Sometimes you just need to let your thoughts know they're not going to win, even if things seem to be looking good for them at the moment."

"Is it possible to bottle your optimism?" I asked, ducking a branch. "I'd love to get drunk on it every night."

Kateri laughed. "You have your own. We wouldn't be out here if you didn't. Are you sure you know where you're taking us?"

My gaze lingered on Rafael as I nodded.

"Completely," I said. "You said he needs light; we'll give it to him."

The scent of golden pine needles and sap hung heavy in the air. I took a deep breath. "You ever wonder how things got this way? Like, where along the line did someone royally screw everything up?"

Kateri paused at the base of a withering oak, craning her neck to peer up at the branches.

"Nothing happens all at once. Not even the universe; it rolls on and on like the sea, slowly unfolding first in stars, then planets. Suddenly galaxies sprawl before us." She paused, lifting one hand to the rough bark of the tree. "It's never on one big moment that everything pivots… It's on the thousands of little choices that slip by without our noticing."

I watched as the tree transformed beneath her touch, becoming once again vibrant and alive. The branches swayed and unfurled mint-green leaves.

"It's scary when you think about it that way," I said absently, shifting Rafael's weight in my arms.

"Why?"

"Because it would mean that every little thing we do—every action, every decision that seems small and pointless—is actually *making* the future." I blew out my cheeks. "Like… damn."

"Don't be afraid of it." Kateri's fingers danced over the bark. "Just make good things. Good thoughts and decisions."

"I wish I were as good at it as you are."

"Shhh—enough of that." She swatted the air with her hand; then she stopped mid-strike.

"What is it?" I came up behind her.

She pointed ahead, where I could now see that the woods thinned out; shafts of early morning light glittered down through the pine boughs. Beyond the trees I caught snatches of a golden meadow. I looked at Kateri, the stubble on my chin catching in Rafael's hair.

"Nearly there," she said. In her voice was a hint of hope.

Cub had already bounded ahead. She tripped over her own paws and tumbled down a mossy knoll. The sky spread open above us in shades of robin's-egg blue as we emerged together into the bright, open meadow. Golden waves of straw ebbed and swayed like an ocean, stretching for a mile in all directions, and the sunlight felt warm and liquid on my skin.

Sage and dried wildflowers stuck up here and there, marking the places where bison bones lay. The remains of what had once been a mighty herd. A symbol of the wild and the free, reduced to wind-whipped ivory.

Kateri stopped in the middle of the field, and I halted alongside her.

"Hang on." She circled around behind me to flip open my backpack and take out the quilt. She unfurled it and spread it over the ground. "Okay."

I lowered Raf gently onto the quilt. His pale lips parted slightly as his head tipped back.

Kateri sat down beside him, and I slid my backpack off.

"So much warmer and brighter out of the woods." I exhaled the words.

"Mmm, it certainly is," Kateri said, leaning back on her elbows and drinking in the warmth. "It feels strange that something can be so beautiful in the very midst of everything that isn't... but some people say it would be hard to recognize light if we did not also know darkness."

I lifted a hand to shield my eyes from the sun.

"Darkness isn't what makes us recognize the light." I squinted, shaking my head. "No, we recognize the light because we have it flowing through our veins."

I watched as water trickled from Rafael's hands and over the ground to snake through the grass, coaxing tiny seedlings up from the crusty dirt. They bobbed and swayed, growing at an astonishing speed.

"Raf's powers seem to be getting stronger," I pointed out, folding my knees to my chest.

Kateri glanced back at him, observing, as tender green leaves sprouted from the seedlings' stems.

"Maybe it's the light in his veins." She gave me a little smile.

"Maybe," I agreed quietly.

"The sky is so blue here."

"There's less pollution at the high elevations. The air's clearer. You know what that means: more stars," I whispered, like it was a secret.

Kateri smiled, turning back to look at Rafael. "Keeg, look."

The seedlings had blossomed into daisies and now flowed through the field like a stream. Suddenly the landscape wasn't so ghostly.

# 54

I SLAPPED HIM. WITH ALL OF MY STRENGTH I SLAPPED HIM, and he just stood there and looked at me.

It made me hate him even more. Nothing, it seemed, could hurt him. Tears burning in my eyes, I lunged forward, pounding on his chest, striking him again and again until my arms grew as heavy as lead, and I collapsed against him, weeping.

For a moment he was stiff. Then I felt one of his hands gently come up to rest on my back.

I jerked away, sniffing and violently wiping away my tears, and turned away from him.

"Sparrow—"

"Don't—don't speak to me." I gasped raggedly. "J-j-just—just leave me alone! Just leave me alone…"

A long pause answered my trembling command.

"If you run, they'll find you."

"I don't give a damn."

"Don't you?"

I shook my head. "I honestly don't care anymore. You can't scare-monger me into staying here—I won't let you keep me here like a caged animal just because you don't want to be alone!"

He took a deep breath. "Sparrow, they're sending out—"

"I don't care!"

"Sparr—"

"Go to hell!"

My teeth clenched, and tears streamed down my face. A moment later I heard the wall retract, then close.

Silence enveloped the tiny room once more. When I turned around, he was gone.

I listened to his footsteps slowly fade out of earshot, leaving me once again alone with my thoughts. I crumpled to the floor, hugging my knees to my chest.

Thoughts circled in my mind like vultures, devouring me and carrying me deeper into the night.

Too tormented to sleep, I paced and ran my fingers along the wall until I finally found the place where the door was. I tugged a few times, to no avail; the door creaked and groaned but didn't budge. My efforts became more violent as I pulled, thrusting my body weight into it until finally the panel slid aside, sending me stumbling backward.

Chill bumps rose over my skin as the cool air swept in. I staggered forward cautiously, leaning against the door frame to look outside. The shack was situated on a steady incline. Gray moss covered the ground, and an army of ghostly pine trees sprawled in every direction like a carpet. The sky was just beginning to lighten with the dawn.

Now was my chance.

I stepped out, and my feet sank into the moist dirt. I slid the door shut, taking a deep breath as I scanned the woods around me.

I started up the incline, hiking as quickly as I could motivate my exhausted body to move. Unlike the strange, crusty ground in District Firehole, the earth here was soft and slick with dew. When I climbed a little higher, I could see the district far below. It was just light enough for me to make out the shapes of the buildings and the wall wrapping around it all like a corral fence to keep the animals in.

I continued farther up the incline; my leg muscles were already fatigued. How was I going to find my way back to the Homestead when I had no idea where I was?

I pushed this question to the back of my mind, putting one foot in front of the other. The woods encompassed me, silent and empty. When I came to a momentary stop, I heard a soft thud. Then another. And another.

*Footsteps.*

My heart raced. I started running as fast as I could up the incline, throwing glances over my shoulder as I dodged trees and ducked low branches. It seemed the harder and faster I ran, the nearer and louder the sounds of the footsteps became.

I slipped and fell, landing on my hands and knees in the slick moss. My heart was pounding in my head, disorienting me as I scrambled to my feet. I heard snatches of voices.

*The search team…*

I pushed myself forward, grabbing onto trunks of trees and using them to propel myself. I could hear the footsteps and voices closing in. I streaked through the shadows of the trees, running faster and faster—until I slipped again.

Two arms caught me. A scream caught in my throat, and a hand slid over my mouth.

For a moment everything froze. My captor pulled me backwards into the hollow of a massive rotting oak, concealing us there as voices shouted and boots thundered over the ground.

My heart thrashed against my rib cage. The hand was still clapped firmly over my mouth, and it remained there until the voices faded.

"Don't be afraid." I felt the warmth of breath in my ear; the voice was gentle and familiar. "It is I."

My eyes widened as his grip loosened and then slid away. I whirled around and saw the outline of his face in the low light, those dark, kind eyes, wrinkled at the corners. "Old man!" I fell into him, wrapping my arms around his neck.

"You made it out," I gasped, holding onto him, burying my face in his shoulder. "But—but how? How did you?"

"Shhh," he whispered back. "We must be quiet now, Sparrow… There are still soldiers around."

"But how did you get out?" I whispered. "I thought you'd drowned…"

"What we think is not always true."

I pulled away to look into his face, still stunned that he was there in front of me.

"I don't know how to get back… I don't know how to find my way back home." I slid to the ground, huddling as far back into the hollow as I could. The old man did likewise. He took off his dark wool cloak and wrapped it around my shoulders.

"You can see things with your eyes that no one else can see, Sparrow," he told me softly. "But you have yet to open your eyes within…"

He touched his fingertips gently to my forehead.

"What do you mean?" I asked.

"Your spirit, Sparrow," he answered.

I didn't know how to respond. I reached for the old man's hand, just as I had on those dark nights in the pit. My fingers wrapped around his and squeezed gently. Cold, numb, and tired, I listened as the voices and the sounds of footsteps grew nearer and nearer. I willed myself to sink farther back into the shadows, pinching my eyes shut. My sense of hearing grew more and more distant as my eyelids grew heavy and darkness overtook me.

# 55

"PRICE, YOU'RE LEADING THIS ONE."

"Me?"

"Yes, you." Bask's expression was stern as he glanced up from the books and papers strewn across the desk in front of him. "Don't pretend you know as little about the ways of sliders as the rest of us."

"I'm ready to do everything I can to retrieve her."

"I'm not interested in retrieving her." Bask sniffed, glancing up from his paperwork—looking up to where he thought I stood. "When you find her, kill her."

I could feel the blood draining from my face. For once in my life, I was grateful to be invisible.

"Sir?"

"We were going to execute her anyway, Price—and now that we know that she observed operations and god knows what else, she *really* must die."

I tried to swallow the sick feeling tinging the back of my throat. "Sir."

He leaned back in his chair and folded his callused hands over his stomach. "You want to prove to me that you're truly on our side, Price? Here's your chance. Lead the team out into the mountains at dawn. I've already mapped a route and filled everyone in." He paused. "Find her and kill her."

I felt sick to my stomach when I stepped out of Bask's office and into the darkness to head for the gates of the district, where I would be meeting the rest of the unit of soldiers. I walked mindlessly down the road, dodging vehicles and prisoners who had no idea I was there. My head was spinning like a hurricane, and Sparrow was in the eye of the storm.

I reached up and touched my cheek, the one she had slapped.

The very idea that she could *see me* and grab hold of me and slap me—the intoxication of it all was enough to make the sting of the slap seem almost sweet. I was beginning to find it harder and harder to dislike her just because she was unfortunate enough to be a slider.

Viner was outside lighting a cigarette when I strode by his shack. I stopped abruptly, dust sprawling from my boots.

"I'm surprised your lungs haven't rotted away from how much you smoke," I joked grimly.

He put his smoke between his lips and cupped his hands over the tip to light it. "Me too. Want one?" He extended a second cigarette and his lighter. I took both from him.

"You're out here late," I pointed out.

"Couldn't sleep."

"Work at the factory treating you all right?"

He looked a little sheepish, then shrugged. "I try my best. It's hard to keep up with everyone else at times. I'm surprised they keep me around, really."

I took a steady drag. "Don't be too hard on yourself."

Viner only tilted his head and frowned.

"Bask's appointed me to take the search team out." I changed the subject.

"Why you?"

I blew out a long stream of smoke, glancing around as I contemplated how to reply.

I couldn't tell him the real reason; he would never look at me the same, and it was weird to say that about a blind man. But the fact was, until Sparrow, Viner had been the only one to treat me like a normal person, because to him that was what I was: as real as everyone else. He could hear me and feel me just like he could any other man. To him I was normal. To everyone else I was a freak. The RGM had told everyone the same pathetic story I'd told Sparrow—that I'd been inoculated with a faulty injection and that it had cursed me with permanent invisibility. However grim this story seemed, though, the truth was far worse. The truth was a *nightmare.*

"Because I'm the one who captured her," I said, tapping the cigarette and sending bits of ash fluttering to the ground. "Bask seems to think that gives me some merit."

"Little does he know you've actually got your head up your ass."

"Shh. You're the only one who's caught on so far."

He double-tapped the side of his nose.

"Anyway, she couldn't have gotten too far," I mused aloud, playing the role. "I'm sure we'll have her neutralized before the day is out."

Smoke streamed out of Viner's nose as he gave a shallow nod. "Good riddance."

The comment pierced my armor, despite the depth at which I tried to keep my emotions buried. I watched Viner through the smoke feathering up from between my fingers—the only sort-of friend I'd had since I'd been transferred to this hellhole. Yet, if he knew the truth, we would never have been friends. In fact, we would be enemies.

I cleared my throat, taking one last drag before I tossed the rest of the cigarette on the ground and crushed it beneath the heel of my boot.

"I'd better get moving."

Viner nodded. "Good luck, Price."

Luck was the last thing in the world I wanted for this mission, because we weren't going to find Sparrow. Sparrow was safely locked away in the shack. Despite what she'd told me, I knew she wouldn't try to run. Even though she was a slider, I was fairly certain she still had some human instincts left in her. Otherwise, the risk of death would be too great.

I led the search team high into the mountains and as far away from the shack as I could manage without seeming to grossly disregard Bask's orders and the coordinates he'd given us to follow. Everything was uneventful up until then; everyone wanted to go back to the district.

As we reached the end of the area Bask had commanded us to search, I was about to open my mouth and announce that we should head back when I heard a stirring in the brush farther up in the woods. My stomach immediately knotted.

"Did you hear that?" one of the soldiers said, and snapped to attention. "Shhh."

"Over this way!" another shouted.

In an instant, everyone rushed forward, deeper into the forest. I took off after them, scanning the woods frantically for any sign of Sparrow. I heard the sound of footsteps again, and this time I could identify them as hers beyond the shadow of a doubt.

"This way!" I shouted, charging forward in the opposite direction of the sound. The rest of the unit followed me.

I guided the team farther and farther away from where I'd heard Sparrow, hoping to god she didn't stumble right into us. We searched the woods for hours to no avail, then hiked back down to the district. It was my fault, I heard them murmuring, but I was too lost in thought to care. I dismissed the team and trudged back to my lodgings, feeling numb from the inside out.

Sparrow was out there in the woods. She'd taken her chances and decided to run.

I stood there for a moment, my back against the door, my thoughts racing.

I had to go back out and find her before someone else did. Sparrow had no idea how much I needed her, but then how the hell could she? Until now I'd been nothing but a dick to her. I'd tried to scare her into staying rather than giving her a reason to stay.

A strange feeling welled up inside me. I turned and threw open the door again, stepping out into the drizzling rain and starting for the gates once more.

# 56

EVERYTHING WAS A DARK, SPINNING CHAOS. THE VOID OF unconsciousness swallowed me whole. Within that emptiness I heard a voice, soft, whispered words:

*"Sparrow, Sparrow, Sparrow…"*

The voice was as soft and fleeting as the wind. It was always the same: a dark shape burst from the branches overhead and leapt into the churning gray sky in a chaos of feathers. A hawk.

*"Sparrow…"*

Like a black hole, it always seemed to swallow me, leaving me to batter around in the darkness in search of an exit I could never seem to find. Maybe it only felt so useless because I knew deep down that it wasn't really the dream I was trying to escape, but who I was—or at least, who Fin had always told me I was.

Could everything Fin had ever told me about my mother, my father and my identity be true?

If Hawk was my mother and Icarus was my father, if I was the daughter of the patriarchs, why would they have left me? If they had actually loved me, if I was worth anything at all, why would they have *left me?*

As quickly as the glimmer of hope had ignited in my heart, it was drowned out by something dark and bitter welling inside me.

Gasping for air, I opened my eyes. I was shivering and wet. Rain drizzled from a dark gray sky. I still wore the old man's cloak, but when I looked to my side, he was gone.

As I climbed to my feet, I saw my breath paint the air in front of me. My fingertips gripped the cold, damp bark of the oak tree as I stood there, my eyes wide as I frantically searched the forest. There was no sign of him.

I was alone and trembling. I felt as though a fire burned in my head—I was hot and cold all at once. My jaw was stiff and clenched, and every bone in my body shook.

*Keep moving… keep moving…*

I pushed myself forward, panting in the cold air. The ground was slick underneath me as I climbed farther and farther up the mountain, clutching the cloak closer around me, pulling it up over my soaked hair.

*Which way? Which way do I go?*

The questions pitched and bent, repeating themselves with each of my ragged inhales. My brain was foggy as I searched desperately for an answer.

I spun, scanning the trees again, wondering if the pines standing in front of me looked familiar. *Do they?*

"Oh, god. Which way…?" The words tumbled over my lips as I whipped around, looking for my own footprints, trying to understand.

*Am I headed uphill or down?*

*Which way did the search team go? What if they're still out here?*

Stumbling forward, I caught myself on one of the pines as the earth seemed to swell and crest like an ocean wave. My fingers clutched at the bark, and my throat tightened as I tried to catch my breath. Each raindrop felt like fire against my skin.

The cloak rippled behind me as I broke into a run. I ran harder, almost blindly now, and it snagged on something, thrusting me to the ground. My forehead struck a rock, sending pain surging through my head. I curled onto my side, gritting my teeth and clamping a hand over my forehead. When I pulled my hand away, it dripped with blood.

I willed myself to crawl to my feet, but every muscle in my body was knotted and burning. I couldn't move. My thoughts flickered, then faded altogether. Wings against the dark, windy sky flashed behind my closed eyelids.

# 57

THE STARS STRETCHED OUT ABOVE US LIKE A CANOPY, blanketing me as I lay there on my back, staring up into the darkness. A few feet away, Kateri slept beside Rafael. I could hear the soft sounds of her breathing.

I couldn't sleep. My mind raced backwards to before all this had happened. I'd taken it all for granted, never having thought I could lose everything in a heartbeat, just like I'd lost my mom and dad. For a moment, Sparrow had ignited my world; now that light had gone out of it, and I was left in darkness.

Rolling to my side, I pushed myself up to my feet. Starlight glittered down through the darkness, throwing their ghostly light over the skeletons of the buffalo, making them seem like specters rising from the ground.

I glanced back over at Rafael, who was lying beside Kateri. Daisies grew around him, looping through his curly hair. Cub had one paw wrapped around him, her head stuffed in his armpit.

The grass parted around me as I made my way through the silver meadow, walking slowly towards the scatterings of dry bones—the remains of the buffalo herd. I stopped in the middle of them; skeletons surrounded me on all sides, encircling me. The wind whipped stronger through the grass, pushing against me, as though the Earth herself were taunting me. I breathed in the scent of sweet sage and balsam fir. My gaze fell on the skeleton of a mother buffalo and her calf, lying side by side.

Slowly sinking to my knees, I felt a shaky sigh escape me. I gently placed my hand on the cow's massive brow bone. It was smooth and cold to my touch.

For a long moment I knelt there, my mind still. Then warmth rushed into my hands, and my fingers began to burn. With both hands, I grabbed hold of the two horns and lay on the ground beside the skeleton, pulling myself up against the massive skull, pressing my forehead against its own. Heat surged from the center of my chest, flowing through my arms and into my hands. The center of my forehead burned as if a fever raged inside me.

I felt the cold bone of the bison's skull pressing against my own. Then a flash of heat burst out around me, taking every ounce of my strength with it.

Unconsciousness swallowed me.

The world was a foggy blur when I opened my eyes. The soft shapes of trees encircled me where I lay on the soft, golden ground, a landscape that was strangely familiar. I slowly sat up and looked around, trying to figure out where I was.

Pieces of boulders studded the ground around me, jagged, worn, and blending in with the colors of the birch bark. I climbed to my feet. Something in my peripheral vision snagged my gaze. At first, I thought it was just a moss-covered knoll, but as I looked closer, I began to realize it was an opening: a cave.

I strode over and brushed aside the thin blanket of vines that hung over the entrance. I stood there for a moment, peering in and listening. In the distance I could hear the pounding roar of water.

*The waterfall.*

*I have to be near the place where we camped…* Finally, I placed it: that was why the trees and rocks looked so familiar to me. This was the place where Sparrow had seen the person in the woods.

Brushing aside the curtain of leaves, I ducked into the cool, damp cave. My fingertips traced along the mossy walls as the cave grew narrower and narrower. I grasped something cool and firm: a doorknob. I pushed, and nothing happened, so I pulled.

With a shrill groan, the hinges gave way, grinding open. A gust of warm, fragrant air blasted in, along with shafts of pinkish-yellow light. In front of me were tall glass windows. At first, I was too blinded to see.

I stepped out into the light. Blankets of wispy fog billowed up from the belly of a ravine; pine trees cascaded down the sides of it, extending their branches like worshiping arms, as though they were paying homage to the golden sun that hung in the bright blue sky.

I stepped forward breathlessly, spellbound and clueless as to where I was. I stood at the window for a moment before turning to face what I discovered was a long hallway that opened up to a platform. I followed it, my bare feet making soft sounds against the weathered wood floor. I stepped out onto the platform; it was massive and covered with a thatched roof. A railing wrapped around the end where it opened to the ravine.

I walked quietly to the edge, stopping to lean over the rail and stare down into the yawning abyss that seemed to reach into oblivion.

I'd never seen anything like it in my life, yet there was a familiarity about it.

From the mist below, two hawks rocketed up into the azure blaze of sky, flying in twisting tandem. I gazed after them, shielding my eyes with my hand. One of them gave a long, shrill call, and it echoed through the ravine like a battle cry, ricocheting off the rock and rolling away.

For a moment I was mesmerized—then I started as a warm hand clapped onto my shoulder. I spun around, and my eyes locked with a pair of bright, almost iridescent green ones.

An old man stood before me. He wore a long brown overcoat. His face was wrinkled with age, a ginger beard swathed his jaw, and the corners of his mouth were curved slightly in a smile that seemed to communicate that he knew something I didn't.

"Who… who are you?" I asked, my voice betraying my inward unsteadiness.

"Do you truly not recognize me?" He continued to stare into my eyes. "Hasn't Fin told you about me?"

"Fin? You—you know my father?"

The old man smiled. "If you were truly raised by Fin, you would know exactly who I am—for if you have looked into his eyes, you've looked into mine also."

"*Sensei?*" I finally managed to whisper.

He shook his head and placed a hand on my shoulder again. "I am your brother, Keegan."

"But you are—you made all of this." I swung my arm in a wide gesture. "You made this… You taught us *everything*. You are our teacher."

He nodded slowly, moving his hand to my forehead to press his thumb to my brow bone. "And I reside here," he said. "And here." He pressed the same hand to my chest now. "The teacher is inside you, Keegan."

"Yet I can't seem to find the answer to what I need to know more than anything." My voice trembled a little.

"What do you desire to learn?"

"To know where Sparrow is, what happened to her…" My voice cracked, breaking off. I blinked back the tears that were burning in my eyes. "I have to find her."

"You love Sparrow?"

"With all my heart." The reply came without thought.

"Then stop searching for her with your eyes. Search with your heart, Keegan."

Before I could ask him what he meant by that, everything began to fade away into darkness. His face was the last thing to vanish from my view, leaving me alone with only echoes of his voice:

*Search with your heart.*

I rolled onto my side, and something soft and fuzzy nudged my cheek. I became aware of warm breath on my face.

My eyes flew open. Two massive brown eyes stared down at me. An enormous form loomed over me as the huge bison lowered her head so that our foreheads touched. She snorted an exhale, and it felt like a gust of wind on my face.

I bolted to my feet, my legs shaking beneath me. My eyes stung as I looked around. The sky was blue overhead, the grass was splashed in deep, lush green—and a herd of living, breathing buffalo surrounded me. The air was filled with the quiet murmurings of the herd as they grazed.

For a moment I stood there, unable to breathe.

"They're… they're *alive.*" A voice split the quiet.

I spun around.

Rafael stood a few yards away, his eyes as wide as saucers and daisies stuck in his hair.

# 58

I SEARCHED THE FOREST FOR HOURS IN THE COLD RAIN. Finally, I noticed something ahead in the trees: a figure sprawled on the ground beneath a long black cloak.

My heart in my throat, I rushed over and dropped to my knees beside her. She was drenched through and bleeding from the forehead. Her head dropped back listlessly as I carefully slid my arms beneath her and lifted her out of the mud.

I couldn't help but curse as I looked down at her face. If only she'd just listened… If only she'd stayed.

Cradling her in my arms, I made my way back downhill as quickly as I could.

When I reached the shack, I slid the door open with my foot and stepped inside. I unwrapped her from the wet cloak and gently lowered her to the mattress. I sat down on the edge of the bed and took her wrist in my hand to check her pulse. She gasped quietly for air and writhed away from my grasp. I felt her forehead and neck. She was burning up.

My mind raced as I looked down at her, brushing the wet strands of hair away from her face. I needed to get her out of her wet clothes.

I propped her up with one hand and peeled off her wet T-shirt. My hand slid to the small of her back as I gently lowered her back down onto the mattress. I took off her shorts and hung her clothes on the backs of the chairs.

Unfolding the blanket on the end of the mattress, I wrapped her up in it and slid onto the bed behind her, folding her in my arms. I stroked her wet hair away from her face. Then I carefully placed a hand over the cut on her forehead. I felt the warm trickle of blood against my fingertips.

It was my fault. I'd been too intoxicated by the idea of being with someone who could actually see me. Like a hunter, I'd torn her away from everything that was true and wild and hers.

*But she's a slider, so it doesn't matter… You're a soldier; you hate sliders. You feel no remorse.*

These were the lies I'd told myself so that I could sleep at night, but now, as I lay there with Sparrow in my arms, all of that fell away, leaving only the sickening reality. I felt like a child who had just taken a baby bird from its nest and killed it by mistake.

Closing my eyes, I began to stroke my warm, trembling fingertips over her wound. A vibrating heat made its way through my hand, seeming to spill into her.

"I'm sorry," I whispered to her softly. "I'm so sorry, Sparrow."

I couldn't get it out of my head, the way she had looked at me when I'd told her that no one else could see me but her, the look of despair that had crept into her eyes when she realized that I was keeping her like an animal in a cage. Preserving her in this hidden-away place for the sake of my own sanity and with no regard for her—no regard for anyone but myself—with no intention of helping her return home.

Maybe it was the look on her face and the way she had cried and struck me over and over again, pounding my chest with her fists. Maybe it was how much time I'd spent thinking about her and talking to her and getting to know what she was really like. I couldn't pinpoint the moment things had changed, but I could see beyond a shadow of a doubt that they had.

Something inside me had changed because of her.

Once, maybe, I could have carried out my carefully arranged plans without thought or feeling, but not now. Not anymore.

My hand slipped away from her forehead to rest gently against her soft cheek. I raised myself up carefully on my elbow and looked: the blood on her face was gone. I closed my eyes, my arms still wrapped around her as I tried to warm her shivering frame. I lay there in the silence broken only by the thundering of the rain on the roof, and listened to her quiet breathing, silently hoping. Praying.

# 59

I WAS WARM; THAT WAS ALL THAT MATTERED. FOR THE longest time, all I had felt was a deep-set cold in my bones, and all I had seen behind my closed eyes were the same dancing visions of the hawk's wings. Slowly, I opened my eyes.

I was wrapped in a blanket and lying on the mattress in Aaron's shack. He was lying beside me. My head rested against his chest, and one arm was wrapped around his torso. He smelled like sweat and pine. His eyes were closed, and his square jaw was relaxed enough to let his chin drop to his chest. His eyelashes were long and dark against his deep brown skin. One of his arms was tucked around me.

My stirrings immediately awakened him. He sucked in a deep breath, dragged a hand over his face, and sat up.

"Sparrow," he murmured, "thank god you're awake—how do you feel? Your fever's gone." He felt my forehead, sounding relieved.

"I… I had a fever?" I squinted and blinked a few times. "When?"

"Last night." His warm hand lingered on my forehead. "I found you in the forest, unconscious."

"I wanted so badly to get away from this place," I murmured in reply, reaching up to rub my forehead. "From you."

"I know," he replied softly. "I'm sorry."

I struggled to sit up, and my eyes widened as the quilt slid down to uncover my bra. I quickly clutched it back to my chest.

"You undressed me?"

"I had to. You were soaked from the rain," he explained flatly. "Would you rather I'd let you die of exposure?"

I considered it for a moment, tucking the quilt snugly under my arms. I was about to retort when my head started spinning. I pressed the heel of my hand to my forehead, squeezing my eyes shut.

"Here, lie down," he said. "Rest. You're still recovering."

I brushed his hand away as he touched my shoulder.

"No, no, I don't need rest—you'll just find any excuse to keep me here, won't you?" I bit my lip and shook my head slowly. "God, I hate you. I hate that something inside me feels sorry for you."

"That's the very last thing I want—for you to feel sorry for me." His voice came out strained and quiet. "I didn't want to tell you the truth for that reason. And because…" His voice trailed off, and he shrugged. "Well, because I knew you would try to run away."

"I'm sorry they ruined you, Price… Aaron. I'm sorry the RGM made you invisible to everyone but me… but you must realize that I can't stay…" I let my words trail off, then began again, this time with greater resolve in my tone. "That I *will not* stay. I will do whatever it takes to get out of here."

Aaron took a shallow breath and nodded sadly. "I know, Sparrow, I… I know."

"Do you?"

He gave the same nod. "Yes. And after almost getting you killed—a few times…" He blew out a sigh, rubbing the back of his neck. "I realize I… I was just thinking of myself. Never of you or of anyone else—not even of the RGM, with whom my loyalty is supposed to lie… God, I threw all of it away just because I…"

He stopped, shaking his head.

"Because you what?" I prodded after a moment.

There was a strange look in his eyes—something vulnerable. Something I'd never seen in him before.

"I guess I was just… tired," he admitted. "Tired of waking up and watching the days and months and years pass… seeing everyone and everything change, but no one ever seeing *me* except the blind prisoner, Viner, as strange as that is." A tired, mirthless laugh escaped him. "To everyone else, I'm not even there…" He paused, steadying his trembling voice. "No one can ever look me in the eyes. No one can ever reach out and take me by the hand, because no one can even see me standing there. To them I'm *not* there; I'm as good as nonexistent…"

Something tightened in my throat.

"It wasn't just because I saw *you* out there in the forest that I wanted you, Sparrow," he went on softly. "It was because you saw *me*. I'd almost forgotten what it felt like to look into the eyes of another human being and know that they're looking back at you… But that was no reason to take you, to capture you and take you to the district, to almost get you killed."

"It was your mission, wasn't it?" I asked.

He nodded a little. "But my mission was to capture all of you. Instead, after Janna, I started to realize that I just wanted *you*. I stopped caring about the mission—for the *first time in my life*. I took you because something inside me craved to be seen again. Something inside me *needed* you."

For the first time, there was something honest in his dark eyes. There was truth in his face and something wounded in his voice. For the first time, Corporal Aaron Price was not an RGM soldier. He was a human. Vulnerable, scarred, and limping, just like I was.

He must have read my thoughts, because after a long moment he looked back to the floor.

"As soon as they stop looking for you, you can go, Sparrow," he said quietly. "I won't keep you here."

I stared at him, wide-eyed, still holding the quilt up to my chest.

"You'll let me go?" I could hardly believe the words that were coming out of my mouth. "Are you—are you serious?"

Aaron nodded slowly. "I just ask that you remain here until I know that they've given up trying to find you," he said. "You need to rest anyway—you took a bad fall."

I winced, finally remembering a little of what had happened before I blacked out. I reached up to gently touch my forehead. My fingers came back clean.

"Yeah," I murmured, still looking down at my hands. "I thought for sure I was bleeding. When you found me, was my head bleeding, or was I hallucinating?"

Aaron hesitated a moment, then shook his head. "No, it wasn't bleeding. Just badly bruised."

I nodded absently, running my fingertips across my forehead again. It didn't feel bruised. In fact, it didn't even hurt.

"So…" I began, my voice hoarse. "That was the RGM's mission from the outset—to capture us all?"

"Bask tasked me with tracking your group as soon as they were detected," Aaron explained bluntly. "He thought I would be the perfect man for the job of hunting down sliders."

I quirked an eyebrow. "Why you specifically?"

Suddenly Aaron cursed. "I have to go."

"What?"

"I've been out all night," he muttered, dragging a hand over the back of his neck. "Bask will have my head—he has strict orders that I be locked in each night."

"Why? What does it matter, when you go and do whatever you like during the day?" I asked.

"It's Bask's way of showing me he still owns me. Or he likes to think he does, anyway," Price replied, already striding for the door. He stopped when he reached it to look over his shoulder at me. "I'll come back later, when I can get away." He faltered. "That is, if you want me to."

"It's your place," I reminded him. "You can come whenever you want."

"But do you *want* me to return?"

I pulled in a shaky breath. "Yes," I answered at last. "I… I want you to. Now leave so I can get dressed."

# 60

"I REMEMBER WAKING UP..." RAFAEL BEGAN. "SOMEONE HAD clamped a hand over my mouth, but I couldn't see anything because it was dark." He shook his head and dipped his chin into the quilt drawn up around his neck. Cub was curled up beside him as we sat by the fire. "At first, I thought it was you or Preston, but then it started dragging me…"

"You saw no one?" Kateri inquired. "Not even when they brought you to—wherever it was?"

Rafael's dark curls dangled into his eyes as he shook his head. "I saw *nothing*. It was all just darkness. I could hear voices, and I could feel cold, damp walls around me. That was all. From what Sparrow told me, it sounded like we were at some sort of RGM prison camp."

I watched him through the firelight, my muscles tensing at the mention of her name.

"Sparrow *was* there with you, then?" I asked, my voice tense. "I tried reading your mind, several times, and I could make little sense of it other than the fact that Sparrow had told you something—that you had seen her."

The look in Rafael's eyes grew distant. "She was the only thing I could see… Somehow, she got them to let me go. I don't know how or why… only that she must have exchanged herself for me. She must have told them she wouldn't give them any of the information they wanted unless they let me go."

"And they *did* let you go?" Kateri inquired.

"The guard took me out into the woods, beat me, and left me for dead."

I rubbed my forehead with my fingertips. Kateri shifted to sit closer to Rafael, looping an arm around him.

"Before that happened, though, Sparrow told me to tell you something," he continued, his eyes slipping up from the fire to meet mine now. "She wanted me to tell you that everything would be all right…"

His voice faltered, cracking. He pinched the bridge of his nose with his fingers, squeezing his eyes shut. A lump formed in my throat as I waited for him to continue.

"She wanted me to tell you that she found something in the forest," Rafael said quietly. "She said it was near where we had camped by the river the night I disappeared."

"What was it?" I asked.

He sucked in a wavering breath and wiped his eyes with the heels of his hands. "A cavern," he said finally. "She said she found some kind of cavern in the woods."

I could feel the hairs rising on the back of my neck.

"She wanted you to look for it," he continued. "She said she wanted you to try to find it."

I swallowed hard, staring at him as my mind reeled back to the dream I'd awoken from that morning. The dream in which I'd been back there, in that exact part of the forest, and found a cavern.

"Did she say what she found there?" I managed to ask.

"She wouldn't tell me, not outright—she acted like she couldn't explain it. She just said that there was something about it." He paused, looking back into the open flame. "Something important."

I pressed my fingers to my lips, leaning forward on my knees; my thoughts scattered like broken glass.

"Do you think you'll be able to find it, Keeg?" Rafael spoke up again after a moment. "Do you think tomorrow maybe we could—"

"Shhh. Hey, you just woke up from a really long nap," Kateri cut in to tease him, gently ruffling his hair. "You need to take it slow for the next few days, all right?"

"Kateri, this is important," he protested, turning to look at her. "Sparrow *told me* it was."

"And I don't doubt it," Kateri assured him. "But we have to be careful about where we go, Raf—how deep we venture into the woods. We told Sensei we wouldn't go beyond the river."

No one said anything for a moment. The fire snapped and spat flecks of gold dust up into the dark navy sky. I craned my neck back to look up at the silver pinpricks of stars, lost in thought.

"This cavern," I began. "Sparrow said it was along the river?"

"By the river where we camped, beyond the falls," Rafael confirmed. "She said she found it in the woods somewhere nearby."

I didn't respond. I thought back to the landscape I'd seen in my dream. I *knew* it had seemed familiar for a reason.

I glanced back up to the stars for a moment and then down to Kateri to find her eyes fixed on mine. She had already deduced what I was thinking, I could tell.

Rafael's eyelids grew heavy. He curled up beside Cub and succumbed to sleep.

Kateri and I sat in silence. Finally, I stood and walked a few paces into the tall, wavering blue grass, gazing through the starlight as the hulking shadows of the herd waded through the meadow. The gentle sounds of their breathing and snorting were the only ones to disturb the deep quiet of the night. I'd never seen such creatures or heard such noises.

I pulled in a breath as I felt the warmth of Kateri's hand on my shoulder blade. She stood there beside me for a moment, listening too. I could see a faint smile on her lips in the soft silvery light.

"They're magnificent," she whispered, leaning her head on my shoulder. "I don't think I could have imagined anything so powerful. Even with the stories and the old pictures."

"Mmm. I'll definitely never forget waking up face-to-face with one."

She gave a little laugh. "The things that come out of your heart, Keegan… They are the most beautiful things I have ever seen."

I turned, my eyes locking with hers.

"You are special, Keegan… gifted…" she continued. "We need you…" Her voice tapered off. She turned to look back out at the dark shapes of the herd. "*I* need you."

"I could say all the same things to you," I whispered back, following her gaze out to the darkness ahead of us. "Where would I be without you to remind me of who I am?" I paused, glancing at her. "But in a dream, I saw the cavern, Kateri. It was the same one Sparrow told Rafael about. It was in the same part of the woods."

"In a dream?"

"Last night, before the buffalo came back to life, I dreamed I found a cavern, and it led to another world… the world my dad has told us all about for so long. I saw the Dimension, Kateri. I saw Sensei there."

"Sensei?" she repeated. "You mean… *the* Sensei?"

"The one my father has told us all so much about. Yes."

"And what was he like?"

"Everything I imagined… So much more than what I imagined."

"And… did he speak to you?"

"He asked me what I desired to learn," I answered, crossing my arms, turning to look up at the sky. "I told him I desired more than anything to find Sparrow. To find her and Janna and bring them home."

"And what did he tell you?"

"Exactly what you've been telling me this whole time," I answered quietly. "To stop searching with my eyes…"

Kateri stepped closer, gently placing a hand on my cheek to turn my face toward her.

"More than anything, I want to tell you not to go," she whispered.

"More than anything, I want you to come back to the Homestead with Rafael and me, to not go beyond the river to look for the cavern. More than anything, I want to keep you safe…" Her voice faded. "But I can already see in your eyes that your spirit has spoken to you, Keeg… and I would never drown out its voice with my own."

I slid my fingers over the back of her hand. I slowly leaned forward, and our foreheads lightly touched. For a moment we stood there just like that, not saying a word.

"Kateri, I will come back," I whispered finally. "I promise… I will find the cavern, and then I will come back."

She took a shaky breath, nodding a little. "I believe you, Keeg."

For a moment we lingered there, our fingers still interlaced. She lifted my hand to press it to her lips, closing her eyes. Then she turned and walked back to the fire.

# 61

I'D TOLD SPARROW I WAS GOING TO LET HER GO, TO HELP her find her way home. And I meant it.

For the first time in my life, I felt as though something had changed inside me. Nothing was different, yet, at the same time, everything was. I'd defied the RGM. I'd finally accepted that I no longer stood on their side, though that only stirred up a thousand other questions…

If I wasn't on their side, whose side was I on? The anomalies'—the sliders who had ruined my life?

No, and I never would be.

It still sickened me in some ways to consider that in helping Sparrow I was, in effect, helping a slider, but I couldn't think of it that way—she *wasn't* a slider to me. She was the only person I truly trusted.

As I walked back to the district, I found I could think of little else. Sparrow filled my mind like a beacon shining into a storm. I couldn't stop thinking about how it had felt to wake up beside her, my arms around her. I'd almost forgotten what the warmth of human touch felt like, the luxury of being *held*. Being a normal human.

I was in a state of confusion by the time I breached the district gates and started down the long dirt road to my lodgings. The factory whistle blew, and the district burst to life around me. Doors opened, guards shouted, and overseers barked orders and wielded clubs.

I dodged around bodies in the churning sea of grimy prisoners heading toward the factory. I bumped shoulders with someone and turned to find Viner walking steadily beside me, a stick extended in front of him. His eyes scanned hollowly back and forth, as they always did, but recognition passed over his face as he clapped a hand down on my arm.

"Price, where the hell were you all night?" There was something serious in his voice.

"Something… came up," I began, but he cut me off, his grip tightening on my arm.

"Bask has been looking for you," he informed me gravely. "Be careful."

My stomach sank.

"I'll be fine, Viner," I told him. "Thanks for the heads-up."

His jaw tightened before he gave a reluctant nod and continued in the surge to get to the factory. I stood there in the middle of the muddy road for a moment and watched the back of him melt away into the crowd, and then I turned and made my way to my lodgings.

I fumbled in my breast pocket for a cigarette, pinching it between my lips. I kicked the mud off my boots and shouldered the door open. Dim light filtered through the grimy panes of glass into the otherwise dark interior. It took a moment for my eyes to adjust as I closed the door behind me.

A dark shape lunged forward. A set of strong hands groped for a moment and then locked around my throat, shoving me back against the door.

"Where the hell were you?" I felt the spatter of spit on my face and the heat of Bask's breath.

I writhed in his blind stranglehold, weaving one arm up, over, and underneath his, tossing him aside and lurching away from him. He stumbled and caught himself on the table, hunching there a moment to regain himself before straightening back up.

"Where *were you*, Price?" he growled. "I already know you were gone all night. I already know everything."

I grunted, rubbing my throat. "You wish."

His face drained of color as he stared hollowly, searching for me in thin air.

"I've proven myself to you," I continued, my voice stony and level. "I'm sick of being locked in. I'm sick of your distrust when it's clear that I've proven mysel—"

"You've proven *nothing!*" Bask roared, striding closer. "Nothing except that you *cannot* be trusted and *never* will be. I know you're hiding something from me, Price." His voice was breathless and trembling, his face beet red. "And if you don't tell me where you were, I swear I will find a way to cut you *deep*."

"I'm allowed to come and go as I please during the day. What does it matter if I'm not here at night?"

"It matters because it is part of the pact between us, Price," Bask snarled. "It is a symbol that you are, in fact, on our side. Something that must *constantly* be questioned. If you break that one simple rule, how do I know that you are not breaking every other?" he went on, his mouth curled into a disgusted frown. "How do I know you *are* on our side?"

His cold, unfeeling eyes shifted back and forth, searching for where I might be. Hot anger welled inside me as I stared at him, my hands curling into fists.

"You *know* that I am loyal to the RGM." My voice rattled. "I have *given my blood* to this cause—without it, you would not even have the power to stand in front of me now! You would be just another gray-faced, no-name prisoner among the thousands of others. You would still be a goddamn war criminal—"

He lunged for me again, but I stepped aside. He pounded his fists against the wall, roaring.

"You might know who I really am, Bask," I went on in a steely voice. "But you seem to forget that I know who *you* are, too. I know I'm the only reason they didn't execute you for having beaten an officer to death. I'm the only reason they gave you back your rank and your position. Why do you think that is, Bask?"

I let the question hang in the air. I watched his fingernails clutch at the wall.

"Because you were the one to harness the power of the invisible man," I finished. "*I* gave you that. And I can take it away just as easily."

He turned around slowly, his face contorted with rage and his lips slick with saliva. "You threaten me and you dare to boast of your *loyalty*? If you're so eager to leave, Price, then why don't you?"

I narrowed my eyes, shaking my head slowly as I walked to the window.

"You know full well, Bask, that leaving isn't what I really want," I said flatly. "You know that's why I stay—because the RGM is the only way I can ever have what I've always wanted. The RGM is everything my father…" My jaw clenched as I swallowed. "It was everything my father wanted for me. It meant everything to him, and it means everything to me. I *refuse* to go down in shame."

Bask's mouth twitched and bent into a dastardly grin. "You *actually* think you'll earn your way back into the RGM's good graces and get your rank back one day, don't you?" He barked out a disgusted laugh. "Price, you are nothing more than a *filthy slider*."

Something inside me snapped.

Heat flooding my body, I snatched the glass shade off the oil lamp on the table, smashing it on the edge and lunging forward to tackle Bask to the floor. I leapt on top of him and laid the jagged glass up against his throat.

His eyes were wide with horror as he stared ahead at nothing. A vein pulsed in his reddened neck.

"Up until now, I have offered no violence." I leaned close enough for him to feel my breath against his face. "But if you ever call me that again—" spit dripped over my lips, my voice trembling "—I will kill you and leave you for the animals to devour." My hand shook, the jagged edge of the shade trembling against his skin. "Do you understand, Bask? Never again."

Bask gulped for a breath, his lips twitching as if he were having a seizure. "Y-y-yes. Yes, I understand."

Everything inside me wanted to kill him, to be free of him. But then the old man's face flashed in my mind, that face that had haunted me for so long. And in that moment, I knew that if I killed Bask now... I would never truly be free of him. Instead, I would be *just like* him.

With a hard jolt, I released him, rising quickly to my feet. In a burst of uncontrollable white energy, the glass shade shot out of my hand and smashed to the floor, disintegrating into shards.

Bask slowly climbed to his feet and dusted himself off. He looked around at the scattering of broken glass, still glowing red hot with the heat that had just exploded out of my hands. A sneer curled his lips: a look that mocked me, laughed at me, reduced my threats to a mere childish tantrum.

I lowered to the bed, a melting sensation filling me, eating away at what little sanity I had tried to preserve. I gripped my head in my hands.

Bask walked to the door and opened it. He took a step over the threshold and paused there, looking back inside.

"You will learn that your actions bring consequences, Price." His voice came out like a lead weight.

He paused there a moment, then the door closed behind him, and I heard one of the deadbolts click into place. Then another. And another, until all of them had been locked.

I sat there listening, clutching my head between my hands as if it would burst. Finally, I crumpled beneath the weight of it all, doubling over and falling to my knees. My fingertips dug into the floor, and my teeth chattered.

*one year after graduation*

I couldn't sleep the night before our first mission. I lay awake in my bunk, too excited to close my eyes. I couldn't stop thinking of Dad, of how honored I was to finally do something I knew he would be proud of: fighting against the resurgence that had killed him—the sliders who had taken his life. This is how I would have my revenge. This is how I would feed the sliders their own poison.

The coming dawn would be my first chance.

I felt sick with anticipation as I lay there, recalling everything I'd learned in training.

I closed my eyes and focused on my breathing. I knew I had to sleep. I had to be fresh and alert for what we were all about to head into. So I began to count silently to myself, listening to the soft sounds of unconscious breathing around me, of my comrades tucked away in their bunks. The soldiers I would fight alongside in only a few short hours.

I could still see Dad's face behind my closed eyes. His dark brown skin and deep-set eyes. His stiff upper lip and resolute demeanor. I could still hear his voice ringing in my ears, even in the quiet. His strong, guiding words blended in with the soft sounds around me, tugging me closer and closer to unconsciousness.

Then the muted sound of footsteps pulled me back to consciousness.

My eyes flew open, my senses rousing to alertness. A dark shape hovered above me.

I lurched backward, gasping. In the light drifting in from the window, I caught snatches of his glimmering eyes as he placed a finger to his lips.

"My son," whispered the old man, "you must listen carefully."

I gaped at him, petrified and unable to move.

"You will never be one of them. You *can never* be one of them," he told me, his craggy voice hushed. "You must not let them break you. You must hold on to your soul with all of your might, my son."

"I am not your son," I whispered. "I don't know who you are—I don't know why you follow me. I… I don't know why no one seems to see you but me!"

"That is because no one *can* see me but you, Aaron," he said, his voice more deafening than the silence. "I have followed you because you hold something special within you."

"Within me?"

I flinched as he took my hand and opened my palm. I watched as he laid his large, leathery hand over mine for a moment before slowly lifting his away again to reveal a dim yellow glow, a swirling light held in levitation between my palm and his.

I stared, spellbound, as the light twisted and grew, illuminating my face. My mouth ran dry as adrenaline surged through my veins, along with a strange warmth.

"Power," he whispered. "You are about to discover your ability, Aaron." The yellow glow reflected in his eyes.

Everything that had, only moments ago, been the most important things in the world to me faded to nonexistence. There was no RGM. There was no war. No walls, no ceiling above us.

There was only light. And for a moment, I held it in my hands.

My eyes searched the old man's, and I remembered the first time I had seen him from across that field on the day of my graduation, seated beside my mother in the chair that should have been filled by my father. My father, who had died, not by a bullet, but by the powerful hand of an anomaly. By an orb of light like the one I now held in my own hand.

Suddenly the warmth inside me chilled to ice. I clenched my hand into a fist, extinguishing the light. My jaw hardened as my eyes bored into his.

"I will *never* be an anomaly. I will *never* be like the ones who killed my father!"

His eyes stay fixed on mine.

"Aaron," he said quietly, "you already are."

My fear instantly turned into rage; scrambling up, I swung violently for his face, searching frantically for him in the darkness. As I grabbed for him, my foot caught on something, and I fell hard, knocking an object off a nearby table. It toppled to the floor. The overhead light clicked on a moment later.

"What's going on?" The familiar voice of one of my comrades cut through the quiet.

I scrambled to my feet, picking up the lamp that had fallen. In the now illuminated room, I could see that the old man was gone.

"I fell out of bed," I grumbled. "I'm sorry to wake—"

"Aaron? Aaron, where are you?"

For a moment I stood there, confused, holding the lamp.

"Aaron, where are you?"

"Right here." My throat tightened. "Can't you see me?"

I'll never forget the look on that soldier's face as he stood there, his eyes wide in horror. He shuffled farther back until he had reached the door. Then he turned, swung it open and bolted, shouting for security.

By now a few other men had awoken in their bunks. I felt eyes burning holes through me. Someone, stammering, finally spoke up. He pointed to the object I held in my hands, jumping to his feet to shout in horror.

"It's floating—it's floating in midair!"

A ringing filled my ears; adrenaline still rattled through my veins.

*They can't see me. None of them can see me.*

The lamp slipped from my fingers and shattered on the cement floor.

# 62

I STILL COULDN'T DETERMINE WHETHER THE OLD MAN had just been a hallucination or if he'd actually escaped the flooded pit and found me in the forest.

*Who on earth is he?*

Questions spun wildly in my mind as I lay there in the shack, shivering beneath the thick quilt. I tried to remember everything the old man had said to me as we had huddled there in the hollow of the tree, waiting for the search team to pass. He had saved me. I would have been discovered and captured without his intervention.

His words echoed in my mind like memories from a dream: *"What we think is not always true…"*

I'd told him that I didn't know how to find my way back home. I'd never forget the look in his eyes.

*"You can see things with your eyes that no one else can see, Sparrow, but you have yet to open your eyes within…"*

He had called it my spirit. I didn't really understand what that meant, but his words stirred me inwardly.

But how had he escaped the flooded pit? When I had awakened in the woods after my dream of Hawk, he was gone, his cloak the only evidence that he'd even been there at all. It still hung draped over one of the chairs to dry.

As I turned the old man's words over in my mind, I began to think of Keegan, Fin, and the Homestead. My heart ached to be back with them.

I pressed my forefinger and thumb to my eyelids and drew a shaky breath. Hot tears welled in my eyes.

Maybe the longing I felt inside me for Keegan was what the old man had been talking about… Maybe that was my spirit. Maybe that was the guiding voice: the whisper that seemed to say that if the old man could escape the cell, then maybe I could escape all of this and find my way home—find my way back to Keegan. Maybe the corporal was my ticket out.

The truth was, I couldn't leave—not without Janna. I'd promised that I would find her and Rafael and bring them back. So far, I'd only been able to fulfill half of that promise—assuming that Raf had made it back all right.

In order to save Janna, I had to get Aaron on my side. I was the only one who could physically see him, and that was more important to him than anything, I could tell. I still couldn't read him. He was fire and ice rolled into one, one or the other, depending on his mood. His explanation about the faulty inoculation had only raised a thousand other questions— how had the RGM even formulated a way to make their units and bases invisible in the first place?

*How can we battle forces we can't see? The anomalies have no weapon to use against the RGM's invisible forces…*

Then it clicked.

*No weapon except… me.*

Brushing back the blankets, I stood and walked to the table. I pulled my shirt over my head and zipped up my shorts. Then I lifted the cloak off the back of the chair and wrapped it around myself, pulling up the hood.

I had to make some headway—I had to at least figure out where they were keeping Janna.

Grabbing the coil of rope off the table, I pushed aside the wall panel and stepped outside. I crept carefully around the side of the shack, pausing to scope out my surroundings and listen. A warm, mighty breeze rolled over the mountainside, drifting down toward the district, propelling me forward through the soft beginnings of twilight.

I moved as fast as I could, coming to a stop every now and then to listen for footsteps.

As I drew closer to the district, I could smell sulfur in the air. I crept around the back of it, painstakingly skirting around the wall until I reached the place where Aaron and I had scaled it before. There were a few footholds here and there, enough to get me up and over just as we had before.

I tied the rope to the stump of a tree at the base of the wall, looping the slack over my shoulder as I began to carefully climb my way up.

I landed hard on my feet on the other side, dropping the slack on the ground. My back was to the wall of one of the lodgings. I could still hear the churning rumbles coming from the direction of the factory. I stood there for a moment, getting my bearings.

My heart rate picking up, I slowly inched my way to the corner of the building, peering around it to the street ahead. The dirt road was devoid of life, and steam bellowed up from the stacks that rose out of the hulking cement structure at the end of it. Lights were on in the windows, informing me that the prisoners were still working.

*This is my chance.*

Clutching my hood to keep it in place, I darted out from behind the building and streaked down the road, darting through the semidarkness to the cover of a building a hundred yards or so away.

I checked over my shoulder and slipped out from the shadow of the building, quickly mounting the steps of the experimentation lab. Through the glass window inlaid in the door, I could see that the building was dark and vacant. I tried the knob. Unsurprisingly, it was locked.

Checking around again, I descended the steps all at once and quickly circled around to the back of the building, scanning the windows above me. The first few were shut tight, but one was ajar.

*Now I just have to figure out how the hell I can get up there...*

I walked to the end of the building where some of the foundation had crumbled away, creating footholds. I started climbing, frantically gripping at the places where the rough cement had worn away. I was halfway up when the factory whistle blew, heralding the end of the workday.

*Shit.*

Climbing faster, I finally reached up and grabbed hold of the edge of the roof. I swung up onto the cool metal surface, flattening myself against it for a moment as the shouts of guards and the murmur of voices filled the air. Inching my way to the ridge of the roof, I peered over it just enough to be able to look down into the district.

A steady flow of uniformed figures made their daily pilgrimage back to the shacks. I could make out the shape of Aaron's lodgings from here; there was a soft light in the window.

*Thank god. He's locked in.*

Suddenly, a door slammed. Bask emerged from a concrete building farther down the street, a club in his hand. He stood there for a moment, seeming to scrutinize the prisoners as they passed, flanked by guards. Then he lifted his club and pointed at one of the prisoners.

"You," he shouted.

When the prisoner Bask was pointing to didn't stop, Mooney lurched forward to seize him by the arm. I noticed that the prisoner carried a stick, extending it in front of him.

"Yes, him," Bask confirmed, nodding. "Execute him."

The prisoner began to writhe violently, dropping his stick.

"No! No, please!" His voice cracked as he shouted. "Please—I—I beg you!"

Bask said nothing. He flicked the club back and forth and watched as Mooney dragged him away. The heels of his boots left lines in the dirt.

"You." Bask pointed the club at a soldier now. "Assemble a search team and head out."

"Sir?"

"I want Sparrow's head brought to me on a plate."

"Yes, sir!"

I felt sick as I ducked back below the ridge and scuttled quietly over the span of the roof.

I dropped to my stomach just above the window that was open. Reaching down, I carefully edged it open. Making sure I wasn't being observed, I lowered myself down, swinging my legs carefully through the opening. I dropped to my feet inside, remaining crouched in the darkness for a moment as my vision adjusted to the lack of light.

When I was satisfied that I was alone in the small room, I stood up, glancing around as I took a few cautious steps forward.

Around me were tables stacked with what looked like medical equipment. A table stood in the middle of the room, a pair of scrubs tossed over the end of it. Up against the opposite wall there was a translucent case filled with glass beakers of clear fluid.

I leaned closer, squinting through the dark to make out the scrawled handwriting labeling each vial.

*Invisibility inoculation.* Each label also featured a string of numbers indicating a date.

I straightened back up and crossed the room. On another table, a binder of papers lay open. I began to flip through it, skimming over patients' names. It seemed as though nearly every patient had been to the clinic for the same reason: to receive an inoculation. All except Price. Written beside his name were the words *blood extraction.*

Chills rose over my spine.

Three days later there was another entry. Price had been in the medic's office again for the same reason: to get blood drawn. Then another one, three days after that.

I turned to look back over my shoulder at the case of inoculations waiting to be administered. The dates on each vial matched the dates of Aaron's blood extractions.

The revelation hit me like a tidal wave.

I eased the door open and slipped out into the silent hallway, scanning the rows of doors that lined either side. Rising to my tiptoes, I checked inside each room as I passed, peering through the small windows high up in the doors. The rooms looked alike: white, sterile, and empty.

When I came to the second-last door, my eyes widened as I peered inside.

Crumpled into a fetal position at the far end of the room, Janna lay sleeping. Her frizzy blonde hair was gone, replaced by a shaved scalp; small metal spheres had been attached to her head.

The door was locked. I tapped on the window, urgently whispering her name.

Janna stirred, her dry, faded lips parting slightly.

I tapped again. This time she bolted upright. Her large blue eyes caught on mine, and I heard her gasp. She leapt to her feet and sprinted toward me, thudding against the door with sickening force.

She gritted her teeth, pressing her fingertips to the glass, revealing two metal spheres adhered to the palms of her hands to match the ones dotting her skull.

"Sparrow!" Her sobs were muffled through the thick glass separating us. "Sparrow, help me! I can't see *anything*, Sparrow…"

I noticed the small keypad lock on the wall beside the door.

I threw a careful glance over my shoulder and then pressed my hand to the window, my fingers aligning with hers.

"Have you told them anything?" I asked quietly.

Janna only stared at me, her lower lip trembling. "I told them everything, Sparrow." She cut me off, her muffled voice ragged, snot dribbling down to the crest of her lip. "They—they said they would kill me otherwise. I-I-I didn't know what to do! What else *could* I do?"

She collapsed against the window, her chest heaving as she sobbed.

"Did you tell them where the Homestead is?" I asked, almost afraid to hear the answer.

Janna's fingertips tensed against the pane of glass, and her expression became twisted, tortured.

*Oh no.* "Janna, you could get them all killed! You played right into their hands," I hissed. "If they know they've gotten everything out of you…"

"Please, Sparrow," she sobbed. "You've got to help me get out of here…"

Suddenly I heard the rattle of a doorknob. Everything inside me froze.

"Janna, I have to go—someone's coming. Buy yourself some time. Invent something they don't know about yet. Let them think you're hiding something."

"Sparrow, please don't leave…"

I placed a finger to my lips. "I'll be back for you."

That was the last thing I said before I fled down the hallway, escaping through the back door. I managed to race back to the wall without detection, dodging behind buildings for shelter and then scrambling up the rope and over the wall.

As I climbed breathlessly back up the mountain in the darkness, one thought repeated incessantly: *I have to warn Keegan… I have to find a way to get back to them and warn them…*

Finally, I caught a glimpse of the shack's darker outline among the trees. I waded through the brush and collapsed against the wall panel, shoving it aside and stepping in.

I slid the door shut behind me and leaned back against it to catch my breath, closing my eyes for a moment. When I opened them again, I gasped.

Corporal Price was sitting at the table in front of me, his chin resting in his hand and his eyes drilling into mine.

# 63

QUIETLY I ROSE AND GOT MY THINGS TOGETHER. I LOOPED my knife holster over my chest and slid into my moccasins. Rafael was sound asleep, his mouth hanging open. He snored softly, one arm hooked around Cub. Color had returned to his cheeks. Already he had regained so much strength.

I walked around to where Kateri lay. Crouching down beside her, I softly brushed her long, wild hair away from her cheek with the backs of my fingers. She drew a deeper breath and rolled onto her back.

"Kateri," I whispered softly, "it's light. I'm going to slip away."

Rubbing a hand over her eyes, she slowly sat up, not saying anything. She looped her arms around me and buried her face in the curve of my neck. I returned the embrace, closing my eyes.

"Take Cub with you," she whispered. "I'd like to know that you're not alone out there."

"Raf will miss her."

"Take her, Keeg."

"Will you need any help getting back?"

"We know our way. Just get yourself back."

"I will… I promise."

Leaving Kateri behind was hard. But I knew that she and Rafael would be safe back at the Homestead.

I made mental notes of the landscape as I hiked, Cub at my heels. I reached the river in no time at all. On the other side, I charted a mental course downstream, heading for the waterfall.

When it grew dark, I curled up on the soft ground, spooning with Cub and absorbing her body heat. I slept restlessly and was up before the dawn.

I pushed on with renewed energy. The forest spilled over to a rocky sheer drop, the place where Sparrow and I had climbed up. I dropped to my belly without hesitation and took out my knives, using the same method to get myself down.

This was where Sparrow had found the cavern.

Leaving Cub fishing on the riverbank, I made my way across the rocks and into the forest on the opposite side. Immediately I began to notice the tall, swaying clusters of birches—exactly like the ones I'd seen in my dream.

A few yards off, standing silently among the trees, was the old man.

I staggered backward, catching myself against a trunk of a tree. "Sensei?"

He gestured me forward. "Come," he said quietly. "We do not have much time."

I followed him through the birch trees and around slate-gray boulders until finally we came to an embankment where vines covered what looked like two rocks leaning up against each other.

"Sensei, how did you know that I would be here?"

He looked at me for a moment, then smiled.

"So many questions." He leaned closer. "Perhaps what lies inside the cavern will answer them."

My throat tightened. Reaching out a shaking hand, I parted the vines and ducked into the darkness.

I heard the curtain of leaves swish behind me as Sensei followed me inside. I felt my way through the darkness and along the dripping walls until, finally, just like in my dream, my fingers brushed against a cold brass knob.

"Open it," Sensei instructed.

Grasping the knob, I turned it. The door groaned open on its hinges, and I stepped over the threshold.

Before me were massive glass windows filled with warm golden light. Beyond them was a stunning view overlooking a ravine carpeted with trees reaching up from either side to puncture the light pink sky. Below, fog rolled, and from it a pair of hawks burst upwards into the sky, a chaos of tumbling wings climbing higher to split the atmosphere with the sounds of their cries.

I walked to the window and placed my hand on the glass.

"The Dimension," I breathed. "It's really... it's really the Dimension."

Sensei came up beside me. "You wished to know who Sparrow is, did you not?" He tipped his head toward the ravine. "How can you find someone when you do not even know where they have come from?"

I turned to stare at him. "Sparrow comes from here?"

"Her parents do," he answered. "And the blood of the split-soul flows in her veins. This is her place of origin—and yours."

"I was not born of anomalies, Sensei. I didn't even know I *was* one until Fin adopted me."

"*All* are born from here," he corrected me. "Though they may not realize it. They may live their whole lives without even glimpsing it. But it's from here that they come, and it's here that they belong."

"Then why not just bring everyone here?" I asked. "Why not just open the Dimension to everyone, Sensei? It would change everything..." I looked back to the velvety sky beyond the window. "It would change the *world*."

I felt the warmth of one of Sensei's weathered hands on my arm. He turned me around to face him.

"This portal is only here because your father created it himself, back when you and he first came here. But I do not want the Dimension to be found out in the woods, or in a cave—that is not where the Dimension truly resides." His hand slid down to my own. He spread my palm and pressed it to my chest. "*Here… here* is where the Dimension can be found; here, eternity waits in silence to be released. Here is restoration. Here is everything that ever has been or will be. *Here…*" He stepped closer. "*Here is infinity.*"

My heart pounded beneath my hand; my eyes locked with his.

"A dimension is not another place, Keegan; it is simply another way to look at something that has always existed. Something inside of which you have always existed. It is all the same universe—all the same Earth. The Dimension is not separate from Earth, Keegan—it is the Earth's truest identity, and yours. It is not separate from you at any time, but hidden between your ribs and tangled with the color in your eyes. It is what you feel on the edge of the summer wind. It's the feeling that swells inside you when you look upon the sea or gaze up into the stars. It is something that burns within you, Keegan." He smiled, tears glossing his eyes. "It is your very spirit. And it is all around you if you only open your eyes to see it."

A mighty roar shook the air. Gazing past the glass, down the ravine, I watched as the two opposing cliffs, with a great groaning sound, seemed to morph together, to join. The trees bowed away as water began to trickle down the face of the cliff, lit up gold with the sunlight. The stream began to gush, tumbling with more force, pounding down into the fog, until reality itself began to morph around me. One moment I was in the Dimension; the next, I stood on the embankment overlooking the earthly waterfall where I had left Cub behind. Like hot melting gold, the two landscapes transformed into one.

The fog that had filled the ravine now flowed over the river, and the fresh life that had filled the Dimension swelled before me. The two hawks soared overhead, and the panes of glass in front of me shattered to the ground to explode into a burst of white butterflies, eliminating the final separation that stood between me and this new Earth-Dimension.

My heart pounded in my chest as I stepped forward, turning slowly to look around at the restored cliffs. The sparkling blue river rushed past where Cub stood on the bank, and the hawks soared above me in a sky no longer tainted by smog. Tears burned in my eyes as I turned and looked back at Sensei.

"The Dimension is on Earth?" I questioned in a cracked whisper. "It has been all along? The separation… the separation is finished?"

"Yes, Keegan." Sensei looked at me for a moment before bowing his head. "It is finished. With this new knowledge, go. Go and find Sparrow. See first with your heart, and your vision will follow."

"But where do I start?" I asked.

"At the place where you felt her but your eyes kept you from believing," he answered. "At the clearing where the ground turned red and geothermal, where you heard the rumbling of water rising from the earth but saw no spout."

I nodded, remembering the strange feeling that had come over me as Kateri and I had stood there, looking out into the wide-open space where the ground seemed to sweat, hissing with steam.

"Yes. Yes, I do remember."

"Return to that place," Sensei instructed. "And listen with your *spirit*, Keegan."

*four years earlier*

I'D LOST TRACK OF HOW LONG I'D BEEN IN THE DISTRICT. Time seemed to escape through the spaces between the bars on the window, leaving me behind to fade away to a hollow shell.

"What are you thinking of, boy?"

The gruff voice came from the shadows on the other side of the cold stone cell. The walls drizzled with moisture, and everything smelled of sulfur. Normally, I wouldn't have answered. But I was empty now; I had nothing to hide. Like a dying man giving up his secrets, I would have answered anything by this point.

"I was just thinking about how much I hate myself," I replied quietly.

"And why is that?"

"Because…" I trailed off, squinting into the shadows. "Because I have become everything I despise. There is an evil inside me that I cannot reverse."

"Being a slider, you mean?" he grunted. "Or being invisible?"

"One begets the other." I felt sick even thinking about it. "They killed my father…"

"And you're one of them," he said, and chuckled. "I'm surprised you didn't kill yourself."

I swallowed. "I am, too," I whispered.

"But maybe it's for the best that you didn't."

I glanced up as he emerged from the shadows to stand before me: a five-and-a-half-foot frame, a swath of thinning brown hair, a jagged, sallow face. He wore a dirty gray prisoner's uniform like I did. His lip was split and bloodied, and a considerable shiner circled his left eye socket. He'd just arrived last night.

"How the hell is that for the best?" I asked, numb.

Though my cellmate couldn't see me, he studied the place where he assumed I was with almost disturbing intensity.

"You're invisible to all the world, Price. Do you realize what you could do with such a power?"

"I never wanted it—I *don't* want it." I swallowed back the lump in my throat. "They'll kill me. I know they will."

"The RGM?"

"Who else?"

The prisoner rubbed his nose with the back of his hand, then crossed his arms over his barrel chest.

"No," he said finally. "No, they won't kill you, Price. Not if you give them something they want—something they need."

"I have nothing they need."

"That's where you're wrong, Price." He laughed coarsely.

My jaw tightening, I shot him a seething glare. "Who are you?"

"The name is Bask."

I tipped my head back against the damp stone wall, watching as he began to pace from one wall to the other and back again.

"Why do you think they haven't already killed you, *hmm?* Why do you think that is?"

"They want to prolong my shame."

Bask rubbed one massive hand over his jaw. Both his paws were meaty and scarred; a few of his fingers hung crookedly, as if they'd been broken before.

"They don't give a damn about your shame or anyone else's."

"What do you mean?"

"I mean that they want something *from* you, Price…"

"That makes two of us. I want something from them, too: I want to be a soldier… not a prisoner. I want my rank and position back."

The only sound to disrupt the quiet cell was the scuff of Bask's boots over the floor as he paced, his dark eyes scanning the air.

"Do you know what I was before I was brought here?" he asked, pausing, looking back to the place where he was pinpointing my voice.

I shook my head. "No. Why? What were you?"

He began to walk slowly back to my end of the cell, coming to a stop in the shaft of pale light from the window overhead.

"I worked as a mutator. *The* mutator, actually."

I stared at him, chills rising across my skin. "You were the one in charge of the—"

"I was in charge of the last three major mutation projects carried out by the RGM."

"Why the hell are you *here*, then?"

"I killed one of the other officers," he muttered, running a hand over his face. "I was having a rough day, and I… lashed out… so here I am. They can take away my position and my rank, but they'll never be able to take away *this*." He tapped one crooked finger vigorously against his temple. "Everything I've ever seen, everything I've learned, everything I *know*… it's all up here. And the only way they can take that away is to kill me."

"Why haven't they?"

The corners of Bask's mouth twitched upward into a disturbing grin. "For the same reason they haven't killed you, boy. Because they think there still may be something of value left in us for them."

"What could I possibly have that would help them?"

Bask squatted down on the damp floor and looked in my general direction. Unbeknown to him, his eyes stared into mine.

"Their thirst to be like you is greater than their desire to kill you." He lowered his voice. "Just as you would give anything to be seen, they would sacrifice as much to not be seen."

"The RGM wants to be invisible?"

Bask didn't answer right away. He let me think about it.

"I've worked on projects like this before, Price… What if I could find a way to give them what they wanted?" he asked slowly. "To extract your powers—"

"You're a mutator." I cut him off before he could finish. "And a murderer."

His lips curled into a sneer. "And you're a filthy slider."

My jaw tightened, my eyes narrowing as I stared at him.

"Yet it would seem that each of us is all the other has. Give the RGM an incentive, Price; something that will make them give you back what you lost in exchange for something they want…" He paused thoughtfully. "We could be a team, you and I."

My eyes narrowed. "What's in it for you?"

Bask sat there in the shaft of light for a long moment, then lowered his voice. "Freedom."

*"Where were you?"*

Sparrow started as she stepped into the shack. Even in the shadow of the hood pulled over her long, wild hair, I could see her dark eyes widen.

"I-I thought they'd locked you in," she stammered.

"I have ways of escaping. Now tell me where you were."

She threw back her hood. "I went back down to the district."

*"What?"*

"I had to! I can't wait until they stop looking for me. I will *not* be the coward who hides in the shadows!" Her voice was stern and defiant. "Since you wouldn't help me, I had to do it myself—I had to find Janna!"

"Sparrow, by now they've sent her to another base," I replied, clenching my jaw. "There's nothing to be done about it—"

"That's where you're wrong—I found her!" she cut in. "I broke into the experimentation lab while no one was there—I found her in one of the cells. Price, they're going to kill her! You have to do something!"

"Like what?" I shouted. "Sparrow, you're out of your *mind* if you think I have any authority here! I have *none*, none at all! I'm as much of a prisoner here as you! Be glad I'm helping *you*."

"Helping me?" Sparrow stepped closer. "If you think keeping me trapped here while my family dies is helping me, *you're* the one who's out of your mind!"

"Your family?" I grunted. "*Your family?* That's what you think they are? Sparrow, they don't care about you. They're not loyal to you—they are *sliders*! They only care about killing us." I thrust my hands against my chest. "You're just a cog in their machine!"

"*Us?* You and the RGM? You aren't one of them, Price. You may try, you may want to be more than anything, but you'll never be one of them."

Every muscle in my body tightened as a familiar fire reignited in my chest.

I lurched to my feet so quickly the chair clattered to the floor. I seized Sparrow by the shoulders and shoved her back, hard, against the opposing wall. She gasped, her eyes wide and only inches from mine.

"I am a *soldier*, Sparrow." My voice morphed to a soft growl as I stared into her face. "A *soldier*. My job is *not* to help sliders, but to *kill* them, to *wipe them off the face of the earth*."

"Then why haven't you killed *me*?" She searched my face. "I saw the inoculations. I saw the entries… I know you're not invisible because of *them*… No, Aaron, *they're* invisible because of *you*…" Her voice lowered to a tense whisper. "You're an anomaly."

My hands were shaking, my fingers still latched tightly around her arms, fire raging between my ribs. Part of me felt like it was dying. I wanted to roar—to shout curses into her face, to tell her it all was a lie.

"Sparrow, you don't understand. I *hate* being a slider."

"I understand that perfectly—I felt the same way."

"No, no, you *don't* understand—they didn't kill your father, did they, Sparrow? No. *They killed mine.* I still remember the day they brought his helmet home…" I swallowed back the lump in my throat. "I hate sliders. I hate everything they stand for… and I despise myself for being one of them."

"They're not all like that," Sparrow shot back. "*I'm* not like that." She searched my face for a moment. "You don't have to stay here, Aaron. You don't have to let them literally suck the life out of you—don't you realize that?"

"I've made Bask who he is, Sparrow. He owes me *everything*—I'm the reason he's not rotting away in a cell," I came back firmly. "He promised me he would get me out of this—that if I helped him, *he* would help *me*. He has not kept that promise. I've raised him up, and now he's the only way I can get out of this. Don't you see that? He's the only way I can get out!"

Sparrow pressed her hand to my cheek and stared into my eyes. "Bask doesn't *care* about you, Aaron. He doesn't care about you or anyone else. He's a *killer*! Before I broke into the lab, I saw Bask pull a blind man out of the crowd of prisoners to be executed. I'll never forget the look of terror on that poor man's face. They'll do the same to Janna… to me, to everyone I left behind. Because Janna told them—she told them *everything*, Aaron!"

"He was blind?" My throat tightened. "The-the man Bask executed was blind?"

Sparrow nodded. "Yes."

I stared at her in disbelief, the strength going out of my body as I backed away slowly.

"Aaron?"

I couldn't answer her. My mind reeled back to that morning, breaking the lampshade and holding it to Bask's throat. His ragged threat resounded in my thoughts.

*"You will learn that your actions bring consequences, Price."*

Without another word, I turned, throwing open the wall panel to step out into the darkness. The last thing I heard was Sparrow desperately shouting my name as I sprinted down the mountain.

Moving more slowly now so as not to kick up dust, I easily bypassed the oblivious guards at the gate and started down the long dirt road. As soon as I was out of their earshot, I began to run again.

As I reached the rows of shacks, Mooney walked toward me. His face was dirty and blood streaked, lit up in the rusty light of the lamp he carried.

A sick feeling twisted in my gut; my hands tightened to fists.

I forced myself to walk past him, picking up my pace once again to dart through the pale light from the lamps hanging at each dirty, decaying cement-block shack. All except one. The lamp beside this door creaked as it swayed in the breeze, empty and unlit.

A cold, heavy feeling sinking inside me, I forced one foot forward. One step, and then two, until finally I stood at the threshold. The door hung open on its hinges.

My boot brushed something as I stepped in. Stooping down, I picked the object up off the ground, turning it over in my hands.

A long stick with a smooth, carved wooden handle.

My throat ran dry as I stood there, my knuckles whitening as I clutched the stick.

*Consequences…*

In a surge of rage, I slammed my fist full force into the wooden door. Winding back my arm, I repeated the action again and again and again.

I dropped the stick, clear blood rivering down my arm, my heartbeat pounding in my head as I collapsed to my knees.

Without a word, I opened the panel and stepped back into the shack. Sparrow's eyes widened a little when she noticed the translucent blood dripping down my arm. I walked numbly to the mattress and sank down on the edge of it.

"He was the man I told you about once," I finally managed, my voice a numb whisper. "Viner."

Sparrow didn't say anything in response, but sat down beside me.

"Bask killed him because of me," I went on quietly. "Because I disobeyed. Because I didn't come back for lockdown. Because I attacked him and put him in his place." My voice faded. "He killed Viner because of *me*."

There was something pleading in Sparrow's eyes as they searched my face. "The very fact that you can see the wrong in it—the hate and evil in what Bask does," she said, "that proves that you are not like him. Can't you see that you are so much more than them?"

She took my bloody, throbbing hand in hers and gently laid her fingers over the wound. Her brown eyes remained locked with my own.

"You are so much more than them, Aaron." Her voice dropped to a whisper. "You don't have to live like this."

"Sparrow, you don't understand." I sucked back tears.

She only shook her head. "You *don't* have to live like this, Aaron. *You don't have to live like this...*"

I felt myself slipping, the ground beneath me seeming to disintegrate until there was nothing left to hold me up, nothing left for me to hold onto.

I watched with tears in my eyes as Sparrow gently took her hand off mine, leaving my knuckles healed and washed clean of blood. A tear rolled down my cheek.

"You don't have to live like this," she whispered once more, her eyes still locked with my own.

I felt like a hurricane inside, a chaos of feelings I thought I'd buried long ago. Sorrow, pain, grief, and regret waged war inside me, pulling me in deeper and deeper until I felt as if I were drowning. As if I would never make it back to the surface for air.

But in the middle of that storm was a calm. In the middle of it all was *Sparrow*.

For a moment, I fought with myself. Then I caved beneath the weight.

I took her face in my hands, and I kissed her.

# 65

HIS LIPS PRESSED AGAINST MINE AS HE SLID ONE HAND OVER my cheek and into my hair, pulling me closer. My heart raced, my body stiffening. Aaron's kiss was desperate and groping like a cry for help. I saw Keegan's face in my mind, and my heart ached.

Gently placing a hand against his chest, I pulled away. "Aaron, please… I can't."

"I'm sorry," he whispered.

I stood, pacing the shack, trying to clear my thoughts.

"So they take your blood and use it for the inoculations?" I asked, clearing my throat.

Aaron nodded heavily. "Bask was the one who figured out how… He'd worked in the labs where they were using the blood of slain sliders to mutate animals. He knew what he was dealing with when he first saw me… except he never actually *saw* me."

"So he used you," I concluded quietly.

"To climb his way out of this filthy hell and leave me behind to rot in it," he said, staring blankly ahead. "He told me that if I helped him… if I prostituted my powers to the service of the RGM, they would take me back. But instead, they just took back the mutator who discovered how to use my blood to make the district and everyone in it invisible. Soldiers and prisoners get an inoculation; objects are misted with a solution made from my blood."

I began piecing everything together in my head. I took a seat at the table, facing him.

"I actually believed he was going to help me get out of this hell." He laughed, running a hand over his head. "I was just a stupid boy. He got what he wanted out of me."

"Then what reason do you have to stay? Aaron, Bask deceived you. They're draining the very *life* out of you. That's all you are to them here: an experiment."

The muscles in his jaw tightened, but he said nothing to refute it.

I narrowed my eyes. "Did you know where Janna was all along?"

"No. I didn't." He drew a shaky breath. "Though I don't expect you to believe a word I say."

"We have to figure out a way to break her out."

"That's going to be impossible."

"Oh? Like it was impossible to break me out of my cell, bring me here, and keep me hidden from the search team?"

Aaron shot me a glance.

"And besides that, I need to get out of here—I need to find my way back to my family. Tonight, I overheard Bask giving orders to send out another search team."

"In that case, the mountains will be crawling with them," he said. "You can't go. Not yet."

The chair slammed to the floor as I got to my feet. "You don't understand. I *have* to get back to them. I have to warn them that the RGM is going to find them! They know everything, Aaron! Janna—Janna told them *every damn thing* about us!"

"You must understand that I can't…" He watched as I paced. "I can't help you get her out of there."

I whirled around to look at him, anger swelling in my gut. "Why? Why not? You just explained to me why—"

"Why I can't trust Bask, yes," he cut in. "But the RGM, Sparrow… Releasing Rafael already made me feel like a filthy traitor. I may not be an RGM soldier anymore, but I'm not a slider either, not by choice…"

I strode across the room and stopped in front of him.

"Is that really how you feel, Aaron?" I asked, my voice shaking.

"You told me only moments ago," he interrupted, "that you knew what it felt like to hate being a slider."

"Yes, I did. Because I do—I do know what that's like. I… I always wanted to just be normal. To have parents and go to school and…"

"Parents?"

Memories of the dreams came flooding back. I squeezed my eyes shut, willing them to depart.

"My parents left me," I said softly. "Right after I was born. They never came back."

I felt naked saying it out loud, small and vulnerable. I swallowed back the lump in my throat as tears stung my eyes. I turned away.

"I'm sorry," Aaron said quietly. "I didn't—"

"Don't feel sorry for me. Just answer my damn question. *Will you help me?*"

He stared at me like it was the first time he'd ever seen me.

"I cannot deceive you anymore, Sparrow," he answered, something softening in his eyes. "I don't know that I will ever accept that I'm an anomaly… I don't know that I will ever do anything except live each day to *fight* it. But… because it means so much to you… because I *care* about *you*, I will help you."

I searched for honesty in his face, wondering if maybe there *was* something in him that I could trust.

"Good. So how the hell are we going to get Janna out of there?" I asked.

"There is no 'we,' Sparrow," he said bluntly. "You can't go back into the district."

"I have to—"

"It's too great a risk! If they find you—"

"They *won't.*"

"*Sparrow.*"

"Aaron, I'm the one who found her. I'm the one who knows where she is."

"*I* know where *everything* is in the district, Sparrow. Just tell me where she is, and I'll find her," he insisted. "You just said that Bask is sending another team out. I clearly won't be leading them this time; you'll have no protection."

"Fine. Fine—if you won't let me go back into the district with you, then I will go by myself," I said, crossing my arms over my chest.

"Sparrow, what the hell? They are out there *looking* for *you*. What part of that don't you get?"

"What I *get*, Aaron, is the fact that everyone back at the Homestead is in danger of getting captured or *killed*," I snapped back, looking him straight in the eyes. "Do you really think I'll just stand by while everyone I've ever cared about is destroyed? No. No, Aaron, I'm not going to do that. So you pick: either I go down there myself, or we break Janna out together."

"You know I could always just tie you up and leave you here, right?"

"I've taken down a cougar before. I think I could handle you."

He smirked. "Please do."

I rolled my eyes. "Are you ready for information, Corporal?"

Aaron pulled out a chair at the table and sat down, gesturing to the one opposite. "Ready."

# 66

I HIKED FARTHER AND FARTHER AWAY FROM THE FALLS; the landscape now sprawled in transformed splendor, pulsating with colors and life. As I kept up my brisk pace, my mind reeled back to my encounter with Sensei, still hardly able to grasp it.

I'd heard Dad's stories about him all my life, but I'd never imagined him like that. I'd never seen a face burn so bright. I'd never known eyes so deep and wise. There was something ancient inside them, something I couldn't name, yet I knew that it was everything I was searching for inside myself. I couldn't help but wonder if Sparrow had met him there too—if that was why she couldn't explain what she had found in the cavern.

Funny how none of us had found it except Sparrow—even though she resented even being a slider. It was almost like we'd been so preoccupied with our own efforts that we had missed what was right there in front of us. We'd missed the Dimension.

Sparrow was the only reason I'd found it. Sparrow, who had never even believed in the mission, yet had stumbled straight into the Dimension by accident. Sparrow the doubter had easily found what we "believers" had spent our entire lives training to search for. Yet, according to Sensei, we needed to look no further than inside ourselves. It had never been somewhere else.

It was almost hard to swallow; it made nonsense of all our toiling and work. It made mockery of the lines we'd drawn. But at the same time, the realization had set me free—and given me a weapon to use against the invisible forces of the RGM. And against the invisible force inside *me*—which was far greater than anything the RGM could attempt to manufacture.

It seemed to affirm what Dad had told me all along: that I wasn't at the Homestead because of anything I'd done to get there, but because I was his *son*. We were there because he *already knew* what was inside us, even if we couldn't see it ourselves.

My mind flashed back to the day he'd placed those seeds in my hand and told me that I came from nowhere yet everywhere.

*Infinity* trapped inside me.

Finally, I understood what Dad meant.

I reached the end of the wash and started up a hillside, veering away from the lake and starting into the woods. I reached down and rubbed my knuckles against Cub's head, letting her race ahead to lead the way. This was where Kateri and I had found her—this was her territory. She knew the way better than I did.

Following Cub became automatic, and my thoughts began to drift. Every time I closed my eyes, I either saw Sparrow's face or the Dimension, and somehow the two were becoming more and more the same thing. It was getting more and more difficult to think of one without thinking of the other.

And still, I thought of the lake. Of kissing her.

I had to force myself not to think about it; I needed to stay sharp and alert. I focused on the forest ahead and keeping up with the cougar in front of me.

"Hey, hey, hey, stop…" I muttered aloud, scanning the trees around me. "We're going deeper into the woods. We should have made it to the tree line by now."

Cub ventured farther and farther away. Sighing irritably, I cupped my hands to my mouth and let out a howl, calling her back. She usually came running. This time she didn't. Instead, a low howl replied to my own.

The lonely, haunting sound split the otherwise silent forest around me. The hairs on the backs of my arms rose as I whipped around. My gaze flashed ahead, where I could still see disturbance in the brush and the tip of Cub's tail periscoped above her.

"Cub! Cub, stop!" I called to her, making my way towards her.

Cub's tail froze in place, then bristled like a porcupine's.

In a flash she streaked ahead, letting out a hiss just as something to my left bolted from the brush and slammed into me with the force of a freight train, leveling me to the ground in a chaos of ragged gray fur.

Jaws snapped for my throat; massive claws dug into my shoulders. I swung a fist in a gut reaction and nailed the wolf in the eye, but this didn't stop it for more than an instant. It lunged more fiercely for my face, and I felt its massive teeth slice through my skin.

Adrenaline surged through me as I writhed violently on the ground, sweeping my arm down in one swift motion to knock one of its iron paws off my shoulder. I struggled to my feet, but the massive jaws latched around my calf and clamped shut like a vise grip.

I went down again, howling in agony. Its weight came crashing down on top of me, and this time I felt teeth sink into the back of my skull.

An almost inhuman sound escaped my throat as I reached back and grabbed hold of its jaws with both hands, attempting to pry them off. He thrashed me back and forth, attempting to break my neck like I was nothing more than a rabbit.

My fingers were still clamped around the massive animal's jaws; I could feel its teeth shredding the skin of my hands.

With a wild surge of warmth, a channel flowed down my arms and burst through my fingers in a wave of energy that sent the wolf flying backward—taking a chunk of my hair with it.

I rolled away and lurched to my feet, channeling another orb as the wolf jumped to all fours. Before the orb had even fully formed, the wolf lunged forward and leapt on top of me. Fire rippled through me as we rolled, its claws slicing through my chest.

Then a shot split the air. The wolf became a dead weight and collapsed on top of me.

Barely able to see past the blood pouring down my face, I shimmied out from under the wolf's corpse and rolled away through the tall grass, crawling on my elbows and knees, sinking behind a tree. I could hear the clomp of boots against the ground.

"Please be dead… Good. It is dead," a male voice muttered. "This should last us a day, at least. Beggars can't be choosers. But damn, I thought for sure it had been attacking something…"

I peered out from behind the tree, searching for the source of the voice, but saw no one.

"Hmm. That's so strange…" the muttering continued. "Holy shit—its mouth looks almost… burnt. Wait until the commander sees this…"

*He's a soldier.*

I could practically feel his eyes as he scanned the woods.

A few grunts, then the footsteps resumed.

Sinking down into the tall grass, I crept forward. Peering through the blades, I caught snatches of blood-streaked fur—the dead wolf was floating in midair, as if it was being carried by someone. But no one was there.

I stared, wide-eyed, as pain rippled through my skull. I felt the brush of fur against my skin. I turned and found Cub crouching beside me in the grass.

I pressed my fingertips to the back of my head, trying to focus on healing myself.

*God, it hurts…*

I needed to act fast—the dead wolf would act as the perfect tracer, the only way I would be able to follow this invisible soldier back to the base. But the harder I tried to channel healing, the more impossible it became. My energy was draining.

Cub's massive eyes wavered and blurred in my vision as I sank to the ground, my head throbbing in my blood-covered hands. I fought to stay conscious—trying desperately to channel.

*Don't close your eyes, don't close your eyes, don't…*

# 67

MY DEFIANCE HAD COST VINER HIS LIFE. HE HAD DONE nothing but serve the RGM to the best of his ability, even with his handicap. He was the only person who had been a friend to me since my arrival at District Firehole. Maybe he would have thought of me differently if he knew what I really was: a filthy slider. Maybe we would have grown to hate each other.

Or maybe he would have accepted me, like he always had. Maybe I was just trying in vain to ease my blood-spattered conscience. I couldn't… so instead, I flooded it with thoughts of Sparrow.

Sparrow, who was the most stubborn, irritating human being alive. Sparrow, who had urged me to return to my lodgings for the night so Bask wouldn't discover that I was gone. Sparrow, whom I lay awake thinking of. Sparrow, whom I had kissed.

Before I was invisible, I'd kissed a lot of other women, yet none of those had ever meant anything to me; puffs of smoke vanishing in the wind. But kissing Sparrow had felt entirely different. Nothing else had existed. The velvet softness of her lips pressed against mine, the warmth of her skin. Eyes that stared up into mine, eyes that could *see* me.

God, it was all I could think about.

I sighed out a curse, running a hand over my face. I wanted to kiss her again, to feel her next to me. She filled my dreams.

When I awoke the next morning, there was a resolve inside me: I knew I'd made the right decision. Though I refused to accept being a slider, I was beginning to realize that I was not an RGM soldier, either.

I'd hung on Bask's every empty promise, waiting for my turn to rise. But my turn was never going to come. Bask was never going to use the influence I'd helped him acquire to get me out of my situation.

I would help Sparrow get Janna out not because I sided with the sliders, but because I was in love with Sparrow. I would take away everything I had ever given the RGM—strip them of their invisibility; there would be no more inoculations because there would be no more of my blood.

I felt myself beginning to smile. It was the first time I'd admitted it to myself: *I am in love with Sparrow.*

I rolled over on my mattress and got to my feet, dressed, and laced up my boots. I heard the bolts retract like clockwork, and when I stepped outside a moment later, I found myself face-to-face with Mooney. My blood ran cold. I wanted to knock the few teeth he still possessed down the back of his throat, but I held back.

"Where's Bask?" I asked as he pocketed the ring of jangling keys.

"Gone." He sniffed hard and spat on the ground. "Won't be back until later."

"Gone where?"

Mooney's eyes narrowed to slits as he studied the place where he thought I stood. "The woods. With the search team that went out last night."

"They're still not back?"

Mooney had already spun on his heel to lumber away. "Evidently not."

I gritted my teeth as I watched him go, my fingers twitching into tight, trembling fists as fire coursed through my veins.

If ever there was a time to get out of here, it was now. And if ever there was a time to break Janna out, it was now, while Bask was outside the wire. It was a rare opportunity that I doubted would present itself a second time.

When the factory whistle blew, I was walking down the long dirt road toward the gates. The door to Viner's vacant shack still hung open on its hinges.

With renewed energy, I walked past the guards at the gate, dodging a soldier who was coming in, a gun slung over one shoulder and a dead wolf over the other.

My thoughts raced back to Sparrow as I headed into the forest: her eyes, her wild dark hair, her lips. I was already beginning to feel weightless when a sudden snap yanked me back down to earth.

I whirled around, scanning the silent, skeletal trees around me, straining to listen. Cautiously, I took a few steps forward, scouring the woods.

*Probably one of the few animals left.*

I hiked the rest of the way up to the shack. Sparrow glanced up when I slid the wall panel open.

"Aaron." She was seated on the edge of the bed. "Is it finally morning?"

I stared at her for a moment, my heart beating a little faster as I nodded.

"God, I thought it'd never come," she said, and sighed. "It was such a long night."

"Bask is gone," I informed her. "He went out last night with the search team and hasn't come back yet. We needed to be down there an hour ago. Now's the time to strike."

"*Shit*—we should have just broken her out last night! Let's get down there now!"

I nodded and slid the panel aside. "Let's take a different path down. I thought I heard something in the woods when I left the district—we don't want to run into the team."

"All right." She hurried past me. "Let's go."

"Just keep your head down," I hissed, yanking the rope to the ground and coiling it up. We sank back into the shadow of one of the lodging shacks.

Sparrow pulled the hood of her black cloak over her head. Staying low, we ran parallel to the long row of dilapidated cement buildings.

"Hey, hey, hey—the lab's actually behind us," I whispered urgently into her ear as I fell into step beside her. "We're going in the wrong direction."

Sparrow didn't look surprised. She halted at the end of the last building, peering out to the street.

"I know that," she whispered. "Keep your voice down."

I latched a hand over her shoulder. "What the hell are you doing?" I hissed.

Sparrow shook free of my grasp, sprinting across the street and falling back behind Bask's office. Stunned, I took off after her, my eyes everywhere as I sidled up next to her.

"Dammit, Sparrow—are you *out of your mind*?"

"There's a window." She jerked her chin upwards. "Hoist me up."

My jaw clenched. "No."

"Aaron—"

"*No.* No, we are not breaking into Bask's office!"

"We *have to.*"

I was about to open my mouth to protest when a voice boomed out, "Who's back there?"

Sparrow froze, her eyes going wide. My heart began to race.

"I said who's back there?" the strong, deliberate voice repeated. "Show yourself *immediately!*"

Without thinking, I grabbed Sparrow by the waist and tossed her up onto my shoulders. She lifted to her feet and balanced there.

"*Hurry the hell up,*" I whispered through gritted teeth, holding onto her ankles while she pushed on the window.

"It's locked!"

"You're a slider—bust it open!"

She didn't answer, but a moment later I heard the *bzzzt* of energy igniting in her hands, followed by a searing *pop* a moment later. When I glanced to my left, I could already see the shadow of the approaching guard on the ground.

In one swift motion, I hoisted her higher and through the window. She struggled inside, and I heard it drop shut.

With a quiet sigh of relief, I sank back against the cool cement wall as the barrel of the guard's gun slid around the corner, pointed straight at me. I stayed where I was, watching silently.

With a jerk, the guard stepped out into the open, his face tense and his eyes scanning frantically around him. After a moment, he relaxed his grip on the rifle and slowly retracted it. I crossed my arms over my chest, standing only a few feet to his left.

The guard muttered curses under his breath, giving the back of the building one last look before he turned and walked back to the road.

I immediately snapped around and jumped up to grab hold of the windowsill. I hung there for a moment, then released one hand and reached up to tap gently on the glass. It slid open.

Latching both hands over the sill again, I hoisted myself inside and dropped to the floor. We were in a storage room. The walls were covered in floor-to-ceiling shelves lined with boxes. I gestured Sparrow forward to the metal door.

Grasping the knob, I twisted it silently, easing the door open to peer out into the rest of Bask's office. I held my breath.

Shafts of golden sunlight blasted in through the windows at the far end of the room, illuminating the hardwood floors, the tall wooden cabinet pushed up against one wall, and the disheveled papers scattered across Bask's vacant desk.

I nodded to Sparrow, opening the door enough to step through.

Our footsteps seemed as loud as gunshots in the silence. Sparrow slid behind Bask's desk, hunching in front of the massive armchair to glance over the heaps of papers. Above me, over the massive fireplace, the buffalo head hung, covered in dust. Its glass eyes seemed to observe us.

My gaze snapped to the windows as I heard a guard moving in the street.

"I can't believe I let you talk me into this," I muttered, ducking away from the windows to circle around to the massive wood-slab desk. "If we don't hurry—"

"I know, okay? I know…" Sparrow began to rifle through the papers.

"Sparrow, we have to go—now."

"Shh." Her eyes widened as she lifted one of the papers to read it.

"The Homestead…" Sparrow's voice came out barely above a whisper. "They have the coordinates… How the hell do they have the coordinates?"

She turned to gape at me, dread lingering in the dark centers of her eyes.

"Janna wouldn't have known the coordinates," she whispered.

I took the paper out of her hand and looked it over for myself, scanning over Bask's trembling scrawl. Beneath the coordinates there was a list of names.

"They must have already scoped the place out—it's procedure," I answered quietly. "They must have already been there…"

"No." Sparrow's voice rushed out, frantic. "No, no, no—that can't be possible! You would have known about it if they'd already sent out—"

"Not necessarily," I interrupted. "I'm not exactly in Bask's good graces right now."

Slapping the paper back down on the desk, I quickly shuffled through another stack, keeping my eyes peeled for a gray folder—the kind my commander always used for mission intel. I found it in moments, but to my surprise there was nothing inside. Nothing but a small, handwritten notation in the corner. A date.

"Dammit," I whispered.

Sparrow leaned closer to peer over my shoulder. "What?"

"Tonight." I tapped the date with my index finger. "That's when they're going to attack."

"That… that's not possible. They couldn't even get out there that quickly."

"They'll be moving nonstop, and they move fast—trust me, I know." I snapped the folder shut. "We don't have much time."

The sound of approaching boots split the silence. Sparrow tensed beside me.

"Quick," I hissed, jerking my head for her to follow as I rushed across the room, over to the narrow wooden cabinet.

I threw open the door and shoved her inside with Bask's dress uniform. Though I knew *I* wouldn't be seen, I didn't trust Sparrow's temper, so I fitted myself into the tight space beside her and closed the door behind us.

"Not a sound," I said under my breath. I felt Sparrow nod, her petite frame fitting easily around mine. She held her breath as the office door creaked open.

A long pause. My heart throbbed in the back of my throat.

A few sets of boots clomped into the room. The heavy door slammed shut.

A voice I instantly recognized as Bask's cursed loudly and slammed something.

"We still have a lot of ground to cover, sir," said another voice.

"She could be *anywhere* by now," Bask replied. "Far beyond our reach."

"Or maybe she's hiding…"

Pacing boots. I heard Bask unscrew his flask, then a soft swish as he drank from it.

"Or perhaps…"

"Perhaps what? Speak up, damn it."

"Perhaps she's being *kept* hidden."

"Hidden? Kept hidden by whom?"

"By one of our own, sir."

I felt my muscles tighten, sweat beginning to bead at the back of my neck.

"What are you suggesting, Corporal?"

A hesitation.

"Only that our resident freak went missing himself the other night," the soldier replied. "And that's not the only occurrence—he's slipped off base plenty of other times when he thinks no one notices."

There was another swish as Bask drank again from his flask, followed by a sudden fleshy thud. A pained cry erupted.

"Corporal," Bask said calmly, "do you suggest that my experimental protégé might be a turncoat?"

"Sir, I didn't mean—I-I didn't mean that—"

Another sickening thud, followed this time by stumbling boots and a crash. The soldier sputtered, gasping, and I heard Bask drag him to his feet and slam him back against the wall.

"To suggest that this is Price's fault is to suggest that it is *my* fault," Bask hissed, his voice shaking. "It's because of my experiment that you're even here, Corporal. It's because of *me* that you even have this job. If Price is blamed for this, it will reflect badly not on him, but on *me*. *Do you understand?*"

I barely heard the soldier's gasping response. That one word was still ringing in my ears:

*Experiment.*

"Now get out of my sight," Bask roared.

The door opened and slammed shut again, leaving Bask alone. There was a long moment of silence, and then an explosion of objects crashing against the floor. Glass shattered; Bask roared. Papers fluttered.

I knew the drill: he'd cleared his desk in one fell swoop—which, in this case, fortunately destroyed any evidence that we'd been rifling through his things.

"Damn you, Price!" he seethed. "I'll *kill you* before I let you betray me..."

I swallowed, hot anger swelling in my chest.

Bask stormed out of his office and slammed the door behind him.

I pushed open the closet door and jumped out. "Come on," I hissed to Sparrow.

We made a hasty escape, leaving the same way we'd come in, and raced to cover behind the building. Once we were sure we wouldn't be spotted, Sparrow grabbed my arm.

"Bask suspects you of hiding me in the woods." Her voice sounded scared. "The soldier said—"

"He has no proof," I cut in firmly. "No one does."

"Yes, but…" Terror danced through her dark eyes.

"I'm not going to let them find you—I promise," I whispered, my gaze locking with hers. "Do you think you can make it back to the shack without being spotted?"

"Yes, but—"

"I'll meet you there as soon as I can."

"Why?" Sparrow asked, alarmed. "What are you going to do?"

"I have a plan." Reaching down, I took her hand and leaned closer. "Trust me."

My stomach churned nervously as I got Sparrow back over the wall and watched her take off alone. It felt like letting a lamb into a lion's den. But then, she was definitely more of a lion type herself.

I glanced away as the slender needle pricked my skin. The medic slowly pulled back the plunger and filled the barrel of the syringe with my translucent blood.

"Glad you were able to make your appointment, Price," he commented casually, breaking the silence.

"I always make my appointments," I replied. "When have I ever not?"

The medic didn't reply.

One syringe down; he placed it to the side and picked up another. Uncapping it, he pierced my skin with the second needle.

"It's just that you weren't in your lodgings the other night," the medic responded finally, jerking me out of my thoughts.

"I lost track of time on a trail run."

"It must be nice to come and go as you like. You enjoy a lot of freedom in exchange for your blood."

I glanced down at the syringe stuck in my arm. "If you call this freedom."

He filled another syringe… and another.

I took a deeper breath and blew it out in an audible sigh. "How many more?"

"Just one. Why?"

I shook my head. "I guess it's getting to me this time—I think I need to use the bathroom. I feel like I'm going to be sick."

He slid the needle out of my arm and capped it, setting the last full syringe on a tray with the others.

"We're done," he said, scribbling an entry down in the book that lay open on the table at one end of the room. "Water closet's down the hall."

I got to my feet, pulling in an uneasy breath. I stepped out into the long cement hallway and closed the door behind me. I walked briskly to the tiny water closet, where I reached in quickly to snap the light on and then pulled the door shut. Then I sprinted down the hallway, trying my best to keep my footsteps as muted as possible. The hallway wound around a corner and abruptly ended at another door. I checked through the glass window at the top to make sure I was clear before I shouldered it open and emerged into a sterile white corridor.

Treading softly, I quickened my pace, recalling Sparrow's instructions in my head as I passed several heavy iron doors. I glanced through the small glass window at the top of each cell as I walked past. Each was vacant.

Finally, I approached the cell that Sparrow had said was Janna's. I stopped dead in my tracks before I'd even reached it. The hair on the back of my neck rose.

The door hung ajar. Metal sensors were scattered across the floor. The cell was empty, and the access panel was melting down the wall.

# 68

*NO... YOU CANNOT FALL ASLEEP.*

Forcing my eyes open, I struggled to get up, pressing a hand to my bleeding head wound. I could see the dead wolf up ahead, bobbing through the trees as its invisible predator carried it away.

For a moment I crouched there in the grass; I felt a liquid warmth rinse over my scalp as the wound began to heal. Smooth flesh formed on the left side of my head where hair had once been. Blood streaked my chest where the wolf had dug its claws in, but there was no time to heal that now. A few claw marks wouldn't kill me.

I staggered to my feet and crept through the trees, tuning into the thoughts of the invisible soldier up ahead. Cub trod softly alongside me, staying just as silent, as I kept the dead wolf in my line of sight.

The soldier's thoughts were a mixed bag, but most of them were about the wolf's burned face and how that could possibly have happened. He wondered what his commander would think of it.

I dodged from one tree to the next, sinking lower each time I perceived the soldier looking around. It was so eerie, watching that wolf carcass hovering in midair.

Eventually the forest opened to a clearing, and I dropped silently into the brush at the very edge of the woods, watching as the invisible soldier carried the wolf out into the open.

This was the clearing where Kateri and I had felt the earth shake and heard it roar, as if it were spouting gushing water, though we had seen nothing.

I watched as the dead wolf disappeared into thin air—swallowed up by whatever strange force obviously occupied the open valley ahead.

I sat there a moment, scanning for the mind of the soldier I'd been reading only moments before, but I detected nothing. I started to rise from the brush, then stopped, startled, as someone else's thoughts flashed in my mind.

*I have to get back to Sparrow… I hope she—*

I flattened to the earth, snatching Cub by the scruff just as she began to venture away, snapping a twig in two.

The thought pattern abruptly ended. I could feel a set of eyes scanning the trees. There was a long pause, then:

*Probably one of the few animals left…*

I lay there, concealed by the brush, holding Cub back until I lost the thought pattern. Just like the dead wolf, it vanished suddenly. Trying in vain to tap back into the channel of thought, I lay still against the ground, listening.

A thousand questions raced through my head in unison: *Whose thoughts did I just read? How does he know Sparrow? Where did he come from, and where is he going?*

Accepting that I was once again alone in the forest, I bent down and rustled my fingers through Cub's soft coat.

"You have to wait here," I whispered.

It took a little convincing, but finally she obeyed.

I crept carefully out into the open, letting my forehead go numb. I listened, just as Sensei had instructed, unable to help but wonder why I hadn't done this the first time, that day when Kateri and I had stood at the edge of the woods, gazing out into the valley. I hadn't trusted myself enough. I'd felt like my judgment had been too clouded by my love for Sparrow. But now, after seeing Sensei face-to-face, after witnessing the Dimension collide with our earthly one, there was no room for doubt in my heart.

I could sense the presence of the invisible soldier somewhere ahead. I dropped to my belly on the crusty, seeping ground and crawled my way closer. There were now three separate streams of thought flowing through my mind, and I followed them like Cub scenting a prey. Aside from the soldier carrying the dead wolf, I detected two others. From the way they were questioning the soldier about the wolf's burned face, I got the feeling they were security guards.

*"Hey, stop—where the hell'd you find a wolf?"*

Lying there in the dirt, I scanned the wide-open space around me, so deceivingly empty. I needed to figure out where the perimeter of this place began. I needed to get the lay of the land. But how? I couldn't see anything…

*But they can.*

I closed my eyes, zeroing in on the channel of thought coming from the first guard who had spoken.

Reading someone's thoughts was an easy task, but letting someone else's mind completely eclipse my own was a different story. I became less and less aware of my own body and senses, and more and more aware of my invisible counterpart's until I could not only perceive their every thought, but I could feel their body as if it were my own: the stiffness of a military uniform, the weight of a gun slung over my shoulder. Through a face shield I could see the soldier with the wolf; I could hear him talking.

"Out in the woods a few miles, not that far—the thing's skinny as shit, but it's better than nothing, which is basically what we've been living on," he explained.

Thoughts swirled in the guard's head as he peered around. I could see a cement wall encompassing a mass of dilapidated buildings. I saw the forest beyond the gates, and as he turned back to look at the soldier, I could make out a long dirt road and a massive factory looming like a giant over the rest of the encampment. The streets were pretty empty save a smattering of guards patrolling up and down the long dirt road.

"How'd its face get roasted?" the guard asked.

"Dunno, really—it was attacking something in the tall grass when I snuck up on it. There was a bit of blood on the ground but nothing else—whatever it was must have done its damage and got away."

The guard grunted. "Figures. Only a lice-bag slider could have done damage like that, and they seem to be coming out of the woodwork these days…"

I got a full panoramic view of the compound as the guard checked around again.

Taking a deep breath, I snapped out of his thoughts. Through his eyes I had seen the area where I was hiding, though he had not detected me hunched in the dried brush alongside the wall; I could see now that that was what it was—a wall.

I had to get past the wall, but there was no easy way over. Closing my eyes, I let my thoughts fade away. I made a mental lock on what I'd seen inside the encampment and slipped into a deep visualization. I opened my eyes to pure darkness. For a second I was stunned. I guessed this was what it looked like to be inside an invisible world.

*This is exactly how Raf described it.*

I crawled carefully, using my hands to feel my way forward. Meanwhile, the ground began to quake beneath me, as if something boiled and churned in the Earth's belly.

I crawled a little farther, then hit a wall. I sidled up against it, quickly letting my mind merge with another nearby guard's so I could get my bearings. Vision flickered back into my senses. Rows of buildings came into view—small cement shacks. The guard didn't notice me; he was too busy thinking about… *other things.* But right away, I detected a smudge of ginger hair peeking out from behind the corner of one of the buildings. I shimmied back a little farther, concealing myself in the shadows and feeling my way along to the back of the building.

I halted, tipping my head back against the cool cement, listening, looking out through the guard's narrowed eyes.

I could see the two guards at the gate, still talking to the soldier carrying the wolf. When he reached the end of the road, he pivoted on the heels of his boots and made a hundred-and-eighty-degree turn to stalk back in the direction he had come from. From this new perspective, I could see the long row of cement-block shacks clearly. An alleyway ran behind them, all the way down to the factory at the end.

Across the street were larger buildings, more lodging facilities, I was guessing. Each had a rusty metal door, sprayed with mud from the road.

Finally, at the far end of the row opposite, I spotted what I was looking for: a larger building with a set of rugged cement steps leading up to it. There was a sign posted beside the door reading "Experimentation Lab."

*Perfect.*

I waited until the guard had passed before I edged my way around the building, feeling through the darkness. I knew from the mental map I was beginning to piece together in my head that I was now facing the street. The additional buildings I'd seen through the guard's vision were directly across from me.

I scanned my surroundings for prying minds, anyone nearby who could possibly witness what I was about to do. After a few seconds, I could tell the street was clear. The guards at the gate had finally let the soldier carrying the dead wolf leave, and were facing outward once again.

I rushed forward, my palms meeting cold, rough cement a moment later. I quickly flattened against it, feeling my way along the side of the building until I reached the back corner. I proceeded carefully until—

*"Hey!"*

The voice came out of nowhere. And every muscle in my body tightened. My mind swept my surroundings and immediately caught on the guard who was standing behind one of the adjoining buildings; everything came into clear focus as soon as I dropped into his mind. He held a cigarette in his fingers and wore a black RGM uniform. He stared right at me, and since I was in his head, I guess that meant *I* was staring right at me.

My bare chest was caked with dried blood and marred by a distinct set of claw marks. One side of my head was bald right down to the skin where the wolf's teeth had given me a close shave.

The cigarette dropped from his hand, and I caught blurry snatches of myself as he ran for me, reaching for his gun. I watched myself reach into my shoulder holster and snatch a knife, hurtling it forward in one quick motion.

*What the—*

Pain fizzled in the guard's head as he stumbled backward, clutching his shoulder where the blade had impaled him. I lunged on top of him, smothering his mouth with my hand before he could get a word out. I could see myself hovering over him as I lifted a finger to my lips and pressed the first three fingers of my opposite hand to his forehead.

I felt my hand heat up, trembling. The guard wrestled under my grasp, his thoughts frantic… then they slowed like a river beginning to freeze. My blood-streaked face wavered and then dimmed altogether.

Then everything was dark again as I was released from his now unconscious mind.

Wasting no time, I blindly unbuttoned his uniform and unzipped his pants. I quickly undressed him and pulled the shirt on, wincing as the fabric touched my shredded flesh. I yanked off his boots and pants, shimmying into them myself.

I propped him up against the back of the cement building and left him there, snatching the beret off his drooping head. I shoved my hair into the cap and pulled it on.

I found the steps to the lab with the toe of my boot. Mounting them carefully, I paused when I reached the top, letting my own mind empty as I scanned for a new channel of thought from someone inside the building.

At first, I didn't pick anything up. Then I detected a calm, concise thought pattern.

*Entries, entries, entries…* I could practically feel the sensation of pages flipping under my fingertips. *Hmm… Price was due for a visit today. Great. That's just great. What the hell am I going to tell Bask when he finds out Price didn't show? Damn it…*

Slowly, I let my mind loose on his, letting the darkness give way to a blinding flash of white. In front of my eyes were a pair of hands; one finger was scanning down a long list of entries. Names and dates and procedures. His finger stopped and tapped one entry in particular, almost absentmindedly.

*Aaron Price.*

The name he'd just been thinking of. Today's date was scribbled beside it. An appointment, it seemed.

My fingers closed around the doorknob in front of me. I pushed the door open and stepped inside. At the sudden sound of the door creaking open, my view lifted from the book and panned swiftly across the sterile white room. I caught glimpses of counters full of test tubes and medical equipment and noticed an examination table standing in the middle of the room. Then I saw a door swinging open and a rough-looking RGM soldier step inside—*me.*

"What the hell happened to you?" the medic asked, giving me a once-over.

*Shit—there's still blood on my face.*

I watched myself gulp air like a fish and wipe my face off with my sleeve.

The medic waved me forward. From his point of view, I could only see his arm; then his gaze flashed away to focus on the white surface of the examination table. "Did Mooney do that?" he asked.

I had no idea what this meant, but I rolled with it, nodding.

"Did you give him back as good as he gave?"

I cleared my throat. "Tried to."

He turned away to grab some cotton off one of the counters. I took advantage of the opportunity to feel my way forward and sit down on the table. When he turned back around, I saw myself sitting there.

He soaked the wad of cotton in rubbing alcohol, then pressed it to my split eyebrow.

I winced at the sting and then cleared my throat. "Bask sent me in to check on the prisoner."

Using the name was a huge risk—I didn't even know who I was talking about here. But from the context of the medic's thoughts, I got the feeling he was someone in leadership, and my hunches were not usually wrong.

"Bask did?" he questioned. "I thought he was out with the search team."

I nodded. "He gave me the order before he left."

"Ah."

The medic dabbed at my eyebrow, saying nothing else for a moment.

"Just a superficial wound. You won't need stitches," he said finally, the room spinning again as he turned around to toss the cotton into the trash and wash his hands. My gaze focused on the warm water in the basin as it slowly turned a rusty color from the blood on his hands. "Bask told you what cell she's in, right?"

I shook my head. "Remind me."

"Cell 014, just down the hall there." He glanced toward the opposite end of the room now, where a door with a plate-glass window opened up to what looked like a dim cement hallway.

"Much appreciated."

Dropping back to my feet, I carefully crossed the room and let myself out into the hallway, exiting the medic's thoughts. Everything darkened once more. As soon as I had closed the door behind me, I extended my arms in front of me to start feeling my way along the damp cement wall, quickly scanning for the presence of anyone who could be up ahead.

I didn't sense anything, only the medic in the office behind me. My open eyes gaped into the darkness, and I continued carefully down the hallway, putting one foot in front of the other until—

I cursed, crashing into something hard. My thoughts became frenzied for a moment, and then I slowed myself down, moving one hand across the surface in front of me. I felt cool glass pass under my palm.

Another door.

I lowered my hand, sweeping it back and forth until my fingertips brushed with the cool, slightly sticky shape of a doorknob. I clenched it and pushed.

I opened the door and stepped through, emerging into what felt like another hallway, except it smelled like bleach now. The walls were smooth.

*How am I going to find cell 014 without sight?*

Running my hands over the walls, I could feel my fingertips pass over a metal door. I paused for a moment, feeling around for a glass window. When I located it, I moved my hand to the door frame, and then to the wall, sweeping my palm over the surface until I finally felt something rigid and embossed under my fingers.

I thoroughly investigated the shapes until I could make it out.

0… 0… 3

*003.*

*Now I'm getting somewhere.*

Quickening my pace, I moved forward, trailing my hand along the wall and counting the doors as they passed underneath my hand.

*007… 009… 011…*

I moved farther down the hallway, rounding a corner.

*013…*

I slammed to a halt. I could detect a new set of thoughts.

*Sparrow said she would come back… Why hasn't she?… Why hasn't she?…*

The thoughts ebbed, exhausted. But I recognized them immediately. A moment later, the hallway echoed with soft, muffled sobs.

I took a few more steps forward, and my fingertips brushed with a cool glass windowpane. I leaned closer, looking through. And this time, I saw more than thick folds of inky darkness. This time I saw a familiar figure hunched at the far end of the room. A thin, shaking frame, her shaved head bowed. Her scalp was covered in little metal disks.

My eyes widened, and I tapped on the glass. "Janna!"

For a moment, she didn't budge; she just kept crying.

I knocked on the glass more deliberately. *"Janna!"*

Slowly, she looked up from the floor and met my gaze. Her wide blue eyes were bloodshot and filled with tears. I saw her mouth form the shape of my name. I nodded.

She lurched to her feet and all but threw herself against the door.

"Keegan! How did you—where did you—"

I placed a finger to my lips, moving my hand through the darkness until I could feel the threshold, then, beside it, the keypad. I didn't touch the sensor, having no clue what to do with it. Instead, I latched my fingers around the device itself, pressing my nails against the plastic. I drew a breath and blew it back out in a surge of energy; I felt it wash down my arm in hot rays, melting the device, which disintegrated with a few distorted bleeps. A moment later, I heard a *tsssttt* as the door depressurized and popped open.

Janna stumbled out, bleary eyed. She fell into me, hanging on unsteadily for a moment.

"Quiet," I warned her, already tugging her forward, farther down the hall. "Stay close and follow my lead."

"I can't see any—"

"Shhh! I know, I know. I can't see anything either. Just keep your mind still. I'm going to transport us out of here."

I was already positioning my still-pulsating fingertips over her forehead. Janna was shaking, and her breathing was unsteady. Letting my thoughts melt away to nothing, I started focusing on the edge of the woods where I'd left Cub behind. I imagined it in detail, rewinding back to the moment I'd been crouching there in the brush.

Chills ran up and down my spine as the walls fell away to open air. My eyes flew open to find Janna staring at me, that same haunted expression in her eyes.

"Keegan, how—"

"Long story," I interrupted as Cub emerged from the brush and bounded over to us. Janna stared down at Cub; she seemed not to have heard me. I gently lifted her face in my hands and brought her focus back up to mine.

"Janna—Janna, I know you're scared, but you've gotta pay attention right now, all right?" I urged her. "Did you tell them anything when they questioned you?"

"I… I didn't… I didn't want to."

My throat tightened. "So you *did* give them information, then?"

"You don't understand." Her voice became watery. "They were going to *kill* me."

"What did you tell them?"

Her nose was running, and tears filled her eyes. "Everything," she said, her voice cracking. "I told them everything, Keegan…"

I squeezed my eyes shut and cursed.

"I'm sorry." Her voice trembled as tears rolled down her cheeks. "I-I'm sorry…"

"So they know our location?" I couldn't hide the fury in my voice.

Janna nodded.

My jaw tightened as I glanced back over my shoulder at the expansive valley sprawling out beyond the tree line. All that "empty" space.

"You have to get out of here—now." My voice was cold. "You have to get back to the Homestead and tell Sensei everything—tell him I said they have to get out as fast as they can. I'll transport you."

"B-b-but what about you?"

"Don't worry about me—just get them out of there. Tell them to abandon the Homestead and get as far away as they possibly can before they're found. Do you understand?"

Sniffing, she nodded fiercely.

"Is Sparrow in there?" I proceeded to the next pressing question, my eyes still drilling into hers. "Did you see Sparrow while you were in there?"

"Ye-yes. Once."

"So she's in there?"

Janna jerked her head up and down in a fevered nod.

"Do you know where they're keeping her?"

"No idea."

"She wasn't in that containment area with you?"

"No, she wasn't. I have no idea where they're keeping her. She didn't say."

Bending down, I picked Cub up off the ground and thrust her into Janna's arms, already positioning my fingers on her forehead again.

She latched onto my wrist and stared up at me. "W-w-what about you?" she stammered. "Aren't you—"

"I'm not leaving without Sparrow," I said resolutely as I glanced over my shoulder at the haunting, desolate valley. "I'm going back in."

# 69

"GONE? GONE—NO. NO, THAT'S IMPOSSIBLE..." I PACED across the creaking floor of the shack. "We have to go back. We have to figure out where they moved her to, or if they…"

My mind raced through every eventuality. Aaron sat on the edge of the bed as I walked back and forth in front of him.

"The RGM didn't move her," Aaron answered at last, pinching his lower lip between his thumb and first finger. "Someone else did."

"What the hell are you talking about?"

"The access panel was fried, Sparrow."

"Fried, as in…?"

"As in dripping down the wall—melted." His voice was grave. It sent chills down my spine.

*Who would be capable of doing such a thing?* I knew the answer, and so did he. I could see it in his eyes.

"It… it can't be," I began, my throat still tight. "There's no way."

Something inside me knew that Keegan wasn't far away.

Rafael must have made it back alive… He'd told Keegan what was going on, and Keegan had found me.

*Keegan found me.*

"What?" Aaron's eyes narrowed. "What is it?"

"How would it be possible for a slider to break into the district? No one can see this place but me." I answered his question by posing another, more puzzling one. "How could anyone possibly find this place?"

Aaron searched my face for a moment, then shook his head. "I don't know. I don't know, Sparrow. It could only be an anomaly—no human could do damage like that."

My mind began to churn.

"Maybe you should head back down there and figure out what's going on—whether Janna is still on the premises or not."

"I wouldn't hold your breath," Aaron grunted, dragging a hand over his face. "Bask won't tell me anything. Not when he suspects me of harboring you."

"But Bask seemed to defend you when the soldier so much as suggested that you were a traitor—"

"Only because Bask hates to be wrong," Aaron cut in.

"You've worked with him a long time. You know him—do you think he knows you're hiding me?"

"I don't know Bask, Sparrow," he concluded, sounding numb. "I can't guess what he thinks or knows. But what he suspects could be deadly enough."

"Deadly?"

I came to a stop in front of him, kneeling down to put myself at eye level with him. His gaze locked with mine.

"Aaron, do you… do you think Bask would kill you?"

"Not if he wants to keep draining the life from my veins," he responded hoarsely. "Kind of have to be alive for that."

"Still, why risk it?"

"*You're* why I risk it." He shook his head, then cursed through a sigh. "Sparrow, I love you." He let go of the words like a kite in gale winds. "You're the only person who's ever seen me—really *seen me* in every way. And I feel like I've seen you too… if that makes sense. I know you don't love me. I guess I just…"

There was something soft, almost vulnerable, in his brown eyes as they searched mine.

"Maybe we shouldn't talk about this now," I began softly. "There's so much—"

"That's why I *have* to talk about it now, Sparrow. I have to talk about it because I don't know what's going to happen."

I took a deep breath, pressing my lips together. "Aaron, I *do* care about you. I believe you are meant for so much more than this life you've been living here. But I just…"

"Please don't explain it." He got up and began to walk the floor like a wolf trapped in a cage. "If you don't say it, then I don't really know, and I can just… hope. If you finish that sentence, I feel like I'll lose something I only just found, Sparrow, so…" He trailed off again, shaking his head feverishly. "Just don't say it."

I sat down on the edge of the bed and watched him pace back and forth for a moment until abruptly he stopped, pounding his fist against the wall and resting his head against it.

"You said you didn't want to accept that you are a slider." His voice came out rough. "That you are an anomaly."

"That's right."

"Why?"

"I always wanted to be normal, I guess. I wanted to live like other people. I didn't want to be the daughter of—" I stopped, clenching my jaw before the words could slip out. "Anomalies."

"Your parents were anomalies?"

My heart beat a little faster. "Yeah. Yeah, but I resented it. And wanted to be everything they weren't. I fought it with everything in me— but life has a way of twisting and turning and bringing you around to where you're supposed to be."

"So now you're all right with who you are?"

I surrendered a small shrug. "I'm not sure I know who that is yet."

"So I guess being a slider didn't make your life a nightmare like it made mine."

"Depends on how you define nightmare."

"Taking away your family, your pride, your dreams—all of that was stripped from me, Sparrow, all at once." Aaron's hands clenched into fists. He walked slowly over to the bed and sank down beside me, looking squarely into my eyes. "I don't think you know what it's like to lose everything that's ever mattered to you. I don't think you get how much like hell it feels to lose your parents."

The words cut deep—deeper than I was expecting them to.

My mind reeled back to Fin, to all the stories he'd told me every night after the other kids had gone to bed. Stories about my mom and dad: the patriarchs. The split-souls, between whom the universe was supported. To all the times I'd asked him when they were coming back; that look he'd get in his eyes.

Pressing my eyelids shut, I took a deep breath to push the memories away.

"I know a little of what it feels like." I opened my eyes again and turned to look at him. "I lost my parents too."

"What happened to them?" Aaron asked softly.

I bit my lower lip, shaking my head a little. "I don't know. They left— they had to leave. Fin raised me."

"Fin?"

"Basically, my dad in almost every sense of the word." My voice was small and tight. "My Sensei."

"Sensei?"

"It means teacher," I explained quietly. "He taught me everything I…"

It was the first time I'd ever referred to Fin as Sensei, but now, looking back, I could see how blind I'd been all this time. Fin had given me everything.

*Oh, god, why hadn't I seen it? Why had I always been so hard on him?*

And now his life was in danger.

"But the old man taught me something too," I whispered, almost to myself, clutching the cloak around me, a stinging feeling in my eyes. "That nothing is impossible if I believe—something I've never been very good at."

"Old man?" Aaron questioned.

"The old man who was sharing my cell—the one I thought had drowned the night of the flood," I explained, a tear drifting down my cheek. "Remember you dragged me away when I wanted to get him out? He survived."

Aaron stared at me. "There was no one else in your cell, Sparrow. You were in solitary confinement."

"But that's… that's impossible."

"There was no one there, Sparrow," he said firmly, almost angrily. "There was no one in that cell with you. What the hell are you talking about?"

"I don't understand. Of course there was someone in there with me! The old man was there the whole time!"

He grabbed me by the shoulders, his eyes wild. "What was his name?"

"He never told me," I replied, jerking backward. "Now let go!"

Aaron released me. I jumped up and backed away a few paces.

"He survived the flood, you say?" Aaron asked, his voice low and trembling.

"Yes, he survived. He's the one who helped me hide from you and your search team in the woods. I was with him before you found me in the woods. He gave me this." I ran my fingers over the soft fabric of the cloak. "He knew I could see things that no one else can…" I trailed off. "I think maybe he could see, too…"

Aaron's dark eyes locked onto the cloak. "He gave you that?"

Before I could answer, he jumped to his feet, striding and seizing a handful of the fabric before I could even react. He ripped it from my body and violently tore it in half down the middle, rage burning in his eyes. He snatched one of the halves and tore it again, then threw the fabric to the floor.

"Aaron!" I grabbed him by the arm, but he shoved me away.

"Don't touch me!" He wrenched around to shout right into my face. "Get the hell away from me—"

"Aaron, what is wrong with you?" I cried, bewildered. "Do you know who he is?"

Aaron slid open the door, then turned to glare at me. "Where is the old man now?"

My heart pounding in my chest, I stood there breathless for a moment, unsure of what to say. "I… I don't know. I last saw him in the woods."

Aaron hesitated at the threshold for a moment and then suddenly closed the distance between us, his heavy boots making the floor shake. He stopped inches from me and stared down into my eyes.

"Why did you never tell me about him?"

"Because I thought you *knew* about him—I thought you knew he was my cellmate," I blurted. "I thought you saw him too! And on top of that, I thought he drowned! I thought he died!"

"Yes, but then you found out he didn't," Aaron hissed, grabbing me by the shoulders again, his fingers digging in. "You *knew* he was out there, and you said *nothing!*"

"Why would I?" I said through gritted teeth as I stared right back at him. "Who the hell is he to you?"

Aaron's hands shook, still frozen in a vise grip around my shoulders. The glimpse of softness I'd caught in his eyes before was gone, replaced by ice. He jerked away and stormed outside, slamming the door behind him.

# 70

I WAS SO CLOSE—*SO CLOSE* TO FINALLY FINDING SPARROW.

I transported Janna back to the Homestead, praying that she and the others I'd left behind would be safe—that Janna would relay the warning I'd given her. I felt like my heart was being tugged in two separate directions as I stood there at the edge of the woods, looking out at the empty space where I knew the prison camp lay. Everything inside me wanted to find Sparrow, but at the same time I wanted to be back there, back at the Homestead, making sure they were safe.

For now, I focused on the challenge at hand: getting back into the camp and finding Sparrow.

This time, instead of painstakingly making my way back across the wide-open expanse, I closed my eyes and locked my focus on what I'd seen through the eyes of the soldiers who had been inside the camp. I focused on the long row of buildings I'd taken cover behind, the run-down shacks that looked like they were being used for housing. I'd only seen them for a moment, but I could still remember enough of the details to make the transport.

I opened my eyes to the encompassing darkness of a strange reality I couldn't see. I could hear the mechanical churning of the factory, the sound of hissing steam and grinding machines. I could hear the voices of nearby guards out on the street. My fingertips brushed against something cool and rough—the cement back side of one of the shacks.

My mind snagged on a rapid pattern of thought from somewhere close. For a moment I just listened.

*He wouldn't betray me. He never has before, not when he's had so much to lose…*

I squinted in the darkness, listening to the soldier's thoughts, slowly letting myself slip out of my head and into his, sweat beading at the back of my neck.

*No… No, Price has never betrayed me. He thinks I'm going to get him back into the RGM. Why would he risk losing that when it's so important to him?*

*Price.* Recognition flashed in my mind as I recalled the entry I'd seen in the experimentation lab's ledger. Slowly, my vision cleared around a view of a desk cluttered with books and papers. Smoke rose from a cigar resting between two meaty fingers. I quickly took in the rest. A rustic office lined with mahogany walls and a fireplace.

*Why would he risk it all now for a girl? Why would he do that?*

The pair of hands lifted the cigar to his mouth and then set it down on a metal tray and started shuffling papers. I caught a brief glimpse of the word "Homestead" on one of the pages as he riffled through.

My heart sank.

*But if he is hiding Sparrow… then how the hell am I ever going to find her?*

The hands scattered the papers, frustrated.

*If I kill him, I'll have no more of his blood, and I'll never find her…*

I dropped out of the man's thoughts. I wasn't sure what it all meant, but I could understand enough of it to grasp the fact that this man was looking for Sparrow. Which meant Sparrow wasn't here. I needed to get back out of the camp and search the surrounding area for her.

I couldn't help but curse as I wiped the sweat off my face. For a moment she'd been so close, and now I felt like I was back to square one.

Suddenly the ground began to shake, and a rumbling filled the air. Startled, I crouched down and braced against the back of the building. I heard the muffled roar of gushing water and was suddenly blindsided by a sickening sense of déjà vu. This was the sound I'd heard that day with Kateri, standing there at the edge of the woods, looking out over the valley: the erupting geyser I'd been unable to see. Now, finally, I knew why.

Carefully getting to my feet, I leaned back against the building and started to focus on transporting once more, back to the woods. I wiped the sweat off my face again and tried to focus. My chest ached from the wounds I still hadn't had a chance to heal. I could feel infection setting in, the skin starting to become hot and swollen.

I brushed these thoughts away and brought my focus back to forming a solid mental image of where I wanted to be, but the harder I tried, the harder it became. I winced and slumped back against the rough cement behind me.

*Why can't I transport?* The question pounded through my head with the nervous energy that was filling my system. *What is going on with me?*

I tried again, forcing my mind to silence, feverishly conjuring visions of the trees. They only seemed to blur and fade with the thudding of my pulse in my head.

I cursed under my breath, clenching my jaw as I pinched my eyes shut. As suddenly as the ground had begun to shake, a whistle blew. The pounding of footsteps filled the air, along with the shouting of guards. I could see nothing, but I could tell by the sound of the tumult that the factory was emptying.

If anyone came off the street and stepped into the back alley behind the shacks where I was hiding, I was a dead man.

I tried again to focus, to imagine the forest and establish a cognitive lock. I felt the power inside me straining and dwindling. With or without my power, I had to get out of there.

Then I remembered that I was wearing the RGM uniform I'd stolen off the soldier.

My thoughts racing, I tried to latch onto one of the soldiers' minds again, giving myself eyes, but I ended up tapping into one of the prisoners' minds instead. They were walking down the long dirt road, lost in the rest of the mob, accompanied by a handful of soldiers. Everyone was dirty-faced and uniformed.

*Perfect.*

Beyond the many heads of the uniformed ghosts, I could see the gate ahead, and on either side of the street I could see the grimy cement office buildings and lodgings. I tried my best to orient myself accordingly, cautiously stepping forward and making my way around the side of the building, edging toward the street. I stayed in the prisoner's mind, watching carefully through his eyes for any glimpses of myself as I moved forward from the cover of the building and onto the street, casually ducking into the rest of the crowd just as the soldier glanced away.

When he fixed his eyes forward again, I saw the back of my head. I marched forward with the rest of the mass, staying directly in front of the soldier whose mind I was reading so I could continue seeing.

My body trembled, and my skin was slick with sweat. I tried to calm my breathing, but I couldn't seem to take in enough air.

"Keep walking," one of the guards shouted hoarsely.

I heard a dull, fleshy thud followed by a pained cry. A moment later, another guard crept up into my peripheral vision, swinging a club. He gave one of the prisoners a glowering once-over, then drew back the club as if to strike him. Instinctively, I winced.

Immediately the guard turned his attention to me, swishing the club through the air and cracking a smile.

"What's wrong with you?" he sneered, getting right in my face.

I kept my eyes straight ahead. He raised his club again, and I braced myself as he stepped threateningly closer.

"Halt!" someone shouted.

All of the prisoners and soldiers stopped, turned to the side, and folded their hands behind their backs. I followed suit, blending in as best I could.

In front of us was a large cement building that looked like some kind of headquarters. The front door stood open, and a man wearing a camouflage RGM uniform stepped out into the street, looking his captive audience over sternly.

I immediately recognized the sleeves. I'd seen them and those hands only moments ago, as their owner sat at a desk, smoking a cigar.

He rubbed his nose and smoothed his mustache, then straightened.

"As some of you may already know, we have a missing prisoner," he announced loudly. "An anomaly prisoner known as Sparrow. She has been missing for several days now, but I have been informed by my men that someone within the district may have information as to her whereabouts—"

The commander, as I'd finally been able to identify him, stopped mid-sentence as a soldier in a black uniform came running over. He slid to a stop at the commander's side and leaned into his ear. I couldn't hear any of what was being said, but I watched the commander's face slowly change, hardening to steel.

He clenched his fists as the soldier stepped away, turning his attention back to the crowd of prisoners standing in front of him.

"It would seem that we are now looking for not just one, but *two* missing anomaly prisoners," he roared, his cheeks reddening. "Sparrow, it seems, has helped another anomaly prisoner escape from the lab. She could quite possibly be on the premises as I speak. You all will spread out immediately and search the district for the two of them—now!" He nodded to the man with the club, who was still standing beside me. "Keep an eye on them. Make sure no one escapes."

The commander turned to gaze at the prisoners once more. "This is a chance to redeem yourselves!" he shouted hoarsely. "To prove to the RGM that you are more than a filthy waste of our time and funds… Find the missing prisoners. Bring me the body of Janna—and bring me Sparrow, still breathing."

My stomach turned at this. As I looked around through the soldier's eyes, I could see that everyone was excited.

"Now get going, all of you!" the commander yelled, spit flying from his mouth. "Search every corner of the district until you find them! Do you understand me?"

A collective roar of excited comprehension rose from the body of prisoners as they dispersed, quickly scattering in every direction.

This was my opportunity to escape.

Picking up my pace with everyone else, I jogged toward the gates. When I got a little closer, I slowed up, pretending to look around until the accompanying guards had passed me. I shadowed the other prisoners who had splintered off, then turned to veer away from them. Working strictly from memory now, I bolted for the gates, breaching the darkness of the district and emerging once again into the light.

The security guards shouted after me, and I heard the crack of a pistol shot, but I didn't stop running. I sprinted forward, my feet flying over the crusty white ground. I ran as hard and as fast as I could—and then slammed directly into something solid.

The impact sent me sprawling to the ground, but I didn't stay there long. Invisible vises latched around my shoulders and yanked me to my feet, dragging me by the collar of my shirt, tightening it until I was choking. I felt hot breath on my face.

"And where the hell do you think you're going?" a voice asked.

I couldn't speak—I couldn't breathe. The heels of my boots dug into the earth as my invisible attacker dragged me backwards, back through the jaws of hell I'd only just escaped. I threw blind kicks and punches but never delivered a blow. After a moment, I heard my captor swear softly with frustration, and suddenly my arm was yanked violently up behind my back.

Gritting my teeth, I bit back a cry as my shoulder was nearly wrenched out of its socket. Then the world went dark. We were past the gates again— back in the camp.

I writhed in his grasp, still wrestling to get away, but my captor only twisted my arm harder. Finally he let go of my arm and threw me to the ground, kneeing me in the back.

I tasted dirt and blood on my tongue as I slammed face-first into the dirt.

"Security!" my captor shouted. "I need security over here!"

I heard the pounding of boots against the ground, followed by a chaos of voices, and then one seemed to rise above the rest. The voice of the commander.

"What is it, Price?"

"This one was trying to escape, and I don't think he's one of ours." The same strong hands ripped my hat off and snatched a handful of my long hair, yanking me up to my knees and jerking my head back. He grunted. "Definitely not one of ours."

My eyes closed. With the last ounce of energy I had left in my body, I forced my thoughts to fall away and my mind to merge with the commander's. I could still see myself kneeling there, blood pouring down my face, my head pulled back. But I couldn't see who was standing behind me. I could feel hands yanking my hair, fingertips digging into my skin. But even through the commander's vision, I could not see anyone there.

*How is that possible? How...*

"Good work, Price," the commander said, sounding satisfied. "I recognize this one. He's on the list. Get him to the lab and find him a cell, then meet me in my office."

The powerful fingers dug into my flesh with renewed ferocity, wrenching me to my feet now. "Very good, sir."

Through the commander's eyes, I saw myself being dragged to my feet, stumbling, and being led away—by a force that even he couldn't see.

The commander then turned his attention to what I could now see was a unit waiting at the gates. He strode over and stopped in front of them, looking at each heavily armed man in turn.

"You all know your mission," he said at last. "I want the ringleader, Fin, alive. Kill everyone else."

I could hear the click of guns and the rhythmic pounding of boots against the ground. They marched past the gates and out toward the forest. I knew exactly where they were headed: The Homestead.

*Oh, god, I hope they all got out in time...*

My exhausted mind flickered, dropping out of the commander's and going blank. The pounding of the unit's orderly march faded out of earshot.

# 71

I SPRINTED THROUGH THE THICK FOREST, HEADING FOR the district.

Sparrow's words rang in my ears like sirens: *"He knew I could see things that no one else can… I think maybe he could see, too…"*

The more I thought about it, the more terrified energy coursed through me. I ran through the forest, tearing through the low brush, violently swatting away branches that were dry and void of leaves. My eyes darted back and forth over the dead landscape, as if the shadows would overtake me and eat me alive.

*"Who the hell is he to you?"* Sparrow's question haunted me, repeating over and over until the woods seemed filled with the echoes of her voice.

She'd had no idea what she was asking, or who she was dealing with. Listening to her describe him with that far-off look in her eyes had pierced my soul with terror and turned my stomach. The way she'd said he had helped her—saved her from the search teams. The way she'd spoken of him as if he was… *good*. He was the furthest thing from good. He wasn't the one protecting her: *I am*. I was the one who had saved Sparrow from her flooded cell. *I* was the one who had brought her to the shack in the woods, the shack *I* had built.

"This is my doing, not yours!" I shouted breathlessly, stopping in the middle of the trees. "This has *nothing to do with you!*"

Spit flew out of my mouth as I yelled up into the churning gray sky, staring it down like it was my opponent.

"*She* has nothing to do with you! Do you understand me? You've taken everything from me—*everything*! Just leave her alone—leave *me* alone!" I threw a fist, punching nothing. I grabbed hold of the trunk of a skinny dead tree, gripping it until my fingernails sank into the soft wood. "For god's sake, just leave me the hell alone…"

My voice drifted and echoed in the empty woods for a moment. I stood there, shaking with anger, feeling disembodied—like I was standing outside myself looking at the nothingness I'd amounted to.

An invisible man. Like a wisp of vapor, here and gone. Forgotten.

*Who is the old man to me?* He was the black hole into which my life had been siphoned. He was a plague that chased me—a shadow that followed me. Sparrow had *no idea* what he was capable of—what he could do. She had no idea how dangerous he was, and now it was evident that he wanted to take her from me too.

I pressed my forehead to the tree, sweat beading at the back of my neck.

"I will never let you have her… *never.*"

I made my way down the mountain, attempting to steady my shaking hands as I wove my way through the trees. Coming to a stop as District Firehole came into view, I squinted down at it.

What *bullshit* Bask had fed me—bullshit I'd believed without question. As if he would *ever* help me… For a while, I'd counted the fact that he gave me so much leash as a sign that he was going to eventually help me. Now, I finally realized that his sole intention was to *hang me* with that leash.

Everything I'd been relying on was gone. I knew nothing for certain anymore. The only thing I knew now was that I loved Sparrow. She was the only real thing I had; whether she loved me yet or not, I didn't really care. I just wanted to be with her and have the chance to eventually win her heart. I was certain I could, and somehow, with that realization, the importance I'd placed on everything else faded.

I walked the rest of the way down the mountain, emerging from the trees and brush to cross the stretch of faded geothermal ground leading to the district. I could hear shouting voices as I reached the gate. Coming to a halt, I listened.

A black blur moved in my peripheral vision. A soldier bolted past the guards, blowing through the gates to sprint directly toward me, oblivious of my presence. When he didn't stop at the guard's command, one of them took aim at him and fired, but missed. He was upon me in seconds—crashing right into me. The force sent him reeling backward and he sprawled to the ground. I reached down and grabbed him by the collar of his shirt, tightening it to a chokehold as I hauled him to his feet.

"And where the hell do you think you're going?" I growled into his face.

He sputtered and choked, writhing violently in my grasp as I spun him around and began to frog-march him back towards the district. He fought me, throwing punches and kicks, but not landing a single blow. Snatching one of his arms, I easily twisted it behind his back, manipulating it into a joint lock. I escorted him past the gates and into the courtyard, where I threw him to the ground and drove my knee into his back.

"Security!" I shouted to the soldiers nearby. "I need security over here!"

Two guards rushed over, shouldering their weapons, and a moment later, Bask's voice boomed out.

"What is it, Price?"

I whirled around to find Bask striding down the long dirt road to meet me. My jaw stiffened, my hands beginning to heat up against my will. I forced my slider instinct to the back of my mind.

"This one was trying to escape, and I don't think he's one of ours." I reached down and firmly yanked the black cap off his head. His hair was long and red, shaved on one side. I pulled his head back. "Definitely not one of ours."

Bask came to a stop in front of the prisoner, spitting on the ground before fixing his gaze on the young man's bloodied face. I saw a flicker of a smile tug at the corners of my commander's lips.

"Good work, Price," he said finally. "I recognize him—he's on the list. Get him to the lab and find him a cell, then meet me in my office."

I looked at Bask, trying to decipher that strange expression he wore; then I wrenched my prisoner to his feet. "Very good, sir."

Bask headed off to address the unit that had assembled at the gates. I needed only one quick look at the amount of gear and ammo they had to know where they were headed.

"You all know your mission," I heard him say. "I want the ringleader, Fin, alive. Kill everyone else."

A sinking feeling filled my gut. The unit was heading out for the Homestead.

I continued forward, shoving the prisoner along with me. I marched up the steps to the lab and swung the door open. The medic looked up as soon as I walked in, though all he saw was the contorted body of my prisoner as I held him in my grasp. Startled, he jumped up from his chair, sending it clattering to the floor.

"I have orders to lock him in a cell," I said firmly.

"B-but this man was just in here! He's—"

I shook my head. "Not one of ours."

"How did he…" The medic trailed off, stroking his jaw.

"What?" I barked. "What is it?"

"The missing prisoner… Janna…" he said quietly. "He must have… I let him—"

"You let him into the containment area?"

The young medic's expression was tortured. "I thought he was a soldier!"

"Well, you apparently thought wrong," I replied through gritted teeth. "Now open that door."

Wordlessly, the medic crossed the room and held the door open for me. I shoved the prisoner ahead of me, still keeping control of his arm. I led him down the long hallway and stopped when I got to the first empty cell, opening the door. I was about to throw him inside when he suddenly went limp. Thinking he was going to faint, I released his wrist, and he spun around and grabbed me by the throat. Shocked he'd managed it, I didn't react fast enough. Gripping me in a firm chokehold, he threw himself into me and drove me backward into the cell, sending me sprawling to the ground. In a second, he was on top of me, his hands even tighter around my throat. I could feel them growing hot and beginning to vibrate.

Gagging, I swung a fist for his face, but he lurched away and grasped my throat more tightly. Shifting his weight, he dug his knee into my thigh, striking a nerve.

Writhing in pain, I coughed and gasped for air, straining to breathe. I felt one of his hands slide away from my throat. His fingertips pressed into my forehead. My vision began to flicker and fade. Gathering all my strength, I threw my head forward, clashing skulls with him and sending him reeling backward.

Pain pounded through my head as I jumped to my feet and ran out of the cell, slamming the door shut behind me before he had a chance to regain himself. I heard the loud steely *click* as the door bolted automatically. I sprinted out of the building and ran down the road, dodging prisoners and guards, my head throbbing with every step I took.

My breathing was ragged by the time I reached Bask's office. I swung open the metal door and stepped inside.

Bask looked up from his desk. "Price." He exhaled a long stream of smoke. "Everything squared away?"

"He's locked up, yes." I tried to calm my breathing as I replied. "It was him—he was the one who freed Janna. Not Sparrow."

Bask looked taken aback. "How'd he get in there?"

"The medic let him in, thinking he was a soldier."

I watched my commander as he tapped the ash off the end of his cigar.

"So Sparrow isn't on the premises after all," he mused aloud, looking in my general direction. "It was another anomaly all along."

"Will you question him?"

Bask bowed his head. "But let's not deviate—Sparrow is still the greater threat. Sparrow is still the one who can see."

I swallowed back the pain still thumping sickeningly through my head and lowered my gaze to my boots.

"Do you not wish to talk about Sparrow, Price?"

I heard his chair scrape back and his boots thudding across the floor. When I looked up, he was standing just in front of me, that same strange look lingering in the darks of his eyes.

"I have nothing to say about Sparrow," I replied, my voice hoarse and quiet.

"No?"

"No."

Bask lifted the cigar to his mouth and took a slow sip.

"But you seemed to enjoy her company."

I made no reply.

Bask's lips parted, dripping with smoke as he exhaled. His eyes probed the place where he thought my face was.

"If you find her and bring her back," he began quietly, "I'll lay the RGM at your feet, Price."

"What are you talking about?"

"Exactly what I just said." He took another long drag off the cigar and tapped the ashes onto the floor. "I'll give you everything you've ever wanted. Everything I promised you when we were both incarcerated. I told you I wouldn't forget, didn't I?"

"I never imagined that you forgot," I replied icily. "I just know that you're not a man of your word."

Bask's expression went blank for a moment; then he cracked a smile. "I'm not. But once again, you somehow managed to get the upper hand, Price."

"If you think I know where she is, why wouldn't you just threaten me and make me bring her to you?" I asked.

"What would I threaten you with? Death?" Bask grunted. "You know

I would never kill you, so how would that benefit me?”

My heart began to beat faster as I watched him through narrowed eyes.

“I need you, Price, you know that—and now you’re forcing my hand.” He puffed his cigar. “I’m forced to cooperate.”

“Cooperate how?”

“I’ll put in a word for you—in fact, Price, I’ll even get you a promotion. You can have an office right next to mine.

“You’ll be an officer, and you’ll manage the district alongside me,” he went on firmly. “And don’t say that you don’t care about the RGM as much as you care about her. I *know you,* Price—you hate sliders, and you have no sympathy for them. If you did, you wouldn’t have prevented that lice-bag from escaping just now.”

“What about the fact that *I am* one of those lice-bag sliders?”

“You’re not. Not in the same way…” His words trailed off, and this time his eyes actually found mine. “You’re not on *their* side, Price; you’re on *ours.* You’ve always been on ours. No matter how many times we’ve betrayed you and punished you, you’ve never betrayed *us…*”

A strange, cold feeling settled into my gut.

Sparrow’s eyes flashed in my mind, resurrecting my dreams of running away with her—of escaping… escaping with her. Being with her. Building a life with her.

“You’re right. You have betrayed me—*many times.*” I nodded slowly. “You took everything I loved away from me, because of something that was beyond my control—something that I never wanted! You stripped me of *everything.* You killed the only friend I had here…” My voice cracked. I bit my lip and looked away. “What the hell makes you think I could *ever* trust you again? What makes you think I would find her for you?”

Bask tipped his chin slightly and looked down his nose at me, his expression unfaltering.

“Because you were born for this, Price—”

“Oh, shut the hell up, Bask. Do you really think you can give me that now?” My voice rose as I stepped closer. “You think you can trample me and spit on me and kick me to the side for years, then get me back into your game with a few sugarcoated words?"

"It *is* all a game, Price," Bask growled. "War is a game. Those who choose to accept that fact can maneuver their way to the top—can own it all. Those who try to save their integrity and play this game clean will go down, Price—that's just the way things are." He narrowed his eyes. "You and I both know it."

Bask stepped closer, and this time, he reached out and found my shoulder, clamping his hand there firmly.

"Your father fought and died for the RGM." He lowered his voice to a whisper. "He gave his *entire life* to the RGM because he knew which was the right side of this conflict, Price—and he believed in it…" Bask trailed off. "Just like his son."

Despite everything, I felt something stirring deep in my heart, among all the ice embedded there: a tiny, flickering flame of pride.

My thoughts lurched back to the day I'd graduated—the day I'd officially become an RGM soldier. When I closed my eyes, I could still hear the roaring crowd—I could still see the black confetti raining down. I could still make out my mother's face, the tears of pride welling in her eyes.

The joy of those memories dissipated as I then remembered the stranger I'd noticed sitting beside her. The old man no one had seen but me. The old man who had made me a monster.

He represented everything I hated. Yet Sparrow's voice had swelled with admiration when she spoke of him.

I pressed my eyelids shut; my body had begun to shake.

I wasn't about to lose someone else to him. Not by a long shot.

No… in fact, I was about to gain *everything*.

"If you hurt her," I began, my voice like steel, "you'll have me to answer to."

"She's a *slider*, Price."

"I *love* her."

"Love is but an irrational emotion, Price." Bask chuckled and shook his head. "Besides, what woman would want to have sex with a man she couldn't even see?"

I made no response. For a moment Bask looked at the empty air; then he staggered back a step.

"Wait a minute…" Revelation flashed in his eyes. "She can see *you*, can't she?"

"Yes… yes, she can."

Bask's eyes widened as he began to pace, rubbing his chin thoughtfully. "Then she's more valuable than I realized…" he murmured.

Silence filled the room.

Bask turned on his heels again to face where I was standing. "I'm prepared to make a deal with you, Price."

I raised an eyebrow. "What would you require of me?"

A smile curved over Bask's lips. "Just one thing."

# 72

FOR A MOMENT, I'D FELT LIKE I WAS ACTUALLY GETTING somewhere with Aaron. There'd been something so soft and vulnerable in his face when he'd confessed that he loved me—something I'd never expected him to say, something I'd often wondered if he was even capable of. I could see the humanness in his eyes, traces of the young man who wanted to belong somewhere—*with someone*. For a moment, I'd seen a flicker of hope beyond the darkness that had seemed to consume him on the inside. And within that hope, I'd caught a glimpse of my freedom.

But in a heartbeat, that had all faded.

Mentioning the old man had been like a trigger. Watching as he tore apart the cloak the old man had given me with fevered, trembling hands had reminded me of his volatility.

After he had gone, I paced the tiny shack, my heart and mind racing in equal measure.

My thoughts kept circling back to the melted access panel on the wall—back to the knowing feeling I still had in my gut: Keegan was close. He had to be the one who had helped Janna escape.

And now he would be looking for me.

Whether they were sending out another search team or not, I had to leave before Price got back. I had to escape and find Keegan before he went back into the district to find me.

Pressing my hands against the rough wood, I pushed the panel open. Fresh spring air swept into the room as I jumped down to the ground and took off at a sprint. I ran down the mountain toward District Firehole, my feet moving so fast that the rest of my body could barely keep up.

The trees parted to reveal the valley below, the agglomeration of crusty, uniform buildings and dirty roads. I could hear the factory whistle even from here. I could see tiny black dots like ants, scurrying back toward the factory at the far end of the compound. The sight alone was enough to hoist a red flag in the back of my mind, one that urged me to turn and run in the opposite direction, to not risk getting caught once again in the clutches of this hell.

But a quieter voice in my heart whispered: *courage*.

Dodging around dead trees and boulders, I continued to the mountain's base, then veered off to one side of it to skirt the perimeter of the woods. My eyes darted frantically from tree to tree, from one brush patch to the next, searching for some sign of Keegan. I made my way farther and farther along the edge, then progressed deeper into the woods, keeping as silent as possible. My own breathing sounded loud in the stillness that engulfed the forest, interrupted only by the distant hissing of fumaroles.

When I reached a small glade, I stopped. My muscles tightened as my eyes caught on the traces of soft green grass sprouting from the desolate ground. I took a few cautious steps closer, squatting down to examine them. They spread out over the dirt in the shapes of familiar footprints. My heart rose into my mouth.

I froze. The thudding of boots echoed in the air around me, drawing closer.

Dropping to the ground, I rolled to a patch of thicker brush at the perimeter of the small clearing, tucking myself in among the dead leaves and branches.

The footsteps passed.

I waited there a few moments, making sure there was no one else.

Then I quietly rose to my feet, carefully scanning my surroundings.

Suddenly a hand clamped over my mouth from behind, smothering my ragged gasp. My eyes widened as adrenaline surged through me as soft lips brushed against my ear. "What the hell are you doing down here?"

My stomach sank. I wrenched around to face him, a fire igniting inside me. With a hard shove, I pushed him backward.

"What do you think?" I asked in a trembling voice. "Getting away from *you*."

His expression didn't change from one of urgency.

"They're still looking for you," he hissed, taking a step and closing the gap between us again to stare down into my face. "Do you want to get caught?"

"I don't care anymore." I tipped my head back to look at him. "I have to get out of here—I can't wait around for you to make up your mind about whose side you're on, Aaron."

His eyes filled with resolve, he leaned in, lowering his voice. "I'm on *your* side, Sparrow."

"*Prove it.*"

Price studied my face for a long moment. "There's a slider in the district."

My throat tightened. "Does Bask know?"

"No, I'm the only one who's detected him," Aaron explained in a rush, already tugging me gently forward. "I think he's looking for you—you need to get in there, find him before someone else does, and help him escape…" He placed a hand on my cheek and looked me square in the eyes. "Then we'll run, Sparrow—the three of us."

I stared at him, my heart thrashing against my rib cage. I searched his eyes for something earnest. Then I shoved his hands away and took off at a run, sprinting through the trees. Everything inside me seemed to pulsate. The woods opened, and I found myself exposed in the dry geothermal valley. Aaron raced up beside me, grabbing me by the shoulders and pulling me lower to the ground.

"Stay down, for god's sake," he hissed, jerking his head to the side.

Together, we skirted the tree line, keeping low and veering away from the gates where guards were posted and sneaking around to the back side of the district.

"Where were you, anyway?" I whispered, breathless.

"I went back to the district. They were all looking for you—they thought you were the one who broke Janna out," Aaron whispered back. "That's when I saw him…"

I followed Aaron as he secured the rope around a dead tree growing at the base of the cracked cement wall. Quickly and carefully finding footholds, we scaled the wall in silence and dropped to the ground on the other side, leaving the rope dangling there.

We came up behind the factory. Aaron lifted a finger to his lips, falling back against the building. I followed suit, collapsing alongside him, barely breathing.

He edged to the corner of the building and carefully peered around it, ducking back almost immediately. His lips formed the word "guards."

I held my breath, flexing my sweaty fingers. A minute ticked by like an eternity.

Finally, Aaron made a small motion with his hand, and we dodged through the small gap between buildings and slipped in next to another one. I dropped back into its shadow and, with my back pressed to the wall, I turned and looked at Aaron. His dark brown eyes were wide and alert, his head on a swivel.

"You're actually doing this?" I whispered. "You're actually helping me save him?"

Aaron didn't look at me; his eyes were still scanning our surroundings. "Why wouldn't I?"

"Why *would* you? You made your feelings pretty clear… I guess I just mean that I… thought I lost you."

"What do you mean?"

"I mean that I questioned why I had ever trusted you," I replied softly. "And now I see that I was wrong about you."

Something faltered in his eyes before he glanced away. He put a finger to his lips, not saying a word.

I edged my way along the back of the building, Aaron right behind me, until I could see the street.

"There." Aaron leaned over my shoulder and pointed. "I just saw him duck behind that building across the—"

"Halt!" A booming voice cut him off.

Everything inside me twisted as I whirled around to look behind us. A soldier rounded the side of the building, his weapon raised in a ready position and his finger on the trigger.

Before I could comprehend anything else, Aaron launched me forward into the street with a firm shove. I stumbled forward and caught myself before I had a chance to fall—taking off in the direction of the small cement-block building Aaron had pointed out. I heard the gun go off an instant later, but I kept running. Everything became muffled, leaving only the pounding of my footsteps to echo in my head.

I rounded the corner of the building—and found myself staring down the long black barrel of a rifle.

"Halt!" the soldier shouted, thrusting the weapon aggressively forward, keeping it trained on my head. "Hands up!"

Numb, I lifted my arms. I could barely hear his voice over the pounding of my blood in my skull.

"Drop to your knees!"

I swallowed hard and did as I was told, lowering my eyes to the dirt. Another soldier came up behind me and latched a zip tie around my hands, tightening it until it stung. Then he grabbed a fistful of my hair and wrenched me to my feet, jolting me forward.

I glanced up as we crossed the street, looking for Aaron, but the soldier nudged me with the barrel of his gun.

"Eyes forward!"

Tears stung in my eyes, but I fiercely blinked them back as we mounted the steps to the lab. The soldier escorted me through the door, across the room and out into the long, familiar hall of cells, his boots echoing on the concrete. We entered another hallway, one that was bright white and sterile smelling.

"Halt." The soldier jerked me to a stop. I felt the cool steel muzzle of his gun at the nape of my neck. "In here."

I turned cautiously and didn't resist as he shoved me into my sterile white cell. I stumbled forward several feet and caught myself against the wall. The door slammed shut behind me and bolted, and I heard his footsteps fading away.

Pinching my eyes shut, I attempted to slow my frantic breathing. My mind could barely process what had just happened. I couldn't believe it…

*What happened to Aaron?* My throat tightened as I remembered the gunshot. *Oh, god, let him be all right…*

Clasping my face in my hands, I pressed my back to the wall and slid to the floor. All I could hear was my heart pounding in my ears.

*Everything happened so quickly… And Keegan is still out there…* My stomach turned at the thought.

I struggled to think back to the moments before we'd been caught, to the moment when Aaron had spotted Keegan across the street, slipping behind one of the buildings. I hadn't seen him, but Aaron had. By the time I'd gotten there, it was too late. He was gone—replaced by the soldiers who had most likely captured him, too.

I lifted my face from my hands as I heard the authoritative clomping of boots approaching my cell. Bask's face appeared in the small glass window at the top of the door. A stern but satisfied expression twisted his lips. I clenched my teeth as the bolt retracted and the door swung open.

He stepped inside and slammed the door shut behind him. He stood there for a moment with his hands on his hips, examining me from a distance like I was a dangerous animal.

"Welcome back, Sparrow." His tone was gravelly and mocking. "Did you enjoy your little vacation?"

I kept my teeth clenched, my eyes locked with his.

"Tell me how you got out of the flooded cell," he commanded at length, his eyes growing harder. "Tell me how you escaped—or, better yet, explain to me how you can see."

Though my hands were still shaking, I forced myself to steady.

"I cannot explain what I do not know," I answered finally. "I do not know why I can see you or anyone or anything in the district. It makes as much sense to me as it does to you."

Bask gave me a long, careful once-over, then nodded slowly. "But regardless, you must realize now that this means we have two options. We either kill you or keep you. Do you have a preference?"

"Yes." The word came out sharp. "To be free."

Bask cracked a smile, chuckling. "No wonder Price likes you—you're a feisty little thing."

He still thought Aaron was a sympathizer. Aaron, who had likely just taken a bullet for me.

I had to make Bask believe he was loyal—even if I knew it was a lie.

"If you like someone, you don't capture them and doom them to a life of imprisonment," I shot back, my voice boiling. "Which is exactly what that lice-bag did."

Bask lifted an eyebrow. "Price was the one who caught you sneaking into the district?"

I nodded, trying my best to look sincere.

"So that was what the commotion was all about?"

Again, I bowed my head in a nod. I felt the heat of Bask's gaze for a moment longer; then he chuckled.

"Interesting." His boots thudded quietly closer. "Very interesting."

I glanced up, startled to find him right in front of me. He squatted down, bringing himself to my eye level.

"So you can see Price, then?"

I froze, unsure how to respond. At length, I nodded.

A satisfied grin twitched at the corners of Bask's lips. "Remarkable."

I pushed myself a little farther away from him, but there was nowhere to go; my back was against the wall.

"I'm not going to kill you, Sparrow," Bask continued in a lower tone. "You're too valuable to waste. You can do things I've never seen any slider do before… and beyond that, there's something about you." He pinched the corner of his mustache, squinting at my face. "Something odd. Can't put my finger on it, but I feel almost as if I've seen your face before in another life."

I swallowed, dropping my gaze. A cold, sick feeling settled inside me as I thought back to Hawk's photograph on the wanted list.

"You could become very useful," he concluded with a cold smile. "Once you learn the ropes… No doubt Price will show you how," he grunted. "Since he's the one who captured you, it looks like you fall to his responsibility."

Bask reached into his pocket and took out a long syringe full of clear liquid. I jerked away as soon as he made a motion to bring it closer to my arm.

"What are you doing?" I asked him frantically.

He seized me by the wrist and jerked me closer. A stinging sensation sizzled up my arm as it pierced my skin; something cool flowed into my veins.

Bask emptied the barrel and retracted the needle. Capping it, he put it back in his pocket. His cold eyes shifted up to mine.

"You just took the first step toward becoming one of us, Sparrow," he replied bluntly. "You're invisible now."

I already knew this—I'd known exactly what was in the syringe—but hearing it confirmed made me feel as though I'd swallowed a lead weight.

Bask narrowed his eyes, seeming to search my face for a moment before rising and crossing the room again. I felt numb as I watched him open the door, then pause in the threshold to look back at me.

"We caught your friend, by the way, the one you snuck back in to save," he informed me flatly. "So at least you can take comfort in knowing that your efforts were entirely wasted."

Everything inside me ignited, burned. I leapt to my feet, hardly feeling the floor pass beneath me as I rushed to the door—just as Bask quickly stepped out and slammed it shut in my face.

"You bastard!" The words roared out of my throat as I slammed my fists against the glass, wishing I were pounding Bask's face in instead.

"Where is he? W-what did you do to him? Where did you take him—*tell me!*"

Bask only watched from the other side, his lips curled into a bloodless grin. Then he turned on his heels and stepped out of sight.

"Let him go!" My throat tightened as I screamed the words, pulling back my fists and pounding the glass again and again. "*I'm* the one you wanted! *Let him go!*"

I pressed my forehead to the glass, tears welling in my eyes.

"Let him go…"

# 73

"STOP!" I SHOUTED, GRABBING THE GUARD BY THE HAND and twisting it into a lock. The gun swung around, firing into the sky before the soldier dropped it and doubled over in pain. I quickly stole a glance over my shoulder to ensure that Sparrow had taken off across the street before leaning closer to whisper in the soldier's ear, "I'm on your side."

He grunted, wincing back the pain. "When the hell have you ever been on our side, Price? You son of a bitch."

"Shut up, you idiot!" I hissed, straightening him back up to his feet, still holding him in a lock. "Bask wants her alive." I released the soldier, and he immediately staggered away, flipping me off as he stooped to pick up his weapon.

Two soldiers were waiting for Sparrow behind the building I'd just pushed her towards. Bask had told them exactly where to wait, and the plan had been going smoothly up until the moment this uniformed private had found us hiding in the alley and nearly shot Sparrow's head off.

Across the street, I heard one of the soldiers shout to Sparrow: "Halt!

Hands up!"

It was over.

A strange feeling came over me as I stood there. My stomach turned, but at the same time I felt as if a lead weight had finally lifted from my shoulders.

I waited at the corner of the building, watching as Sparrow was escorted across the street and into the lab at gunpoint. Bask went in a few moments later.

Keeping my gaze on the lab, I walked steadily to the center of the street, stopping there to catch my breath, adrenaline still coursing through my veins.

Part of me couldn't believe what I'd just done—handed Sparrow over to the wolves. Yet another part of me had been expecting it all along. Part of me loved her, and part of me wondered why it had taken me so long to realize the opportunity she had created for me. She was everything Bask wanted—and now he had her because I had given her back to him. He was in my debt.

I scanned the buildings surrounding me. My gaze caught on Bask's office and remained there for a moment as I imagined having my own office alongside it. My stomach fluttered with anticipation.

I felt as if I was seeing District Firehole through new eyes: no longer a prisoner, but once more a soldier.

A *soldier*. Oh, *god*, how good that sounded. I couldn't help but wonder what my father would have thought of me. What my mother would think when she heard: I would be the first slider to be acknowledged by the RGM.

The warmth of pride swelling in my chest abruptly faded as my eyes caught on the empty shack where Viner had lived. I was about to turn away when something caught my attention, a blur near the threshold of the door, which still stood open. A figure.

Alarmed, I stepped closer, narrowing my eyes. The shadowy form remained for a moment, then vanished back inside before I could make out who it was.

Dodging the soldiers, who were still buzzing around like hornets disturbed from their nest, I crossed the road and came to a halt in front of Viner's shack. The cold feeling returned as I hesitated there, giving the dilapidated front of the building a solid once-over.

I pushed the door open a little wider and stepped over the threshold. It groaned mournfully on its hinges, letting in a dim, overcast shaft of light that sliced through the darkness. I stepped farther in, glancing around. Wind had blown the crusty, faded dirt over the floor and scattered papers and litter across the room.

"Hello?" I spoke into the darkness, straining to see. "Is someone there?"

No answer.

I stopped in the middle of the room, standing at the edge of the shaft of light that fell across the floorboards. Flecks of dust floated like microscopic ghosts in the soft gray light, settling over the floor and the untouched furniture. One of Viner's shirts still hung over the back of a chair.

A floorboard creaked, and despite myself, I started.

"Who's there?" I demanded, the hairs on the back of my neck rising. "Show yourself immediately, or I'll call security."

The only answer that came from the darkness was the door slamming shut behind me. I jumped, spinning around.

Even in the dimness, I could see the whites of his eyes. Those haunting eyes.

Quickly recoiling, I stumbled into a chair and fell over it, crashing to the floor. I scrambled backward, still on my ass. The shafts of cool light from the grime-coated windows on either side of the door slowly ignited the rest of the old man's features: his dark brown skin, his wrinkled face, his long dark robes.

My back hit the wall, knocking the air out of me. I stared across the room at the ghostly figure, who still hadn't moved a muscle or spoken a word.

"What do you want with me?" I choked in a whisper that quickly escalated to a yell. "*What do you want!*"

My voice echoed for a moment before it was consumed by the tomblike silence.

The old man remained where he was, but his eyes didn't leave mine.

"Aaron." His voice was quiet, yet it seemed to fill the room. "What have you done?"

"Nothing to do with you," I growled. "Now get out! Get out and leave me alone—haven't you taken enough away from me? I never want to see your face again!"

The old man stepped closer. "I have only ever given, Aaron. It is you who have taken your life away." He raised his hand to gesture around the room. "And the lives of others."

Hot anger welling inside me, I leapt to my feet. Snatching the chair that had clattered to the floor, I hurled it at the old man. It passed easily through his body, as if he were no more than vapor. I felt nailed to the floor; my eyes widened in disbelief.

The old man only looked at me, something undecipherable in his eyes. I began to feel like the air was being sucked out of the room. I felt like I was suffocating.

"Have a care, Aaron." The old man's voice was as hushed as a whisper. "A seed placed in the ground remains a seed no longer... It lays down roots." He took a step closer. "It grows."

I swallowed as he stepped up in front of me, looking firmly into my eyes.

"Beware of what kind of seeds you plant, Aaron."

Anger and terror pulsed through me in equal measure. I wanted to speak, but I couldn't.

"Who's in here?" came a gruff voice from outside.

The door burst open. Mooney stood in the doorway with a club in his hand.

"I said who's in here?" he barked, looping the club threateningly through the air. I remained silent, and after a moment or so he gave up, turned, and walked away, grumbling to himself.

I let out the breath I'd been holding the entire time, reaching up to drag a trembling hand over my face. I found the room empty once again. The old man's deep voice haunted my thoughts.

Sick to my stomach, I tore out of the shack and into the light of day. I squared my shoulders and took a deep breath, glancing over at Bask's office just in time to see the door slam shut.

He must have just finished with Sparrow.

Picking up my pace, I waited for a vehicle to roll past before jogging across the street. Bask glanced up, lighting a cigar, as I opened the door.

"You'll have to thank her." He spoke through his teeth, taking a few small puffs.

"Who?"

He shot me a dubious glance.

"Sparrow?" I asked.

"She just made everything remarkably easier for you—saved your reputation, in fact." He flicked the match into the ashtray.

"How so?"

"In an attempt to save your ass, she just told me that *you* were the one who caught her sneaking into the district. That you were the one who captured her." He chuckled, smoke seeping out through his teeth. "She's a good little actress, I'll give her that. She really sounded as if she hated your guts, Price. How the hell'd you earn her loyalty?" He paused, blowing out smoke.

I leaned back against the wall, stunned.

"S-Sparrow told you *I* was the one who captured her?"

Bask laughed, collapsing back into his leather chair. "She did. Apparently, she thought I would behead you if I thought you had anything to do with her escape…" He trailed off, lifting the cigar to his lips. "Truth is, I would even now if I could reproduce your blood. But *c'est la vie.* Instead, I'll work with you, Price… if you work with me. Isn't that how it's always been?" he grunted, shooting me a mocking glance. "Haven't we always been a pretty good team?"

I swallowed back a sick feeling, trying to process it all. Sure, Sparrow didn't know that I was the one behind her capture… but never in a million years would I have expected her to stand up for me like that—to think of me even as she stood at the mouth of hell.

The old man's words continued to echo in my head:

*What have you done?*

"So now we're happily spared having to invent a story to cover your actions, Price, which no one would have believed anyway," Bask continued. "Now we have a cover story straight from the prisoner's mouth."

"So what are you going to do with her?" I asked hoarsely. "Experiment on her as you have on me?"

"I haven't decided yet," he said, taking a long, sizzling drag. "For now, she'll be our secret weapon."

My jaw hardened. "I want her to be more than that."

"Fine. You can have her at night, then."

I slammed the wall with my hand. "You bastard."

His eyes hardened as he blew out a long stream of smoke. "I'm not the one who lured her back under false pretenses."

"You're the one who told me—"

"You had a choice: Sparrow or the RGM. You made the call. You know where your allegiance truly lies."

I took a few weak, shaking steps toward him, anger and regret warring inside me.

"I *love* her," I whispered. "And I will not allow you to… I will do *everything* to protect her."

Bask smirked, like this was a schoolboy joke. He bobbed his head in a nod, as if playing along. "And I look forward to observing your endeavors."

Anger rushing through me, I took a breath to speak, but Bask interrupted before I could say another word.

"Now, where exactly would you like your new office to be?" He unrolled a map and spread it out on the desk in front of him. "I think right next to mine may be a little too much of a good thing… There's a very nice little plot of ground over here, though." He tapped an upper corner of the map, clenching the cigar between his teeth as he lifted his eyes in my direction. "We just buried Viner there."

Every muscle in my body tightened as I stood there, staring into his dark eyes. The room seemed to swirl around me.

I wanted to kill him then and there.

Instead, I jerked away. My boots pounded across the floor as I crossed the room and threw the door open. I heard his laughter as the door slammed shut behind me.

# 74

I WAS SO EXHAUSTED AND IN PAIN I COULD BARELY THINK straight, and when I did, it was about Sparrow and the thoughts I'd read in the invisible soldier's mind that were all about her. When I'd attacked him and finally managed to place my fingers against his forehead, I'd recognized his thoughts immediately. They were the same as the ones I had detected at the edge of the woods as I'd lain there in the brush, hiding.

Within seconds I'd confirmed my suspicions: he knew where Sparrow was. He was the soldier the commander was concerned about—the one he thought had betrayed the RGM and helped Sparrow escape. He had—he was hiding her in the woods. He was keeping her from the RGM, but I hadn't been able to read deeply enough into his mind to find out why. But it made sense—that was why the commander had everyone looking for her. She was no longer in the district.

I needed to speak with the soldier who had captured me, the one I hadn't been able to see even through the eyes of the commander. I needed to find out where he was keeping her, whether I discovered that by mind reading or by force. I was prepared to do either.

Breathing heavily, I lifted a hand to my face, wincing a little at my own touch. I quieted the thoughts that were hammering along with the pain in my head.

Slowly, I felt a tinge of warmth in my fingertips as healing trickled into them. I imagined golden liquid spilling over my face and healing me. I felt the warmth make its way into my skull, easing the pounding. Exhausted, I wanted to sleep, but knew I could not. I needed to stay awake and alert. My thoughts became more and more tortured as the night wore on. With every passing moment, the unit was getting closer and closer to the Homestead.

Just as I had begun to slip away into the seductive arms of unconsciousness, I heard something: a faint thudding against the concrete floor, growing closer and closer. A moment later the door unlocked and swung open with a low groan. There was the tread of boots as someone entered. Then the door slammed shut.

"Your face is recovered?" The voice belonged to the commander. "It's Keegan, isn't it?"

I tipped my head back against the wall and looked up into the darkness.

"How do you know my name?" I already knew the answer—but I wanted to hear it confirmed.

"Your friend told us," he answered, sounding satisfied. "She told us quite a few things about you, actually—you and your fellow healers."

My stomach twisted.

"That is what you are, isn't it?" he continued. "An anomaly specially selected to be trained in ways of healing—so that 'Earth may be restored'?"

"I was not specially selected, no," I replied. "Everyone is able to heal. They just don't realize it."

The commander was silent for a long moment. Then he chuckled. "Indeed… indeed." His voice lowered to my face level. "Keegan, what *is* your power, exactly?"

"I would sooner let you execute me than tell you," I answered flatly, not looking away from the place where I knew his face was. "I will not tell you anything."

"Keegan, listen to me…" the commander began again, taking a quieter tone. "Your school—the Homestead, I believe it's called. Janna has told us all about it. In fact, my men are already en route to that location—they'll kill the students and take Fin prisoner."

The muscles in my jaw tightened.

"Yes, Keegan, *your Sensei*," he went on. "Soon he will be joining you here. Soon there will be nothing left of your school hidden away in Section West… Soon the 'healers' will be no more." He trailed off and paused, as if letting this sink in. "So, you see, Keegan, yours is the losing side. The anomalies of Earth will not last forever, and this is the beginning of the end."

"Why are you telling me this?"

"Because I am giving you an opportunity to abandon the losing side, Keegan."

"And what? Join you—join the RGM?"

"Why not?"

"I could list the reasons, but it would take an eternity."

He gave a fake laugh. "Keegan, it is in the RGM's interest to recruit what anomalies we can."

"I'm sure."

"I am offering you a way out. There is nothing you can do to save your friends and teacher now—"

*Little does he realize.*

"—so surely you must see that the wisest thing you can do now is to work *with* us, not against us. I know you feel loyal to those people, but they are delusional," he went on. "Fighting a battle that will never be won. If you leave them behind, Keegan—if you can let go of them—then arrangements can be made."

"Meaning what?"

"Meaning that perhaps we will be… lenient with you."

"As opposed to putting me to death?"

He hesitated. "As of right now, you will be executed at the coming dawn.”

I took a deep breath.

“If a war waged between good and evil,” I began slowly, my voice quiet, “between light and darkness, hope and despair… If you knew with all your heart that goodness and hope and light were the truth, would you ever *once* consider deserting, even if darkness and evil and despair seemed to have the upper hand?”

“Indeed, I would. For the sake of my own preservation,” he replied bluntly. “Wouldn’t you?”

I shook my head. “I would sooner lay down my life—because in abandoning all that I knew to be true, I would already be putting the deepest and truest part of myself to death.”

The commander was silent. I could practically feel him tense. He strode back across the room to the door.

“Have it your way, you filthy slider,” he muttered. “Enjoy the few hours you have left on Earth.”

The door creaked open and slammed shut a moment later. I listened in the darkness as his footsteps faded away down the hall. The sound was replaced with the pounding of my own heart. I tipped my head back against the wall and squeezed my eyes shut.

*Oh, god, I hope they’ve left the Homestead by now…*

I’d transported Janna myself; I was confident that she’d made it back to the Homestead all right. Which meant she would have warned Dad, and of course Dad would have gotten everyone out of there already. They were probably miles away by now.

I blinked the tears back. Then, in the stillness, through the wall, I heard something: a whisper like the wind. It came and went in a heartbeat, and for a moment I strained my ears, trying to detect it again. I heard nothing beyond the silence.

I leaned back against the wall again and began to listen with a deeper sense than hearing. I began to listen with my heart. I heard it again: a whisper. A soft, familiar voice. One I knew better than my own.

*Let him go… Please, please… Please just let him go…* Thoughts seemed to waft through the wall like ghosts to fill my brain. *How could I let this happen? How could I…*

Leaning closer to the wall, I pressed my ear against it. I kept my eyes closed.

*I love him… Oh god, I love him so much… I wish I could have told him… I wish I could have…*

I pressed both my hands against the wall, my throat tightening and my heart warring in my chest. *Sparrow is here…* She hadn't been only hours ago, but she was *here* now, in the cell right next to mine. I could hear her, feel her.

"Sparrow?" At first my voice came out in a whisper. "Sparrow, can you—can you hear me, Sparrow?"

As I stared into the darkness, it was like something inside me caught fire.

"Sparrow!" Her name poured out like a battle cry. "Sparrow, *can you hear me?*"

Clenching my hands into fists, I pounded the wall, shouting her name over and over again.

"Sparrow!" I pressed my forehead against the wall, a sob swelling in my throat. "*Sparrow…*"

Silence. Then, a muffled voice from the other side. A word I could only make out because I heard it deep within me.

"Keegan…?"

Tears flooded down my cheeks. "I'm here, Sparrow." My voice came out broken. "I'm here, my love."

I knew she couldn't hear me like I could hear her. I wasn't listening to her muffled voice; I was listening to her thoughts.

*Keegan, I'm so sorry… I'm so sorry…*

"It's okay… I love you." My voice was a broken whisper.

*I'm so sorry…*

"It's okay," I repeated, my voice barely there as a tear traced down my cheek. "I love you… I love you, Sparrow."

# 75

AT FIRST, I COULDN'T HEAR ANYTHING OVER MY OWN voice as I lay there, crumpled on the floor, sobbing. Bask's words rang through my head, crushing me with the reality that Keegan hadn't escaped—that he'd been captured. At first, all I could hear were echoes of my own exhausted sobs. But as I lay there, I heard something. I wasn't sure what.

A soft, almost inaudible thudding echoed through the thick wall, followed by a familiar voice. I couldn't make out what he was saying, but I recognized the syllables of my own name.

"*Sparrow!*"

Scrambling frantically to my feet, I ran to the wall, throwing my hands against it.

"Keegan?" I shouted, my voice trembling.

I heard the muffled sound of his voice through the wall. I couldn't make out what he was saying.

Pressing my forehead to the cold concrete, I felt hot tears blurring my vision and pouring down my cheeks. "Keegan, I'm so sorry... *I'm so sorry…*"

The remnants of his voice faded.

Shaking and weeping, I curled my fingertips against the wall. "I'm so sorry…"

Time seemed to stand still. Hours must have passed, yet it was all irrelevant; nothing seemed to matter anymore. I remained kneeling on the floor, my body pressed up against the wall, sobbing until I was empty of tears, hollow.

The room grew as cold as I felt inside.

"Why are you crying?" a voice asked quietly.

For a moment, I wasn't sure if someone had spoken from the darkness or if it was a voice inside me.

"They captured Keegan," I whispered. "More than anything, I had hoped…"

I covered my face with my hands and shook my head, unable to finish.

"You had hoped that he would escape?"

I started to look up.

"Do not look at me, Sparrow… Stop looking outward," he whispered. "Look inside you."

"But I don't know what to do!" The words rose from my throat in a sob. "I tried to save him, but it was too late! You—why didn't—why didn't you do something? If y-y-you can appear to me like this, at any time—if you can do *so much*, why the hell didn't you save him? Why don't you save him now?"

For a moment all I heard were the painful echoes of my own voice.

"Sparrow, I am only ever what you allow me to be," he whispered back. "I am inside you, a part of you—waiting to be freed by your imagination. Waiting for it to expand—to believe and create…" He paused. "No, Sparrow, I cannot do anything apart from you. I can only ever be who I really am through you… *with you.*"

I sniffed, sucking back tears. "B-but I don't understand. You saved me from the search teams—"

"Because you expected me to be there."

My throat tightened with a sob.

"Sparrow, if you believe Keegan should be saved, then you must save him yourself."

"I don't know how!"

"It is not about knowing, Sparrow. It never has been. It's always been about believing… believing in who you are. Believing that you are who you have always run from and fought and denied…"

I listened, tears rolling down my cheeks.

"Believing you were born of a Sunrise and a Sunset, that you are made of light, even when you are surrounded by the darkness. Believing that you are capable of all things…"

Slowly, I lifted my face from my hands. I couldn't see him in the darkness, but I didn't need to.

"And believe that I am with you, Sparrow," he finished, his voice fading to a whisper. "That I will *always* be with you…"

As suddenly as his voice had come, it was gone.

I took a long, shaky breath and straightened up. Wiping my tears away with my forearm, I got to my feet, steadying myself against the wall. In the distance I heard footsteps.

I squared my shoulders, fixing my eyes on the window inlaid in the door, expecting to see Bask's face there at any moment.

Instead, I saw Aaron. The dim lights in the hall washed over him to illuminate his rich, deep brown skin and those dark eyes studying me through the glass. Then he reached over to the keypad, and the door unbolted, swinging open. He stepped inside, his eyes meeting mine gravely.

"I have failed you, Sparrow." He spoke before I could say anything.

"You haven't."

"You have no idea."

I felt the sting of tears in my eyes again. "I was the one who didn't get to him in time," I said, my voice shaking. "You did everything you could."

"Sparrow." I felt his hand on my shoulder.

Just my name, but it was enough. I collapsed against him, sobbing. He folded me into his arms, caressing my hair with his hand.

"Shh, it's okay…"

"It's the furthest thing from okay," I sobbed. "You don't understand."

"I understand that I'm not going to let anything happen to you, Sparrow. I promise you," he whispered, kissing the top of my head. "I'm sorry."

I pulled away, sniffing back tears. "For what? Trying to help me? Trying to help Keegan?" I shook my head. "You don't have anything to be sorry for."

He said nothing, his eyes shifting down to the floor.

"Aaron, what is it?" I stepped closer. "What are they planning to do?"

He took a deep breath and gave a heavy sigh, shaking his head.

"Aaron, please… *please* tell me."

He was silent for a moment longer before he finally lifted his gaze from the floor to look at me again. "They're going to execute him, Sparrow."

"W-what?" My heart sank.

"Bask tried to talk to him—tried to get him to open up and—"

"Keegan would *never* betray us." My voice was steely. "He would never tell Bask anything—just as I will never tell him anything!"

Aaron lifted a finger to his lips, checking over his shoulders before leaning in closer. "I'm not asking you to cooperate with them, Sparrow. I'm just asking you to play the game."

"The game?" I spat. "Is that—is that what this is to you? *A game?*"

"Sparrow, no. I—"

"You sound just like Bask!" My icy words cut through his. "You always act as though you hate him, yet sometimes you sound *just like him*."

Aaron's face froze and then hardened. "I am nothing like him, Sparrow. *Nothing.*"

I tipped my chin defiantly, looking up at him through my tears. "Prove it, then," I whispered.

He studied my face, then shook his head. "No. No, you can't ask me to—I can't get him out of here, Sparrow."

"Aaron, please!"

"Bask bought your story, Sparrow!" he hissed, looking me straight in the eyes. "He actually thinks I'm still loyal to the RGM—that *I* captured you. He believed everything you told him. If I ask for a prisoner to be released, what is he going to think, Sparrow?"

"Everything I said, I said to protect you—to make sure they didn't kill you! I did it for *you*!"

"I know you did!" His voice rose, cracking.

I bit my lip, shaking my head as I looked at him. "Please, Aaron."

"Sparrow, you have no idea how dangerous this situation is. If the RGM suspects that—"

"I will do anything—*anything* you ask of me if you save him." I cut him off, my voice a trembling whisper. "I will do *anything*."

Aaron studied me for a long moment, his eyes probing mine.

"You say that you love me, and that you will protect me from them, but if you let them execute Keegan, it will kill me, Aaron." My voice broke, and tears rolled off my chin. "It will *kill me*."

"Bask will give up nothing, Sparrow, no one," he answered firmly. "The only way I could ever go to him and request such a thing is if we had something of equal value to give him in return. Something to set a seal on my loyalty to the RGM." He faltered. "*Our* loyalty."

A cold, sick feeling twisted in my gut, but I swallowed it back. "Like what?"

Aaron was quiet for a moment; I could see the gears turning behind his eyes.

"Bask believes I captured you—he thinks that I'm loyal to him now." He exhaled the words in a rush. "What he wants to know now is whether *you* will be loyal, Sparrow."

"I *never* will."

"He doesn't need to know that. He just needs to *believe* you will."

"And what on earth would make him think that I am or ever would be loyal to—"

"Let me tell him that you'll marry me."

My eyes widened. Everything I'd been about to say turned to ashes in my throat.

"I-I can't—"

He lifted a finger to his lips. "I know that you don't love me, Sparrow, at least not yet, but that's not what I'm asking for—"

"Aaron, you don't unders—"

"Your idea of marriage is far different from the RGM's," he interrupted. "It has nothing to do with love and romance—it's about forming an alliance. Proving our loyalty, Sparrow."

"And you?" I asked quietly. "Is that all it means to you?"

Aaron searched my face for a moment before he answered. "I do love you, Sparrow."

"But I do not love you—doesn't that mean anything to you? I could never be happy!"

"You'll be happier than you will be if they…" His words trailed off. "Sparrow, you have only seen the beginning of what they will do to you. At least this way—"

"What? You can protect me?"

He shook his head. "You will have something to shield yourself with. It would form an alliance between us—Bask would see that. You won't be abused as a slider. They would think I converted you."

"But it wouldn't be true of either of us!"

He leaned closer, his eyes wide and urgent now. "It wouldn't matter—can't you see?"

I said nothing. The cold feeling inside me was growing more ominous now.

"It's the only way Bask would ever even consider letting him go…" He lowered his voice. "He sees you as a potential asset, Sparrow—because of your powers. Keegan he sees as merely another lice-bag he's going to slaughter and leave in a pit to rot."

My eyelids sank shut beneath the weight of his words.

"Your allegiance in exchange for Keegan's release," Price explained softly. "Our marriage will be a symbol of your loyalty. That's how I will present it to Bask."

I sucked in a shaky breath, my mind racing along with my heart. "And if he agrees, Keegan will be freed?"

Price hesitated a moment; then I felt the warmth of his hand on my cheek. He bowed his head in agreement. "Keegan will be freed."

I felt as if I stood at the very brink of darkness. I was terrified to take that leap and let it consume me. But I knew I was not alone on that ledge; Keegan was there, too… and the darkness required one of us to be sacrificed.

"All right." I pulled in a shaky breath, forcing myself to nod, wiping away the tears. "If Bask agrees to release him, I'll do it… I'll marry you."

"Absolutely not—are you out of your mind? How can *you*, of *all people*, ask such a thing?"

"Because in marrying me, Sparrow would become even more solidly one of us."

Bask slammed a hand against the mantel of the fireplace and stared down into the flames. "That sounds like surrender!"

I stared at him, shaking my head in disbelief. "You're missing the point, Bask—you're overlooking what an incredible opportunity this will be to harness her power, just as you've harnessed mine!"

"That's completely different."

"I see no difference."

"You wanted to be one of us more than life itself. Sparrow, on the other hand, is already indoctrinated by sliders—already brainwashed to think and act and *be* just like the rest of them, Price. Surely you must see that."

"*No*—no, that's where you're wrong," I protested. "I've spent time getting to know Sparrow. She resents being a slider, just as I do."

"Then why is she so eager to have this prisoner released? He's a radical," he muttered, taking his flask out of his pocket and unscrewing the cap. "If Sparrow's so attached to him, it says something about her."

My jaw tightened. It was nothing I hadn't already thought myself—but it got under my skin even more hearing it spoken out loud.

"Sparrow will come around," I said resolutely. "I *know* she will."

Bask sipped his whiskey, lowering his gaze back to the flickering flames in the hearth.

"If you don't let him go, Sparrow will fight you, Bask—what will you achieve then?" I questioned. "Keegan is nothing—*no one*. Let him go back to the Homestead and perish in the forthcoming ambush. We have nothing to lose or gain by keeping him. He has no power that will benefit us, and he has seen nothing, unlike Sparrow, who *has* seen us, who knows us, and through whom we have much to gain."

"Sparrow will conform eventually because she will be forced to do so—whether I free this prisoner or not."

"Yes, but she wouldn't be my wife."

Bask took another swig. "Which is your main objective in all this, isn't it?"

My silence was affirmation enough for him.

"You want Sparrow? Fine." His voice was cold, calculating. "Here's the ultimatum: you tell Sparrow you're going to release Keegan—meet her demands." He screwed the cap back on his flask. "Then you take him into the woods and shoot him."

"What?"

"It's the opportunity you've been waiting for, Price—a chance to prove where your loyalties really lie. A real RGM soldier wouldn't think twice about executing another soldier if he had to—a best friend, a brother—never mind a *filthy* slider," he answered, his hard, suspicious eyes scanning the room for me. "You think you're really cut out for this life? Prove it. Tell Sparrow you'll save Keegan's life, then put a bullet through his skull."

I swallowed back a sick feeling. Burned into my mind was an

afterimage of Sparrow: her pleading eyes as she had begged for Keegan's life—promising herself to me if I'd only get Bask to let him go. In her eyes, I'd caught glimpses of the same disease I had—the possession that had taken hold of me that first day I'd seen her out there in the woods… the day *she'd seen me.* She loved him. She loved him enough to give up everything she cared about for him. She was prepared to do for him exactly what I *wouldn't* do for her: sacrifice herself.

I was laying her on the altar while I got away clean.

Something cold settled inside me as I stood there, sweat prickling the back of my neck.

Bask's eyes narrowed as he waited for an answer. "Well, Price? Do we have a deal?"

My trembling fingers curled into fists. "One bullet or two?"

Bask cracked a grin. "You know we always double tap." He opened his flask again. "Beat him first. Now get the hell out of my office before I change my mind."

I didn't need to be told twice.

Stepping back out into the crisp night air, I closed the door behind me. I was startled to find Mooney standing there, waiting for me in the darkness. His lips parted in a gaping grin, his eyes searching hollowly for me.

I shoved him out of the way, sickened. "What do you want from me?"

"Bask's orders, *sir*," he said, with clumsy emphasis on the last part. "Said you were to beat him and shoot him, didn't he?"

"That's no concern of yours."

I felt something thud against my arm. I turned back to Mooney as he extended his club to me. My gaze stayed frozen on his face for a long moment before lowering to the weapon in his hand. The wooden club was heavily stained with splatters of blood.

"Take it," he urged.

My eyes shifted back up to his. "Do you actually think I would take the weapon that you used to kill my friend?"

He snickered, then spat on the ground. "RGM soldiers aren't friends with the prisoners."

I stared at him for a moment before lowering my gaze once again to the club in his hand.

"Now take it." He thrust it into my arms. "Prove to us you can really be who you say you are: *a loyal soldier.*"

My muscles tensed. I grasped the club and pulled it from his hand. I wanted to smash his skull open with it, but instead I just stood there and watched as he scuttled away like the roach he truly was.

When I turned, I could already see the soft yellow glow of the lights in the windows of the lab, melting through the twilight as if to coax me closer, like a moth to a flame.

Giving myself no time to think, I strode down the long, familiar dirt road. Off to one side of the gate, a unit of soldiers had already begun to congregate. I could hear the robust voice of one of their superiors as he briefed them.

I rubbed my forehead and took a fortifying breath, climbing the stairs to the lab and shouldering the door open. I hardly noticed the floor passing beneath my feet as I walked, barely comprehended the doors filing by to my right and left. I stopped at the door to the sterile white cell where Keegan was being held. His face was the first thing I saw when I stepped up to the small window in the door.

He was seated on the floor, his long reddish hair hanging down into his face as he leaned against the wall that divided his cell from Sparrow's.

My grip around the club tightened. I could hear Sparrow's desperate plea for his freedom ringing in my ears, the way she had spoken his name.

God, I wanted to open Sparrow up and dig him out of her soul. I could erase him from the face of the Earth, but not from her heart.

I stood there for a moment, the club trembling in my clenched fist as I observed Keegan hunched against the wall. Then I lifted my free hand and pressed my thumb to the access pad. The bolts immediately retracted, and the door swung open before me.

He didn't glance up as I stepped inside and slammed the door.

"You're to be released, Keegan," I announced bluntly. "I'm here to release you."

Slowly, he turned in the direction of my voice, revealing his face, which was now completely healed.

"I don't want to leave."

"You *do* realize they're going to execute you, don't you?"

"At dawn, yes."

"Why would you want to stay and die?"

"I can't leave Sparrow." Keegan's voice weakened at her name.

"You'll do as you're told," I said through gritted teeth.

"*You* don't," he said, glancing up. "You kept Sparrow hidden up in the woods, shielded her from the rest of the RGM even when they were looking for her."

My insides lurched as I stared down at him.

*How the hell does he know that?*

I pushed the blunt end of the club against his forehead. "Careful what accusations you make."

"I'm not afraid of being beaten." His eyes steeled. "I'm not afraid of *you.*"

My knuckles whitened as rage welled in my chest. "You should be."

With one blow, I sent him sprawling, grasping his upper arm where the club had impacted.

"What is your connection to Sparrow?" I shouted, raising the club over him again. "Tell me, now!"

Keegan pressed himself up off the floor, slowly standing. "There is nothing between us."

"I find that hard to believe. Do you love her?" I demanded.

Keegan tipped his head back, staring defiantly at the place where he was pinpointing my voice. "With everything I am."

"What if I told you that she really loved me—and that I'm in love with her?"

"If you truly loved her, she wouldn't be locked in that cell right now—and by *your doing!*" he shouted, his voice steel. "You know nothing of love—*nothing.* Love is a foreign concept to you!"

I swung the club, and the dull, sickening thud of wood on bone filled the cell. Crying out in pain, he doubled over. I brought the club down on his back over and over again. I stood there breathing heavily for a moment, satisfaction flushing through me as I listened to him whimper.

Then I looked down at the club in my hand and noticed a new splotch of blood—blood *I'd* drawn.

I swallowed hard, my stomach turning. My mind flashed back to Viner's empty shack, the blood I'd seen on Mooney's face, the club in his hand. The club I was now holding in *my* hand.

*What have I done?*

The floor seemed to shift beneath my feet as I staggered backward a few paces. I closed my eyes and forced myself to take a deep breath, swallowing back the wave of nausea. With a few sputtering coughs, Keegan climbed back to his feet.

"Sparrow has requested to see you before you go," I informed him coldly. "You will say nothing of how you were captured, or of who captured you."

Keegan stared into the empty air, blood trickling from his nose.

"You mean you don't want her to know that it was *you* who captured me?" he shot back defiantly. "That *you're* the reason she's here right now? Because *you* lured her here?"

His words were like triggers, snapping something inside me. I lunged at him, driving him back against the wall, thrusting the club up against his throat.

"It's for her sake that I am allowing you to see her before I release you," I hissed into his face. "You will say *nothing* to Sparrow about me: you will not tell her that I captured you, or that I'm the one who beat you. I will be listening and watching the entire time. You will tell her absolutely nothing—do you understand? If you do, she'll be the one who pays for it."

His wild eyes stared like he could see into my mind. "Then you don't really love her," he whispered, choked.

I let him go with a jerk, and he dropped back against the wall. I straightened my shirt and turned for the door.

"Why are they letting me go?"

I glanced over my shoulder. "Why don't you ask Sparrow?"

WHEN THE DOOR HAD SLAMMED SHUT, THE REALITY OF what I'd just agreed to began to sink in. My heart raced as I grasped my head in my hands.

No part of me could imagine being joined inseparably to Corporal Aaron Price in the name of "solidifying an alliance" between the RGM and me. I would be binding myself to a man I did not love, but, even worse, I'd be damning myself to slavery—working alongside the brutal forces that sought to kill those I loved.

*I can't do it, I can't, I can't, I can't…*

But there was no alternative: anything else would result in Keegan's death. My choice was between an enslaved life or one without Keegan's existence. Was there even a choice to be made, when I would give up far more than just my freedom for him?

*I have to do it… I have to.*

I attempted to steady my breathing as I paced from one end of the room to the next.

Aaron had promised me that I could talk to Keegan before he was released. The thought was enough to make me lose my mind—I'd spent so many nights longing for this moment; now it was finally here and to serve one purpose only: to say goodbye.

But I knew Keegan. I knew that no matter what I said, he would never stop trying to get me out of the RGM's grasp. Giving up wasn't in his nature. But if he came back, there would be no second chances: if they didn't kill him now, they most certainly would if he ever showed his face again.

*Oh, god, what would I tell him? What would I say?* I wanted nothing more than to empty my heart to him—to throw my arms around him and bury my face in his chest and feel his arms around me. I wanted nothing more than to hold onto him and never let go—ever. But I couldn't. No, if I wanted to keep him safe, to make sure that he never returned, I had to do the *exact opposite.*

I squeezed my eyes shut before the tears had a chance to well there, cursing under my breath. Hurried footsteps came into earshot, and a moment later the door opened. Aaron stepped inside, halting in the middle of the room. He bowed his head in an affirmative nod, a flicker of warmth in his eyes.

"Bask said yes?" I whispered.

"He's ordered Keegan to be released," he confirmed. "Not… without sufficient punishment, but—"

My heart sank. "Bask beat him?"

"I'm afraid anything else would be against his nature," Aaron said quietly. "Perhaps you shouldn't speak with him."

I shook my head, already rushing forward. "I have to see him, Aaron, please." My voice crumbled. "*Please.* You *promised* me."

He remained where he was for a moment, the only thing standing between me and the door. Finally, he stepped aside and gestured for me to follow him.

"You have two minutes," he said firmly. "Ask him nothing."

I nodded quickly, scarcely able to catch my breath as I followed him out into the hallway. We walked only a few feet before halting at the next door. Aaron stopped to turn and look at me, his thumb hovering over the access pad. He studied me wordlessly for a moment, scanning me up and down like I was a puzzle he couldn't solve. Then he pressed his thumb to the scanner.

The bolt retracted with a loud click. Aaron pushed the door open, but I grabbed his arm before he could cross the threshold.

His gaze snapped back to mine. "What?"

"Could I…" I trailed off, swallowed. "Could I go in alone?"

He shook his head. "Bask would never allow it."

"Bask isn't here," I reminded him. "He left this in *your* hands."

Aaron remained where he was, barring me from the threshold. Drawing a shaky breath, I stepped closer to look up into his eyes.

"Aaron, from here onward, you will always have me…" I paused to steady my voice. "Let me have these two minutes alone."

"Sparrow—"

"If you *truly* love me," I cut in emphatically, "you'll give me this."

Aaron's dark eyes held mine a moment longer. Finally, he stepped aside, holding the heavy door open for me. I slipped past him and into the small room, my heart pounding in my chest.

Keegan was seated on the floor at the opposite end of the room. He was wearing an RGM soldier's uniform streaked with dirt and blood. Half his head had been shaved down to the skin, his face was swollen, and crimson dribbled from his nose. His eyes opened when the door clicked shut.

"Who's there?" he whispered in a weak voice.

For a moment I couldn't answer his question. I could only stand there, watching as his green eyes flickered back and forth, searching the empty air between us instead of meeting my own.

Feeling sick, I curled my fingers around the place on my arm where the long, slender needle had pierced my flesh. A bruise was forming where Bask had given me the injection.

*I'm invisible now. He can't even see me anymore.*

"W-who is it?" He climbed slowly to his feet, keeping one hand pressed against the smooth white wall.

Without answering, I crossed the room and came to a stop in front of him. His glistening green eyes searched the air. Tears burning in my eyes, I placed one hand to his chest. A hot tear rolled down my cheek.

As if melting beneath my touch, he carefully closed one hand around mine. Lifting my hand from his chest, he spread my palm open and, pressing it to his face, he kissed it. For a moment I felt nothing but the warmth and shape of his face in my hand, the wetness of his tears.

He kissed the palm of my hand, the back of it, my knuckles, and then reached up to gently take my face in his hands, moving his thumbs over my cheeks to wipe away tears he couldn't even see.

"Sparrow." His voice was barely above a whisper.

I couldn't speak. I could hardly breathe as his forehead made gentle contact with mine.

"Did they—have they—"

I shook my head before he could finish. "They haven't hurt me… but they've given me an injection. That's why you can't see me."

"An injection?"

"Ask nothing," I whispered, my voice desperate. "Please."

I felt the warmth of his breath as a gentle sigh pushed past his lips. His body melted against mine as he pulled me into his arms. For a moment I was folded up in his warmth; I could feel the rhythm of his pulse as my face pressed against his chest. For a moment I had everything.

"Oh, god, I wish I could see your face." His voice was like the wind. I felt everything inside me beginning to crumble. Wiping back the tears, I pulled away.

"Keegan, stop," I whispered, trying to steady my voice and my hands at the same time. "I-I can't."

Something like pain flashed in his eyes as I jerked my hand away from his.

"What is it?"

I shook my head, my voice swelling to a sob in my throat. "I-I can't be like this with you."

"Sparrow, what are you talking about?"

He took a step closer.

"Don't," I told him coldly. "That is an *order*."

I felt like someone had jammed a knife into my chest as I watched his face fall.

"I can never be the slider you want me to be—I never have been, and I never will be." I tried to keep my voice from shaking. "You don't understand."

"You can't possibly believe that." His tone became urgent. "Sparrow, you belong with—"

"I belong *here*, with Corporal Price." I severed his sentence, my voice as sharp as a knife. "I belong with the RGM, Keegan."

"Sparrow! My god, what have they—"

"I mean it!" My voice filled the room, startling us both. Tears spilled from my eyes as I pulled in a trembling breath. Thank god he couldn't see me. "Keegan, what I felt for you was a childish infatuation—it was *nothing*. *We* are *nothing*," I whispered, my voice stone cold. "I don't love you, and I never have. You have to leave this place and forget about me."

For a moment he just stood there, looking as if he'd been struck. Then his eyes narrowed, and he shook his head. "I don't believe you."

I clasped my face in my hands, pressing my fingertips to my forehead.

"Well, you should." My lower lip trembled uncontrollably. "Because I love Corporal Price."

His jaw tensed, and he shook his head again. "Sparrow, I know you don't—"

"He asked me to marry him, and I said yes." My voice rose again as I looked into his glistening green eyes. "I could *never* love someone so devoted to being an anomaly. Price hates the fact that he's an anomaly, just like I always have! I've never been one of you—ever!"

Keegan reached out to try to find me, but I yanked away as soon as his fingertips made contact. "Please, Sparrow—*please* don't do this!"

"You don't love me, Keegan. You only love who you thought I was— which was a figment of your imagination! It's not who I really am!"

"I love *you*, Sparrow—not an anomaly, not a slider—*you*! For *all* that you are…" His voice rolled out like a hurricane, echoing off the walls. "I *know* who you are, and I *love* you…"

Everything inside me screamed: *I love you too.*

"Well, I don't love you." The words spilled out in a rush. "And I *never will.*"

He didn't move. A tear rolled over his lips and crested his chin.

"And if you care about me as much as you claim you do, you'll leave me in peace and never come back," I finished icily. "And tell Fin to do the same. He never could believe that I knew my own mind… I never want to see any of you again."

The color had drained from Keegan's face. Finally, he sucked in a breath. The fire that had flared in his eyes only moments ago was gone, replaced by a heavy hollowness.

My knees were shaking as he stepped closer. I didn't move as he leaned forward and found me with his fingertips, then took my face in his hands once more. He pressed his lips to my forehead and gave me a soft, lingering kiss before he pulled away, a cold feeling replacing the warmth where his lips head been. He bent his head to whisper into my ear.

"I want you to be happy, Sparrow—and if that means never seeing me again, so be it…" He hesitated as his voice cracked. "But you must never… *never* let them find out who you really are."

My heart stopped, chills racing over my skin. I stared up into his eyes. *He knows? He knows who I am?*

The door swung open so hard it hit the wall.

"Time's up." Aaron's voice was like a thunderbolt. "Come."

He didn't wait for Keegan to respond; instead, he strode across the room and seized him by the arm, dragging him forward. I felt everything inside me lurch, almost causing me to stumble, as if Aaron had grabbed hold of me and not Keegan.

"Guards—assist," Aaron bellowed, his voice ricocheting off the cement. The door at the end of the hallway burst open, and two armed guards rushed down the corridor and stepped into Keegan's cell. "We're taking him to the perimeter and throwing him out," Aaron told them. "Bask's orders." Without a word, the guards grabbed Keegan and hauled him out of the cell.

Tears streamed down my face as I rushed out into the hallway. I stopped just outside the door, shaking as I watched them drag Keegan away. His green eyes stared back down the hallway in my direction until the guards jerked him roughly over the threshold of the security door. I saw his face for a moment through the glass, then the guards jolted him forward, and he slipped out of sight.

I felt like I was dying. Crumpling to the floor, I buried my face in my hands. The once silent hallway filled with my echoing sobs.

# 78

MY HEART POUNDED AS I DRAGGED KEEGAN PAST THE district gates. A full moon glowed over the desolate valley ahead of us as I jolted him forward, slamming the butt of my rifle into his back. I guided him into the looming forest.

When we halted in the shadows, Keegan turned, looking straight at me.

I raised my rifle and cocked it. "Turn around."

"You promised her that I would be released," he countered without moving. "Does your word mean so little?"

I stared down the sights of my weapon at him. "Sparrow will never know."

"If you actually think she won't find out, then you don't know Sparrow at all." His voice was steel. "She can see things that no one else can. She'll sense it. She'll know. She'll know that you *lied.*"

"You don't understand."

"I understand that if you *really* loved her, you wouldn't do this."

"Shut up!" I barked, the rifle trembling in my sweaty grasp. "Turn around now!"

"Why? Are you scared?"

"Why should I be? You are powerless against the RGM."

"Then don't shoot me in the back." He took a step toward me. "Look me in the eyes and pull the trigger. Kill me. Follow your orders—if they really mean more to you than she does. Because you'll never really hold her heart. She'll know—she'll feel it. And she'll never love you."

He trembled in the crosshairs as my arms shook. He continued steadily toward me.

*Pull the trigger.*

He stopped right in front of me, at point-blank distance.

"What are you waiting for?" He reached out and grabbed hold of the barrel of the gun. He steadied it, aiming it straight at his own forehead. "Go ahead… Pull the trigger."

My stomach churned; sweat was dripping down my back, the rifle shaking in my grip.

*Just pull the goddamn trigger.*

Keegan's eyes searched for me in the shadows and moonlight. I stared right back at him, willing myself to pull the trigger—cursing myself, raging inside.

But Sparrow's eyes haunted my thoughts—her begging, pleading words. The promise I'd made her.

My moist fingertip rested on the trigger, ice cold.

I jerked the barrel from his grasp and fired into the air. The shot echoed in the night, then faded away. I drew a trembling breath.

"If you ever come back here," I whispered hoarsely, "I *will* kill you."

"No," he said, his eyes trained on mine. "Not if I kill you first."

My jaw clenched as I raised my rifle again, but he vanished into the shadows of the trees, evaporating into the night. I stood there for a long moment, staring after him, my heart pounding, barely able to keep a grasp on my weapon.

"Coward," I cursed under my breath. "You damn coward."

I turned around—and stopped dead.

Standing at the forest's edge with a wide, gap-toothed grin, was Mooney. His club rested on his shoulder.

"Coward is right," he sneered. "I knew you didn't have the balls for it, Price."

The blood drained from my face as he stepped into the shadows, his face darkening as he laughed maniacally.

My muscles tightened as I raised my weapon.

"You'll never be a soldier, not when Bask hears of this," he growled. "You never were—you're just a prisoner…"

My heart pounded in my chest as I watched him make his way toward me in the moonlight.

"You're no better than your dead blind friend." He twirled the club in his hand. "And you'll die just like he did…" His words trailed off, his crooked lips curling into a smirk. "Like a dog."

My jaw clenched as my finger closed over the trigger. "No, Mooney." My voice hardened to steel. "You will."

I squeezed the trigger.

Blood splashed from the center of his forehead. I watched his body drop through the crosshairs, smoke wafting up from the hot barrel of my rifle. My cheek still pressed to the stock, I listened to the echoes of the shot ricochet off the distant cliffs and then die away.

Slowly, I lowered the gun and stepped over to Mooney's dead body. A crimson puddle seeped into the ground around his head.

"You fool," I said softly. "You know we always double tap."

"The deed is done?" Bask asked as I stepped into his office and closed the door behind me.

I licked the sweat from my upper lip. "Keegan is dead, yes."

"I'm… impressed."

"It was nothing."

"It didn't bother you?"

"Bother me? Why should it?"

He gestured toward a chair, turning to open a bottle of whiskey.

My rifle over my shoulder, I crossed the room and took a seat.

"Killing one of your own." Bask splashed the deep amber liquid into two glasses and handed me one. "Executing your own flesh and blood, in a sense."

"You're mistaken—he was a filthy slider. I am a soldier."

My voice was hard—confident. I threw back my head, draining the glass and slamming it down.

A small smile began to form on my commander's lips. "In that case—" he opened the bottle again "—we should celebrate."

"Celebrate?"

He swallowed his own drink and poured us both another round of shots.

He raised his glass. "To your upcoming union to Sparrow, and to the future of the RGM." His lips curled into a grin. "I always knew I'd get you in the end, Price. I always knew we'd do great things together…"

My sweaty fingers curled around the shot glass as I raised it. I sat there, stiff in my chair across from him. It was everything I'd ever wanted to hear.

Yet my stomach was turning.

"To a future without sliders," he finished with a gruff laugh, and drained the glass.

For a moment I just watched him, my hand trembling. Then I threw back my head and took the shot, swallowing back the storm raging inside me.

# 79

IT WAS LIKE PUSHING AGAINST GRAVITY, RUNNING farther and farther away from Sparrow. Her words pounded through me with each of my footsteps as I raced across the valley, just a flickering shadow in the moonlight.

I sprinted faster than the wind itself, it seemed, and I comprehended nothing; not the ground passing beneath my feet, not the trees or the branches that struck me, or the brush that tore at my legs, or even the cool night air as it whipped against my face.

Once I was deep in the woods, I stopped. Leaning back against one of the towering pines, I pressed my eyes shut.

Though I hadn't seen her face when she stood before me, I saw it now, etched into my memory along with every single razor-sharp word she had spoken.

Tears streamed down my face as I began to create a cognitive lock on the Homestead, imagining home. But it wasn't home anymore—it never would be. Not without Sparrow.

She was my home.

In my mind's eye I caught glimpses of a richer, restored forest around me, lush and healed, just like the ravine had been… the ravine where I'd witnessed something my mind still grappled with. Something I couldn't comprehend.

Soon, the glade opened before me. That achingly familiar clearing, in the center of which our beautiful little cabin rose like an arrow reaching for the sky. The garden slept peacefully, washed in the pale, white glow. The windows were all dark, and the front door hung open lifelessly.

I breathed a sigh of relief as I opened my eyes, the transport complete. I took the cedar steps all at once, rushing into the house and stopping in the middle of the front room. I looked around in the darkness, over the floorboards blanketed in the glow of moonlight. I swallowed back the lump in my throat as my eyes traced all the familiar shapes around me, as I breathed in the scent of mahogany mixed with cotton and lavender.

*Empty. Thank god—they had made it.*

I could already see the flickering of lights in the woods as I stepped back outside. The unit was nearly to the clearing. I could hear them, distantly.

Breathing hard, wiping the blood off my face with my forearm, I circled around the cabin to the barn. I wasn't surprised when I found the door hanging open on its hinges. Kateri had let all the animals go.

I peered inside, expecting to find it as vacant as the house had been. Instead, I started when I noticed two yellow eyes gaping out from the darkness.

For a moment, I froze.

"Holy sh…" I trailed off, breathless, then stepped inside to grab hold of Cub by the scruff of the neck. "Why didn't you run off? The door's open…"

Quivering slightly, Cub didn't resist as I quickly, carefully scooped her up into my arms. My thoughts began to churn.

"Were you waiting for me?" I whispered, more to myself. "Do you know where they went?"

Cub tensed in my arms as we heard the shouts of the first soldiers emerging into the clearing. I held my breath, listening for a moment, then set Cub on the ground and darted for the cover of the trees, whispering to Cub to follow me. We melted in among the shadows and sank down into the brush. When the coast was clear, I crouched and circled around to the front of the cabin, Cub padding at my heels.

The pounding of boots came into earshot as invisible soldiers flooded the clearing around the cabin. All I could see were dozens of flickering flames bobbing and weaving through the darkness. They rushed into the cabin and I heard commotion from inside—the sounds of breaking glass, splintering wood. The soldiers overturned the furniture on the porch and trampled the gardens.

"No one's here!" one voice shouted. "They've gone!"

Someone cursed.

"No—no, they have to be here. Search again…"

The search carried on a while longer, accentuated by more thuds and smashing glass from inside.

I waited in the shadows, watching as several of the flames moved back into the cabin's dark interior, only to reappear a moment later in the window. The curtains that hung behind the glass ignited. The air filled with the raucous laughter and shouts of the soldiers standing outside. A few clapped.

My jaw tightened as I crouched in the shadows, Cub shivering at my side.

Within moments, the windows raged with amber light, black smoke rolling out through the panes as they shattered.

Tears burned in my eyes as I watched the flames climb the exterior walls of the cabin, reaching into the early morning sky, lighting up the clearing in a haunting orange glow. I could feel the radiating heat even from where I was hiding.

One by one, the voices of the soldiers vanished back into the woods, their lights flickering after them.

I rose slowly from the brush, standing there, staring at the burning cabin. A shrill snapping pierced the air, escalating into a deafening, whooshing roar as the roof collapsed in on itself, sending a storm of golden sparks up into the air.

I turned my face away, swallowing hard.

I wanted to scream, to sob, to tear apart the darkness with my bare hands; I felt like *I* was the one who was on fire.

But instead, I just stood there. Empty.

Suddenly I became aware that I was alone. I spun around, searching the undergrowth, and spotted brush moving as Cub trotted away into the deep, lush forest. The little cougar halted, perhaps sensing that I was watching her, and turned back to stare at me. Her eyes were wide, almost pleading.

"You know where they are, don't you?" I whispered, my voice cracking. "That's why you stayed…"

Cub looked at me for a moment before turning away again and scampering deeper into the trees.

I looked back at the cabin, at the massive plumes of orange and angry red consuming the last of what I held dear.

I wiped my tears and took a deep breath. I forced myself to turn away.

Cub halted in the brush, far ahead now, waiting for me. Drawing a painful breath, I fixed my eyes ahead, following after her, putting one foot in front of the other until I, too, began to lose myself among the trees.

I left the burning cabin behind. I didn't look back.

*Sparrow and Keegan will return in*

# SPARROW
# RISING

*Stay updated on new releases at:*
*www.kaemmons.com*

# ABOUT THE AUTHOR

K.A. Emmons is the author of *The Blood Race* series and co-host of The Kate & Abbie Show – a podcast she produces with her sister. When she's not writing, you will probably find Kate outside: hiking, surfing, practicing kata or heading to the climbing gym. Visit her online at:

WWW.KAEMMONS.COM

ALSO FOLLOW KATE ON:

- youtube.com/kaemmons
- facebook.com/kaemmonsauthor
- instagram.com/lonehawkwriter